UNRAVELED

UNRAVELED

STRANGER MAGICS, BOOK SEVEN

ASH FITZSIMMONS

Print Edition ISBN: 978-1-949861-15-0

Cover design by BespokeBookCovers.com

www.ashfitzsimmons.com

FORWARD

On January 15, 2016, the Arcanum—the mortal realm's most powerful magical organization—installed Helen Isadora Carver as its newest grand magus. Her ascension, which had seemed almost inevitable since childhood, was accomplished by the thinnest of margins. Yes, Helen had exhibited impressive talent from an early age and had excelled in her studies. Her elderly predecessor, Greg Harrison, had trained her himself and assured the Council that she was a fine wizard and would make a great leader. Had he been in a position to step aside three years earlier, the transition might have succeeded. But such would have been impossible; at the time of her ascension, Helen had only just turned twenty-two, and young wizards did not come of age until twenty.

And so, in those last years of Helen's education and preparation, the Council watched as the golden girl was tarnished.

There was, of course, the matter of her younger brother—her half brother, really, the talentless dud who'd grown up in the Arcanum. The Council knew the truth about him, but why Grand Magus Harrison felt the need to inform the *boy* of his parentage was baffling to many magi. In fact, Aiden Carver was no dud—he was witch-blooded fae, cursed with wizard and faerie blood in equal measure. Worse, the boy was a high lord, half brother to the new king of Faerie, Coileán. And when he learned the secret of his parentage—that he'd been born of the late queen, Titania, and not of the respectable wizard who'd mothered him—

he fled to his brother's realm.

Had Helen done the sensible thing, she would have disavowed her traitorous sibling and helped maintain the fiction that he was a dud, shipped off to a mundane school to prepare him for life outside the Arcanum. Instead, she stubbornly stood by him, even when he, through some strange pact with the soul of Faerie itself, suppressed their father's effect on him and embraced his mother's gift. He had the audacity to out himself at her magus ceremony—an enchantment-wielding, iron-fearing *faerie* in the heart of the silo, reigning as regent during his brother's convalescence— and yet, she refused to disown him. If anything, rumor suggested that she had become *friendly* with Lord Coileán himself, a distressing development to that wing of the Council that would have liked nothing more than to wipe Faerie from the map.

And then there was the matter of her boyfriend.

The Council had been less than fond of Joey Bolin as a potential spouse for their future head. At best, the young man was mundane, potentially sabotaging the talent of Helen's children. At worst, he was Coileán's friend, living in the king's backyard and raising a dragon. Having become fast friends with Aiden, he had done himself no favors with the Council. But they'd held their noses when Helen and Joey announced their engagement—that is, until it came to light that Joey was not only lesser fae but also descended from the old king and queen, Oberon and Titania. Yes, his ancestry came as a shock to both of them, but Helen should have broken off the relationship. Rather than do her duty to the Arcanum, however, she'd *eloped* with him, marrying in Faerie and practically daring the Council to object.

The vote had been tight, but in the end, the Council had allowed her to ascend.

Perhaps, if there had been a cooling-off period, if Helen had appeased the Council over the following years with sound policy and peace, then they might have grudgingly wished the happy couple well. But a minority faction of the

Council had grown stronger and more determined in the face of Helen's brazen defiance of all norms. She would never have a chance to prove herself as grand magus.

An alliance was struck with Coileán's patricidal daughter, Moyna. Joey, mortally wounded in the fight against her uprising, saved himself by accepting the same sort of augmentation that Faerie had offered Aiden...and he revealed as much to his pregnant wife within full view of the silo's security cameras. That proved to be the final straw for the last holdouts among the conspiring magi.

On March 28, after barely two months in office, Helen was kidnapped and locked away, victim of a coup. After she was secured, the conspirators seized control of the Arcanum, named James Mulligan the new grand magus, and attacked the Fringe, the mortal realm's comparatively defenseless alliance of witches and lesser fae, using Harrison's credentials to break into the Fringe's database and hunt them down. Some, like Helen, were taken as hostages to ensure that the powers in Faerie stayed out of the mortal realm. Some were murdered. A fraction of their number were evacuated to Faerie, and the rest went into hiding to escape the Arcanum's assassin corps.

To the Fringe, that day became known as "the unraveling," echoing the code word that Harrison had used to warn them. In the months that followed, two of their surviving members would return to the mortal realm with an untrained faerie and a well-meaning mundane to begin the search for the missing. But as would soon become apparent, there would be no easy resolution to the precarious standoff between the Arcanum and the Faerie courts—and the magical community, once unraveled, would never be the same.

—YEAR ONE—

APRIL: TOULA PAVLI

I didn't notice that night had fallen until the music snapped off.

Looking up from my reading for the source of the disturbance, I spotted my brother, Val, silhouetted in the warm hallway light from the open door, rising from a crouch as he dropped the borrowed boombox's plug. I marked my place with a strip of scrap paper and tried to suppress my annoyance at the interruption—the work couldn't wait. "You could have just pressed the power button, you know."

It was difficult to see the details of his face in the darkness, but I could imagine the look that Val was giving me, a lift of the eyebrows and tilt of the head that silently asked, *Really?*

I couldn't be too hard on him. Val had come a long way over the previous two and a half years, quietly studying Joey and Aiden's toys and sneaking back to me with his questions. He was doing well for a guy with two millennia behind him, and besides, few faeries were ever wholly at ease around electronics. But the boombox was at least a couple of decades old—I'd found it in one of the many piles in the sprawling palace library that Coileán had yet to sort through—and I assumed that Val had never seen its like. At least he hadn't hexed it into silence.

"How can you think with that shouting?" he asked as a glowing white orb appeared in the air between us. "More importantly, how can you see without light?"

"Eyes adjust, and it's not *shouting*, it's AC/DC."

With the orb illuminating the room, I got the full force of his look that time.

"Have you eaten?" he asked, picking his way around the stacks of books I'd pulled and piled on the rug.

"Yeah."

"Today?"

"*Yes*, Val."

His gaze drifted toward my empty water bottle and the plate of crusts from my breakfast toast. "Take a break. You need food and sleep."

"I'm fine," I protested, but Val shook his head.

"If you don't eat, you can't think, and then this reading will be for nothing." He glanced at the open book on the table in front of me, a tenth-century French magus's treatise on theoretical wardwork in cramped, faded Latin, and grimaced. "*Rest*, Fotoula. You cannot solve the problems of the world by yourself tonight. You've barely slept for two weeks."

One corner of my mouth ticked. "Want to give me a hand, then?"

He chuckled. "Ah, yes, all of my great expertise on *wards*. I can offer companionship and food delivery, but this…" He patted the page and shook his head. "You might as well ask Stuart's opinion."

Fat chance, there—I doubted that the wannabe wizard could even read Latin. "Better not let the boss catch you touching that," I chided. "Bet you didn't wash your hands first."

"In that case, I'm sure there's a preservation spell you could throw together to save me from his wrath." He stooped and kissed my temple. "Come. You've been in here all day. At least eat dinner and step outside the building."

"Thanks, but I'm not hungry."

"Toula—"

"This isn't going to read itself."

Val sighed, then lit a few lamps before heading to the door. "This isn't your fault," he said before leaving, his nightly refrain that week. "You know that. It's not up to you to fix this alone."

"Goodnight," I replied, and rose to plug the boombox back in.

Strictly speaking, my brother had a point: I hadn't been the catalyst for this mess. I hadn't conspired with James Mulligan and his traitorous Council buddies when they planned the coup that had upended the Arcanum and life in the mortal realm for most of us on the magical spectrum. I hadn't been there when they kidnapped and disabled Helen Carver or when they named Mulligan grand magus in her stead—Helen had sent me away the day before, just in case my presence annoyed the respectable people of the silo more than it usually did. I hadn't guided Helen and Joey to a spot near a security camera so that Joey could tell his newly pregnant wife *and* the silo's security team that his tiny taint of fae blood had been amplified beyond all redemption. I certainly hadn't been the one who gave the order to start abducting witches and murdering lesser fae.

But I was the one who'd last worked on the wards around Arc 1. I'd tightened them beautifully at Greg Harrison's request, preventing anyone without a built-in exception from accessing the silo by gate. I'd left in an exception for Helen, and one for her and Joey together, but I'd been ordered to lock myself out. My wardwork—*mine*— was now helping those sons and daughters of bitches. In trying to prove to the Arcanum that I could be a team player, I'd hamstrung us all, and that fact kept me out of bed and buried in Coileán's library.

Mulligan had us where he wanted us: if he detected a faerie presence in the mortal realm, then he'd kill his hostages. Sure, Coileán and Eleanor could have stormed the silo, overloaded the wards, and fought their way inside. Had full-blooded faeries held the thrones, the standoff would have been over the day it began—after all, what were a few hundred or thousand mortals' lives to a faerie? But the king and queen, like my brother, were half fae, blessed or cursed with somewhat human sensibilities. Eleanor's late husband had been a witch, and Coileán knew at least a few of the missing. And then there was the minor matter of Helen— grand magus, yes, but also Joey's wife and Aiden's half sibling, which made her almost family to Coileán. Even if he'd been willing to sacrifice the other hostages, I knew he wouldn't risk the life of his little brother's big sister. Thus, we were trapped, unwilling to even create new gates into the mortal realm for fear of causing a spike on a background magic detector.

Had I been next to the wards, I could have dismantled them. Instead, I was stuck in Faerie, glad to be alive and safe but feeling so very guilty about the part I'd played in this fiasco.

And so I read. If the answer was anywhere in the realm, it would be in Coileán's library—or, more accurately, in his mother's hodgepodge of books, artwork, and anything else that had caught the old queen's eye over the centuries, including the boombox and half a dozen cassettes. I'd snagged a generator from Aiden's workshop and made camp in the library, telling myself that I'd find a way through my wards.

If I were truly my father's daughter, I'd make this right.

Three nights later, Coileán stopped in to check on me.

Well, I *think* it was three nights later. In all honesty, that April was a blur the color of old paper and brown ink. I do know for certain that I hadn't showered since before Val insulted my musical selection, but my library catnaps had wreaked havoc on my internal clock. I was too busy to eat, sleeping only when my brain shut itself off in desperation, and still no closer to a solution.

And then there he was in his usual Oxford-and-jeans uniform, leaning against the doorframe with his arms folded, surveying the mess around my nest of codices and dirty plates. "Hey, Glinda," he said. "Haven't gone cross-eyed yet?"

I was too exhausted by then to complain about the nickname—he *knew* I hated it. "Nope," I mumbled, squinting at him in the gloom.

He came in, carefully avoiding my book piles, which were organized based on a logic understood only by my sleep-deprived mind. "You've got to get some rest."

"I'm fine."

"Hardly. You look like shit." He took an exaggerated sniff, then added, "And you're somewhat more odiferous than usual. Go on, go to bed."

I shook my head. "Got reading to do."

"That wasn't a request."

At that, I locked eyes with him and held my ground. Staring down a faerie with a bit of age is uncomfortable at best, nerve-racking when said faerie is a king, but my lack of sleep had made me fearless. "You're not the boss of me."

"No," he replied, shrugging, "but I'm worried about you. So's Val."

"And I'm worried about Helen and half the damn Fringe," I retorted, and turned back to my book. "Coffee?"

He let me be, but not before leaving a quart of steaming Arabica within my reach. I drank two-thirds of it, slapped my cheeks to wake up, and tapped my pencil against the table as I sought an impossible solution. I could find it. I *had* to find it.

My late, reviled father had done the impossible when there was nothing more at stake than his sense of justice. Surely I could do as much with lives on the line.

When I hear people complain about growing up in the shadow of their parents' accomplishments, I *laugh*.

My father, the only parent I knew as a child, was Apollonios Pavli, the mass-murdering psychopath housed in a secure cell deep in the silo while he awaited his execution. By the time I was old enough to form memories of him, whatever internal fire that had driven him to kill forty-three innocent wizards in one night of terror had died down to cooling embers. He was a wiry man of average height with thinning, close-cropped black hair and sunken brown eyes that seemed to regard me with resignation during my annual two-hour birthday visits. His nose was twisted from a poorly healed break, and he never smiled. When he spoke, his voice was low, his affect flat, a near monotone colored by a trace of his Greek accent, so different than the voices I heard growing up in Montana. He endured our visits, him on one side of the bars and me in a folding chair on the other side. Once I was given my first wand, he'd ask me to show him what I could do, and I'd be struck with unaccustomed stage fright as I tried to perform like a trained dog for the most hated man in the Arcanum. I shouldn't have cared—he'd given me nothing but a name and a lifetime of baggage—but I'd craved his approval, and the pressure of casting while he watched with those expressionless eyes made me stumble.

Well, that, plus the bind.

I might not have been so desperate to impress my father if anyone else in my life had given a damn about me. By the time I turned eighteen and left the silo, I'd been fostered by half a dozen families, most of which had grudgingly taken me in for a while in exchange for the promise of a promotion. At least one of my fosters made magus because of his benevolence in seeing that I ate breakfast and dinner for four years. I tried to be a good kid—I never skipped class, never used anything worse than pot, made honor roll throughout my years at the county school up the road. Under other circumstances, I think I could have made my parents proud of me. But the Arcanum feared that I'd inherited my father's capacity for evil, and so they bound me, just as they bound him. He was rendered powerless, but I was permitted access to a taste of power—enough to warrant giving me a proper magical education, but not so much that I'd ever pose a threat. I grew up on a dragonscale wand, practically a witch among wizards, but I worked hard to overcome my handicap. While my classmates were lazy in their casting, secure in the knowledge that they'd have the necessary power to make their spells coalesce, I researched and practiced focusing techniques, mastering the technical side of spellcraft even if I lacked the oomph to fully realize my work.

A little commendation might have been nice. A pat on the back every now and then would have been appreciated. I'd have liked to have been applauded instead of regarded as a burden to be endured. But praise was in short supply, no one wanted me, and I had no friends to speak of—just a couple of mundane girls at school who didn't fit in, either. We were friends of convenience, kids with good grades and low social prospects. When I started wearing all black and spiking my hair with gel, they went goth with me, wearing ankhs and pentacles they'd acquired from cousins in more cosmopolitan places. It was the nineties, no one cared what I did, and so I wore black eyeliner like war paint and silently told the world that it could go fuck itself.

But under the costume and jagged edges, I wanted to impress my father. Just once, I wanted him to smile and tell me that I'd done a good job. Sure, he'd been a powerful wizard in his prime, and I was an angry little shit with a dragonscale wand, but I so wanted him to approve of me.

He never did. He didn't keep the drawings I'd made for him when I was a kid or the research papers I'd aced and brought down to show off or any of my angsty, morbid teenage poetry (though I can't fault him for that). I wasn't even good enough to be remembered by my father, who went to his execution without leaving me so much as a note. Happy eighteenth birthday to me. And four months later, once I'd walked across the gym stage for my high school diploma, I'd packed my few belongings into black garbage bags, slung the mess into the back of the fourth-hand van the Arcanum bought me to facilitate my exit, and headed east to make my way in a world where I might be seen as more than Apollonios's loser daughter.

For seventeen years, I got by with odd jobs and a bit of magic, making the best of the little talent I had while waiting tables and tending bar to pay the rent. I kept studying whatever books I could get my hands on and practicing new techniques, hoping that if I kept my nose clean, the Arcanum might finally break my bind. Maybe then I'd be strong enough for an ash wand, or even a maple. No one ever called, though, and I'd almost given up when I saw a particular book in an estate sale catalogue in 2013 and convinced my book-dealing friend, Meg, to purchase it.

That March, Meg unwittingly managed a next-to-impossible feat: she acquired the long-lost diary of Simon Magus, the Arcanum's founder and possibly the most talented wizard who's ever lived. I was going to offer it to the Arcanum in exchange for my freedom. Instead, Meg and her changeling daughter got trapped in Faerie, that realm was sealed off, and when I drove over to her house to check on her, I found her old boyfriend drinking in the basement, bemoaning the fact that he couldn't get a gate open. Meg hadn't known that her green-eyed Colin Leffee, who'd gotten her pregnant and skipped town before either of them was the wiser, was a high lord.

In the interest of saving Meg and magic as we knew it, he and I had teamed up. When magic eventually ran out, my old bind fell apart. And when we finally went to Montana for help, Grand Magus Harrison let slip the tiny, insignificant matter of my maternity. I hadn't been bound because my father was a mass murderer, but rather because my mother was *Mab*, exiled queen of Faerie...and my folks had, apparently, joined forces to do the unthinkable: create a combination spell and enchantment so powerful that it had thrown Faerie into lockdown. The bind the Arcanum had put on me wasn't incomplete as a kindness—they *couldn't* fully bind me. I was the hypothetical witch-blood with both parents' abilities instead of neither's, as was usual for my kind. When I finally crossed into Faerie, surrounded by magic and unchained for the first time in my life, I discovered that I was at least my father's daughter in terms of talent. Maybe not my mother's—she was a queen, after all, and I was just a freakish witch-blood—but *fuck*, did it feel good when reality bent to my whisper.

Long story short, we saved the day, Coileán got himself a throne out of the deal, and Greg took me on as his assistant and a liaison to Faerie. It made sense—I mean, no one else wanted to deal with the courts, and Coileán and I didn't exactly hate each other. I wouldn't go so far as to say we were *friends*, but we'd killed each other's homicidally inclined mother, and that's the sort of thing that brings people together.

Of course, once back in the silo, I was reminded of the many reasons why I'd fled in the first place. I was Apollonios Pavli's little girl again, all grown up and still spiking my hair, but suddenly unbound and not at all in need of a wand. I tried to be polite—I even made small talk with my former classmates when I ran into them in the canteen or around Greg's office and looked up my former foster siblings—but the stares and whispers were worse than ever. People didn't know about Mab, but they didn't need to; my father's legacy was damnation enough. And now that I was at full strength, they didn't just revile or pity me—they *feared* me. I was the bomb waiting to explode, the snake coiled in the basket, the potential killer in their midst. For years, I'd insisted that I wasn't my father's daughter, but no one believed me.

You know, it hurts to walk down a corridor and see people pull their children away from you, shielding them as if you might reach out and slit their little throats at any moment.

I suppose that's why I was so eager to get to know my half brother when we met a few months later. Val was excited to meet me and knew absolutely nothing about my father. Honestly, I wasn't sure how to deal with the novelty of having someone in my life who cared whether I was getting enough to eat. He fretted when I told him in no uncertain terms that I was going along with him and Coileán to the Gray Lands, and then, when Oberon invaded Faerie, he stayed behind and insisted that I remain in the mortal realm, where it was safe. Of course, I wasn't going to sit idly by while Faerie went to pieces. Five days later, I had a death warrant on my head, courtesy of my fan club back in Montana, and I went on the run with assassins one step behind me. We straightened the matter out two months after that, but by then, I'd done what I had to do to survive.

People don't look at you the same way once you rack up a couple dozen confirmed kills, particularly not when said kills are wizards. I was well on my way to matching my father's record, and to make matters worse, word of my mother's identity had finally gotten around. As a rule, the Arcanum doesn't care for mongrels, particularly not overly talented ones like me. But I tried. I used friendly shades of hair dye and kept my wardrobe semi-professional. I took pains to do nothing that could be construed as enchantment while I was in the silo, and I *never* mentioned my brother or my frequent trips across the border during Coileán's convalescence. I reworked the silo's wards in the cold of winter, freezing my ass off while doing the sort of complex casting that most wizards could never manage, much less singlehandedly. And as ever, I continued to protest that I wasn't my father's daughter, even though my actions suggested otherwise.

Then came the coup—Helen captured, Fringers killed or taken or evacuated to Faerie as refugees, and a note on my phone from Missy Harrison that read almost like a deathbed confession. My father hadn't killed forty-three wizards on a lark. He'd killed forty-three *assassins* at a training program when Greg wouldn't give him justice for the Arcanum-sanctioned murder of the faerie who'd raised him—the woman to whom I was a namesake. He'd loved me, though his bind had prevented him from showing it. To keep up the pretense, his jailers had thrown away all his keepsakes of me before giving me his effects. And he'd gone to his execution begging them to let him see me one more time. It was my birthday, after all.

I'm not sure what the hell I was supposed to do with *that*, but Val had held me while I cried.

Whatever else he was, my father had been a complicated presence in my life, simultaneously the thing against which I contrasted myself and the person whose approval I desired most. I'd run from the Arcanum, I'd returned to it to try again, and I'd been cast out when it evolved into something monstrous. Now, innocent people were in danger, and the only thing between Mulligan and a full-scale attack from a pissed-off faerie horde was the ward system I'd rebuilt. All I had to do was find a way to bring it down from a distance—quickly, cleanly, and without giving Mulligan time to make good on his threats against the hostages.

There was just one problem: to my knowledge, what I wanted to accomplish was impossible. Even if I were on the ground outside the silo, tapping into the wards and doing everything in my power to overload them, it would take time to bring down a system that complex, especially since I'd built multiple failsafe measures in. Technical magic had long been my forte by necessity—I'd just gone on to larger projects once I had my full talent at my disposal—and now it had bitten me in the ass.

But my father had done the impossible. Spellcraft and enchantment don't work well together under the best of conditions, yet he and Mab had created something so stable and powerful that it had sealed Faerie away. Eight Arcanum theorists had already asked me for my notes on the trap's construction. If he could pull that off, then well…maybe I could be my father's daughter after all. *Just once*, I thought, *maybe the world needs a Pavli.*

Two nights after Coileán tried to coax me out of his library, he returned to find me sitting in the middle of a ring of stacked books, rocking back and forth with the heels of my hands pressed over my eyes. The headache that had been nagging me for nearly a week by then had become blinding, and even the smell of decaying paper was an indictment.

Failure.

I didn't know he was there until he pulled my hands away from my face. As I squinted in the dim light, I could just make him out in front of me, kneeling between two stacks and holding on to my wrists. "Enough," he murmured, and slipped his grip to take my hands. "No more, Toula, not now."

"I need more coffee," I protested. "I'm okay, I've got to keep reading…"

There was a flash of guilt in his old eyes, and then I saw the enchantment form around me, too quickly for me to fight in my mild delirium. It solidified into a disorganized, glowing web, and I had only a fraction of a second to contemplate the powerful chaos of faerie-made magic before I lost consciousness.

When I woke, I was burrowed in the bed in the guestroom that I'd nominally claimed, though I'd barely wrinkled the sheets since coming to Faerie. Pushing back the thick feather duvet, I let my eyes adjust to the light of the low-burning bedside lamp, then rubbed the grit out and swung my feet to the rug. The world spun for a moment, but when equilibrium returned, I rose, stretched my stiff limbs, and crossed to the window. Though the curtains had been drawn, it was dark outside, a typical cloudless night beneath a dome of scattered stars.

Tricky bastard had hit me with a sleeping enchantment. At least he hadn't taken my clothes off, I noted—I was still wearing that week's T-shirt and leggings, which admittedly had begun to exude a certain funk. I didn't want to think about the state of my hair, gone limp and falling around my face in clumps made dirty with oil and old gel.

As I mulled over all the ways I was going to chew Coileán out, someone softly knocked, and I turned to see Astrid, his head cook, poke her head into the room. "Oh! You're awake," she said, smiling. "Are you hungry, dear?"

I paused to think about the question, then recognized the angry gnawing in my midsection. "Famished, actually."

Astrid opened the door a little wider, revealing a trolley in the hallway. "Chicken and rice? Or would you like something—"

"Nope, that's great," I interrupted, and headed for the door to take it from her.

"*Sit*," she ordered, pointing to the overstuffed armchair by the window, then wheeled in the food and created a wooden tray table with a flick of her finger. The aroma wafting from the covered dish made my mouth water, and I realized how thirsty I was. As if reading my mind—easy for a faerie, though I'd have felt the intrusion had she tried—Astrid produced a large tumbler of ice water and a straw. "Drink up, now, it's good for you," she said, pressing the glass into my hands. "And here's a napkin…cutlery…"

While she fussed over the place setting, I glanced out the window again, trying to discern how long I'd been asleep. The stars were no help, however, and I soon gave it up as futile. "How late is it, anyway?"

She made a face—telling time in Faerie is more an art than a science. "A few hours past sundown. Before midnight, I'd think. Why?"

"Just trying to figure out how long I napped."

Astrid chuckled and added tiny salt and pepper shakers to my tray. "About a day."

"A *day*?"

She patted my shoulder, firmly coaxing me back into my seat before I could upset the food. "You were exhausted, poor thing. Feeling better now?"

I glowered at my dinner, shoveled a bite in, and

swallowed. Delicious as usual, and I hurried to fill the void in my stomach. "Gonna kill him," I mumbled with my mouth full.

"Don't worry, no one's touched your books," she replied, sidestepping my declaration of intended regicide. "And he's in his office, should you need a word with him— *ah*, sit," she said as I started to stand. "Eat, Toula. The king's not going anywhere, and that's far less appetizing cold."

"I can reheat it."

Astrid folded her arms and stared down at me. "Listen to your elders, young lady, especially when they're trying to keep you from fainting with hunger. Yes?"

It *was* good chicken. I took another bite, then tried not to inhale the rest. But with my baser animal need satiated, my mind had resources to return to its ever-louder refrain from the last few days: *Failure*.

The thought, when it hit again, was almost enough to kill my appetite. I didn't deserve this—I hadn't earned a bed and a chicken dinner and a babysitter to watch me eat, not when I had yet to find a single passage of use in all of my reading. Oh, I'd come across theoretical musings and hypothetical postulates, but none of them had borne fruit. I'd set up tiny ward systems in the library, shielding lamps and books and a marble statue that I had a strong suspicion was a Michelangelo, but my distance experiments failed. Nothing was sufficiently fast or precise, even from a few yards away. Simply put, I needed my hands to be within inches of the ward lattice to work major changes on it, and even then, I couldn't muster the power I would need to bring it down in a sudden stroke.

Failure. Like always. Never good enough, too blind to see the truth behind my father's bind, too well-behaved to break my own chains, too slow to see the danger roaring toward us like a tsunami.

Of course I wasn't my father's daughter. He would have known what to do.

As Astrid had promised, I found Coileán in his firelit office, working late on the continual stream of complaints. Petty grievances like party noise could turn deadly in Faerie, as we'd witnessed in recent months, and he and Eleanor had their work cut out for them to manage their courts, a people with incredible magical ability and the emotional intelligence of surly toddlers. I didn't bother knocking, but he didn't seem peeved at the intrusion. "Sorry about the sneak attack," he said, gesturing to his pair of blue leather couches in invitation. "You were becoming a danger to yourself."

"Warn me next time," I muttered, sinking onto the nearer couch.

"See, then it wouldn't be a sneak attack." He rose from his desk and headed for his substantial bar. "What are you drinking?"

"Doesn't matter."

Coileán paused and studied me for a moment, then frowned and reached for the tequila. After pouring himself a double of bourbon, he joined me and slid my drink across the coffee table. "Still groggy, eh?"

I shook my head and drank.

He hesitated, watching me, and pushed his glass aside. "I swear, I knocked you out because you looked like you were on the verge of a break with reality. Please don't be angry, I thought you were on your way to hallucinations and hurting yourself…"

If he had more to say, I didn't hear it. I squeezed my eyes closed against their sudden burning and broke down into a fit of sobs that left me shaking. Somehow, my tequila ended up on the table instead of soaking into the rug, and I covered my face as I rocked on the couch.

I don't know when Coileán took the seat beside me, but I soon became aware of his hand running up and down over my shoulders in an ineffective attempt at comfort. And then, when I came up for air in the space between spasms, I heard him murmur near my ear, "May I see?"

I nodded and dropped my mental defenses, and he slid

into my thoughts like a needle through gauze, quick, deft, and painless. He couldn't have been in there more than a few seconds before he withdrew. Pulling myself together, I rubbed the worst of the tears from my eyes and wiped one hand under my running nose, suddenly conscious of how *naked* I'd let myself be. I'd never voluntarily allowed anyone but Val inside my mind, and reaching that point of trust had taken me months. After all, armor's no good if it isn't impenetrable.

I'm not sure what I expected to see in Coileán's expression when I looked up again, but incredulity hadn't been on the list. "Moon and stars, woman, you haven't failed anyone," he said, shaking his head in disbelief.

My eyes pricked, and I dug my fingernails into the meat of my palms to stop the fresh tears. "Nothing's working. I'm looking everywhere for a solution—"

"To an impossible problem."

"*He* did it!"

Coileán took a sip of bourbon while I wrestled myself under control, then asked, "How do you know it was your father's work?" When I didn't immediately answer, he continued, "What your parents did together was incredible, I'll grant you that. But what makes you think that Apollonios was the architect?"

"I…you know, he…" I began, stuttering as I groped for an argument. "I mean—"

"How long could he have worked on it, really? Months? A couple of years, maybe?" He took my hand and squeezed. "Mab had a millennium to work through the kinks. I'd wager a million that she had most of the project working by the time she met him. Sure, your father was talented, but that wasn't the sort of project a kid his age could have thrown together in that little time." He leaned closer and waited until I met his eyes, then said, "She had *centuries*, Glinda. You've been working for twenty-three days. You haven't failed anyone." Sitting back, he released me and reached for his tumbler again. "Give yourself credit. You're attempting the impossible. If you'd made headway already, it would be extraordinary."

He was missing the point, and I struggled to put it into words until I managed to blurt, "So what good am I if I'm not extraordinary?"

Coileán paused, his glass halfway to his lips. "Who said you weren't?"

"If I can't get through the damn wards—"

"You're *trying*. Whether you succeed or fail doesn't make you any less remarkable." He threw back the rest of his drink, and the glass refilled as it returned to the table. "You know, I've read most of those books in there. Studied wardwork."

"*Why?*"

"Why not? It doesn't come naturally to me, the Arcanum's pontificated on the subject for ages, so why not read up and see what translates? And after all that reading, I still can't hold a candle to you."

I sniffed and reached for my drink, then let the smooth burn run down my tight throat. "Your building's network was pretty tight."

Coileán snorted. "Tinkertoys next to the silo wards. I still don't know how you worked those on your own."

"Just practice and concentration."

"And a hell of a lot of talent." He paused, frowning to himself, then gripped my wrist. "I'm going to be honest with you. You're the finest wizard I've ever met, and I've run across *many* magi."

"Hardly," I replied, "but thanks."

"I'm not just blowing smoke," he insisted. "What you can do is phenomenal, Toula."

"Except my father could—"

"Your father was a fool," Coileán interrupted. "The genius teamed up with Mab, got to shoot a few people, and spent the rest of his life in a cell, and *you're* the one who suffered for it. Whatever talent he had, it was inversely proportional to his planning abilities."

I wanted to rebut that, but I couldn't find the words.

"You think I don't want to attack the silo?" he asked. "Hell, I'd *enjoy* it. Ellie would be right there with me, and to be blunt about it, your wards couldn't keep us out forever. But we've got to be smart about this. Apollonios was hasty, and look what happened to the two of you. Mab forgot to plan for any scenario in which you wouldn't kill me the second you had the chance, and she's not around anymore. Let's do better than that. Live hostages beat dead victims any day."

He waited for a time while I struggled with my thoughts, then said, "Let's design a proper apartment for you. A bedroom, a kitchen—you know, the important things you've been neglecting this month. A sound system that plays more than cassettes. Take whatever you want from the library, but take care of yourself, yes?"

A thought bubbled up, apropos of nothing, and I smirked to keep myself from laughing. "Don't try to buy my affection with a library, Gramps. Won't work."

"Alas," he replied, rolling his eyes. "Should have sprung for a ladder on brass rails, shouldn't I?"

"And I want a practice room. I need space to run tests."

"Whatever you like. For the time being...mi casa, et cetera." He smiled, then patted my shoulder. "We're going to find them, and we're going to get them out alive. After that, if you'd like to go full Pavli on the Council, be my guest."

"And there it is again," I said, flopping back into the cushion. "Why does everyone assume I'm always *this* close to homicidal rage, huh?"

"Personally? I'm probably projecting," Coileán admitted. He drank his second bourbon, then leaned back beside me, both of us staring at the stone wall while the fire burned low. "Here's to good old Mom and Dad," he said, raising his empty glass, "and all the shit they force us to carry long after they're gone."

I looked into the shadows and could almost envision

Apollonios watching me through the bars, forever trying and failing to be his daughter's father.

"Hear, hear," I murmured, and drank.

APRIL: HELEN CARVER

It's quiet in the void.

I would call it womb-like, but wombs are noisy places. Isn't that what they tell you at prenatal classes—your baby can hear your heartbeat, the gurgling of your stomach, the rumbling of your voice? But in the void, most of the time, you hear nothing. You hang motionless in space, cradled by nothingness, bobbing below the surface of awareness like a sleeping whale. Every so often, however, you rise to breathe, and that's when consciousness returns...and everything that goes with it.

It was voices, mostly, that pulled me back into my personal hell. There's no need to be quiet if the patient's in a coma, is there? I couldn't open my eyes to see my jailers, but I knew them by timbre and accent.

James Mulligan, baritone, silo-reared with an upper midwestern cadence to match, a pleasing voice if you disregarded the rest of the treasonous package.

Russel Mulligan, a low tenor with a tendency to slip into fry, a silo boy like his old man but with less of the distinct vowels that made James sound like he was auditioning to be Canadian in his next life.

Once or twice, Howard Carver—my dad—his familiar deep rasp turned strange until I pinpointed the problem. Before, Dad's voice had usually been gentle with me, paternal, proud. What I heard instead were the clipped tones he'd reserved for Aid, and when the Mulligans gave him a moment alone with me, he cursed me to my unmoving face.

I had my arguments lined up and ready: *I fell in love with a bright, brave, kind man who looks at me like I hung the moon and would follow me off a cliff. He protects my little brother in ways that I can't. When he really smiles, even with the beard, he looks about twelve, and that drawl makes my heart melt because it tells me I'm home and safe. Why should it matter who his great-great-grandfather was?* I wouldn't have brought up in my opening salvo the minor detail that Joey had been living in Coileán's backyard for the better part of three years, or that he had no plans to permanently abandon Faerie because of Georgie, the draconic other lady in his life. I *definitely* would have avoided discussing Joey's recent augmentation, though even that could have been excused: he was a newlywed with a baby on the way, and he'd been shot through the chest. What other option did he have but accept the realm's offer to save him? He was still the man I loved, albeit with a newfound capacity for enchantment and a metal allergy that meant I'd never need to pick out a silver pattern. I would have told Dad that we'd make it work, had I been able to speak. But stasis binds are difficult enough to break when only two people are involved, let alone six. Mulligan and five other magi had poured themselves into my bonds, ensuring that I'd stay under even if a few of my captors were disabled. I might have overpowered one, but six was overkill. And so I lay there…wherever I was…unable to do anything but listen to Dad tell me that he wished I'd never been born.

It was the fourth voice that hurt the worst.

Though she spoke softly, my mother's voice sliced through my mental fog like a flashlight in a cave. The first time I heard her, I rejoiced—Mom would set me free, Mom would make it better. I lay there, powerless to do otherwise, and waited for the bind to be released. Instead, I heard Mom's quiet conversation with Mulligan, her tone betraying nothing but professional confidence, and felt the chill of a stethoscope on my chest, the pressure of an inflating cuff on my arm, the sting of a needle at the bend of my elbow. I listened with mounting despair as she explained medical visualization spells to the magus. Mom wasn't a doctor, but silo medics knew how to see what was happening below the surface. I felt it when the spell finally kicked in—she must have gone slowly so as not to upset my bind—and then I heard her say, "We have a heartbeat. It's still alive."

It—my baby.

"Helen's pulse just spiked," Mom said, sounding troubled. "Can she hear—"

"Bits and pieces," Mulligan told her, and patted my cheek. "She might even be dreaming. No way to tell."

I wanted to scream at him, to rise up and claw out his eyes, but my muscles wouldn't respond to my frantic attempts at motion.

When she spoke again, Mom didn't sound entirely convinced. "Next week. We've got a baseline—let's give it a few days."

And that had been that. The voices had grown distant, the door had slammed, and I'd drifted back into insensibility, my only means of staving off the insanity of solitude.

But I wasn't alone—not entirely. Unable to do more than breathe and pump blood, cut off from all sound but the rushing in my ears, I concentrated and tried to feel the faint stirrings of my baby fluttering against me, kicking and punching in its watery world. I'd sneaked off to my old college OB/GYN in Nashville during the early days of my pregnancy, and by her calculations, I'd moved into the second trimester before I'd been attacked. Baby Bolin and I had made it through the worst, but now, I couldn't feel a single twitch. They'd bound my baby, too.

We'll make it through this, I thought, carrying on a silent conversation with my little roommate. *Mommy will get free, and Daddy will help us, and everything will be okay, very soon. Mommy won't let anything happen to you. Don't worry about a thing. I'm here. Please live.*

When I heard Mom again, I assumed it had been about a week, but I had no way of knowing. "No change," she said to Mulligan. "It looks like development stopped with the bind. The fetus is alive, but it's not growing. I don't think it's hurting her."

His reply chilled my heart: "Can't be too careful."

When they left, before nothingness claimed me again, I sent my plea into the universe: *Help us, Joey. They're coming for our baby, help us.*

Joey wouldn't let me stay locked away for long, I told myself. He and Aid had hiked through the wilderness of Faerie for weeks when Coileán was bound—surely they'd come for me, too. I spoke comfort to myself, insisting that the next time I heard voices, they'd be my husband's and my brother's.

I told myself a lot of things down there.

The next voice I heard was Mulligan's, followed by Mom's: muted mumblings, all business. And then, as I woke, I began to make sense of the sounds.

"It's quite secure," Mom said. "We used it just last year at Arc 5 when one of the aides needed chemo and found out she was pregnant. Baby went almost to term." She paused. "Of course, you understand that the odds of a successful transfer would be *much* better if I had some help."

"Just do the best you can." Mulligan replied. "If it fails…well, no great loss there."

Mom didn't answer him. "I need you to step back, please. Can't even disinfect properly in here…"

As she muttered to herself, I felt my shirt pulled up to my breasts and my pants lowered ever so slightly—an elastic waist, I realized, and briefly wondered what I was wearing before I felt cold liquid being rubbed over my exposed abdomen.

A disinfectant. It had to be a disinfectant of some kind. And that meant…

In vain, I struggled to move, to flinch, to make a sound, but my body was unresponsive, even as I yelled inside my own head.

When Mom finished, I heard the rustling and snap of gloves. "Well, this is about as far from sterile as you can get, but we'll call it field surgery. Now, I'm just going to numb her—"

"No, don't."

"Excuse me?"

"Don't," Mulligan repeated. "She's insensate, it'd be a waste of effort."

"Still," Mom protested, "just in case…"

"We've got enough spells in play as it is without adding a superfluous numbing spell to the mix. Let's not tax the bind, Rachel, eh?"

For a long moment, Mom said nothing. I couldn't even hear her move, and I started to visualize her reconsidering, stepping away from me and telling Mulligan that she wouldn't stand for any of this.

Instead, I finally heard her murmur, "Yes, Grand Magus."

The thin scalpel was cold against my skin, shaking ever so slightly in Mom's hand…and then it burned like a branding iron as it cut me open.

I couldn't scream, couldn't move, couldn't even retreat into my foggy blackness in the face of my agony. My universe shrank to encompass the path of the scalpel, the fissure left behind it, and my pain and fear. *Not my baby*, I wordlessly begged, *please, Mom, not my baby, don't kill my baby, let us go, make it stop make it stop—*

The scalpel finished its work, and Mom began to whisper a spell. I could feel the concentration of power along my bleeding wound and knew her wand had to be somewhere just above me. The coalescing spell tingled against my skin, and I luxuriated in the welcome reduction in pain, momentarily pushing aside worry for the sheer joy of physical relief.

And then the spell took effect.

The scalpel was as a papercut compared to the wrenching, twisting torture of that damn spell as it opened me wider and pulled the baby out of me. I tried to kick, to shout for help, *anything* to make the pain end…

"Her finger twitched," Mom said.

"What?"

"Just now. Are you sure I can't numb her?"

"Do as I ask," Mulligan snapped.

I heard his footsteps moving away, a sharp ring against the hard floor, and then I felt Mom's breath in my ear. "I'm sorry," was all she whispered before the pain swelled again, and then, with a *pop* like a rubber band released, it subsided into a dull, throbbing ache.

As the blackness rose around me like a warm blanket, I heard Mom say, "Fetus is stable. If you want to take the bind off it, I'll close her up."

No, I tried to say, *no, Mommy, bring my baby back, I'm sorry, I'll be better…*

The last thing I heard was the squeal of a sticky wheel on what I took to be a medical cart, and then the door closed.

I was alone. Truly alone and hurting, my wound seeming to pulse in time with my magically slowed heart.

Joey, can you hear me? I thought as the void took me again. *They stole our baby. You have to find it. Please, Joey.*

Please find me.

My mother never returned to visit me. Maybe Mulligan was afraid she'd go soft on him, or maybe Mom was as disgusted by me as Dad kept insisting he was. I couldn't say for sure either way.

As a rule, I didn't dream much in the void, but my subconscious came up with a short movie to console me: my mother, tied to a boulder like Prometheus, screaming as an eagle ripped her open and gorged itself, over and over again. *Welcome to hell, Mom,* I thought each time, just before I floated off into my silent solitude.

APRIL: AMY LEVEY

"You know, you're safe here," said Miss Beatriz. "You don't have to bring that along every time."

That was my black Glock semi-automatic pistol, my last birthday present from my parents, which accompanied me everywhere in its hip holster those days. A ten-round magazine loaded with 9mm ammo might not stop a truly determined wizard, but it would at least slow him down.

Miss Beatriz didn't like guns—she'd made that much clear during our first meeting three weeks before, when one of my fosters dragged me in for counseling. I'd carried a rifle that day as well. Better safe than sorry until you know the terrain, and as far as I was concerned, Faerie was the Wild West.

Focus, Daddy used to tell me. *Always keep an eye on what's around you.*

On the surface, our settlement looked safe enough. The Fringe refugee camp had grown up into a town in the last month. The original building, with its rows of beds and screaming kids and hallways that echoed with the sounds of people sneaking off to cry in private, had disappeared after the first week, replaced by a carefully laid out Main Street and a growing neighborhood of comfortable houses. The place was a little *too* nice, a carless version of small-town perfection—like one of the weirder planned communities, but for the short brick wall surrounding the place. I wasn't sure whether the wall was supposed to keep us in or curious faeries out, and so I never went walking without a gun. Not at first.

We didn't even have a real coordinator anymore. The adults didn't talk about it much around us, at least not in the group home, but I picked up bits and pieces from scattered conversations. None of the coordinators had made it across during the evacuation scramble. Many of them were confirmed dead. The only coordinator I knew was Mr. Slim, who lived a few hours north of my family in Virginia and was a crafter like Mama. He'd been running the evacuation from his place, but he was taken before the end. Miss Vivi wasn't a coordinator, but she'd been working with Mr. Slim from Faerie, and I guess people figured she was good enough in a pinch. She was a weird case, even by Fringe standards: both of her parents were half fae, but Miss Vivi seemed to have gotten almost every last one of their human genes. I could commiserate—both of my parents were witch-bloods, who'd gone into making me with the hope that I'd favor one side or the other.

Ha.

Miss Vivi was young for a coordinator, even a de facto emergency coordinator, but she apparently knew the king, and since we were camping on his turf, that seemed to give her a smidgen of authority. She also knew the queen—technically, Miss Vivi should have belonged to her court—and the queen had given some of Miss Vivi's brothers a pass to help us out. They were nice enough, if a little standoffish at first, but I couldn't blame them. We weren't exactly a happy bunch of refugees, even though the town they built for us was lovely.

Among the first buildings to go up downtown were offices for the psychologists, therapists, and grief counselors—really, anyone remotely qualified to sit and listen to people cry with a box of tissues on hand. There weren't enough of them to deal with our collective and individual traumas, and they were booked solid.

I'd been assigned to Miss Beatriz, and judging by the bags under her dark eyes, she hadn't slept well in the month since the evacuation. She was pretty, a Brazilian lady in her early forties who favored floral capris and wore her dark hair braided and coiled into fantastic updos, and she was sympathetic while I talked. But I never felt like saying much, even when she tried to pry it out of me. I chalked it up to a linguistic thing at first—we conducted our sessions in Fae, though we'd only just learned it on arrival. The words still felt strange in my mouth, and Miss Beatriz and I sometimes had to puzzle over each other's accent. Portuguese and southern American English didn't always play nicely together.

"So," said my therapist, crossing her long legs, "how are we doing today?"

Focus. Breathe.

I shrugged and sat, reassured by the pistol at my hip.

I'm sure that Miss Beatriz tried her best, but I wasn't in a talkative mood that month.

"How are you sleeping?" she finally enquired after a few minutes of receiving nothing more than monosyllabic responses from me.

Honestly? In fits and starts, short spurts of exhausted unconsciousness punctuated by screaming nightmares.

"Fine," I told her.

She didn't look convinced, but she let it slide. "I heard that you've moved out of the group home."

"Yes, ma'am."

"Any particular reason?"

Because I can't take another night of waking up to little kids sobbing for their mamas in ten languages. I can't stand sitting around the tables and pretending we're a big old family when we're just pieces of lost puzzles tossed into a box and forced together. If one of the fosters snaps at me again, I'm going to punch a hole in the wall.

"I need to concentrate in order to craft," I said. "Takes some quiet. I can't do that in a shared bedroom."

"You could have a workshop and still go back to the house at night," she suggested. "I don't like the thought of you being on your own." Miss Beatriz pursed her lips and flipped through my thin file. "You're...sixteen?"

Two weeks ago. Halfway to my real driver's license. I was going to go out for a fancy dinner with my friends the following Friday. We would have dressed up like for prom, and Mama promised to rent a limo for the night, and there was going to be chocolate cake and fake champagne back at my house. My dress was pink and layered like a flapper's, and my high heels made me five-foot-five. Daddy was going to take me hunting for wild hogs the next day, just the two of us.

"Yes, ma'am."

"That's young to be fending for yourself, Amy. Don't you think you'll be lonely?"

Some of the little ones have regressed to wetting the bed, and their end of the building smells like pee all the time. The older ones cry and scream at night, just like me. We sit around and stare at each other, no one eager to make friends because we don't have it in us to take on someone else's grief. The walls are thin, and one of the girls in the room beside mine talks in her sleep. I think it's Spanish, but whatever she's saying, she's pleading with someone. My roommate cuts herself. I don't know if it makes the ache go away, but it gives her something else to think about. One of the ten-year-old boys is on suicide watch after he was caught trying to make a noose out of a bedsheet.

"I'll be fine," I said. "And there's supposed to be school in a few months, if we're still here after the summer, so...you know?" Miss Beatriz said nothing, and after a moment, I filled the silence. "People need wands, right? That's important. Lots of folks didn't even have a chance to grab theirs before they left." I paused, then asked, "Do you need one? I've got some of Mama's still, if you want to try them."

She smiled slightly and shook her head. "Lesser blood, but thank you."

"Oh."

Miss Beatriz was still smiling, but I'd seen it there, in the way her face tightened when I talked about crafting. She wouldn't *say* anything, of course, and if I'd asked, I'm sure she would have denied even thinking about what had to have flitted through her mind: *mongrel.*

Other Fringers were nice to our faces, but Mama and Daddy warned me not to expect too much from them. The ones who came by needed wands, which only witch-bloods could make. Of my parents, Mama had the talent, and so her customers spoke kindly and shook my parents' hands and made polite conversation while they tested wands or Mama put the finishing touches on their orders. And folks always said hi to them on the Fringe network, where they were Picasso and Deputy, the crafter and her husband who held down a mundane IT job to keep the mortgage paid. But most of them weren't exactly *friendly.* Some people didn't care that we were witch-bloods, but we made a lot of them uneasy. Mr. Slim didn't seem to have it as bad as we did, probably because the eastern third of the country looked to him for help in times of crisis. But Mama was just a crafter, not a coordinator, and I was a double witch-blood, something that should never have been born.

With all of the commotion and upheaval, I could have passed as a dud without a problem—I didn't even have a network code name yet to give me away. Instead, I'd gotten the go-ahead from Miss Vivi to open my own workshop, the third in town. Mr. Robbie, one of her brothers, had helped me design it down to the paint colors, and it was sandwiched between a new bakery and a café, so at least I wouldn't go hungry. Still, I was striking out on my own *and* outing myself as a mongrel, and that was a decision that someone like Miss Beatriz couldn't understand.

Focus, pumpkin.

The digital clock on the table between us beeped to signal the end of our session, and I stood and adjusted my gun. "Thanks. See you later," I said, and headed for the exit.

"Amy," she called after me, "wait a minute. We need to schedule our next meeting before you leave."

But I'd already reached the door, and the thought of returning for a fifth half-hour of light conversation and awkward silences didn't sit well with me. Miss Beatriz meant well, but our little talks hadn't done anything to make the dreams go away.

"I'm going to be busy," I replied, and depressed the handle. "Maybe later."

The boy who'd been waiting in the vestibule slipped in behind me before she could protest, and I saw myself out into the warm afternoon. Another perfectly pleasant day in Faerie, just like all the ones before, and I smiled at the people who passed on the newly laid sidewalk.

I wanted to shoot something.

It's the faerie in you, Daddy had told me when I was little and lashed out in tantrums that left me with bruised knuckles from punching my bedroom walls. *You've just got to put it on a leash, pumpkin. Like a big dog.*

I didn't have a dog to practice with—Mama had terrible allergies to dogs, cats, and almost anything else with fur—so Daddy took me hunting instead.

Hunting takes patience, he explained, and focus. You have to learn to be absolutely still and listen, picking out the rustling of your quarry within the background noise of the woods. If you're doing it right, you'll be in a blind or a stand in the cold dark of a winter morning and the swampy heat of summer alike, depending on what you're hunting, and you have to accept the discomfort as part of the experience. Your shivers and sweats don't matter—you keep focused on the task at hand. He taught me to clear my mind and shoot straight, to exhale before firing, to pull back on a bow and wait, arm quivering, until the target was perfectly aligned. He explained the hunting seasons and what we could and couldn't take, and how important it was to follow game rules and safety regulations alike. Daddy was a responsible hunter and an excellent shot, and I wanted to be just like him. We spent our long Saturdays together out in the middle of nowhere, master and novice, and then, back home, whenever my anger boiled up until it was too big for me to keep inside, Daddy would dodge my fists and hold me steady, telling me to focus. Picture the deer in the brush and be still.

It gets better, baby, he'd say when I was spent and crying. *I promise, it gets better.*

And it did, eventually. I learned to recognize a coming wave of rage before it crashed over me, and in time, I could keep my feelings locked down instead of letting them drag me under. Most of my days were good ones—I remember being a happy kid—but as for the bad days, I grew to a point where I didn't let emotion overwhelm me. I wore a smile as a shield to keep the anger from bursting forth.

We had it worse than many, Mama and Daddy and me. No two witch-bloods are quite the same, and my parents had inherited strongly fae tempers. Mr. Slim didn't have that problem—I heard the three of them talk about it in the kitchen early one afternoon when I was supposed to be napping—and neither did many of the lesser fae. *You know it's a crapshoot*, he'd said while they sat around drinking coffee. *She could have ended up almost fae.*

At least then I'd have had an excuse. Instead, I was a witch-blood with anger management issues, learning to control the feelings that were too big for me. Instead of letting my anger vent in physical ways, I allowed myself to dive into the darker corners of my imagination, picturing all sorts of violence enacted upon people who crossed me until my conscience caught up with me and gave me a good shake. I was ashamed of the bad thoughts, but since it's preferable to imagine someone being hit in the face with a tire iron rather than actually carry it out, I accepted the thoughts as part of my particular curse.

On occasion, I wondered about my grandfathers, both of whom had been fully fae, and what their tempers must have been like. I'd never met them—we only knew what they were because the Arcanum had checked out my parents when they were babies, making sure that the situation was as bad as my grandmothers feared. My parents were the product of rape, but even though I was the product of love, my grandfathers' little gift came to me, too.

And so I learned to put on a smile so as not to scare people. There was no need to let on about what lurked beneath the surface, especially not to a nice lady like Miss Beatriz who probably already thought I should never have been born.

The ability to craft was the one perk to being a witch-blood, and even then, not all of us could do it well. Daddy never had the knack, but Mama's wands brought people from far and wide—even wizards knew the Levey name. Daddy would call her the Stradivari of crafters, and she'd swat at him with a polishing towel but blush with pleasure.

I wasn't Mama's equal, not by a long shot. Mama was a master crafter, and I'd been her apprentice, learning my woods and cores and the concentration needed to make everything come together and spark in the right hands.

It's like breathing.

Mama's focusing methods were different than Daddy's, but after my years in the woods with him, I'd picked the basics up pretty quickly, and I could make serviceable wands. It was the little details that set Mama's wands apart: the perfect varnish, the ideal weight, the fine balance between the components. Mine might be too short, too heavy, too core-focused, or streaky where I used tongs during varnishing. *You're doing great, honey*, Mama always told me when I showed her my imperfect offerings. *All the rest will come in time. I'll show you everything, don't you worry.*

I'm sure there was plenty she never got around to passing on, but it was too late to wonder what she'd forgotten—my apprenticeship had ended prematurely. Still, despite my relative inexperience, I was Amelia Levey's daughter, and when I went to Miss Vivi two days before my last counseling session and said I could craft, she agreed to have a workshop set up for me, whatever I wanted. So many of us had fled with the clothes on our backs, and good wands were in short supply. I asked to move out of the group home to have more time and space to work, and she agreed, though she'd given me a look of doubt like Miss Beatriz's.

Mr. Robbie had come by the next day and taken me to my new workshop, a white-brick building on a tree-lined side street. The place was nothing but a shell when we arrived, but he'd designed the whole thing with me standing there, giving directions. My workshop was on the street level, and it had only two rooms, a narrow waiting room and the main workspace. He'd put a double row of wooden chairs in the waiting area, then added a sturdy concrete floor to my workshop and lined three walls with shelving units too tall for me to fully use without a stepstool. The fourth wall was a plate-glass window overlooking the sidewalk, and though he seemed pained by the request, he tinted the glass red. Sure, it made the inside of the workshop look a bit like the bowels of Hell, but crafting could be a sensitive business, and some of the more experimental materials were liable to go *boom* if the conditions weren't just right. He'd gestured a long wooden workbench into being and a couple of stools to go with it. I'd laughed at that and asked if he was planning to come by and help me, and he'd tugged my braid and called me cheeky before creating stairs to the upper floor. My creativity had reached its limit by then, and so I'd stepped back and let him section off a bedroom, bathroom, den, and kitchenette, all nicely furnished and painted with muted neutrals. The wood floors were a pretty touch, and he'd given me big windows and a skylight, but I found it hard to get too worked up about things like rugs and cabinetry. Still, Mr. Robbie had been patient with my ambivalence, and when he'd finished late that afternoon, I had a respectable apartment and workshop—even Wi-Fi, he'd explained, thanks to a tiny gate in Lord Coileán's palace and the sort of enchantment I'd never fully understand. I didn't have a computer to go with the Wi-Fi, but it was a small comfort to know it was there, all the same.

When all of my supplies were loaded onto the shelves and my few other belongings had been brought over from the group home, Mr. Robbie had taken a last glance around the workshop, then given me a worried look much like Miss Vivi's. "Have you got dinner plans?" he'd asked. "I'll send one of the boys 'round tomorrow to stock your pantry, but tonight…"

I'd shrugged. "There's sandwiches next door, I think."

That idea hadn't sat well with him. After a quick phone call, he'd opened a gate to a long, fancy dining room—burgundy walls, a thick rug, two chandeliers, and a mahogany table ringed with at least twenty ornate chairs. "Come with me," he'd said, beckoning toward the gate. "Mum's made shepherd's pie, and there's roughly enough for an army."

Daddy had been the cook in our family, and his shepherd's pie had started with a jar of sauce from the imports section of Publix and a box of instant mashed potatoes. "Real bits of shepherd in every bite?" I'd asked, letting the words slip out before I'd remembered that Daddy wasn't there to joke back at me.

Mr. Robbie had stiffened in surprise, then chuckled. His smile was like his sister's, wide and friendly.

I couldn't keep all the Stowes straight that night—eight of the twelve brothers had come for dinner, and since everyone looked about twenty-five, it took some doing for me to even remember which was Mr. Robbie's dad. Miz Rohese, his mom, was petite like me but smotheringly kind, fussing over me to eat more and asking me all about crafting. But dinner conversation was tough, as none of the normal questions adults ask teenagers could be answered without complications.

"Where are you from?"

South Carolina until last month. I just moved out of a group home that might as well be renamed "PTSD Place."

"Any siblings?"

One mongrel was bad enough, don't you think?

"What year are you in?"

Well, I was finishing tenth grade when the Arcanum murdered my parents. Now, I guess I'll have to catch up when I go back to school. If I go back to school.

One of the brothers had asked if I had any court ties, and Miz Rohese had given him the same sort of glare that Mama once gave me for loudly farting during a quiet movement at the symphony. I'd tried to make him feel better and just said I'd never looked into it, since *I don't really care who my rapist grandfathers swore allegiance to* didn't seem to be a nice thing to say at the dinner table.

Miz Rohese's shepherd's pie was pretty good, but it wasn't Daddy's. I'd thanked Mr. Robbie again once he brought me home, and when he'd closed the gate behind him, I'd burrowed beneath the blankets of my new bed and cried myself to sleep.

When you're on the cusp of sixteen, death is something that happens to other people—*maybe* a grandparent if you're unlucky, but certainly no one in your immediate family. I mean, logically, you know that your parents are going to die someday, but if you think about it at all, it's a blur in the far distance, maybe an old person peacefully going to sleep and never waking up. It's an awful eventuality, and it you think about it too long, you might choke yourself up, but it's a thought that can be pushed to the mental back burner, something to wrestle with once you're grown and graying yourself.

Or at least it was for me until the assassins came by.

I'd gone to Catholic school since kindergarten, and without fail, we got Easter Monday off, a bonus day of vacation at the end of spring break. Daddy had made lamb for dinner Sunday night, and the three of us had stayed up late watching Monty Python movies and acting out our favorite scenes from the comfort of the couch. Mama had pointed out that it seemed *slightly* sacrilegious to watch *Life of Brian* on Easter, but she made popcorn anyway and settled in beside me, sandwiching me between her and Daddy until we started falling asleep and dragged ourselves upstairs.

I didn't roll out of bed until eleven the next morning, but both of my parents were still home when I shuffled down for food. Mama's workshop was in the basement, and Daddy had decided to take the day off to get a jump on the yard before the height of spring. I microwaved pancakes and lazed around while I ate, keeping Mama company while she polished a new batch of wands, and then I decided to go for a run—my cross-country coach had stressed the importance of conditioning before the fall season. Mama told me to watch for cars, like always, and Daddy, who was coming inside to make lunch, waved as I put in my earbuds and took off on a two-mile circuit.

When I jogged back onto the sidewalk in front of our house, I was sweaty but pleased with my time and finishing condition. Draping my earbuds around my neck, I let myself in the front door and called to my parents to signal my return—or started to, at least. I don't know how much of the planned *Hey, y'all, I'm back* made it out before I started screaming.

Mama and Daddy were sprawled on the gray tile floor of the hallway heading toward the kitchen, staring at nothing with twin expressions of horror. I remember too many details of that tableau. Daddy was still in his grubby yard clothes, his hands and arms scrubbed clean but for the dirt around his cuticles. He had a thin streak of mud down one cheek, the result of a careless swipe against sweat, and his brown hair stuck up in odd tufts. In his right hand, he held a steak knife. Mama had a trace of varnish on her fingers and was still wearing Sunday's black eyeliner, smudged with sleep. She hadn't showered yet, and her hair, blonde like mine, was pinned back in a messy bun with a blue claw clip. I could tell they'd been surprised—Mama had been working in her pajamas, and she'd never have answered the door without a bra on, at least not without putting a bathrobe on first to make her more shapeless. She lay behind Daddy, closer to the kitchen.

As my emotional brain tried to shut down, my logical side stepped in with clinical dispassion. I could piece together what had happened: the door had opened—probably loudly, given Daddy's improvised weapon—and he'd gone to investigate. Mama had come up from the basement through the kitchen and been attacked after Daddy was neutralized. Clearly, the perpetrators had used wands; both of my parents had blast holes the size of dessert plates through their chests, though neither seemed to be bleeding, thanks to the bolt-cauterized edges of their wounds.

Having made that assessment, my logical brain ceded the floor, and I sank to my knees and howled.

I might have stayed there for hours, staring at the bodies and trying to will them to life, had a familiar alarm not begun to wail in the kitchen. The sound snapped me back from the brink of a full breakdown, and I heard Daddy's voice somewhere deep within me: *Focus, pumpkin.*

The network alarm.

Skirting my parents' bodies, I ran into the kitchen and found Daddy's laptop open on the island—he liked to listen to music while he cooked, and his pasta was still boiling on the stove. I turned off the eye and clicked the icon for the Fringe network's emergency app, which was tested on the first of every month in case of disaster. This was most certainly not a test.

The network opened to me without credentials, at least as far as the emergency communications portal. The edge of the window pulsed red in time with the alarm, and when I clicked on the message notification at the top, I heard Mr. Slim warning about immediate danger. Little video windows began to pop open on the left side of the screen, while the right, a long chat window, filled with text—messages of confusion, panic, horror. I watched for a few minutes, almost numb, then pulled myself together and opened a video window of my own. "Please help me," I said to the laptop camera's steady red light as I struggled not to cry. "Someone just killed my parents. I'm alone, and I don't know what to do, and…and I need help…"

A response window popped open on my screen, and I recognized Miss Vivi—Mr. Slim had brought her down a few months after the siege on the Arcanum silo to introduce her to my folks. "Amy?" she said, straightening her glasses. "Honey, are you hurt?"

Never had I been so grateful to see a familiar face. "No, but Mama and Daddy—"

"You're sure they're dead?"

I nodded.

"*Shit.* Are you home?"

"Yes, ma'am—"

"Okay, I remember what your house looks like. We can aim a gate with that. Don't go anywhere, and *don't* answer the door. I'm going to send one of my brothers to get you, okay?"

"Get?" I asked, dazed.

"The Fringe is evacuating. You've got about ten minutes—go pack what you can carry," she said, and closed her window.

Focus, pumpkin.

Ten minutes may seem like a long time, but not when you're having to maneuver around your parents' corpses while you rush to throw your life into bags. I tried to be methodical. My bowhunting gear was ready to go at the back of my closet, I pulled my firearms from Daddy's gun safe, and I raided the storage closet for ammo. Into the den went my rifle, shotgun, and compound bow; the pistol went straight onto my hip. Grabbing another duffel from the closet, I tossed in a few clothes—the ones I'd worn that week and left slung over a chair—a little jewelry, and my purse, then dumped the contents of my medicine cabinet in on top, finishing with the family photos on the fridge and the framed ones Mama had set up around the den. With five minutes to go, I raced into the basement, grabbed a couple of reusable grocery bags, and began to raid Mama's shelves, swiping finished wands, empty rods, jars of core material labeled in her cramped hand, tamping rods, a magnifying visor, cans of varnish, and even a few pieces of lumber, which I carried upstairs under my arm. Last was Mama's sample case, one of each of the five primary wands to be used in determining what a customer needed. She'd told me that I'd be ready to call myself a crafter when I could make my own case to her satisfaction, but I realized as I dragged hers into the den that she'd never have the chance to judge my work.

As I finished stacking my mound of gear, a crackling sound in the hallway made me draw my gun and spin around, only to find myself staring down a blond man in a blue polo and chinos, who took a step back toward the rip in reality behind him and manifested a shield between us. "Easy, now, *easy*," he said, showing me his empty hands as I kept the gun high, trying not to let my arms shake. "You're Amy, yes? I've come to fetch you. Stephen Stowe, I'm Vivi's brother."

At that moment, all I knew for sure about him was that he was British and unnerved to be facing the barrel of my Glock, but his apparent youth and ease with wandless magic suggested he was at least half fae. "You're *Fringe*?" I asked doubtfully.

"Not exactly. Drafted for the occasion. Ehm…" He reached into his back pocket and pulled out a battered leather wallet, then showed me a card from inside. "Bar Council membership card, if you like, or I've got better ID in here. Finally got back around to using my real name."

"Bar Council?" I echoed.

"I'm a barrister. Not going to hurt you. Could you point that somewhere else, please?" When I lowered the gun, he dropped his shield and stepped into the room. "Vivi said that you—oh, *fuck* me," he muttered, catching sight of my parents. "Oh. Oh, that's…"

"Mama and Daddy," I mumbled.

"Right. Yes." He sounded shaken, and he grimaced as he looked away from them. "I'm terribly sorry, truly I am. That, ehm…that's your gear, then?" he asked, pointing to the pile behind me. I nodded, and as he gestured, the bags floated into the air and through the hole—which, I could see on closer inspection, seemed to lead into a noisy, stone-walled room. "Off you go," he said, cocking his thumb toward the hole. "It doesn't hurt a bit."

But I hesitated on the threshold. "What about my parents? I can't leave them like that…"

"No, we can't," he agreed, and gestured again.

I cried out when they vanished, and he gripped my shoulder before I could run to the places where they'd been. "What if the police find your parents dead and you missing?" he said, holding me back. "You're a suspect. Better for the three of you to mysteriously disappear. Come on, now, child, we haven't got long."

He steered me through, and I looked back in time to see the gate shrink and seal itself, severing me from my home. And that was how I came to Faerie: puffy-eyed, bereaved, and still wearing my sweat-damp running shorts. I was cold and disgusting and a few heartbeats away from a meltdown, and as I stood with what remained of my worldly possessions and looked around for a life preserver, a pretty woman with a platinum-blonde bun and a stained white apron hurried to my side. She took one good look at my face, then enveloped me in a tight hug and murmured, "You're safe, little one. It's going to be all right."

That was how I met Miss Astrid: sobbing on her shoulder while my heart shattered. While the Stowe brothers continued to deliver Fringers through gates opening all around us, she held me until I began to calm down, then shrunk my bags down to the size of dollhouse miniatures, put everything into a plastic baggie for safekeeping, and ushered me off to a shower. Not until I was clean again did I realize that I'd left my phone and earbuds in the hallway where they'd fallen, but there was no going back.

After leaving Miss Beatriz's office, I returned to my workshop and locked the door behind me. People needed wands, and I'd stalled as long as I could, rearranging my materials on the shelves and carefully packing Mama's salvaged wands into the new wand boxes Mr. Robbie had made for me. I carried the basket of unfinished wands to the bench, then pulled down the appropriate core jars: powdered dragonscale for the rowan wands, unicorn horn for the oak. A nice varnish to finish. Sandpaper. Plugging resin for the base. I wouldn't try to carve anything, just make functional wands that wouldn't tarnish Mama's legacy too badly.

And I was scared to death.

I'd never crafted without her reassuring supervision. Mama had always been there to guide me, to check my cores as I packed them and help me polish my beginner's wands until they gleamed. She'd corrected my mistakes, never letting me fail and promising me that it would all make sense in time.

She was gone now, and so was Daddy, though I still had so much to learn: how to balance a wand just right, how to bake perfect lasagna, how to butcher a deer without making a mess of everything.

How to smile at people who might not call me a mongrel to my face but would certainly whisper about it out of my hearing.

How to make the nightmares stop.

How to say goodbye.

People were looking to me for help, but I wasn't ready. I was still a million angry, grieving, *slightly* homicidal shards, and not a damn thing Miss Beatriz had said had helped me piece myself back together.

But as I stared at the tools of my craft, I heard those familiar voices somewhere deep inside once more:

Focus.

Breathe.

There would be time for tears and violence, for self-blame and revenge fantasies, but for now, I had work to do. I slipped on Mama's magnifying visor, then willed my rage to heel and reached for the first rod.

JUNE: ELEANOR

My dearest,

We've had the first bit of good news in nearly three months: Detective Parsons is alive and well. I'm sure you met her on the network—Badger, the northern coordinator? She looked into your disappearance last December, and she was very kind about the situation, even after Coileán let my "little secret" slip. She brought the rest of you back to me, you know, and for that, I am eternally grateful. I can't imagine that you'd be pleased to find yourself spread about.

Anyway, she arrived last night with the Endicott twins, so that's three more Fringers safe. Do you remember the girls? You showed me their picture on the network a few years ago—Marty Endicott was going to refurbish that dresser we found at the charity shop, the one with the nice shape and that horrid robin's-egg paint job. For the guestroom, if you recall. He did lovely work, I think. I'd have given it to the girls now if not for the fire—they should have *something* from their mum and dad. Poor little lambs are terribly burnt, but they're alive, and these days, that's enough. They have their granny here—incidentally, she's one of my people, which still seems like such an impossible thing to say—and she's eager to have them, so at least they won't be going to the group home in the settlement.

I couldn't tell you how many children are still living in the group home. Isn't that terrible? I'd thought to get involved at the start, you know, really dig in and have things organized, but there's always *something* with the court. Someone's taken two steps onto someone else's land, and now there's a war about to break out. Or someone wasn't invited to a party and demands justice for the insult—I'm serious, a *party*. Remember that bit in "Sleeping Beauty" where one faerie isn't invited to the christening and curses the baby and the kingdom in revenge? That's quite nearly accurate. I knew there was pettiness in them, love, but not to this degree. Half the time, I've got to stop myself from laughing when I hear their grievances, and the other half, I'm gobsmacked at the triviality of it all. The Arcanum has been holding heaven-knows-how-many hostages for three months, the Fringe here is still working out what to do with all the orphaned children, and my people are reaching for the dueling pistols over the tiniest social slight. Of course, if you try to point out to them that their problems are miniscule by comparison, they look at you like you're speaking Greek. Like the robots on the telly used to say, it does not compute.

I wish my father were still alive. Not because of late-blooming sentimentality—the man was my sperm donor, nothing more—but because if he were still here, then this bloody stupid court would be his problem, and you and I would be back in Durham, back in our house and our office suite, and we'd be *happy*.

Or perhaps not. Maybe the Arcanum would still have gone mad, and I suppose they would have come for you. Even if I could have kept you safe at home, you'd have wanted to help—the Montana siege was one thing, but this "Unravelling" business would have been so personal. Would you be here now, in a neat little house in the settlement, having Rufus over for a pint? (He has a girlfriend now, you know—I think you'd like her.) And if you'd come over, would Coileán have let me come along?

But pretend with me that none of that would have happened. Where would we be if my father were alive? You and Rufus might have finished your book by now, and we'd be making plans for Paris, wouldn't we? I was so looking forward to that anniversary trip we'd talked about. Darling, I know it made you insecure sometimes thinking about the spouses I had before you, but please, *please* believe me when I say that you are the only one I've ever truly loved. I'd take a long weekend in Paris with you over a year with any of the others. I married them for mutual convenience; I married you because my heart couldn't bear the alternative.

You don't know how it terrified me to come clean with you in December. I never thought the subject of my paternity would ever create such a fuss—if something happened to Oberon, there was always Robin waiting in the wings. But Robin got himself killed, Oberon got what he deserved by partnering with that she-demon, and I...

I'm sorry, I've got to go—my aide says that one of my guests is beginning to stir, and I'm sure they'll both want breakfast. He may be a problem, but more later.

Much love,
Your Ellie

My dearest,

Where do I begin?

When Detective Parsons arrived last night, she brought another detective with her. She's quite obviously smitten with him, and it seems to be a reciprocal situation. He's not Fringe, but I wouldn't mind allowing him to remain here with her, were it not for the fact that he's Mab's half-fae grandson.

Yes, *that* Mab.

I've told you about the realm and her moods, haven't I? Well, she's beside herself now, and she's been shouting at Coileán and me since they arrived. The poor boy barely understands what's happening—he's only known that he's fae for a few days, and he's in desperate need of a basic education before he accidentally kills himself. I can't in good conscience turn him out to the mortal realm for that reason alone, never mind the Arcanum's threats regarding what will happen if they detect faeries running around over there. Detective Parsons trusts him, and he seems harmless enough. But God, the realm will not *shut up* about it, and I can't tell her where to get off because she's in my bloody head.

That's one problem. The other is Detective Parsons, who seems hell-bent on going back across the border as quickly as possible in search of other Fringers in hiding. Admirable, yes, but foolish—she's only a witch. I wish you could talk sense into her, though I fear you'd tell her to take an anorak and keep an eye out for suspicious wands.

To make matters worse, I've heard word that she's recruited another Fringer to the cause, a teenage crafter. What am I to do, sit back and wish them good luck? They owe me no obedience, but still...

I wish you were here. All the time, I wish you were here, but now especially. I'm not sure of myself, I don't know if I'm about to make a terrible mistake, and I need you to remind me to trust my own judgment. You'd do that, wouldn't you? I know I'm not perfect, but would you tell me I'm doing the right thing?

My bed is wide, with a perfect mattress, and I keep rolling to my left, expecting to feel you beside me. The sheets are always cold on your side of the bed these days, and I can't stand it. I don't want to do this alone. What's the use of immeasurable power if it can't give you what you want the most?

Much love,
Your Ellie

My dearest,

I can't shake the feeling that I've sent four people to their death. Please don't think me a monster.

Detective Parsons couldn't be dissuaded. As it happens, she's actually a *wizard*—undertrained most certainly, but Toula says she has ample talent. Amy Levey—that's the little crafter—went with her, as did Seamus Malone, the other detective. I can't say that I'm entirely sorry to see him leave, though I'm told he needs more training. I suppose he'll pick it up the way I did, piecemeal, though his aunt and uncle aren't thrilled about it. (Toula and Valerius, you know, I'm quite sure I've mentioned them in a previous letter.) Our Fringe and Fringe-adjacent trio have assured us that they'll stay off the Arcanum's radar. They returned via a pre-existing gate, and as long as they stay away from Arcanum installations, they may avoid detection. I understand the impetus for their return—there are so many missing Fringers—but thinking of what could happen if they were to be caught makes me ill. At best, Mulligan would surely kill them. At worst…well, I tell myself that he wouldn't execute all of his hostages, but of course, that's no guarantee.

The fourth in their party is Stuart Purcell—you know, the nutter who thinks he can learn to be a wizard. We sent him transformed. Magical constructions on living things break when entering Faerie, as you and I know all too well, but going out is a different matter. Stuart now has a new face and identity, and he intends to go to Montana and see what he can learn. If you ask whether he's brave or stupid, the answer is yes. But he and his poor cats are back in Virginia for the moment, and all I can do now is pray that he's a better actor than wizard.

After they left this afternoon, I had the *pleasure* of arbitrating between two of my brothers, Hugo and Karl. There was a soiree last night at one of our sisters' homes, and Karl apparently made eyes at a woman Hugo had been pursuing. Neither of them has any claim to her—relationship-wise, they're all barely acquaintances—and yet, to hear Hugo tell it, you'd think that Karl had absconded with his dearly beloved wife. Honestly, I've seen end-of-term freshers strung out on coffee and Adderall who displayed greater maturity and emotional sensitivity than those two. But I did my duty: I told Hugo to stop being irrational and Karl to stop gloating, and I sent them on their way, hopefully without bloodshed to come.

I miss those freshers, Walt.

I miss you so much.

I only wish I knew how to send you my letters.

Much love,
Your Ellie

JUNE: KIP

It's difficult to tell the days when you're blindfolded. The rag that my captors—an etalre hunting party—tied around my eyes was thick and wide, covering the area from above my eyebrows almost to the tip of my nose, and whichever one of them knotted it did so securely. Even when I rubbed my head against my legs, I couldn't budge it. They gagged me, too, using another thick rag that tasted coppery like blood. I couldn't do more than grunt—nor could the rest of my family—but blind and speechless, I quickly learned to tell them by their muffled voices: my father and mother; my eldest sister, Azcara, and her mate, Kotima; my other sister, Tido, and her mate, Tardur; and my brother, Hib, his mate, Kanu, and their two-year-old son, Jol. Ten of us all together, our arms bound behind our backs, our legs tied together and lashed to carrying poles. The etalre broke at least one of our legs each, so there was no point in trying to escape. None of us could run, and besides, the etalre had bows. I'd seen how effective they could be.

We called them etalre—raiders—because no one knew what they called themselves. Nor did anyone care to learn. They fell upon our villages like a plague, pale, thin, hairless creatures with fangs and claws and all manner of weapons, riding astride their strong black mounts and heralding death.

When they came for mine, they did so in the night, setting fires and shooting anything that moved. By the time we woke and realized the danger, some of them were upon us—only four, but swift and strong. They tied each of my family to a thick pole, then forced our torsos forward and tied them to our front legs. I hadn't understood why until I felt my pole hoisted and hung between two of the raiders' guronts, their black-scaled mounts. With my body bent, my head couldn't drag the ground, but still I swayed on my pole, bumping into the bodies hung before and behind me. I didn't get a good look at the guronts before I was blindfolded, but they had to be huge to support so many of us, even carrying poles in tandem. I knew how we were being held—one of our hunting parties had surprised and killed an injured etalre and its mount when I was small, and I'd seen the massive saddle, which covered the guront's back and came with slots for five poles. I'd been frightened of it then, but finding myself experiencing captivity firsthand made my childhood fear seem like a bad joke.

The guronts didn't run while they bore us, but then I don't suppose there was any need for speed. As the etalre conversed in their strange tongue, I listened and tried to determine who was around me. Toward the front was Tardur, whose voice was deeper than anyone else's. Hib hung behind him, then me. Kotima was behind me—I could smell my sister's perfumed soap on him—and Father brought up the rear. Mother, my sisters, Kanu, and Jol were carried on the other pair of guronts. The baby cried throughout most of the day, but I couldn't blame the little one. We were all terrified, sore from the injuries the etalre had given us and from continually swaying into each other, and eventually hungry and thirsty.

I suppose that Jol's hysterical sobs annoyed our captors, however, as they ate him first. Before they unloaded the rest of us for the night, they pulled him down and slit his throat—or so I assume. I heard him gurgle his last and heard his mother's wails, but I saw nothing.

After they ate, one of them came around with a water skin and gave us each a mouthful. I sucked the moisture from my gag and twitched in my bonds on the ground until I nudged into my brother's back. Hib made no sound, but I could feel him convulse with silent weeping.

They finished eating Jol that first night. Mother was next, and she took three days to consume. Even hanging from the other guronts, I could smell the stench of her open corpse as we traveled. Judging by the others' grunting, I think they carried her at the back of her line, but she still swung into Kanu or one of my sisters all day. When they'd eaten the last of her, they took Father next, and Kotima hung beside his corpse for the following days. I couldn't see, but oh, could I *smell*.

When one is injured, bound, blinded, gagged, starved, and forced to listen as one's family is killed and consumed, one's mind tends to go in odd directions. At first, mine tried to be rational about the situation. Jol was killed first because he was young and loud, Mother was the eldest female, and Father was the eldest male. They weren't feeding us, so they would logically kill the weakest first—though whether they would select the women or men, I couldn't predict. Would I go next, or would I be carried for days, waiting as each of my loved ones was slaughtered in turn?

Faced with those depressing uncertainties, my mind went somewhere else. As I was unable to speak, unable to see, and too shocked and numb to truly grapple with the death around me, I found myself repeating the old prayers in my head—not in hopes that anything would hear them, but to save myself from yet another useless fit of panicked thrashing. *Give her rest in the far land. Her soul is pure and fit for reward. Take him to the place where there is no hunger, no thirst, and no tiring. May his ancestors receive him there with joy.*

I couldn't always distract myself, however. At night, lying tied up by the etalres' fire, I grew particularly conscious of my wounds, my thirst, and my gnawing hunger. My stomach felt like it wanted to eat me from the inside out, but I could do little more than twist and try to nibble at the grass around me, unsatisfying as it was.

I cannot describe the full depth of the soul-killing horror of smelling my sister's roasting flesh and beginning to salivate. No matter how strongly I recoiled at the notion, starvation didn't care about love or kinship.

During the long days and hungry nights, I told myself their names like a litany, adding to the list as each was killed and butchered in turn. Most were good for three days' food; Kotima and Tardur lasted four. I cannot now be certain of the days, but I believe it was the twenty-fifth when Hib and I were finally separated, each of us carried between a pair of guronts, and I knew that one of us would die that night. I wanted my older brother beside me, even if only for a few more hours, but we were denied the comfort of each other's company.

Finally, the day cooled toward late afternoon, and I heard one of the etalre give the command they used to call a halt. I hung helpless in my bonds, trembling and trying to be brave, but to my surprise, when the etalre began their evening preparations, I heard Hib grunt in panic, then scream…and then nothing.

Three days, maybe four. Surely we'd lost weight during our torture. They would begin eating my brother that night, and when he was nothing but bone, they would come for me. A horrible thought, but at least I had the small comfort of a time window. No matter how miserable the next days would be, only a few remained.

When they put me on the ground, I felt sand on my skin and tried to deduce where we had stopped. It was no use— my mental map of my homeland grew fuzzy around the edges, and I didn't know where we might be after a twenty-five-day trip. Exhausted and almost too numb to grieve for my brother, I lay still while the campfire crackled and hoped I might die in my sleep, just to hurry the inevitable along.

And then, something high above me exploded.

Whatever it was, it was loud, and it threw my captors into a flurry of shouts and running footsteps. As they began to ride away, another explosion went off nearby, and I heard a guront scream in pain. Smaller, sharper sounds followed that, and another guront fell. Then the etalre began to scream in turn, a high, agonized sound. Desperately, I wriggled in the sand, but the ropes were as strong as ever. Every twist chafed at my skin, and I almost cried out when I rubbed against my broken leg, but panic gave me the strength to try.

I heard voices then, male and female, their tongue unintelligible but definitely not the etalres'. One of the females spoke softly and touched my shoulder, and I strained to escape before the knife could find me. I heard her move away and speak to what sounded like an agitated male, and then their voices drew close to me once more. One of the unseen creatures pinned my neck to the sand, one touched the side of my head, and I heard the male whisper above me just before a blast of lightning went off behind my eyes.

I cried out in shock, and I heard them step away as my hearts raced. And then, after a brief moment, I heard the female speak: "Ehm...hello?"

Not death at all, but rather my salvation.

They cut the ropes and removed my gag and blindfold, and I squinted in pain, my eyes sensitive even to the campfire's light. The lead female sent the other female—though really, she seemed nothing more than a short blur—to fetch water, and she and the male gave me the truth I already knew: Hib was beyond help. I tried to stand, but twenty-five days bound and starved left me weak and wobbly, and my broken leg couldn't take any weight.

The female introduced herself as Hannah, the male as Seamus. She offered to take me to safety and treat my injuries, and she asked me to trust her.

Every instinct told me not to. My people are rightly wary of strangers, and my rescuers were unlike anyone I'd ever seen: passably kadalin from the waist up, but they only had two legs like the etalre and the insakut, the purple-skinned deep dwellers who hunted us with magic. Had I been whole and healthy, I'd have run, *especially* once I saw Seamus throw fire from his fingertips. But I was a wreck in every sense of the word, and there was a softness in Hannah's dark eyes that I recognized as pity. I could stay in the desert and die, or I could trust the strangers who'd freed me and killed the etalre.

I cast my gaze to the heavens and was shocked to see hundreds of lights pocking the black dome, like fires burning impossibly high above me. Hannah pointed to a hole hanging in space on the far side of the campfire and explained that I'd left my homeland, though I couldn't fully comprehend the ramifications at the time. Instead, I told her what the etalre had done to my family, trying not to weep in front of her.

Much of the rest of the night is lost in the haze of memory. There was food and water, and a short ride in an incredibly cramped space that I would later come to know as an SUV, and a bath of sorts outside a dwelling, and then they splinted my leg. I know I told them my name at some point, but the details between the time they released me and the time I fell asleep in the glow of dawn are little more than shadows.

When I woke, I didn't know where I was or why the light was so bright, and I yelped when I sat up and saw the brilliant yellow fire in the alien blue sky.

"It's okay, it's okay," a voice soothed, and I turned to find the smaller female from the night before hurrying my way. "You're safe, Kip, it's okay."

At a loss for words, I gestured frantically upward, and she shielded her eyes as she glanced in that direction. "What am I looking at?" she asked.

"The *sky*!" I finally managed. "That...*that*..."

"Oh. *Oh*," she said, drawing out the word as comprehension registered. "Gray Lands, duh. We think y'all have a constant layer of cloud cover. That's what the sky looks like on a clear day."

"What *is* that?"

"The sun," she said slowly. "Source of all daylight?"

I tried to study it, but I couldn't stare at it for more than a second before my eyes stung. Yes, I knew daylight, but it was diffuse, a glow from within the familiar gray sky. This was hot and bright and focused, and I was already growing warm.

The female crouched next to me, her legs bending outward as she balanced. "Really, you're safe. Mr. Jim's come back with a trailer, and we're going to take you to his sister's house. She'll fix your leg. Remember?"

"Vaguely," I replied, feeling the unfamiliar words roll in my mouth. "How…how do I speak—"

"Magic," she said, shrugging, as matter-of-fact as if she were discussing the weather. "Mr. Seamus did it. I've had that happen to me, too—feels weird as heck, doesn't it?"

I nodded.

"You get used to it. Souvenir of your vacation in the mortal realm, if nothing else. I'm Amy, by the way."

"Thank you," I murmured. *Nice to meet you* didn't seen entirely sufficient that morning.

"No worries. You thirsty? I've got a fresh batch purified."

I started to rise and follow her, but she motioned for me to stay still and lugged over a large container of water, then told me to wait and disappeared into the house. When she returned, she had a perfectly transparent glass in her hand, still hot and dripping. "Sorry, just came out of the dishwasher," she explained, filling it from the jug. "I don't think this is sterile, but it's as close as we're going to get."

I didn't know what she was talking about, nor did I care. The glass was almost warm enough to burn my palms, but the water was balm on my parched throat. I gulped down three glasses, and as I went for the fourth, Amy cautioned, "Take it slow. You don't want to throw up."

"I have not had this much to drink in days," I protested.

"Exactly. Don't make yourself sick. It's not going anywhere. Hungry?"

I laughed at the absurdity of the question, and Amy frowned until I patted the ground and explained, "I will eat this grass if there is nothing else."

"We can do better than the lawn," she replied, making a face. "Do you eat meat? Eggs?"

"*Anything.*"

"Don't move," she ordered, then headed into the house. I was on my sixth glass of water when she returned with a plate piled high with yellow lumps and toasted bread. "Cheesy scrambled eggs," she said, offering me the plate. "I'm not a great cook, but I can make those pretty reliably."

I recognized the utensil she handed me as a fork of sorts, though with four tines instead of the usual two. I didn't care—I would gladly have scooped the mess up with my bare hands—but I tried to show basic manners as I shoveled it in as quickly as I could. The eggs were strange but not unpleasant, and I could have wept for joy to fill my stomach. When the plate was clean, Amy took it inside and brought it back loaded with another unidentifiable dish. "Leftover enchiladas," she told me. "Hope you don't mind a little heat."

They were the best thing I'd ever tasted, though in truth, I felt that way about anything I put in my mouth that morning. Amy sat beside me while I ate, then quietly asked, "When did you last get a good meal? I can count your ribs."

I stifled a belch and wiped my lips with the back of my hand. "The...*raiders*, I suppose, is the word...they did not feed us."

"How long were you with them?"

"Perhaps twenty-five days. It was difficult to keep count."

"Twenty-five *days*?" she cried, going to her feet. "Keep eating, I'll at least get the rest of the bread—"

I tugged on her leg covering to stay her. "No, thank you,

with the water…"

"Getting full?"

I nodded but took another bite, and she sat again. "Bet your stomach shrank," she said. "I promise, wherever we're going, I'll make sure you get enough to eat. Miss Hannah and Mr. Seamus will understand."

I was nearing the point of licking the last traces of sauce from the plate when Amy murmured, "Miss Hannah said that was your brother back there."

"Yes," I mumbled.

"I'm so sorry."

She looked older in that moment, not just sympathetic but burdened with a wearying understanding. "You've lost a sibling?" I asked, putting the plate in the grass.

"Only child," she said, shaking her head. "My parents were murdered three months ago." She hesitated, then said, "Those raiders…did they…"

"My entire family," I replied, trying to suppress the surfacing memories. "Killed and ate them. They killed Hib just before you arrived."

She covered her mouth, then jumped to her feet and threw her arms around my neck. Her embrace was awkward—she was shorter than me on her knees and taller when she stood—but her grip was tight, her body warm, and I held on to her as I began to tremble. Neither of us spoke, but then no words needed to be said.

There are certain disadvantages to being kadalin in a world built for humans, among them transportation. I was in no mood to protest that day—I was too busy alternating between gratitude to be alive and guilt and sorrow for the ones I'd lost to complain—but for road excursions, there are far more comfortable methods of transport than a rusty, straw-bedded horse trailer, particularly when one has no choice but to sit and stare at the metal walls. But there was no better option, and so Hannah—or possibly Badger, I was still unsure about her name—levitated me inside with the aid of a polished stick. In retrospect, facing backward was probably not my brightest idea, but I was too sore to try to manage the turn in the narrow space. Before Hannah closed the door, Amy climbed inside the trailer with me, carrying a bag and brushing off her elders' safety concerns, and settled in with her back to one wall as we began to move. When I tensed at the jostling, she crawled over and took my hand. "It's okay, it's just like last night," she soothed. "The SUV's motorized, and it'll tow us up the road. Nothing to worry about."

"They were concerned for you," I countered.

"Because folks aren't supposed to ride back here. No seatbelts." She swept one arm around the trailer, then shrugged. "Not my first time riding unrestrained. If I go flying, try to grab me, huh?"

I smiled in spite of my anxiety and watched her make herself comfortable. Amy seemed small, even by the strangers' standards, and far paler than anyone I'd known, a blonde with greenish-brown eyes and skin like bread dough barely held to the fire. But her face was pretty in spite of its odd coloration. I could see little of the rest of her—for some reason, the strangers shrouded nearly every part of themselves in cloth—but her hands seemed normal enough. The part of her that most piqued my curiosity was her feet, but those she kept encased in soiled white and blue shoes that seemed far longer than necessity would have dictated.

"Snacks?" she asked, opening her bag, and handed me a bottle of water. "I've mostly got dehydrated fruit—the Wigginses didn't have a ton of junk food," she added apologetically—"but better than nothing, right?"

She passed me a packet of sweet dried berries, and I thought of my mother's preserved summer harvests, laid out to desiccate and set aside for the colder season. "Good," I told her, my throat clenching.

She popped one into her mouth. "Yeah. Daddy used to put these in my lunchbox. Kind of like candy, but it's a health food if you squint."

I hesitated, trying to interpret her suddenly pensive expression, then asked, "Hannah and Seamus, are they your kin?"

Amy barely chuckled. "Nope. I've got no one. But they came back here to find our people, and I want to help—I mean, it's better than sitting around and just *hoping* that everyone's okay."

I frowned. "Your people?"

"Oy," she muttered. "Ever heard of a wizard? Witch? Faerie?" When I shook my head, she stretched out her legs and stared up at one of the tiny windows at the top of the trailer's sides. "Well, short version, about three months ago, a bunch of wizards decided that folks like Miss Hannah and me had outlived our usefulness. Want the long version?"

"We are still traveling, are we not?"

"True." She pulled a bottle of brown liquid from her bag, opened it to a hiss and rush of bubbles, and took a long sip. "So, let me tell you about the Fringe."

When Amy finished her long explanation, her drink was almost gone, as was the bag of berries. "Anyway," she said, hugging her knees to her chest, "that's why I'm here. I could be back in Faerie, making wands where it's safe, but if I get a chance to go after the Arcanum…"

"You are brave," I told her.

"Nah. Just angry." She dug in her bag and produced a slim device, the back of which was bright pink. "Want to play Yahtzee?"

"I…do not know how," I replied, eyeing the device with distrust.

"It's easy, I'll teach you. Aiden made me this," she said, pushing a button on the device's side. The front half began to glow, and she tapped and slid her fingertip around it. "Never needs to charge, has great reception, and the app store is totally free. I left my old phone at home, but this one's better. Here, let me download the game…"

After a tutorial in both gameplay and touchscreen usage, she beat me for three rounds in a row, then offered to find another game. I declined—by then, I was determined to best her, and focusing on the numbers and patterns kept my thoughts from returning to the sounds of my sisters' screams as their throats were cut. Amy wedged herself between me and the wall, the better to pass the phone, and kicked off her shoes as we started the next round.

I tried to stealthily glance at her feet when she was taking her turn, but all I could see was white cloth—she'd worn an additional layer between her body and shoes. To make matters worse, Amy finished quickly and noticed the direction of my stare. "Are you admiring my *very* sexy tube socks?" she teased, wiggling her feet.

I hoped she couldn't tell that I was flushed. "Sorry, I—"

"You're curious?" She pulled one sock off and flexed her bare foot. "Not much to see. I need a pedicure."

Though it was rude, I couldn't help but stare. Her feet were akin to misshapen hands, long, with digits like stubby fingers. "How…" I began, studying her foot as she rotated her ankle.

"How what?"

"How can you *walk* on those?"

Amy laughed, long and loudly. Until then, I hadn't seen her full smile—it was beautiful, and her cheeks dimpled as she grinned. I felt myself smiling in spite of my embarrassment, and Amy freed her other foot from its wrappings while I took my turn in the game. "May as well let the dogs breathe," she said as I handed her the phone again. "That's what my daddy used to say. Mama always wore shoes around the house, but Daddy said you have to go barefoot every now and then."

I thought of Mother and the basket of picks she kept by the door, always nagging my siblings and me to clean our feet. The back ones took careful maneuvering, and half the time, we'd do the front two and hope she wouldn't notice.

I would have given anything to hear her nag me about my dirty feet one more time.

"Your turn," said Amy. "And yes, that's a large straight, thank you very much."

I squeezed my eyes shut until the film of tears no longer blurred the screen, then tapped the button to begin.

AUGUST: STUART PURCELL

The man in the mirror still wasn't me.

Oh, he moved with me—he was a cooperative sort of fellow. His eyes flicked around the bathroom as I willed, his hands grasped my toothbrush and half-spent tube of paste, and his mouth opened in a yawn as my mind dictated. But he was a full two inches taller than me, plumper around the chin and softer in the belly, and his hair had gone gray. His eyes were brown like mine, though several shades too light, like stained pine instead of mahogany. It wasn't an unpleasant face—he had crow's feet around his eyes that crinkled when I wanted to smile, thick gray eyebrows, a slightly upturned nose, and a shallow cleft in his chin. When I touched his face, I felt all the irregularities of skin—the spots of papery dryness and oilier patches, the rough bristles of morning stubble, the sore place in the deep crevice beside his nose where a pimple was trying to break free. His was an ordinary face, generally inoffensive, tanned from the better part of two months painting en plein air, and it moved as I wished as I started to brush my teeth. I wouldn't have instinctively run from him in terror, had I met him in a dark alley.

But I was *wearing* his face, and it made my skin—or his, perhaps—crawl.

A wizard does not run from danger—he runs *toward* it, defending the helpless with the full power of the Light. Or so my mentor told me back in California. His name was

Benjamin Hogarth, but professionally, he was Benjamin the Celestial, gifted (or so he claimed) with extraordinary powers of extrasensory perception and a master of the tarot. While my abilities were nothing compared to his, he instructed me in the arcane arts from the back room of his yoga studio, teaching me the techniques of successful spell casting and potion brewing, how to hex and heal, and how to use candles and crystals to best effect in my efforts. He guided me through my difficult first lessons, encouraging me to persevere—after all, no successful wizard was trained in a day. *You have it in you, Stuart,* he used to say, pressing his hand to his breast. *We all do. It's simply a matter of learning to tap that innate power.*

I had no reason to disbelieve Benjamin. My mother visited him regularly to have her cards read, and my father had studied reiki in one of his weekend seminar series when I was just a toddler. Dad died of a heart attack when I was nine, and Benjamin had stepped into the void, serving as a reassuring male presence in my life. Looking back, I think that he and Mom went out a few times—she had quite a few evening solo sessions with him that necessitated calling a babysitter—but nothing came of it in the end. Mom and Benjamin remained friends, and when I was thirteen, he began my instruction in magick.

Always spell it with a k, he insisted. *Magic with a c is what stage illusionists do. You and I are meddling in the great forces of the cosmos, Stuart.*

And oh, I could meddle with the best of them. I was an awkward child, short and skinny, with slightly protruding eyes that always made me look like I had been caught unawares. "Frogface" had been tossed around by my fellow fifth graders. By tenth grade, I had full-blown acne, I liked to read, I was teaching myself the basics of oil painting, and I had no idea how to talk to girls—the perfect recipe for a hellacious educational experience. But Benjamin was always there, steering me through the roughest patches and giving me the confidence I so dearly needed. Sure, I couldn't have gotten a date if my life had depended on it, but I was privy to the secrets of the universe, mysteries so deep that my classmates couldn't have begun to comprehend the extent of their ignorance. They ignored me as a freak, and I ignored them as foolish children, and somehow, the majority of us made it to graduation.

Instead of college, I began working full-time in Benjamin's studio, overseeing his esoteric wares while he tended to the teaching side of the business. He brought me as many books of magick as I desired, and in my downtime, I read and researched, at first looking for unifying principles and then seeking to make the knowledge I'd gleaned easily accessible to practitioners with a more limited library. I'd written my first book by twenty—*Simplifying Spellcraft*, a beginner's guide to incantation and intention—and Benjamin paid for a New Age press to publish it and sold it in his store. I was inducted into the Sunset Circle at twenty-one, a white wizard in my own right and a growing presence in magickal society for my writing. *Intention and Meditation* followed two years later, then *Potent Potions*, *The Secrets of Trees*, *The Novice Guide to Crystal Healing*, and my personal favorite, *The Yankee Bestiary: A Compendium of American Cryptozoology*. Aside from one rather humiliating incident with a brazier and a polyester robe at a meeting in Sacramento that burned down half a house, I was known for the right reasons, accepted—even celebrated.

And then my mother died, T-boned in an intersection by a drunk driver who walked out with barely a bruise. Not cursing him to a life of hell on earth took every ounce of my resolve, but I managed to hold myself together and preserve my integrity. Benjamin helped me through the messy business of tidying Mom's affairs, and when I sat down with her attorney, I learned, to my utter surprise, that my parents had established a trust for me. The money managers had traded wisely, and at the tender age of thirty, between life insurance and the dividends, I had roughly five thousand dollars a month going into my account. Even in California,

I could have gotten by on that alone, especially with the family home paid off...but I needed a challenge.

With Benjamin's encouragement, I spun off the retail work I'd done for him into my own shop: The Endless Knot, a hodgepodge of books, tools, and bric-a-brac for practitioners and the curious. I had a basic website made, advertised by word of mouth and in the bookmarks I sent to purchasers of my books, and soon had a comfortable living. I had a place to go during the day and my research pursuits at night—what more did a young wizard need?

Companionship, as it turned out. Connection. The six cats I'd adopted from the local shelter were good company but not the same as having another human around. Of course, there was the slight problem of my continued unpopularity with the ladies—the ones who ran in my circles were generally too old or not compatible, and the few I met online thought my profession was a joke.

And then I thought of Auntie Eunice.

I had little family that I knew of, and fewer still whom I'd met, but Auntie Eunice was my favorite of the lot. She was, technically speaking, my grandaunt—my mother's father's only sibling, windowed and childless. Mom and I had flown across the country to Virginia to see her a handful of times, and I'd always found her little town charming in a quaint sort of way, a seaside enclave off the beaten path. She ran a teashop on the ground floor of her building and kept an apartment above it, and by all accounts, she was getting along just fine. Like clockwork, I received a Christmas card from her during the first week of December every year.

I was lonely, I realized—and what about Auntie Eunice, seventy-eight years old, all by herself in that little town, with no family to rely upon since Uncle Nate passed? I decided that it was up to me to see to her welfare, and so I bid a fond farewell to California, announced my relocation to the Sunset Circle's sister, the Mid-Atlantic Circle, and purchased an empty building in little Rigby just a few blocks from Auntie Eunice's place. She was surprised to see me when I stopped by unannounced that August, and though she was kind and asked about my plans for my store, I sensed that she was a touch miffed that I'd moved in, as if I were suggesting she needed a sitter. I assured her that I'd come to town to be there for her in case of emergency and set about unpacking my wares, planning to dive into the research I'd begun for a new book on fairies. Auntie Eunice wasn't exactly encouraging when I told her about the project, but I chalked it up to her being more conservative in her beliefs than my parents had been.

I had no idea.

Across the street from Auntie Eunice's building was a tidy secondhand bookstore called Ex Libris. I've always enjoyed browsing—one never knows what might be lurking on an overlooked shelf—but what caught my eye in that shop was its proprietor. Meg Horn was a stunner, a vivacious redhead two years my senior with a full-throated laugh and eyes of pale winter blue. I didn't hold out much hope at first, but unlike so many in Rigby, she didn't immediately dismiss me when I told her about my work—rather, she seemed to take an interest, asking intelligent questions about my shop and my research. She spoke little about her own past, though I learned that she'd originally come from Arizona and had a teenage daughter, the result of a young marriage that had ended too soon.

Our relationship was still in its early days, but I was beginning to think that I might have a chance with Meg when *he* rolled into town.

The problem, I discovered, was that the lady had a boyfriend, a dark-haired man with several inches on me, better muscle tone, and, shall we say, looks that skewed more toward the "classically handsome" end of the spectrum than did mine. He poo-pooed my calling and my work, rolling his eyes whenever I discussed magick—and by some ill chance, he was friends with Auntie Eunice. I didn't know what she saw in Colin, but I wasn't about to sit back and let him walk all over me. Meg had an open, clever mind, and she deserved better than a perpetual skeptic. Besides, it was obvious that Meg's daughter hated him.

I came around the bookstore more frequently, trying to catch Meg alone and show her that a better option existed. I defended her against an attack by unnatural forces—she was considerate enough to walk me home when I was injured in the process—and she accompanied me to a paranormal convention in Richmond. While Meg insisted that she was happy with Colin and seeking only platonic companionship, I told myself it was only a matter of time. She would see her beau for the pedestrian skeptic he was, I would open her eyes to the mysteries of the universe as my old mentor had opened mine, and she would come to view me as more than just her neighbor.

But then, in November, everything went precisely to hell.

Magick, Benjamin used to tell me, is about intention. A wizard casts his spells and sends out his intention into the greater universe, and in so doing, change is effected. It might be less visible than he'd hope, but if his purpose is clear and his technique proper, then change will come.

I believed that wholeheartedly until the moment Rigby's surliest bartender put a Dud Defender in my hand. The rod had no moving pieces, but it was carved with runes that glowed in warning just before I accidentally shot a fireball through a closed window and blew up a trash compactor.

That Monday morning had been uneventful until I heard bellowing screeches in the distance. Puzzled, I'd gone up to my flat roof for a better look, only to spot half a dozen...well, *monsters*...converging on the town. I can't be more descriptive now—I remember brownish creatures two stories tall, and that godawful shrieking, but I suspect that the zoological part of my brain shut off as I ran downstairs, preparing to do battle. This would be my finest moment, the event to which my extensive training and study had been building: I would save Rigby from the forces of darkness.

There was no time to waste on proper ceremonial garb. I donned a silver circlet that had been charmed for clarity of thought, slid on my bracelets for focus and power, and grabbed my best wand, intending to go into the street once I'd prepared my mind. Instead, a squeal of brakes interrupted my meditation, and I looked out the store's window to see Auntie Eunice's car pull up by the door. She was still wearing her bathrobe, and of all people, she'd brought Slim, the bartender, and Colin.

Their timing couldn't have been worse. My store was about to be the epicenter of a magickal battle—it certainly wasn't a safe place for my elderly grandaunt and a couple of ignorant skeptics. Still, I directed them into my protective circle and offered them protection, at which point Colin had the gall to criticize my setup. I finally snapped at him—there were lives on the line, after all, and only one of us was the learned wizard in the room.

Colin disagreed.

And then, with a flick of a finger, he opened what I would later know as an inter-realm gate.

I tried to retake control of the situation—seeing magick that immediate and powerful shook me to my core, and there was Auntie Eunice to think of—but he continued to mock my efforts and sent Auntie Eunice through the gate before telling me to join her.

I insisted that a wizard sworn to the Light doesn't run from danger when innocents are in jeopardy.

He and Slim seemed less than impressed by that declaration, and then they dragged me through another gate into the next town before giving me a choice: go to safety or fight the giant monsters. Naturally, I did my duty, fighting to the last until the danger was neutralized. By then, when Colin suggested that I join Auntie Eunice, I was too strung-out to say no.

I don't remember much of my first twenty-four hours in Faerie because I remained, to be charitable, tipsy for most of the period. But I had good reason to drink: aside from the damage to Rigby—I'd seen my wrecked building on a news report—my world had been shaken to its foundation. I'd been studying magick since childhood, I held myself out as an expert in a number of sub-disciplines, I was a certified *wizard*...and I'd finally seen real magick, something powerful and tangible that my best spells couldn't touch. All of my research on fairies was for naught; instead of tiny wingèd creatures, I got an eight-hundred-year-old smartass who looked down on me metaphorically *and* physically. To top it off, Meg was fae as well—she'd been humoring me, and I'd never had a chance with her.

It was enough to drive a man to the bottle, and there was a *copious* volume of alcohol on hand.

My general funk didn't improve when I was shipped off to the Stowe homestead in Alaska with Auntie Eunice and the less magickally adept two days later. Our hosts were gracious but obviously fae, and the ease with which they manipulated magic only served to remind me of how ineffective my own skills were. Late that night, as I sat alone in my guestroom with the glass of port I'd been nursing since dinner ended, Rohese, the lady of the house, stopped by. "Vivi told me about your...*situation*," she said, regarding me with evident pity. "I know this is difficult for you, dear, but it's not the end of the world."

"It's only my life's work down the toilet," I protested.

"Your life's..." She shook her head. "How old are you, thirty?"

"Thirty-six," I muttered.

"*Child.* You have time to start again."

I hesitated, trying to gauge her mood, then said, "I'm a fairly disciplined practitioner. If you could show me some techniques…"

Rohese grimaced. "I'm sorry, but it doesn't work that way. This can't be taught to someone without a generous dose of fae blood," she said as a white fireball burst into being in her palm.

"What about one of your wizards, then?" I pressed. "There was a woman with us, Toula something—"

"Unlikely. I could be mistaken, but it's my understanding that spellcraft can't be taught to mundanes. Magic isn't something you just pick up unless you've got the inborn ability," she explained, "and if you *had*, you'd know it by now." She smiled gently and gestured toward my unused bed. "Sleep on it, dear. There's a wide world of options open to you beyond…well, whatever sort of magic it is you think you've been using."

I went home the next day to a half-smashed building. Per Toula, Meg was dead, her daughter—and, incidentally, *Colin's* daughter—was on the run, and Colin had fallen apart. While Rigby continued to dig itself out from the rubble and tie blue tarps onto its roofs, I salvaged what I could of my wares, put my stock and most of my furniture into a storage unit, and drove up the coast until I found a shop with art supplies. That week, I set up an easel in one of the beach pavilions and rendered the sea in oils, calling upon the muscle memory I hadn't used in years. My canvasses weren't masterpieces, but each was slightly better than its predecessor, and focusing on the interplay of light and water kept me from dwelling on the fact that my life was meaningless.

Auntie Eunice invited me to Thanksgiving dinner. We sat at her dining room table with a catered meal, drinking dry white wine, and she asked me how I was doing. I told her about my paintings, and she asked when I was planning to reopen my store. "Why bother?" I replied. "I'm a laughingstock."

She sipped her wine in silence for a moment, then said, "Stuart, hon…maybe you don't actually have talent, but if that store makes you happy, you don't have to give it up."

"But Colin said—"

"Colin doesn't know *everything*. Maybe he's right and you'll never do real magic"—I winced at her assessment—"but maybe he's wrong. Maybe you're just a late bloomer."

I bit the inside of my lip until my throat unclenched. "Thought you didn't approve of my store."

"It's not my cup of tea," she admitted. "But you know, there are a lot of people in this town who ran or hid when those things came through. You were ready to stand and fight, and…well, I mean, that was *crazy*, Stuart, you should know better than that, but…" She shrugged. "If you think you can do some good with that magic of yours, then I suggest you get a contractor out there to look at your building."

As it so happened, my building was a total loss, but Colin gave Meg's building to Auntie Eunice a month later, and she let me move in and reopen, rent-free. And so I began to rediscover my center, reaching out on our message boards and filling my backlog of orders. Once more, I turned to research, but on a different tangent—and this time, I told no one in the Circle what I was investigating.

I contemplated telling Benjamin what I'd witnessed and learned, but I ultimately decided against it. Had I told my mentor about fire-shooting rods and realms beyond our own, he'd have thought I was crazy.

Instead, I braved Slim's bar late one afternoon in early January, when the worst of the drunkards had yet to stumble in, and requested information. "I'm not asking for your tools," I explained as he set up glasses and regarded me warily. "I just want to know how they work. What drives them. How they're made."

"You can't replicate them," he warned me. "Hell, *wizards* can't do it."

"I'm not trying to. Really, all I want is to *know*."

He had pity on me. Over the next week, I closed the store at lunch and met Slim in his basement workshop, where he showed me the tools of his trade: wands, rods, experimental devices for detecting fluctuations in background magic. He permitted me to take notes, and then he passed me off to Vivi Stowe, his protégée in the Fringe. She proved to be a more willing teacher—her boyfriend was mundane, after all—and at our third meeting, she gave me a palm-sized brass sphere carved over with an intricate pattern. "I told my brother Rufus what we're doing," she explained. "He found this years ago, I don't know where, but it's an Arcanum commission."

Vaguely, I recalled Rufus, a college professor with whom Auntie Eunice had seemed unusually smitten. I passed the ball from hand to hand, tracing the lines of the crafter's marks. "What is it?"

"Summoner. It's like a Dud Defender, it's preloaded and ready. All you have to do is clear your mind and think about who you want to summon, and it should do the rest—theoretically. I've never played with one," she admitted, "and you might show this to Slim to double-check, but Rufe said that if you take on another eldritch horror, you should have the ability to phone a friend."

I thanked her and took it home, where I put it in the drawer by my cashbox beside the new gun I'd purchased. Having seen what could come stomping through town, I decided that prudence called for a level of protection that my subtler sort of magick couldn't provide. Over the next two days, I took the ball out and rolled it around, mulling over whom I'd call in case of emergency. Something counseled against taking it to Slim for an inspection—honestly, I was afraid he'd try to confiscate it—and by the middle of the month, my curiosity got the best of me.

I set up candles around the protective circle I'd drawn on the floor of my new shop, just as Benjamin had taught me for ritual work. I donned a ceremonial hooded robe—white, like my intentions—and the proper amulets for protection and strength, shooed my curious cats out of the way, and then I held the ball until it warmed and thought of

Colin.

I almost had a heart attack when he appeared—finally, I'd done something real with my craft, and the know-it-all was trapped in the middle of my protective circle. *That* conclusion was swiftly disproven, as he simply stepped over the line and smacked me upside the head to drive the point home. "For the last time, *you are not a wizard*," he told me.

I told him that I was trying.

A wizard doesn't run, after all.

I don't know what swayed him—maybe the hour, maybe boredom, maybe being back in Meg's old bookstore—but he stuck around that night, drinking and answering my questions. We walked down to the deserted beach—I kept my robe on against the cold—and he spoke of thaumaturgical principles I'd never considered, properties of magic beyond Benjamin's teaching, and books written centuries ago by wizards I'd never heard of. "I've read more than my share of treatises on theoretical and practical spellcraft," he said, shoving his hands into the pockets of the jacket he'd pulled from atoms. "If you want the titles, I can give you a list—Vivi probably knows where to find copies. But if you think that reading the books will make you a wizard, I'm sorry to disappoint you. It doesn't work like that."

"My mentor always said that it comes down to intention," I replied.

"Sure, that's a lot of it, but you have to have power behind the intention. You can steer a car all you like, but if there's no gasoline, you won't go anywhere."

I hugged myself in the wind. "And you couldn't have mentioned any of this last fall?"

"Why bother? You were delusional but harmless, and you wouldn't have believed me." He cut his eyes toward me, then snorted. "The Cottingley Fairies? *Really*?"

"You could have said something."

"You were too busy expounding upon the mysteries of the universe to give two shits about anything I'd have said."

"But had you explained that you're—"

"I had a cover to maintain. As does everyone you've met in the Fringe," he added with a note of warning.

I said nothing for a time as I shivered in the sand, listening to the waves crash and hiss, and then I ventured, "I'm, uh...I'm sorry about Meg."

Colin sighed and slowly nodded. "So am I."

Knowing who and what he truly was, I found it disconcerting at first when Colin popped in every couple of weeks to visit Auntie Eunice, but I kept my thoughts to myself and assumed he'd stay across the street—that is, until the day the windchimes over my door tinkled and I looked up from one of Vivi's books to find him contemplating my center display table of quartz points. "That still isn't fooling anyone," he said, cocking his thumb toward the artificial ficus in the corner of the shop. "Why not invest in spider plants? Start small."

I closed the book—a slog written in early modern English, one of the few from Colin's list that I could read in the original. "I take you're not in the market for a wand."

"Nah," he replied, considering the dreamcatchers on the wall. "Checking up on the place. And Vivi said she'd loaned you a copy of Alcester." He crossed the room and peered down at my book, frowning. "That one's in rough shape as it is. Read it on foam—you'll better preserve the spine."

"Come again?"

A pair of green foam wedges appeared on the counter. "Like this," he said, carefully opening the book and resting it atop the supports. "Ooh...*cheap* printing. Alcester had a moment of popularity—there are a few copies from the quality first run still in existence, and then there are the reprints." He closed the book again and lightly tapped the cover. "Do you suppose Vivi's in love with this binding?"

I couldn't say, though the flakes of disintegrating leather were a nuisance. "Probably not."

His finger twitched, and the crumbling cover was replaced with a supple brown leather, the title stamped in neat gold letters instead of the faded black of the original. "At least you shouldn't be shedding pages now. Learning anything?"

I flipped my laptop toward him, showing him the copious notes I'd been taking as I made sense of the text. "Plenty of theory. References to people I've never heard of—I've made a list."

"Show me." He glanced over the page I pulled up, then went down the column. "Grand magus, grand magus, magus, magus, magus, should have been a magus but for politics, hermit, guy who thought he knew a hell of a lot more about magic than he did, another grand magus, and *she* was brilliant, but good luck finding a translation from old Hungarian."

"I've actually tested some of the techniques in here," I said, turning the computer back around. "Building wards and such."

One of Colin's eyebrows inched toward his hairline. "And?"

"*And* I'm not sure of the result, but I'll keep experimenting—"

"Wards, you said?" he interrupted, then waved dismissively at the windows until the shades descended and the front door locked. "There's a ward system still in place around this building, but I won't power it up because you wouldn't be able to control it. Let's start with something smaller. Put together a practice ward for me."

I hadn't had such performance anxiety since my certification testing, but I used my best wand, followed my notes from the book, and cast what I thought was a decent ward system around the chalk circle on the floor. "There you go," I told him, stepping back from my work. "I think that's a decent approximation of the technique."

"Classic Alcester procedure," he agreed, and waved one hand back and forth over the circle. "But no dice. You can't see magic, can you? Raw magic, I mean."

"Well…I'm not sure," I admitted. "What does it look like?"

"You'd know it if you could see it. Colorful, I'm told. I smell it instead. Not nearly as useful for complex casting, but it can't be helped."

"*Smell?*"

"Inactive and active magic smell slightly different. Regardless, if there were a ward system here, I'd feel something," he continued, patting the air above and just outside of the circle. "This isn't going to be neat, but here…"

After a moment of silent gesticulation, he said, "Put your palm near the edge of the circle."

I did as instructed. As I tried to pass my hand over the line, it encountered resistance like the skin of a balloon, painless but firmer the harder I pressed. "What…"

"*That* is a ward," said Colin. "Active, and as I said, not particularly neat or efficient. If you were sensitive to magic, you'd perceive it in some way without having to run into it."

I withdrew my hand and scowled at the invisible wall. "Suppose I need more practice."

"And talent. You can master the techniques, and you still won't be able to do jack shit." He flicked two fingers toward the circle—erasing his work, I assumed—and folded his arms. "Stop torturing yourself. You can't study your way into becoming a wizard."

"I *am* a wizard," I insisted, copying his stance. "Maybe not the kind you're used to—"

"The kind that can actually cast, you mean?"

I didn't rise to the bait. "When confronted with a problem, a wizard doesn't give up. He doesn't run. He works out a solution."

He rolled his eyes and turned toward the door, gesticulating the shades back onto their spools. "Better hope you don't meet too many wizards, Stu. They'll just disappoint you."

Thereafter, about once a month, Colin dropped in on me after visiting with Auntie Eunice. He seldom stayed long, but he answered my questions about my painfully slow reading and continued to repair Vivi's books. Most times, I'd try a technique I'd been practicing, but he never detected so much as a flicker of active spellcraft. "Look, if you could master wizardry from books alone, you'd be well on your way," he told me in September as yet another attempt at wards produced nothing. "But you don't get points for persistence."

I'd be lying if I said my continued failure wasn't disheartening, but I persevered—and I kept my studies a secret. Benjamin and members of the Mid-Atlantic Circle had begun to express concern when I went quiet on our forums at the end of the year. I chalked it up to difficulty with my insurance company and contractor in the wake of the alleged chemical explosions in Rigby—apparently, something hallucinogenic had been included in the mix, and people reported having seen monsters smashing cars and destroying property—and I made it a point to reestablish my presence. I dispatched orders in a timely fashion and answered novice questions on the boards, doing what it took to stay in business, but my heart wasn't in it. Even as I insisted to myself that there was utility in the magick to which I'd devoted my life, nagging doubt plagued me. Still, I made it out to a convention in the early fall, where I spent two days in a hotel ballroom smiling and talking shop with other practitioners like old times. Benjamin had come with some of his students, and he gave me a hearty hug when we met. "This," he told the others, "is my finest pupil. You'll have to look long and hard to find another wizard like Stuart Purcell." His praise gave me a long-missed feeling of pride—in myself, in my craft—and as I drove home at the end of the weekend, I tried to remember that feeling, telling myself that I would continue my clandestine studies and become a wizard the likes of which even Benjamin couldn't imagine.

And then October hit like a meteor.

Oh, it started promisingly enough. The storefronts in Rigby had been decorated with leaves and jack-o'-lanterns, and the new coffee shop off the main square was putting a sprinkle of pumpkin spice onto anything that would hold still. A few of my associates in the Circle who were practicing pagans had invited me out to their Appalachian retreat for a Samhain celebration, which sounded better than sitting up again with Auntie Eunice and passing out candy to trick-or-treaters. But on a Saturday mid-month, I got a panicked call from Vivi: "All hell's broken loose in Faerie, and we need a safehouse to regroup. Are you in?"

I agreed, and she gave me the details. Colin had been incapacitated, and a few people in the know were trying to sneak folks out of the Arcanum silo in Montana, as the Arcanum had refused to get involved with the Faerie situation. That galled me—one sworn to the Light must always step up in times of conflict, and though Colin and I had our differences, I'd gradually decided that he wasn't quite the asshole he'd seemed. The next day, my store was full of anxious refugees and conspirators, most of whom had the decency not to make cracks about my merchandise. Auntie Eunice brewed tea and plotted with us for a time, and then she went back across the street to bed.

The Arcanum sent an assassination team in the middle of the night, ostensibly to arrest Toula. Auntie Eunice went out to confront them, and they murdered her in the street.

Something in me died that night—my naivete, perhaps. Benjamin had always told me that those wizards sworn to the Dark were few and far between, but here was an armed, organized band of them, sent by what was ostensibly the most powerful group of wizards in the world. I'd read the Arcanum's scholars, tried to make sense of their practices…and they'd blasted a hole through an old woman in her nightclothes.

When the assassins were dead, my guests did what they could, removing Auntie Eunice's body and putting a copy in her bed to be discovered, as if she'd peacefully died in her sleep. I was whisked back to Alaska for an uncomfortable week with the Stowe clan—the amenities were fine, but our hosts were understandably tense with a group of Arcanum hitmen in the front yard. When the Fringe got word that there was trouble in Montana, my companions decided to head south and see what they could uncover. "You're welcome to stay with us," Rohese offered, "but I can't in good conscience send you back to Virginia until this business is settled." I thanked her for her hospitality and opted to join the others in Montana.

A wizard doesn't run.

Though I'd been working on my new techniques for months by that point, I decided that the silo siege was the wrong time to assert myself as a proficient wizard, especially seeing as, compared to some in the Fringe camp, I was next to useless with magick. But I was a decent cook—Mom had seen to that—and between trips back to Rigby to work through Auntie Eunice's affairs, I did what I could to help the cause.

The siege broke in early December, but only because Colin's little brother, Aiden, showed up with an army and a newfound abundance of power. Colin remained indisposed, and so I packed up and went home, intending to read my borrowed books in peace and try not to look across the street at Auntie Eunice's darkened windows. Just after Christmas, however, I was surprised when Aiden came in out of the cold late one afternoon. "Got a proposition for you," he said, holding the door open as he knocked the snow off his tennis shoes.

I put down my duster and waited until he'd finished cleaning himself up. "I don't know what Colin's told you about me," I began, "but if you're looking for magickal assistance—"

"Not in the slightest," he said, to my relief, and pulled

out his phone. "How would you like free Wi-Fi?"

The problem, Aiden explained, was his inexperience. While Colin had left him with a working smartphone, he hadn't bothered to set up general network access in the palace, and Aiden, who was all of sixteen, was tired of relying on his phone as a hotspot. Wanting something more reliable, he offered to reimburse me and pay the rest of my cable and Internet bill if I'd allow him to hook up a router or two through my building.

That hour we spent going through plans and packages was the most competent I've ever felt around a faerie. Within a few days, Aiden had a router in Colin's office, plugged into my wall through a tiny gate hidden behind a picture frame. He proved to be a good neighbor, generally quiet, and every now and then, I'd give him notices about upgrades to consider. Money was no object, and I had no idea what to do with four hundred channels, but I didn't mind helping the kid. The gate was unobtrusive, and if anything, I thought it might bring me a bit of luck in my work as I brewed potions and tried to formulate new spells for my customers.

I was completely wrong about that, but at least I got to enjoy HBO for a while.

Colin woke the following December after his year-long nap, disoriented but content to keep up the arrangement Aiden and I had made. He spoke to me infrequently over the following few months, and I assumed he was busy regaining his bearings and didn't make a fuss. If he wanted to talk about theoretical magick, he knew where to find me. In the meantime, I had a conference to attend—I was a speaker on a panel about cryptofauna, and though I could have added several chapters to *The Yankee Bestiary* by then, I kept my mouth shut. While I enjoyed seeing some of my associates from the West Coast, I found myself unable to enjoy the panels and discussions about magick, which had once been my primary reason for making the trip to those affairs. The participants seemed so *smug*, confident that they'd unraveled the mysteries of creation, and they had no idea what was hiding under their noses.

I started to wonder if I'd sounded like that before magic dropped into my life like a nuclear bomb. Maybe that was why I hadn't exactly had friends as a younger man—had I come across as an arrogant prick? Was that why no one in Rigby but for the occasional Fringer ever had much to say to me?

The mirror of truth seldom reveals what we'd like to see, and the reflection I saw was unpleasant and humbling. I resolved to do better, to *be* better—not to give up on my quest for true magick, but rather to approach life embracing the possibility that I didn't have all the answers.

But before I could do much in the way of self-improvement, Easter hit.

The northern part of Virginia aside, the state is still very much part of the Bible Belt, and I knew that my shop wouldn't see high traffic over the holiday. Instead, I took the opportunity to do inventory and a deep clean, getting the dust and cobwebs out of the places I overlooked during my weekly tidying. The spring clean carried over into Monday, which was no great loss to business—really, most people in Rigby who came to my store seemed to do so on a dare—and after lunch, I tackled the long oak counter where I kept my cashbox. It was one of the few pieces of furniture that Colin and Meg had left behind, and it was in need of a good polishing.

Through some kind chance, I was on my knees behind the counter when the two Arcanum assassins blasted my locked door in. Even now, I can't describe precisely what happened. I know that I grabbed my pistol from its place by the cashbox, and I must have surprised them, as I shot them before they could shoot me. I emptied the gun to be sure, and then, seeing Auntie Eunice in my mind's eye, I grabbed a handful of athames from the display, and...

Well, there was blood all over me, and the wizards didn't get up.

I don't remember how I made it down the street to Slim's bar, but he let me in, gave me a cup of strongly laced coffee while I shook and tried not to be sick all over his white carpet, and called Colin for help.

It was the little Internet gate, we decided later. They must have come looking for Slim, picked up on the outflow of raw magic in my building, and gone to the wrong address. But the two who'd broken into my store weren't the only assassins who'd been deployed—the Arcanum had turned on its leader and the Fringe in a devastating surprise assault, and the only sane thing to do was evacuate. I could have stayed behind—I *should* have stayed to help Slim—but I'd never before killed another person, and my skin and clothes were sticky with someone else's blood. It was all I could do to pick up my crated cats and shuffle into Faerie at Colin's command.

That evening, once I'd had a chance to shower and throw up, I told Colin to send me back to the mortal realm. Someone needed to be in Montana to keep an eye on the silo, and no one in the Arcanum's new leadership was likely to know me.

Colin said I was crazy.

I reminded him that a wizard sworn to the Light must always fight the Dark, and whatever else I might be, I was a wizard.

Three months later, the king and queen agreed to let me spy in Montana, but only under heavy disguise. My name and face had been in the compromised Fringe network, they explained, and so if I returned, it would be under a transformation bind.

The new face they chose for me looked nothing like mine. For the first two weeks of my undercover existence, I could barely stand to look at myself in mirrors, as a stranger's face stared back at me and mimicked my motions. Once I parted company with the other members of the returning party—Badger, an untrained wizard, Seamus, an untrained faerie, and Amy, a competent crafter—I had nothing but a panel van of questionable vintage, a bag of enchantment-made cash, a small satchel of clothes, and some forged identification to my name.

I stopped at a public library in a small town in Kentucky to send a final e-mail to Benjamin, explaining that I'd be out of contact for a while doing research and not to worry. After that, I drove down the street to a thrift store and began sorting through the clothes, looking for pieces to fit my new frame. Somewhere between the fraying uniform pants and faded T-shirts, I found a blue caftan, a curious garment at the best of times but thoroughly unexpected in the middle of nowhere. I'd never worn one before, but it seemed to fit the persona I was creating, and anyway, it was only two dollars.

The caftan was surprisingly comfortable, and while people stared, they didn't bother me when I wore it around. I stopped at art stores along the road, then sought out more caftans to expand my wardrobe. I loaded the van with paints and canvasses, clay and bits of metal, glazes and thinners and all manner of odds and ends, then drove out to a national forest, rented a cabin for a few days, and set up camp. Quentin Galloway was an artist, and he needed something to show for it.

Over the rest of the summer, I traveled among the parks and scenic spots, filling the back of the van with a portfolio of landscapes and giving my new clothes an authentic spattering of paint stains. And then, in mid-August, once I'd made enough paintings for a small gallery show, I drove on to the tiny town of Wright's Mill, Montana.

Little had changed about the place since my brief stint there during the siege a year and a half before. Our magically enhanced headquarters had been returned to a ruin before we cleared out, and a drugstore was going up in its place. I puttered around the area until I found a modest house for rent, then called the owner, Bobby Gillespie, and introduced myself. I was an artist, I explained, looking for a change of pace and a simpler life. I said that I'd thrown a dart at a wall map, and fate had taken me to Wright's Mill. He sounded unconvinced, but cash beat an empty house, and I settled in the next morning. A trip to the local thrift store netted me a couch to sleep on—it was a start, in any case—and I'd just made up a makeshift bed that evening when Bobby stopped by with a casserole from his wife. He studied my paintings for a few minutes—I'd hung them around the former dining room in lieu of a proper gallery—and then he cleared his throat. "Got any interest in teaching?" he asked.

As it so happened, Bobby was the principal of the local school, which was in desperate need of an art teacher. I explained that I wasn't certified in any sense of the word, but he seemed unfazed. "Can you pass a background check?" he pressed.

"Maybe," I admitted, reluctant to test my luck with my forged documents.

Bobby just grunted. "Any felonies I should know about that would prevent you from legally being around children all day?"

"*Heavens*, no."

"Then I can offer you thirty grand off the books. I'll throw in the rent here, too," he offered.

The odds of anyone inviting me into the silo for a portrait session being microscopically thin, I decided that my next best way of learning information might be from careless children—and the Arcanum had sent their kids to the county school in the past. "When would I begin?" I asked.

"Three days from now."

We made a gentleman's agreement with a handshake, but my new boss paused before seeing himself out. "That, um…"

"Caftan?" I offered.

"Yeah. You wouldn't have any, like, *pants*, would you?"

"I find that I work best unencumbered," I fibbed. "And this garb is much healthier for men. Let me tell you about sperm production—"

"Nope—*no*, thank you," he interrupted, as I'd hoped. "Whatever. Just...you know, *kids*."

I told him I understood and smiled as the door closed behind him.

For that first morning, I wore sweatpants under one of my cleaner caftans, a royal blue number that had a light sprinkling of brown stains around the sleeve of my right arm. Or rather, Quentin did—these were his caftans, this was his new job, and *that* strange visage in the mirror was his face.

I checked our reflection one last time in the yellow bathroom light. Quentin's eyes squinted in the glare, and his chest rose and fell in time with my breathing.

Magick.

Magic.

Stuart's books and talismans and amulets were far behind me, his messages unanswered. His book on fairies would never be written. I was Quentin now, and Quentin would not run.

I flipped the switch, grabbed my keys, and set off to confront the Dark.

OCTOBER: FAERIE

My realm is both palace and prison. Within, I am almost limitless, conscious of the smallest movement, the most secret thought, and all such lives as have ever been spent within my borders. Without, I am little more than a hand reaching through the bars, present on the margins as a shadow of myself. I perceive, though, and in desperate times, I can find a method of making my will manifest.

The Arcanum believed its precious silo to be impregnable, a fortress protected by spellcraft and threat. What is spellcraft, though, but a mortal's manipulation of the lifeblood of my realm? Gates between the realms had been opened too many times near their stronghold, and the barrier between us was soft, weak—not yet to the point of spontaneously ripping, but patched over like oft-scabbed skin. It was a liminal place in spite of itself, and I slipped through those gates too small to be noticed, the pores between our worlds through which magic flows.

I found the child easily enough, floating in a womb made of spellcraft. My children's blood calls to me, and whatever else she might become, she was my child, too. I felt her parents' gifts within her, her mother's bright and powerful, her father's more subdued. That was expected—his bloodline had been diluted, and he had shown little ability until I amplified the potential within him.

I considered doing the same for his child. It would have been simple. Augmentation of one who has been born and formed is akin to chipping at a block of marble, every cut permanent and an act of violence. But the womb is a truly liminal place, and manipulation at that point is more properly compared to working with clay, forming and smoothing and remaking as necessary. My predecessor, Faerie's former consciousness, had done so to me—I saw the technique in our shared memory—and although she had the benefit of molding me within our realm, I could exert sufficient influence outside myself to shape the child.

I could have suppressed her mother's gift entirely, allowing her to access all of the instinctive power of enchantment from birth. I could have done for her what I had done for Coileán and Eleanor and Aiden, poured part of myself into her and given her power beyond her age. She could have been a titan from her first breath, a creature with catastrophic rages and talent beyond anything the little Arcanum had ever witnessed.

And they would have killed her. This was the problem. Had there been an obvious faerie born within the Arcanum's stronghold, she would have been destroyed.

I needed her alive, and so I took a subtler approach.

For all of my reservations about Mab's witch-blooded daughter, Toula was a wonder. I had studied her, trying to find the secret to her equal facility with her parents' gifts. She was stronger than she should have been, perhaps a side effect of their blood's interaction. Witch-bloods were so often untalented, but in her, the warring talents had fit together like a key in a lock, and what they had opened was without parallel. I wanted to replicate that with the child, but my attempts were imperfect—a broken skeleton key in a faulty lock. I could give her more or less of her father's gift, but I could never achieve the perfect balance that chance had struck with Toula.

But I did what I could. I kept her mother's strong talent alive in her, and when I slightly amplified her father's, I played with the two until they coexisted, neither sabotaging the other's effect. She would discover spellcraft first, I assumed, but in time, if she were sufficiently exposed, her other abilities would come forth.

And I'd be watching.

I bore silent witness when her grandmother birthed her, dissolving the spells around her and holding her as she wailed in protest at being delivered into a cold, alien world. Her grandfather stood by sullenly, as did the one called James Mulligan. Neither man spoke while she was cleaned and catalogued, and then Mulligan asked her name.

"We decided on Roslyn," her grandmother replied. "Roslyn Ella Carver."

Her grandfather winced at the name. I remembered why. Almost twenty years before, Ella Carver, a pretty young witch, had been kidnapped from the mortal realm and given to Titania as a changeling plaything. Seldom gentle, the queen had gone too far, and by the time Ella's brother had stormed into Faerie to rescue her, the girl was dead. I'd pitied the brother then—Howard Carver, a brave, terrified, *stupid* boy who'd been thrown back into the mortal realm with his sister's body, having been used against his will for Titania's pleasure. I'd regretted what the queen had done to them both, and I'd watched with concern when Valerius eventually spirited the child Titania had conceived to Howard's doorstep.

Having seen what Howard had become, however, I pitied him no longer.

"A fine name," Mulligan replied, and clapped them on the shoulder. "Congratulations. She's beautiful."

And she was, in the manner of the newly born, red but less misshapen than she might have been, as she'd been spared the trauma of a natural birth. Her head was covered with a damp, pale fuzz, and her eyes, barely slit open in the bright light of the room where she'd been incubated, were blackish-blue, portending a shift to brown.

Her father dwelt within Faerie then, as did his parents, evacuated from the mortal realm to save their lives. Looking through his mother's mind, I located her memories of Joey's birth—the pain and numbness and pressure and anxiety, the mewling bundle placed in her arms, the surge of joy and relief as she memorized the details of his tiny face. He had looked much as his child did.

My children, both of them.

The blood was strong.

JANUARY: FATHER PAUL MCGILL

I could have had a grand cathedral, had I wanted it. I've heard it said that it's every architect's dream to build one, and from the designs Robbie Stowe showed me, I'd say he fit the stereotype. But I'm just a priest—I'd never even been assigned a parish to oversee on my own—and the sweeping neogothic lines he suggested were a tad ostentatious for my blood. The final result was modest but traditional and tasteful, a church for perhaps three hundred with beautiful stained glass and the best acoustics I'd ever enjoyed. Had we had an organ, I'm sure it would have made the rafters shake. But we were refugees, and there was no competent organist among my small flock, let alone someone able to explain to our eager architect how one was constructed. We made do with a baby grand piano and an ecumenical musical team: a dedicated Methodist pianist, an assortment of volunteer choristers from across the spectrum, and Ruth Greene, a soprano who'd previously served as her temple's cantor and didn't mind pitching in for psalms.

Having studied Hebrew at seminary an age ago, I tried to reciprocate her favor for the few practicing Jews among the Fringe once a month. Those services weren't traditional in any sense of the word, but people seemed to understand and forgive whenever I tripped up. Our little town's unofficial motto was "Make the Best of It," and though I was no rabbi, at least I had more than a passing familiarity with the Torah. The Muslim contingent was another matter—I spoke no Arabic, for starters—but Robbie erected a building for them adjacent to the church, then put the temple next door. Across the street went similar facilities for the Hindus and Buddhists among us, plus a sixth catchall building. Folks just laughed about the odd situation—whatever else they professed, they were Fringers, and multi-faith potlucks became the norm.

As for me, the sole Christian clergyman of any stripe in town, I did my best. Protestants were tricky for me—I didn't know their liturgies, and for many, there was no set formula. But since people in crisis often turn to their faith for support, I began to notice larger crowds at Mass, even during the weekday services, and I tried to be inclusive. There was one part of the church where only the Catholics seemed to venture, however, and that was the lone confessional. It was an unobtrusive wooden piece set against the wall, two red-curtained stalls with coordinating kneelers flanking the central compartment, and I advertised availability for an hour or so after lunch daily.

It had been a quiet Wednesday, and I was taking advantage of the silence to read in the confessional when I heard footsteps on the stone floor, then the rustling of the curtain to my left. I put my book aside while the newcomer got situated, then leaned closer to the wooden screen and waited.

"Forgive me, Father, for I have sinned," came a soft voice I knew instantly. "It's been...um...ninety-four days since my last Confession."

Joey, my prodigal. I wanted to jump out of the box and hug him, but I stuck to the script. "Make your Confession, my son."

"I've missed Mass for the last...fourteen weeks, I think?"

"Missed you at Christmas," I added.

He sighed. "Not exactly in the best place right now, Father."

"I know. What else?"

"I haven't been praying of late."

Nothing unexpected there. "Anything else?"

"I've taken the Lord's name in vain. I really don't know how many times, but it hasn't been an occasional thing."

"Okay."

He hesitated, then murmured, "I still want to kill them, Father. Very much. I…I think about it a lot."

"More so than usual?"

Joey went silent for a time, and I was about to prompt him when I heard him sniff. "It's our anniversary today," he whispered. "Our first. And…"

I opened the door, tugged back his curtain, and pulled him into my arms. "Ten Hail Marys, ten Our Fathers," I said as he quietly wept against my shoulder. "Come on, let's go to my office."

I'd seen so much of myself in Joey Bolin when Immaculate Conception sent him to me as a seminary intern. He'd been quiet and a little hesitant at first—a clean-cut blond in pressed slacks, armed with a notebook and pencil—but then it takes a special sort to feel fully at ease around an exorcist, let alone me. As we'd chatted about his classes and family over pizza and beer in my little apartment, however, he'd begun to open up, and I'd caught a glimpse of the true man. He told me about summers on the Ren Faire circuit, about a childhood learning to ride and joust and "liberate" unattended liquor, about a campus priest at CUA who'd mentored him as he began to explore his calling. He wasn't put off by what I did—curious, rather, and eager to be of assistance. The longer I watched him, the more certain I became that Joey was my intended successor, a young man sufficiently strong in his faith and unwed to the rules to be introduced to Colin Leffee.

Some priests hand down vestments or crucifixes or missals. I, on the other hand, was the latest in a long line to hand down a well-meaning faerie lord.

Six months into Joey's internship, I gave him his first taste of dealing with Colin, then passed off my notes to answer his many, *many* questions. I should have said more at the time, but I was worried about my old friend, who'd just learned that his mother had stolen his former flame's baby sixteen years before, and who had decided to return the girl to her mother in person. Anticipating disaster, and seeing as Joey was on his way to a jousting gig over spring break, I'd asked him to check in with them. Ten days later, when Colin brought Joey back to me, the poor boy was a wreck, having spent his vacation shooting at faeries and doing questionable things with a merrow. I made excuses for him with his professors while he recuperated in my guestroom, but I knew he'd been pushed too far. Joey dropped out of seminary the next month and set off to clear his head, then wound up in Faerie, working for Colin, who was by then struggling with the ins and outs of kingship.

I was apprehensive when Joey showed me his dragon, but I quietly celebrated for him when he and Helen Carver became an item. No, she wasn't a good Catholic girl, but she seemed mature and responsible, and she made him so happy—I only had to look at him when he talked about her to see that. As I've never been one to stay strictly within the lines, I eagerly agreed to officiate at their wedding. And I did—at the rushed version, at least. Instead of the spring wedding they'd planned, they eloped in Faerie, spurred on by the unexpected revelation that Joey was kin to both Colin and the new queen—a death blow to Arcanum approval, but nothing that bothered me. I was as fond of Joey as I was of any of my six siblings' children, and I was happy to do my part to get the kids hitched in a hurry.

They didn't have three months together before the Arcanum turned upside down and the Fringe evacuated. Since then, I'd seen little of Joey. I knew from his mother and father that he was wrestling with his demons, but the young man sitting on my couch, holding a cup of coffee in both hands, was a gaunt-eyed shell of himself. Oh, he looked healthy enough—he'd put on muscle since seminary, his hair had grown out long enough for a ponytail, and his short beard added a few years to his face—but what I saw in his stare chilled me.

"It's my fault," he said as I took the chair opposite him.

"Nonsense," I replied, putting my coffee on a cork coaster. "The Arcanum was a simmering pot. You just happened to be there when it finally boiled over."

But Joey shook his head. "He's punishing me. If I hadn't..."

His voice trailed off, but I knew where his mind was going. "Son, you did what you did to survive," I said, keeping my gaze on him until he glanced up. "For Helen and the baby."

"Not just for them." The guilt in his eyes was unmistakable. "I...I justified it, you know? I had to be there for Helen, for our child, but..."

"But you didn't want to die?" I prompted.

He nodded miserably.

"You're twenty-eight, right? I don't know of many people your age who are eager to end it," I said. "There's no sin in wanting to live."

Joey cut his eyes back to his untouched drink. "Maybe not in wanting, but I acted on it."

I sat and thought for a moment, searching for guidance, as nothing in my training or experience had prepared me to deal with his circumstances.

Two days before his wife and a good portion of the Fringe were kidnapped, Joey had gone into battle. I didn't know the specifics—all I knew was that someone had blown a hole through his chest, and the sentient realm had offered to save his life. The only way to do so was for the realm to somehow magnify the inhuman part of Joey until he was, at least from a practical perspective, fae. My polite, inquisitive seminarian had become an immortal with magical abilities and a nasty metal allergy, but at least he'd been able to come home to his pregnant wife.

In general, I had no problem with faeries—I'd called one a partner and friend for most of my career, after all. But if

Colin had concerns about the state of his soul, he'd always kept them to himself. Joey had been my mentee, however, and his modified state weighed heavily on his mind.

"I don't think you're being punished," I eventually told him. "Not for that. You are what you are, Joey, and that's not anyone's fault."

"What if you're wrong?" he countered. "What if it's a sin? How do I do penance for *that*?"

"Well, for one thing, you can stop thinking about killing yourself." His head shot up, and I snorted, seeing his shock. "Do you honestly think you're the first suicidal person to darken my door? And since one does not make amends for one sin by committing another, put that out of your mind."

His cheeks began to color. "I thought…you know, if I'm being punished, then if I'm not here anymore—"

"You're not going to free Helen by putting a bullet in your head."

"I would do it," he mumbled. "If it would free her, I'd do it."

"You do remember that suicide is a mortal sin, yeah?"

"Yes, Father."

"*Good.*" I slid forward in my chair, wincing as my arthritic knees shifted. "Now, you listen to me. I don't have all the answers for you. I wish I did, but there's been no revelation from on high, and I am *quite* literally only human—"

The corner of his mouth ticked. "Don't be so sure."

"If I hear otherwise, I'll be in touch. But Joey, what I do know is that whatever self-preservation instinct may have kicked in, you also did it out of love. You wouldn't be sitting with me right now if your heart wasn't broken. I don't know what to tell you other than that love is not, on its own, a force for evil. And I do *not* believe that this many lives would be ended or shattered as punishment for one man. Remember," I added, "long before she loved you, she loved her brother. You didn't make the Arcanum blow up by yourself."

"I threw kerosene on the fire," Joey muttered.

"It was already burning." I pushed myself up, then joined him on the couch and squeezed his shoulder. "I pray for you both," I told him. "Every day. And I pray that the right thing happens at the right time. I don't know when that might be. Colin sure doesn't. But in the meantime, why don't you come back to Mass, hmm? Can't hurt."

He smiled tightly. "Don't think I'm exactly welcome around here, Father."

"Why would you say that? Last time I checked, this building is full of sinners. Kind of why I've got that confessional out there, you know?"

"No, I mean..." Joey struggled briefly, then said, "People around here, they know me. They know what I am. I, uh...I scare them."

I didn't need to ask to know how he'd reached that conclusion. The faerie ability to peer into minds was no secret among the Fringers, and I'd come to expect it from Colin.

"You're hurting," I replied. "You need to be here. And if anyone doesn't like it, I celebrate Mass daily. They've got plenty of other options." I squeezed his shoulder again, then gave it a pat. "Come home."

He sipped his coffee, then slowly nodded. "Okay."

"Sunday?"

"Yes, Father."

"Remember that lying is a sin," I told him, and rose again. "Now, if I were you, I'd go back in there and spend some quality time for the last few months' absence. Got a rosary on hand?" He pulled one from his pocket, and I smiled. "Good man. Go on, the sanctuary is open. I'll leave you to it."

Joey went on his way, and I sat down to work on my next homily. When the shadows grew too long to read, I turned on a light, put my notepad aside, and wandered back into the church to check on him.

It was dark in there—all but before the small bye-altar

to the Virgin, where every votive in the rack was glowing in the gloom. Of Joey I found no sign until Sunday morning, when he approached the rail behind his parents with his arms folded across his chest. I made the sign of the cross over him and watched as he returned to their pew, troubled once more as I'd periodically been for the previous four years.

Forgive me, Father, for I have sinned, I prayed as I put the wafers away. *I didn't mean to break that child.*

—YEAR TWO—

MARCH: COILEÁN

I should never have let Robbie put bells in, I thought, trying to ignore the steady peal in the distance. From the sound of it, someone had been up in the settlement's church tower since dawn—Paul, I'd wager—and the funereal tolling hadn't abated all morning. It wasn't loud in my office, not at that distance, but it served as a constant stimulus, reminding me of the date every time my thoughts strayed.

Judging by the pucker in her brow, Ellie wasn't enjoying the bells any more than I was. "Town?" she finally asked, looking up from the papers we'd spread across the low table between us.

"Mm." I beckoned a bottle of whiskey over from the bar and topped up my well-laced coffee.

She watched with faint disapproval as she sipped her unadulterated tea. "Is that helping with the noise?"

"Not yet."

"Well, do keep me posted."

It would have been a moment's work to block out the bells, but that seemed crass, like spitting at passing mourners. It was the one-year anniversary of the Fringe's so-called Unravelling, and they had every right to remember the ones they'd lost.

When I woke to the bell, I'd assumed they would peal it once for each of the dead—an hour's work, I estimated. But the tolling had continued, leading me to believe that they'd included the missing in the list. With the bell having gone on for five hours by that point, I knew they were well beyond the missing by then and just pealing for the sake of it. I didn't want to think about how loud that incessant ringing had to be in the settlement.

At least none of my people had come by yet to complain about the noise. I lived on the far northern edge of my court's agreed-upon territory, and I could only hope that the sound would fade past the edge of annoyance before it reached the next estates. I had enough on my plate that morning without adding gripes about the Fringe. Our people—mine and Ellie's alike—already felt somehow imposed upon because we'd given the refugees shelter and a community of their own, despite the fact that we'd placed it well out of the way. The Fringers kept to themselves for safety, and Ellie kept a Stowe boy or two at the wall to watch for faeries in search of easy entertainment, which I suppose is what peeved our courts. Picking on the Fringe town would be tantamount to shooting fish in a barrel, but as far as the courts were concerned, that was *their* barrel and *their* fish, and we were the buzzkills withholding the guns.

Ellie absently rubbed her ear and turned her attention back to the complaints on the coffee table. "We should never have allowed them to mingle again," she said with a sigh. "Those six months were almost peaceful."

"Except for the intra-court conflicts, you mean."

"At least I can handle those without cross-checking matters with you," she replied. "You know, I'm tempted to put up that wall after all and tell everyone the border is closed."

"We'd look weak—"

"As if we don't already." She pointed to the window, angling her finger toward the north and the bell. "You mean to tell me that none of yours have suggested that you steamroll the silo and be done with it?"

"Actually, mine suggested a blast crater," I muttered, and drank my coffee.

She waited until I lowered the mug, then said, "It's not a horrible idea."

"*Ellie*—"

"Hear me out. I know that Carver means a lot to Aiden and Joey, but she's one person."

"With God-only-knows how many Fringers being held as well," I retorted.

Her lips tightened. "I don't like it, but we need to consider the cost of waiting. If we allow those idiots in Montana to order us about…what message is that sending to the courts? Your mother never would have stood for it, nor my father."

"I am *not* my mother."

"I'm not saying you are," she soothed. "I'm only suggesting that we think about preventing a coup of our own. Do you honestly think we could stand up to both courts by ourselves? Even with the boost?"

"No. Which is why we keep them distracted with each other," I replied, sweeping one hand over the papers. "As long as they don't decide that we're their common enemy…"

"I suppose," she murmured after a long moment. "If we just had some sign of *progress*…perhaps something from Toula?"

She let the question hang, and I shook my head. "If she finds a way, you'll know as soon as I do. For now…" I picked up the closest petition and gave it a quick scan. "Who's Cinotu?"

Ellie made a face and glanced at the ceiling. "His mother was a lady, I *think*, but she wasn't of the blood. Or was she? Honestly, I need my notes," she said, reaching for her tablet.

"You need Toula," I countered. "Have her do for your court what she did for mine. It makes these family grudges infinitely easier to follow."

She paused and regarded me curiously. "You think she would? Mass aural analysis can't be a quick project."

"She'll do it if you ask nicely."

"Would you mind being the intermediary? She's living in your house, after all," she hastily explained. "The two of you have a history. I'm sure she still thinks of me as the histrionic bitch who's out to kill her old friend's wayward little girl."

"She thinks nothing of the sort," I said with an incredulous chuckle. "And our 'history' is built off of reciprocal matricide. Hardly makes us bosom buddies."

"Regardless, she's in *your* house," Ellie replied. "Do me this favor, won't you?" She held up the paper with Cinotu's version of events, set it alight, and smiled. "Tit for tat, hmm?"

When I stopped by Toula's apartment late that afternoon, she almost didn't hear me knock, as she was blasting Janice Joplin from the stereo array Aiden had built her. "Bells, huh?" I asked as she closed the door behind me.

"The first few hours did a thorough job of reminding me of my continuing failure. After that, figured I'd get some work done." She led me into her den, a spacious room with two walls of bookcases and a floor-to-ceiling eastern-facing window, through which I spotted a thin bank of pinking clouds. As usual, her table and two of her three couches were covered with open books, while her laptop sat on an ottoman near the humming generator. "Thought I might have been on to something with Matsuoka, but her theory didn't pan out so well in practice. Oh well, what's one more dead end?" She folded her arms and leaned against the open wall beside a decorative tapestry, a piece she'd found rolled up in the library and appropriated with my blessing. "Need something?"

"Not personally. Ellie wanted to know if you'd be willing to do an aural census for her court."

"Sure," she replied with a shrug. "If she can wrangle everyone in, I can do the analysis. Happy to. It'd be nice to do something I can succeed at again," she added, scowling at her unhelpful books.

I started to respond, then paused as I noticed the odor of beef and bay leaves wafting from her little kitchen. "Is that…*pot roast?'*

"Yep. Astrid taught me how to make a slow cooker."

"*You* cook?"

Toula laughed. "Woman cannot live on Easy Mac alone—not if she doesn't want scurvy. I'm pretty good at throwing things into a pot and walking away, if I do say so myself," she added, brushing imaginary lint from her shoulders. "How about it? You hungry? Should be out in an hour."

I had no grand plans that evening, and as I was already salivating at the smell, I took her up on the offer.

While the pot roast finished, I lingered in the doorway of Toula's practice room, a padded space off the den that she'd copied from the silo. She called up a visualization spell, showing me the complexity of the silo wards she'd rendered in miniature, then demonstrated her latest half-dozen potential techniques and explained why they failed to break through. "I feel like I'm tilting at windmills," she admitted as we arranged the table on her balcony for dinner. "But if the answer's in one of those books, and I'm too lazy to find it…"

"You're anything but lazy," I protested, producing a brass candelabrum. The bell had ceased at sunset, and the cool evening seemed almost eerily quiet with its absence. "And no one should fault you for failing to find a non-existent solution."

"Unless it does exist," she replied, and put out ceramic flatware. "But that's a problem for the morning. Merlot okay?"

I'd created a fire pit near the table to take off the chill when she brought out the food, which was surprisingly good. "A few tips from Astrid, a few more from Pinterest," Toula explained. "Nothing fancy, but it's tender."

That it was, and we spoke little until the first helping had been cleared. "My compliments," I said, lifting my wine stem toward her. "And thank you. I wasn't expecting to dine with company tonight."

"The guys told you not to wait up?"

"Not in so many words, but Aiden let it be known that he was going to the barn with the Wii, so you know what that means."

Toula nodded and sipped her wine. "If he can distract Joey, good for him. I take it Val's supervising?"

"Someone needs to be there to lose in spectacular fashion."

She grinned and helped herself to the potatoes. "Good. Those two should get to beat him at *something* every now and then."

"Be nice to your brother," I mock-chided. "He puts up with me."

"Poor baby. I'll make him a medal or something," she replied. "Mina and I actually talked about doing that once. Like a tiny trophy, yeah?" she said, holding her finger and thumb two inches apart. "'World's Craziest Boss,' we were thinking."

"Put that on an espresso cup, and I think he'd appreciate it more." I followed Toula's example and attacked the meat platter. "So, I realize this is none of my business, but you and Mina…"

"Not friends, but getting closer."

"You're not back together?"

"*Hell*, no." She drank deeply and put her glass aside. "Mina cheated on me, and she wasn't even sorry about it. Why would I go back for more of that?"

"Merely   curious.   She   seems   pleasant enough…competent, reasonably attractive…"

"And the latest in my string of short relationships that ended poorly. But hey, at least my track record remains intact."

I snorted and took a bite. "Women."

"*Men*, too," she said primly. "The worst was this guy named Trevor. I had a shitty little apartment in Chicago, and he lived a few floors above me—one of those relationships of proximity. Anyway, we'd been seeing each other for about a month, and we were going to meet at this Italian restaurant after he got off work. So I dress up, and I'm sitting there like an idiot for an hour, and then I start to think that he's hurt or dead or whatever, and I run up to his place and cast the door open—never underestimate the utility of lock-picking—and I find him passed out in the den with this blonde skank…no, seriously, she was a skank," she insisted as I tried not to laugh. "Looked like she'd done her ink all by herself. They're both naked, and they're curled up around each other on the carpet…long story short, they'd been smoking pot all afternoon, and they started chasing it with Jack, and they fucked and fell asleep."

"I'm sorry."

"I'm not. At least I didn't catch anything," she muttered.

"You *are* somewhat fae," I reminded her. "You can't catch anything."

"And occasionally, that comes in handy. So that was Trevor. There was Adriana," she said, counting off on her fingers, "who hid her heroin addiction for a few weeks…Dawn, the recovering Baptist who wasn't convinced that we weren't going straight to hell every time we kissed…Noah, who heard 'bi' and thought that was code for 'I'll bring along another girl and jump in on the fun'…Damian, who had a delightful anger management issue…oh yes, and Micah. Best relationship I've ever had," she continued, smiling to herself. "We tended bar together, and he did a drag revue on the side. *Super*-conservative family, though, and he needed a beard for his brother's destination wedding in Hawaii, so I got an all-expenses-paid trip to Oahu and pretended to be madly in love with him for a week. Even dyed the highlights out and flattened it," she said, gesturing toward her gelled, purple-tipped tufts of black hair. "I ended up sneaking out of our room while he hooked up with a groomsman. Last I heard, he'd settled down with a nice boy from Boston, and I wish them the best." She drained her wine and refilled the glass, then asked, "What about you?"

"Not much to share," I replied, leaning back to look at the first stars. "Flings—'hookups,' I suppose you'd call them—but nothing serious."

"*Nothing?*"

"Not until Meggy. Is that pitiful or just pathetic?"

"Surprising," she said, and I glanced back at my companion in query. "All that time, and you never fell for *anyone?*"

I drank while I chose my words. "Fairly early on, I understood the…*complications*…of getting involved with a mortal. You can't ever be honest, and you know in the back of your mind that your time together is severely limited. Really, I don't know how Ellie kept doing it," I said, reaching for the wine bottle. "And you saw how broken up she was over Walt. Imagine going though that every few decades. Safer to keep things casual. Less painful, I suppose."

"Except Meg?"

"Except Meg," I replied. "I wish I'd never met her."

Toula huffed her disbelief. "You don't mean that."

"I do. Think about it: if we'd never met, she'd still be alive, Walt would be alive, *Moyna* wouldn't exist, Mother and Oberon would probably still be around to manage this circus, Helen would have had a smooth transition to grand magus, the Fringe would probably still be intact—"

"*Mab* would still be around," she interrupted, "Aiden would be hiding in his bedroom if his little sadist buddies hadn't killed him by now, I'd still be bound, Simon Magus's diary would probably be in a storage unit…" She shrugged. "Good and bad, man. That's life. And I see you've had a chance to ruminate on this to the point of absurdity."

"It's not absurd—"

"Oh, come on. Why stop with you two? If Meg's mom had never gone to that bachelorette party, Meg would never have existed. If your dad had been a little better about his vows, then you wouldn't have been part of the problem. Hell, keep it going. If Titania's parents—who were they?"

"Damned if I know."

"Doesn't matter. If they hadn't made her, then think of what a different place this might have been. You can't just decide that one summer in the nineties was the ultimate flashpoint."

"Maybe not," I replied between sips, "but it's the one I could have controlled. If I'd been honest with her…"

Toula waited while I stewed, then said, "It's not like I've announced to every one of my partners that I can point a stick at things and make them go *boom*. Actually, I think Mina's the only one who's been in on my little secret."

"This was slightly different," I muttered. "But thanks for trying."

We ate for a moment in silence, giving me ample time for a fresh round of recrimination. I'd loved Meggy—I should have told her the truth about myself. She had a right to know what she was getting into. All of the excuses I'd cobbled together—it wasn't safe, we weren't that serious, she was planning to marry someone else—were just the lies I'd told myself to get past the fact that I'd been too afraid to lose her to come clean.

"Selfish, really," I said to Toula. "If I'd been honest, she wouldn't have wanted me. She'd have run screaming."

"You don't know that—"

"I do!" I said, laughing weakly. "That's *exactly* what she did!"

"She came around," Toula protested.

"Yeah, just long enough to decide that she hated me." I considered my plate, then folded my napkin and stood. "I'm sorry, I didn't mean to ruin dinner—"

She touched my arm to stay me. "You didn't. Sit down."

"I should—"

"*Sit.*"

That took me aback, but Toula's face suggested that she would tolerate no dissent. "If you leave now," she said, "you're just going to go back to your office, drink alone, and wallow. Tell me I'm wrong."

"You're not," I grudgingly admitted after a moment.

"Uh-huh. So why not stay here for a while? I mean, if you leave now, who's going to play Monopoly with me, eh?"

"*Monopoly?*"

"Found a set in the library. Looks like an early edition. Got anything better to do? I should warn you that I don't lose."

True, there was still a stack of petitions waiting in my quiet office, but the night was fine, the fire pit was warm, and the company was regarding me with a smirk of challenge. "If you could go over the rules," I said. "I've never played."

She laughed aloud. "Are you kidding? How have you never...you know what, don't answer that," she said, shaking her head. "Help me clean up, and I'll teach you. It's not hard. Two house rules to learn off the bat," she added, gathering her plate and utensils. "Free Parking gets the pot, and I play the racecar."

"I have no idea what that means, but okay."

"And another thing: no cheating. You can't just pull money out of thin air."

I followed her inside, then caught her guilty glance toward her open books and abandoned computer. "Let it go. You're not going to change the world tonight," I reminded her, patting her shoulder.

"I know," she said with a slight sigh, heading back to the balcony. "But when it gets quiet, I start hearing that bell again."

The night was still—crickets, the crackling fire, the soft rustling of the breeze through my orchard and the forest beyond—but if I listened long enough, I could almost hear the distant trill of Meggy's laughter.

I held the door open while Toula carried the platters inside and watched her will the leftovers into plastic containers. "Hey, Glinda?"

She grunted acknowledgement as the plates turned clean and floated into their cabinet.

"I'm glad you're here. Not just for the pot roast."

The corner of her mouth twitched. "Careful, now. That sounded dangerously close to...*nice*."

"And we wouldn't want that," I said, stepping out to bring in the rest.

I watched her through the window as she tidied, willing her slow cooker clean and the garbage into the ether. There was a grace to her movements, I realized—a fluidity I hadn't noticed before. I wondered if she danced in there when no one was watching her.

The accursed bell began to peal again in the distance, but only briefly before segueing into a familiar five-bell pattern. "Evening service," I told Toula as she popped out to investigate. "Paul must be doing something for the occasion."

We stood together at the railing, listening as the tones rose and fell, neither speaking until the last echoes died away.

APRIL: KIP

The dreams only worsened as spring passed.

I'd experienced their like before—I suspect that every male has, in one form or another—but not since I was a boy coping with the first confusing stirrings of manhood had I been so embarrassed by my nocturnal fantasies. I thanked my protective ancestors and any caring deity for the fact that I seldom talk in my sleep, as the thought of having to explain myself made me want to crawl into a hole and never emerge. Badger and Carey could travel in their dreams, but as far as I knew, they couldn't see mine—which was good, as I feared that if they learned where my mind was going, they'd never let me sleep in the bunkhouse again.

In my dreams, I found myself at the kenorib—*season* was the closest translation I could manage, but it meant so much more than that. The kenorib, the annual gathering of the villages to celebrate the cycles of life. Most women had their children during the festival, with midwives and female relatives on hand to assist, but for those my age, the kenorib meant one thing: the chance to meet a mate. I'd been too young at my last kenorib to do more than admire the girls, but I was a grown man now, unattached and available for consideration, and my dream-mind knew it.

Asleep, I walked around the bonfire at the center of our traditional meeting place, freed from the transformation bind that locked me into human form, steady on four legs once again. I met the eyes of the girls around me, noting who was paring off and who still wore the braided grass garland of the searching. As I walked, I realized that Hib was beside me, steering me past the prettiest daughters of the neighboring villages and toward the far side of the fire. "This one is special," he told me, guiding me by the elbow. "Hurry, Kippet, before she makes up her mind."

The crowd parted, and then there she was in the flickering light—the most beautiful woman I could imagine, at least seen from behind. She was petite in her proportions but well formed, her hind legs long and muscular, her glossy tail like glass, reflecting the dancing flame. All of her hair was the same shade of blonde—somewhat like the color Zeb called palomino, but uniform and more yellow than brown. She wore her hair braided with purple flowers, and it flowed into the soft mane down her spine. Her skin, though, was striking, far too light to be of our people, and when she turned toward us, I saw that she was Amy—a kadalin version of Amy, but unmistakably her. She wore only the garland, draped around her slender neck and over her small, firm breasts—a product purely of my imagination, as I'd never seen her in anything more revealing than a bikini. She stamped and cocked her head, giving me a look of invitation comingled with desire, and her tail began to flick...

...and I woke with a start, panting, aroused, and thoroughly humiliated.

I couldn't lie to myself—I wanted Amy, though I knew I shouldn't.

I found her on the couch that morning, asleep in front of the bunkhouse television. She'd promised that she only wanted to watch for an hour before bed, but we knew the likely result of *that*. Amy had been hard at work crafting for the Minor Arcanum over the last weeks and months, and when she crashed, she crashed hard. She was still wearing her "lounge sweats"—a pair of faded, stretchy black pants that had seen better times and a T-shirt that dwarfed her frame, her uniform of choice when working. It doubled as sleepwear, apparently, though I couldn't have said why.

The intricacies and impracticalities of human apparel

were still mysterious to me, though I'd at least grasped the general premise of never exposing any parts of oneself that could be construed as generative. Honestly, I didn't mind that rule as it applied to me—through some bizarre design quirk, no part of their male organs could retract, and so covering them seemed most logical. The women insisted on covering their breasts as well, though, which was a pity. My mother and sisters had worn chest slings on occasion, especially if there would be heavy running, but the notion of sitting around in a climate-controlled room, fully swaddled in cloth, would have been as mystifying to them as it was to me.

Amy was not a beautiful sleeper that day. Her face had squished against a pillow at an odd angle, and a thin line of drool had escaped. Her hair was mussed and oily, and she'd buried her feet beneath the pillow at the other end of the couch for warmth. I covered her with a blanket, and she snorted restlessly, readjusting to the slight weight and sudden warmth, then settled back into deep sleep.

I could have stood there, watching her, but knowing how creepy that would have been, I went outside into the pleasant morning.

Our bunkhouse sat behind Zeb and Carey's home, a short walk from the two barns and fenced pastures where they kept their rescued and rehabilitated horses. As I'd expected, I found Zeb in the closer barn, feeding and watering the few of his charges in the stalls, but I waved and kept my distance. The horses *hated* me, and my transformation bind did nothing to disguise my true nature from them. Seamus said not to take it personally—they feared and hated him, too, as well as anything else not fully of the mortal realm—but it was frustrating to have to watch my steps, knowing that if I strayed too close to the herd, I'd incite a mass panicked flight. I'd done so five times already, though it was never my intention to give our hosts more work.

Unlike Seamus and me, Amy didn't trigger their fear. She

was technically half fae, but whatever made her unable to use magic also seemed to fool the Joneses' herd and pets. Shortly after we arrived at the ranch, Zeb put Amy on a horse's back and began to teach her to ride. She'd been awkward at first, stiff and fearful of falling, but after months of work, she rode more naturally, moving her body with her mount's instead of fighting for control. Watching her ride around the practice ring, I almost laughed at times—she was so slight, and the horses Zeb selected for her training dwarfed her in stature—but slowly, Amy had learned how to lead them with nudges and commands and tugs of the reins.

I'd carried her twice before my transformation, once when her first mount bolted, then again a few days later, trying to help her recover from that incident before her new fear could take root. Though she'd weighed so little, she'd been an awkward burden, stiff as a tree and clinging to me as if the ground below us had turned to fire. At the time, my decisions had seemed sound—Amy was one of the few friends I had in that strange place, and I didn't want to see her come to harm.

I'd since grown less sure of my choices.

While Amy had practiced her riding, Zeb had spied me lurking near the fences and had tried to make me less wary of the creatures. He'd described the structure of the herd, identifying the mares and their grown children, explaining why all of the males but one had been gelded. He'd told me where the horses had come from, which had been abused and which born on the ranch, and let me watch from a safe distance as he tended to them. He even taught me the names for their colors—bay and buckskin, pinto and cremello, and a handful of other varieties.

I wondered sometimes whether he thought of me as a redhead, like some of the refugee Fringers who'd passed through the bunkhouse on their way out of the realm, or as a chestnut.

Before the etalre swept through and destroyed my family, I thought I had life fairly well mapped out. I was the youngest, the beneficiary of my siblings' advice as to the getting and maintenance of mates, and for all of his brotherly teasing, Hib was always ready to answer my questions. I'd grown tall and broad, hardened by working the farm, and my sisters assured me that I would have no trouble with the girls at the next kenorib—my debut would be successful, they predicted. I had much to offer a mate: a place in my family's comfortable home, a bountiful farm, and, if my sisters were to be trusted, an appealing face and form. I assumed that I would take a mate within a year or two and complete my mother's happiness.

Of course, that was not to be. My family had been eradicated, and if my home, let alone my village, still stood, it was unknown to me. I'd been fortunate beyond reason to wind up at the ranch, safe and healthy once more, well-fed and rested, a useful member of the little team. But I was hardly the boy I'd been a year before—troubled by nightmares now, slightly rope-scarred around my wrists and even around the ankles of my unnatural legs, and hypersensitive to unexplained noises in the night.

And I'd lost all of the boy's confidence.

I'd had no concept of humans—or faeries, for that matter—prior to my unexpected arrival in the mortal realm, but they had stories about my kind. Centaurs, they called us, though I gathered that the conception in their legends was somewhat different than my reality. In any case, they had no clue what to do with me. Had I shown myself to their unsuspecting world, I'd have been labeled a monster, or a cryptid at best. For centaurs weren't simply centaurs in the human imagination, but rather amalgamated creatures, half human and half beast.

I hadn't fully understood this at first, but as I learned more of their culture and tales, I began to fear that they thought of me as something *less* than they, even after I learned to balance on their ridiculous legs. I might pass, but those who knew me knew all too well what was hiding under the transformation bind…and how much it resembled the temperamental horses out in the pasture. Parts of my reflection that had once secretly given me pride were now things to be hidden and never spoken of. Perhaps it was irrational that I feared they'd consider me to be no better than one of their animals, albeit a mouthy one, but then again, little of my first year in the realm made complete sense to me.

I'm sure I'd have gotten past my insecurity and my desperate need to belong in my new quasi-family much sooner had Amy not been in the picture. Within days of meeting her, I'd learned to look past her odd legs; within weeks, I found her smile to be the most beautiful thing in my world. Within months, I admitted to myself that I'd fallen for her, though part of me recoiled at the thought. Amy wasn't kadalin—had my family known of my desire for her, I mused, they'd have been appalled. Yes, she had a pretty face…a charming laugh…a clever mind, a strong arm, a steady aim, and a smile that could send me to my knees, yes, all of that—but she wasn't of my people. I should have been disgusted by the idea of taking her to mate, but I couldn't extinguish the fire in my blood.

But if Amy wasn't kadalin, I certainly wasn't human. The bind was only a convincing illusion—it had changed nothing about me in truth. Still, part of me whispered, did that matter? Perhaps Amy felt about me as I did about her…

Of course she didn't, I reminded myself, always cringing at my stupidity. Amy was learning to ride horses, and whatever I might have thought about myself, *she* surely thought of me as near kin to the beasts. She would have been horrified had she known of my feelings…which was as it should be. She didn't want me, and I *shouldn't* want her—but I couldn't lie to myself, and I couldn't stop the dreams of Amy waiting for me, unencumbered and eager.

I was disgusting. A deviant. An embarrassment to my family, my village, and all my many ancestors.

And so I stood at the fence to the training ring, watching the herd graze in the distance and wishing—not for the first time—that I could be back in my body, free from the bind, when I felt arms encircle my chest and jumped.

"Boo," said Amy, and I glanced back to see her grinning up at me. "Sorry, you looked like you were a million miles away. Couldn't sleep?"

Her hair was still a blonde snarl, her chin marked with a white streak of dried saliva, and a spot of varnish had somehow ended up above her left eyebrow, but my hearts leapt at the sight of her.

"You were snoring so loudly, I feared the bunkhouse would come crashing down," I teased.

"I was *not!*" she protested, laughing as she punched me in the arm. "Badger snores, not me!" With a little huff, she clambered onto the fence and gazed at the pasture. "Felicia's out there."

"Yes, but she still hates me."

Amy shrugged. "Her loss, then."

I glanced down at her and saw something curious in the curve of her smile.

Was that…

Did she…

Don't be stupid, Kippet, I told myself, and took a seat on the fence beside her, trying not to think of how she'd looked at me in my dreams.

AUGUST: HELEN CARVER

In the beginning, the world was dark and formless and eternal, black nothingness like an endless sea.

And then a spirit moved upon the waters, and a voice like thunder shook the heavens: "Hello, there. It's Badger Parsons. I'm here to talk to you."

The voice paused, and my soul cried out, silently pleading with her not to go.

The voice tried again. "Helen?"

I'm here, I hear you, I wanted to say, but my lips wouldn't move, my throat wouldn't work, and I had no gift for telepathy.

As my consciousness surfaced, I could have wept for joy, had my eyes been willing to cooperate. Badger—how had *she* found me? I remembered from my Fringe notes that she was a police detective, but she was a weak witch at best. How had she made it into the silc? Surely Mulligan hadn't left me unguarded…

While my mind raced, I felt her take my unresponsive hand. "Helen, it's Badger," she said. "If you can hear me—"

I hear you, I hear you, don't leave me!

"—this is a dream, but it's not a normal one. I'm so sorry that I can't free you…"

A dream. A *dream*? By turns, I was devastated and perplexed—how the hell were we having a conversation in a dream? What sort of magic had Badger stumbled upon?

"You haven't been forgotten," she continued, her voice tender. "The Arcanum is using you as a hostage, along with many of the Fringe, and no one's quite figured a way to get you out of here yet, but they're trying."

Though I couldn't move a muscle, I felt her warm breath on my face as she hovered close. "Joey loves you, dear," she murmured. "He's beside himself, but he's safe. So is Aiden. Joey's mum and dad are with them. I know Joey's desperate to find you, and I'll tell him you're alive—"

My husband, my brother. I hadn't heard their names spoken in a seeming age, and I clung to the news that they were free somewhere beyond my prison walls.

When she spoke again, Badger seemed perplexed. "You're not pregnant any more, are you? Did you have the baby? Did you lose it?"

They took it from me, they pulled it away, you have to find my baby—

But she remained unaware of my end of the conversation. "No matter," she said. "I don't know when, and I don't quite know how, but we're going to rescue you, dear. And until then…we'll be out there. Maybe it seems like it now, but you're not alone."

I tried to beg her not to leave me, but it was too late, and once again, I was smothered in nothingness.

At first, I wanted to sob with frustration, but when the initial feeling passed, I focused on what a precious gift that too-brief visit had been. The only contact I'd had since my child was ripped from me had been the Mulligans, father and son, sometimes singly, sometimes in a pair. When James came alone, he was quiet, almost clinical, and his visits were brief. It was from him that I knew my baby had been born, though he wouldn't so much as tell me the child's name.

"Don't worry," he once said, "when the brat's grown, I'll send it over the border to avenge you. Faeries killed its poor mommy and daddy, you know—I'm sure the kid will be eager to strike back in your name. Assuming it's not a total dud, I mean. If that happens…" He'd sighed in mock sympathy. "I know what a difficult time your mongrel brother had. Maybe the kid could meet with an unfortunate accident. Wouldn't want it to suffer, would we?"

When the Mulligans came together, they rarely stayed more than a few moments—I think James was trying to teach his son the complex casting holding me down. But when Russell came alone, I was reminded in full that while I couldn't move, I could still *feel*.

Aid had been Russell's favorite toy, and I'd stepped in at every opportunity to take it away from him. Compounding matters, Aid had spent a year as regent for Coileán, and he'd lashed out at Russell with his newfound power, humiliating his tormentor. While I'd had to step in professionally and ask my brother to please stop slamming wizards into walls, personally, I thought the little shit had it coming to him.

But now I was the helpless one, and as Aid was unavailable to Russell, he took his anger out on me. Slaps across the face were a warmup. He'd punch me in the stomach, knock me in the head, and even threw me onto the floor when no one was around to stop him, where he could kick me to his heart's content. He never tried to undress me—his father had forbidden it, telling him that it might affect my bind. I had to wonder at James's thought process on that. Russell regularly left me bruised and bleeding, so why did James fear that a hand down my pants would have given me supernatural strength to fight back? The last time I checked, I didn't get a power-up when my fragile female virtue was threatened. Still, I was grateful for his misplaced caution. Physical abuse and emotional torture were bad enough without adding sexual assault to the mix.

I couldn't have guessed how long it was before Badger returned, but I was overjoyed to hear her once more—I'd begun to fear that I'd hallucinated the whole thing.

"Hello, love," she said, patting my cheek. "It's Badger again. How're we doing?"

Oh, you know, it still hurts to breathe from the last time Russell kicked me in the ribs. Same old same old.

"I'm sorry that last visit was so brief. Best to keep these short—I'm getting better at control, but there's no sense in pressing our luck." She sighed softly. "I'll bring you up to date, then, if you can hear me. It's the thirteenth of August. You've been under for approximately sixteen and a half months."

Sixteen? I wanted to shout. Time had little meaning in the void, but still—I'd missed more than a year already? Then my baby…

I knew she couldn't hear me, but still, I almost imagined that Badger had read my mind. "I located your baby. I'm sure it's yours—she glows mostly gold in the dream space, but she's got a little white in her mix."

She.

"I'm sorry, but I haven't yet got her name. I'm trying, but it's not safe to stick around long. Judging by the nursery furnishings, really. Either it's a girl, or your mum and dad *really* like lacy baby things."

My blood boiled at the mention of my parents.

"Anyway, she's living in your parents' flat. Pretty little baby. Blonde, but she hasn't got much hair yet. Chubby cheeks," she added, and I heard the pity in her voice. "She looks to be healthy enough. Unharmed. I'm sorry I don't have more for you, but I'm trying."

I could have kissed her for bringing me those priceless scraps.

"Here's the situation," said Badger after a moment's pause, taking on a clipped tone that reminded me of her mundane career. "Once you were disabled, Mulligan named himself grand magus and send out assassin squads against the Fringe. We believe he forced Greg Harrison to give him access to our network, and he raided our member database. We had no warning in the first wave, and then there was a mass panic." She paused and cleared her throat. "Coileán worked out a short cease-fire, and Faerie evacuated as many of our people as they could reach, but they only got about five hundred in time. At this point, we don't know how many are dead. The official tally is six hundred forty, but so many are still missing. We've been hunting the stragglers down, but we know that Mulligan managed to snag some, and I can't find any trace of them."

Before I could give form to my question, Badger seemed to realize what she'd neglected to mention. "It's only a few of us who're working in this realm: me, my partner—he's Toula Pavli's nephew," she said, as if that explained everything—"a crafter, a centaur we found along the way—long story—and my cousin Arnie, of all people. Arnold Lowe—I trust you know him."

I would have laughed aloud, had I been able. Of course I knew Magus Lowe. He was one of the junior Arc 2 magi, and he'd always struck me as the dependable sort, talented but bookish. I hadn't known that he had a Fringer cousin, and I couldn't picture him as the face of the resistance, but then I was getting brought up to speed by a witch in a dream, so really, who was I to scoff at the improbable?

"You're probably wondering how I'm here," she continued. "Long story short, I'm a wizard. Magic's *loads* easier when you're not working with a shadow alder wand."

I grimaced internally. Shadow alder was expensive and forbidden, the one known wood that could dampen a wizard's power. Then again, it came from the Gray Lands…

Wait, what *centaur?*

"The Minor Arcanum has been helping us. I don't know if you've heard of them. They, ehm…well, they don't have much use for the Arcanum, to be frank, but at the moment, neither do we. They're a loose confederation of wizards and witches. Amy—that's our crafter, Amy—she's bought their help with wands, more or less, but we *did* just stop Nath from invading, so there's that."

My mind whirled. I had a million questions I needed to ask her, but I couldn't force the first sound from my lips.

"Anyway, love, that's nothing for you to worry about," said Badger, patting my arm. "There's a skill some of the Minor Arcanum have that the rest of us seem to have forgotten. They call it sleepwalking, but basically, it's projection into this dream space. Wizards glow gold here, faeries glow white, Gray Landers with any sort of skill glow blue—the color-coding helps. It's what Simon Magus used to conquer the New World, incidentally, so they'd really rather that you lot not figure it out."

Noted.

"But I've got the knack, so I've been using it to find Fringers. We're evacuating them before Mulligan can hunt them down." She paused again, perhaps collecting her thoughts. "He's said that if he detects interference from Faerie in this realm, he'll kill you and his other hostages. We have no reason to doubt him, so those of us working to find the missing are staying well away from the Arcanum installations. We're not trying to endanger any of you," she hastened to add, "but there are still assassins about, and we're hoping to get as many targets to safety as we can without revealing ourselves to the Arcanum."

Guess you know where to find me now.

"The king and queen are biding their time, but...but that's why Joey hasn't tried to break into the silo yet," she said, picking up speed. "I told him I'd found you alive. If you can hear me, he loves you, and he's so sorry. You know he'd come if he could. They're trying to figure out a way through the wards so they can extract everyone safely, but they've been at it for...well, I suppose sixteen months. They want to free you, but they'd rather have you *alive*, and I trust that would be your preference, too."

Tell him I love him, I tried to say. *Please tell him I love him.*

Badger touched my face again, her fingers warm against my skin even if only a dream. "I'll be back, I promise. I'll keep you in the loop, Helen. Stay strong."

And then she was gone.

I sank back into the blackness and let myself drift away, feeling like a fucking useless princess in a goddamned tower as I waited for someone to save me.

AUGUST: ELEANOR

My dearest,

I'm sorry to have neglected you; forgive my recent silence. Matters here have been *tense*, shall we say, in recent days. Coileán only just left me for the evening, and since the old boy has borne the brunt of it, I couldn't in good conscience turn him away tonight. He is not one of those people who drinks in the company of others and insists he doesn't have a problem because he's merely a social drinker—no one with an office bar like Coileán's could make that claim with a straight face. I don't begrudge him his bottle; I have done as much or worse (and there are so many stories I purposefully neglected to tell you of my time before you, darling, as I fear you would have been appalled). But I suspect that Coileán's walls were closing in, and if he needed a quiet room and the pretense of a drinking companion, well, I could spare the hours. In truth, I didn't mind joining him.

As I mentioned previously, Badger located Helen, which is excellent news. After more than a year, it's reassuring to have confirmation that the girl is, in fact, alive. But by Badger's account, she's bound, which makes sense—Helen is talented, and I don't like to consider the sort of spellcraft necessary to subdue her. Badger can't see the contours of the spell, either, which complicates matters. She's only been able to visit Helen in dreams—don't ask, I haven't a clue how it's managed—and she can't see the workings of the bind from that perspective. Helen is no help, as she's been unresponsive to Badger. Coileán insists that she's unlikely to be insensate. (He speaks from experience, and I shudder to think of it. A bind sufficient to keep one frozen inside one's own body is a terrifying notion.) At the moment, it seems improbable that she'll be of much assistance in freeing herself. If she were older and stronger, and if her bind were linked to only one wizard, suppose Mulligan, then she might have a chance of accomplishing it if he could be sufficiently distracted, as Aiden suggests. But Badger's cousin Arnold, the magus, supposes that the bind runs through multiple anchors, as it were. No one magus is stronger than Helen, and besides, they would have learned from my father's mistake with Coileán. In other words, any rescue of Helen must come from the outside.

Here's the wrinkle: Badger can cast in her sleep. (Again, don't ask me how. From our conversations, it seems that *Badger* doesn't fully understand the mechanics.) Hypothetically, she could break Helen's bind, and then Helen would be free to get herself out of the silo, assuming that her exception in the wards holds. To no one's surprise, Joey has been *vociferously* advocating for this plan, consequences be damned, and while Aiden's been quieter about it, I assume that his heart lies with his sister. Badger and Toula have pushed back, however, as Joey's overlooking all manner of complications.

First, this plan hinges on the assumption that Badger, working alone, can break the bind. She's only been at her full power for a little more than a year, and she doesn't trust her training. It's possible that she could bring another wizard or two from the Minor Arcanum along to help her, but my understanding is that her allies are, with reason, reluctant to do anything that might draw the Arcanum's attention. Should the attempt fail and the dreamers be detected, one assumes that Mulligan would try to track the culprits.

Second, assume that the bind could be broken. Mulligan and any other anchoring wizard would know immediately, which would mean a narrow escape window for Helen. We don't know her physical condition—Coileán says binds like that are exhausting, especially if she's fighting it—so whether Helen would be strong enough to remove herself from the room where she's being housed is uncertain, particularly if, as we must assume, there are spells on the door.

The third problem is the matter of the silo wards. Toula built in an exception for Helen, but would her captors have left that open? Perhaps Badger could free Helen, and Helen would be strong enough to stand and move about...and she would still be trapped in the bowels of the installation. Whether she could fight her way out is an unknown variable.

And even if everything worked perfectly and Helen extracted herself without being caught, what would become of the Fringers? Badger is still searching for Mulligan's other hostages, but her scan of the silo has of yet turned up no sign of them. Should Helen escape, surely Mulligan would suspect our involvement. I don't know whether he would kill all of his hostages, but I can't imagine that he wouldn't make an example of at least a few. Vivi is adamant that nothing be done concerning Helen that would jeopardize her people, and I must concur—saving the one at the expense of the many would be grossly unjust. We cannot risk their lives merely to free Helen.

What, then, if Badger locates them? These are witches and lesser bloods, and someone needs must free them—but how would we get them through the wards? When Toula last worked on the silo wards, she left in a pass-through exception for Helen and one for Helen and Joey traveling together, I suppose in case Helen were incapacitated. We can probably assume that the Arcanum have closed the first exception, but the second may have been too complicated to bother with, as Helen and Joey are trapped in different realms. If we freed Helen first and brought her here, perhaps she and Joey could open a way for the Fringers...*if* everything worked. I don't like the odds.

Coileán has been trying to explain this to Joey, but the boy has been adamant that we make the attempt and angry at the perceived delay. Coileán finally played his trump card this afternoon: the baby. Even if everything goes well, even if Helen can escape and she and Joey can return for the Fringers…what about their baby? Helen's parents have the child, per Badger. What would Mulligan do with her? Coileán told Joey that if they act now, Joey's probably signing his daughter's death warrant.

I hate that. Joey's a good kid, and no one wants to add to his heartache, but if it means keeping him from trying to stage a one-man silo rescue, then so be it.

Coileán told me tonight that Aiden came to him with an alternate plan: if Badger can cast in her sleep, then she can kill. The boy's been talking to Amy, and as he understands it, Simon Magus could kill in dreams—why, then, couldn't Badger? If we could locate the Fringe hostages—if we knew where they were and how to reach them—then the suggestion might have merit. But I can't imagine the toll it would take on Badger. Coileán tells me that Aiden wasn't the same after he conducted mass executions—understandable, that—and now we're to propose the idea to Badger? "Here, Detective, why don't you just descend upon the silo like the Angel of Death, only don't stop with the firstborn? There's a good girl."

I suspect she'd be horrified. She might do it—desperate times, et cetera—but that's a great deal of blood to put on her hands. And for purely selfish reasons, if she truly can kill in her sleep, I'd rather not give her a taste of the experience. Toula thinks Badger may top out a more powerful wizard than Helen, and if so, I'd prefer that Badger not think of dream assassination as a practical solution to life's problems.

But all of this is hypothetical, of course, as we don't know where the Fringers are. Until we find them and decide how to free them, we can't further jeopardize their safety.

Still, you see why Coileán needed a drink tonight.

As for me, well, I'm not in the midst of the storm like he is, but I have my own problems on the periphery, not to mention the continual aggravation of my people. Today, at the end of five hours of holding court and hearing ridiculous gripes, I had to deal with my idiot brothers, Hugo and Karl. Karl built a new manor a few weeks ago, and Hugo essentially copied it, only on a grander scale. Karl built an addition, Hugo did likewise, and the two have been locked in an architectural war ever since, which culminated last night in Karl setting Hugo's house on fire. Hugo was unharmed but understandably peeved to have lost a wing. I brought them in today, told Karl that imitation is the sincerest form of flattery, told Hugo to stop being a twat, and told them both that I'll blow up their damned houses and bury them beneath the rubble if they don't knock it off. They went away sulking like children.

I can appreciate why my father ran off to Florida. Inebriates at a bar couldn't be worse than my people's constant petty squabbles.

I've got to find a way to establish peace in this court, Walt. I haven't got the first notion of how I'm to go about doing it, but something must be done. There's always the matter of Moyna lurking somewhere beyond our borders— I don't need a rebellion here, too. I *won't* have a rebellion. When I feel as if they aren't listening to me, my thoughts spiral back to that morning with you in the box, dearest. I've never felt so helpless as I did then—so completely out of control. That cannot happen again. I will have peace and order among my people, and I'll have it on my terms.

Getting to that point is another matter.

So yes, I joined Coileán in a drink tonight. I believe I've earned it, wouldn't you agree?

> Much love,
> Your Ellie

SEPTEMBER: AMY LEVEY

I didn't use to have the screaming nightmares.

I'd usually slept well in the Before. That's how my life seemed to have fractured itself in those days, a clear Before of suburban adolescent problems like term papers and negotiated curfews and bitchy upperclassmen versus an After of hiding from assassins and trying to hold myself out as an adult businessowner at the tender age of seventeen. Before, the worst nightmare I could remember had come the morning of my first big cross-country race, when I'd dreamed that I'd lost the trail and was being chased through dark, unfamiliar woods by something unseen but monstrous and nearing. My nightmares in the After were of a different tenor. Sometimes I was chased, but more often than not, I was back in my childhood home, with my parents' bodies cooling downstairs, hiding in a closet as the wizard who had killed them returned for me. I sat behind my longer dresses in the back corner with my knees to my chin, rough carpet pressed against my sweaty shorts, and tried to muffle my thunderous breathing. But I'd just returned from a run, after all, and my heart and lungs were working overtime. And then he heard me. The closet door was yanked open, the clothing swept aside, and a figure in a black helmet leveled a wand at my head. As I sat paralyzed with fear, the figure took the helmet off, revealing Daddy's rotting face, and I screamed and screamed…

"Amy. *Amy*," a voice insisted, and the nightmare shattered as I panted in Kip's arms. He'd pulled me up from the pillows and held me against his chest, and he rubbed my back and murmured comfort as I grounded myself.

Virginia. I was in Virginia, not South Carolina. This was my windowless bedroom just behind the wall at the back of my store; the dim pink glow of the salt lamp I'd picked up on a lark reminded me of the door's location. The door was wide open—Kip must have heard me and come running. It wasn't the first time he'd darted next door to yank me from sleep—and I'd certainly returned the favor—but my nocturnal terrors arose more regularly than his in those days, which was just embarrassing. I'd prided myself on being cool and collected, and sweat-drenched sheets spoiled the effect.

"I'm okay," I said, wriggling from his grip, and Kip rose from his perch on the edge of my bed. "Sorry."

"No need to apologize." He hesitated, then asked, "Your parents again?"

"Close enough." I glanced at my phone on the bedside table. It was just after five a.m., but I knew that falling asleep wasn't an option. "Going for a run," I said, untangling myself from the blankets.

"Do you want company?"

"Only if you're out of good options," I replied, and fumbled for the nearest lamp.

I don't know what, exactly, spurred me to transition to barefoot running, but our sudden proximity to the beach probably had a lot to do with it. Before, I'd religiously broken in my running shoes and kept tabs on their condition like a pit crew chief gauging tire tread. I'd heard of going shoeless—I'd even seen a few such runners in our local 5Ks, tanned from endless hours outdoors and almost horn-footed—but I'd never been tempted. After, however, I wanted to feel the ground beneath me as I pounded it, and so I'd blithely left my shoes at home one day, only to discover a new world of pain as seldom-used muscles in my feet and legs were put to work. I'd limped the next day, then limited myself to shorter runs as I built up my strength. By early September, I could go for several miles without a problem, running up and down the hard-packed sand at the edge of the sea until my focus narrowed to physicality, putting me in tune with the bellows in my chest and the warning fire creeping up my legs. When I reached my personal zone, I existed purely in the moment, a body without concerns beyond oxygen and glucose. I didn't think about the Before, didn't worry about my future, and didn't allow my mind to replay my troubling dreams.

I had no need of companionship on my runs—the rush and hiss of the waves and the cries of the seabirds provided sufficient background noise. To my surprise, though, when I started my regular beach runs, Kip often tagged along.

My slow speed had to be killing him. I was a decent distance runner, not a sprinter, and I kept my pace around the eight-minute-mile mark. Even hampered by his transformation bind, Kip could have lapped me several times over, had he wanted to. Instead, he plodded along beside me in silence, letting me set the tempo. I'd figured he just wanted an excuse to go down to the beach—he'd grown up with lakes, but nothing like the Atlantic, and the breakers seemed to fascinate him. But once Kip confirmed that what I felt for him was reciprocated, I saw his presence on those runs in a new light.

Yes, looking back, it was obvious, but I was *seventeen*, and he was the twenty-year-old, theretofore unobtainable object of my affection. Smart, sweet, strong, and with a smile that made my heart flutter, he'd been my companion and confidant for months, but I'd been blind to the fact that he wanted to be with me as much as I wanted to be with him. Finally, Badger and Seamus had taken pity on the clueless kids in their midst and helped us along.

That he was kadalin hadn't really bothered me. I'd grown up knowing I wasn't precisely human, appearances aside, and so the fact that he wasn't, either, wasn't a deal-breaker. From the beginning, Kip had been...well, *Kip*, the one person on our team who understood me. Arnold and Seamus and Badger and the Joneses were kind, but he was the only one to whom I felt equally comfortable revealing my tears and my dreams of revenge. He knew both himself—maybe not in precisely the same form, but the contours were similar. It was with Kip that I allowed the narrow focus that got me through the day to widen, reminding me of the trauma I had yet to fully move past. It was with him that I felt myself breathe, as if I'd unlaced a corset and allowed my lungs to fill.

I wanted to think that my parents would have approved, but part of me suspected that they'd have been aghast at the situation.

Kip had taken to barefoot runs almost as soon as he learned what I was doing, but then he viewed shoes as more of a necessary annoyance, one more shortcoming of weird human feet. He jogged beside me down the predawn sidewalk, staying well away from the spot where we'd found a broken beer bottle glittering in the streetlight three mornings before, then followed me across the beach access boardwalk, a rickety structure of graying, salt-weathered boards that seemed one good storm away from collapsing onto the scrubby dunes. When my feet hit the soft sand, still cool and pocked from an early-morning drizzle, I headed for the water, then veered left before I could run into the inky sea. Kip fell in step beside me, splashing through the dying waves, but said nothing. Morning runs were my quiet time.

At least *he* had gotten the memo. Though I tried to switch off my brain that morning and reach that hyperaware state of my body as it moved and protested and existed in space, my mind wouldn't shut up—and it continued to replay, in a sick loop, Daddy's dead and disapproving face as he'd prepared to blast me.

I knew what my subconscious was telling me. Of course

my parents wouldn't be happy with me if they could see what I'd become in the year and a half since their deaths. Before, I was an A student at a respectable prep school, nearing the end of my sophomore year with college in my sights. I was signed up for my first AP exam and already studying for the SAT. I wasn't the captain of the cross-country team yet, but that was looking more like a real possibility down the line. And if—*only* if, Mama insisted—there was nothing else I wanted to do after four years of college, then I could join her in her workshop, and we'd have a little family cottage industry of crafters. In the meantime, I'd focused on my grades, knowing that it was best for me to avoid romantic entanglements—witch-bloods shouldn't breed, much less a second-generation abomination such as myself.

And After? Instead of a senior, I was a high-school dropout. I'd never had the first in my long list of slated standardized tests, and the notion of college had lost its luster. I was crafting wands and removing viruses from computers—no one in Rigby had yet come to me for my advertised web design services—and occasionally taking up arms against creatures from outside the realm. The family into which I'd fallen was one of circumstance: a pair of cops, a magus with a conscience, and the two kids they shepherded along, if you could still call us that. Kip wasn't a teenager any longer, and I felt a decade older than the girl I'd been Before. And foolish, irresponsible, me—instead of letting my tainted blood die out, I was practically engaged. So what if the odds of our having kids seemed statistically insignificant? I might be on my way to not only propagating my genes but mixing them beyond recognition with those of someone out of the Gray Lands.

What would Mama and Daddy have said? Even if it felt right to me, by the conventional metrics, I was a colossal failure.

We ran on as the eastern horizon began to lighten from black to blue, both of us silent and sweating, and only turned for home when the low-hanging clouds above the rim of the sea had flashed pink with the imminent sunrise. Still, Kip kept my pace, splashing to my left as if standing between me and the immensity of the ocean.

I was so proud of him, and more than a little awed. He'd stumbled on bleeding feet until he'd managed the trick of two-legged walking, and now he matched my strides as effortlessly as any seasoned runner. He'd tried so hard to be one of us, to be useful, to the point that I hadn't even known what his people called themselves until Badger had brought it up a month before. I should have asked him, and it embarrassed me that I hadn't done so. I'd gleaned bits and pieces of Kip's culture by then, but he'd seldom volunteered information. In hindsight, I could see his motive: if he never brought it up, then maybe we'd forget that there was anything different about him.

I wondered if I'd done something to contribute to his reticence. He had nothing to be ashamed of—his bind was a concession to life in a world that didn't understand that humans weren't the only intelligent creatures in existence. All of us hid our true nature in one way or another; Kip's difference was simply more obvious than the rest of ours.

I wanted to believe that my parents would have loved him, too, had they known him as I did, but I couldn't be sure. Then again, they were gone, I told myself—why should they get a vote in my happiness? My subconscious, of course, saw things differently.

That morning, I sneaked glances at his face, trying to discern whether Kip also feared the disapproval of dead parents. Surely his wouldn't have been thrilled, had he brought me home—I would have been small and grossly misshapen in their estimation, hardly a fit mate for their son. Hell, I could sit atop him without making him break his stride. Take my guns away, and I was a pasty, weak creature beside him. Did he, like me, write speeches in his head to deliver to an outraged family about why we should be together? Did he defend me against the deep-seated voices in his mind?

Before we reached the boardwalk, Kip stopped me, then grinned mischievously and waded into the sea. I watched at the shore, cold waves lapping at my toes, until he'd disappeared to his waist and bobbed with the rolling chop. "Come out!" he called, cupping his dripping hands like a megaphone. "It's brisk!"

I've never been one for cold showers, but I sucked it up and headed in, shrieking with the cold. Kip laughed and waited while I picked my way toward him. My shirt, damp with sweat, was soon drenched with the waves slapping against my chest—Kip had more than a foot on me, and I realized that I would be treading water where he stood. Still, I struggled on, not paying as much attention to the current as I should have, until a big wave plowed into me and knocked me off my feet. In an instant, I was flailing in the brine, clawing for the surface, and I rose sputtering, ineffectively wiping the water from my eyes with my wet hands.

I felt Kip grab and hoist me up, and I clung to his neck, wrapping my legs around his waist to steady myself. "Are you all right?" he asked, holding on to me as I rested my head against his shoulder and caught my breath.

"Yeah, just soaked," I said, feeling my ponytail drip down my spine.

"Want to go back?"

The water, though cold, was growing more tolerable with exposure. "We don't have to," I replied, closing my eyes. "Don't let me go, okay?"

He chuckled. "Never."

And there we stood, drenched and chilling in the morning breeze, until the pieces of my nightmare began to burn away like fog. I felt it when Kip began to walk, but only when the air hit my legs did I realize he was heading for the shore. He carried me all the way in, and as the beach sloped upward, I began to squirm to drop down. "I've got you," he murmured, tightening his arms around me, and started up the lonely stretch toward home.

"Really, I can walk—"

"You weigh nothing."

"You're a *bad* liar," I protested, but he adjusted his grip and walked on.

As we crossed the boardwalk, I said, "Hey, Kip?"

"Hmm?"

"Do you think your mom would have liked me?"

He said nothing at first—I suppose I caught him off guard with the question—but as he stepped onto the sidewalk, he said, "I don't know. Does it matter?"

Maybe it should have mattered. Maybe everything we were doing was wrong, and we had no business pledging ourselves to each other.

But my head fit perfectly in the hollow of Kip's neck, and as for Daddy…well, even when he was alive, he'd never been able to convince a wand to work.

"Nope," I said, and sighed, finally quieting my troubled mind and focusing on the warmth of his encircling arms.

He whispered something incomprehensible into my ear, and I looked up from his shoulder, perplexed. "Sorry, what was that?"

"Si nialta," he repeated hesitantly.

And though I didn't speak a word of the kadalin tongue, the look in his dark eyes was all the translation I needed.

"I love you, too," I said, and smiled back at him as he beamed.

—YEAR THREE—

APRIL: BONNIE

In more than twelve hundred years, I'd never been bothered by the urge to procreate. Other women seemed to succumb to it at an early age—mortal girls in particular, women barely more than girls themselves with the first two or three of a litter already crawling around them—but I'd remained untouched by the compulsion to get pregnant. Certainly, babies were cute little things when they were cooing or laughing or sleeping, but they could be unholy terrors when displeased, and I had no desire to yoke myself to *that* business. I had far more entertaining things to do in Faerie than soothe squalling brats.

But before I could even mark my two hundredth year, my queen rose up against the rest of the Three and got the court expelled from the realm for her pains. She ordered us to follow her into the Gray Lands. Some went willingly, some by force. Me, I ran, and I wasn't the only one. The mortal realm wasn't Faerie, but it sure as hell beat the alternative.

Among those of us trying to avoid Mab, many immediately struck out on their own, trying to dodge her notice by isolating themselves. Others of us banded together in temporary clumps as we felt out the contours of the world into which we'd been banished. It was the end of the tenth century, I'd wound up in the southern reaches of what's currently France, and no one looked kindly upon strangers who spoke with odd accents and could produce gold from thin air. We had our first brushes with iron weapons. After half a dozen of our number lost their lives in a nighttime ambush outside a particularly hostile village, we split up as our wiser brethren had already done and tried to make our own ways.

Socially speaking, there weren't many methods of advancement for a woman in those days, particularly not one without a title and land. I never went hungry—enchantment has its benefits—but after a time, I began to long for something more than mere sustenance. I wanted *people*, connection, friendship. I'm one of the half-blooded, after all, and unlike our fully fae peers, we can be afflicted by such drives.

And so I created a history for myself that withstood scrutiny, called myself Marie instead of Bonnaura, and found a kindly widow in a small village willing to take in a young woman to help out around the place. She was advanced in years by mortal standards—she was barely a third my age—but her mind was sharp, her hands clever, and she taught me the skills a woman such as myself would need to know: hand-spinning, sewing (my needles were necessarily of bone), cooking, planting, and keeping a tidy home. Her goats wouldn't tolerate my presence, which concerned her—I believe she caught on to my ruse in time, but she was sufficiently desperate for help to overlook my shortcomings. The most useful things she taught me were herb craft, the knowledge of which plants, properly prepared, could treat illness and injury, and midwifery. All of the village women had rudimentary skill at the birthing bed, but the widow had expertise. She knew the signs and portents of an imminent delivery, she could turn a breech, she'd saved three babies born too soon, and once, when the mother had died in labor, she'd cut her open and extracted a healthy son. As her assistant, I stood at her side, learning her tricks and techniques. Several years later, when she died of pneumonia one bitter winter, I stepped into her place.

Though I had no desire to press on, I knew that my time in that village would be finite. Aging myself with glamour, I lingered until I was ancient in my neighbors' estimation, then created a copy of my body to be found in my bed and slipped away during the night, once more unglamoured and young. I didn't go far—I made myself useful in another village five miles away, with a fresh name and a tale of a dead husband—but every so often, I'd see one of the many children I'd helped bring into the world during a festival or at a market. They grew, they had children and grandchildren of their own, and they died, never knowing that the old woman of their childhood was still watching them. I tried not to let their inevitable deaths pain me, but I'm not unfeeling stone, and some touched me deeply. They were like slim candles, quick to light and even quicker to burn out.

I wish now that I'd thought to write their names and stories. I had the knack—written Fae isn't a complicated system—but I hadn't bothered, assuming I'd always remember my favorites from among them. But time fades all, even for us, and I can only imagine how many once-brilliant memories I've lost along the way.

In time, I moved beyond southern France, wandering into the Alps and then as far as Mongolia before turning back to the west and exploring the northerly lands. I finished my European tour in England in 1712, where I bought passage on a ship bound for the New World and the Virginia colony. When my alias grew too old to sustain, I abandoned it and headed west as war loomed, hiding in the remotest corners of the Appalachians until the muskets ceased firing. I returned to the coast as the new nation tried to put itself together, and there I remained until 1848. The Republic of Texas had joined the United States, and wagon trains were heading west. I bought and provisioned a wagon and managed nicely on my own. The oxen hated me, of course, but by then, I'd learned to overpower their will with enchantment, and I held my tight grip on them until I could sell them off. The experience was unpleasant for all parties—binding a living thing without its cooperation is never a simple matter—but I did what I needed to do. Once again, I settled in as a surrogate doctor, setting bones, treating injuries, and birthing children. The young women came to me for advice in the night—how to calm a colicky infant, how to make milk flow, how to stop a husband's wandering eye. I did what I could for them, surreptitiously enchanting as needed, and life went on as it always had. The nation ripped itself apart and began its long rebuilding, automobiles replaced wagons and carriages, and along the way, I settled in a farming community in Texas called Red Plank, roughly in the middle of nowhere.

And all of that is to explain how, in the first years of the new millennium, I came to work in the St. Andrew's United Methodist nursery on Sunday mornings.

For much of my life, it was foolish, if not dangerous, not to profess the faith. I was never convinced, but I wasn't stupid—an unmarried, independently wealthy woman who could heal the sick was a prime target if she didn't go to church and look like she meant it. While I managed to avoid the hysteria in New England, I dodged my share of witchcraft accusations over my centuries in Europe, which I've always found amusing. Certainly, I used magic, but *spellcraft?* Please. Faeries have a gift for enchantment. In time of trouble, a wizard may wave his stick and come up with a complex spell, but a faerie will simply turn the problem into a crater.

There's a good reason why I was never killed as a witch. There are also a few hamlets across Europe that ceased to exist under mysterious circumstances around the time that certain accusations were leveled against me.

Still, even if I'd wanted to avoid church, it would have been difficult. In small towns, the church tended to be the center of the community, particularly in the little settlements that served as the nexus of a cluster of farms. Attitudes gradually shifted, of course, but in a place like Red Plank, which barely deserved to be called a town, if you didn't make an appearance at St. Andrew's or First (and only) Baptist, then you might as well have been a recluse. I chose the Methodists because there was less chance of the preacher getting wound up and sermonizing into the afternoon and because my nearest neighbors, the Rockwells, had invited me when I was new to town and sweetened the pot with a chicken casserole. I'd bought the abandoned Brown place and was already doing my own brand of home improvement to the eyesore cottage, and the ranchers next door were more than friendly.

Burris Rockwell was a giant of a man, probably six and a half feet tall with a voice like thunder and a belly laugh that could shake the room. His wife, Katie, was wide-hipped and dimpled, always cheerful if exhausted by her four sons, and she never declined a nip of sherry when she paid me a call. The boys grew into men like their father, hard workers all of them, though three left for greener pastures: Steven to Houston, Lee to Dallas, and Conner down to the oil rigs in the Gulf. The eldest, Sam, remained to work the family farm and eventually inherited it, buying out his brothers' share in 1985. By then, he'd married a pretty girl from two towns over, Roxie Cole, and they settled into the old ranch house to raise cattle and a family.

I was on hand during Roxie's first pregnancy to help her through the morning sickness and the swelling, but the girl was a trooper, delighted in the prospect of a child. She walked next door to proudly show me the ultrasounds—a girl, she reported with a broad grin. They'd decided to call her Audra.

When I saw Sam's beat-up Chevy race down the road at a quarter of three one morning, I smiled, awaiting the good news. Two days later, however, I got a visit from the preacher's wife. Roxie had died in delivery—she'd bled out, though the baby was healthy. Sam, as could be expected, was beside himself. She asked if I wanted to be added to the visitation roster. I told her to hell with that, jumped in my truck, and sped off to the regional medical center.

My heart broke for that boy—I'd patched him up after his childhood scrapes and fed him apples from my trees out back when a bigger boy stole his lunch at school, but I could do nothing to heal *that* hurt. He seemed to have aged ten years, and he watched with glassy eyes while I fed and swaddled Audra. "I know it hurts, honey," I finally told him as I put the baby in his arms with a fresh bottle and showed him how to hold her. "But this little girl needs you, and you've got to be strong for her."

Well, he looked at me with such bewilderment that I did the sensible thing and moved in to help him raise that child. And it was a good thing I did. While Audra was a beautiful baby, she was sickly, and I nagged Sam until he took her to a proper hospital for testing. He came home with more gray hair and a diagnosis of cystic fibrosis. She had a lifetime of chronic lung infections, malnutrition, and hospitalization ahead of her, and probably a short one at that. But she was a scrappy little thing, and she took to her treatments well— and when those didn't help, I worked healing enchantments to ease her breathing. I couldn't cure her, but I could lessen the symptoms.

I'd assumed that Sam would remarry, but Roxie had been his heart, and he had no desire to seek another wife. So it was that Audra grew up with her daddy and her Miss Bonnie. While Sam kept the place running and provided for her, I taught her what she needed to know to be a woman— not the cleaning and cooking bits, but how to be strong, how to look after herself, and where to hit an attacker to make him regret it.

Sam never clued in that there was anything unusual about me—after Roxie's death, he kept his attention on the ranch and on Audra, never giving much thought to anything else. But Audra was more perceptive than her father, and even though she couldn't see magic, she seemed to know when it was in play, when she was feeling better in spite of her medicine and not because of it. When she was nine, almost too big to believe in such silliness as magic, she'd asked me point-blank if I was a witch. I'd denied it, but the calculating look she'd given me had told me that she sensed a loophole.

"I swear to you, I'm not a witch," I'd told her, "but I do have some…abilities, let's say."

Her little face had puckered. "What *kind*?"

"Do you trust me that I would never hurt you?"

She'd nodded.

"Then you know what you need to know, baby, and that's for your own good."

She'd let the matter drop—Audra was smart enough to know when to stop asking questions—but every now and then, I'd catch her studying me, trying to make sense of the mystery in her guest bedroom. I didn't mind. My baby was a clever one.

When Audra was seventeen, Sam dropped dead of a heart attack in the far pasture. She comported herself with grace, and while I helped her make the arrangements and deal with the family's lawyer, she kept her wits about her and saw that the ranch continued to run, even as she finished high school and coped with a lung infection. I was damn proud of her, and on her eighteenth birthday, I told her I was giving her the gift of privacy—I would move back down the road full time and let her live her life without constant supervision. She smiled, and I knew my girl was ready.

Though I'd told Audra she could call me day or night, I tried to give her space after that. We'd invite each other for dinner on occasion, she'd call with funny stories from town, and I was always on hand if her symptoms flared, but I wanted her to have the room to grow into an adult—and, if she so desired, to settle down. Audra had dabbled with dating during high school, but none of the boys had held her fancy for long. I wondered if she was trying online dating, but it was none of my business, and I didn't pry.

When I spotted Audra out with a young man at the county fair one late October night, I'd been happy for her.

Resolving to keep out of her hair, I'd sat down with a funnel cake along the midway, making plans to see the bluegrass band play in an hour's time. As I people-watched, I saw them coming toward me—Audra, beaming like her grandma, and her redheaded beau, who had wrapped his arm around hers like a proper gentleman and was escorting her down the straw-strewn lane. I didn't know him, but then again, the fair drew people from all over. Still, I couldn't help but check him out. Mental investigation isn't difficult if one is fae, and I wanted to see what his intentions were with Audra.

To my surprise, I was blocked.

As they passed, he turned to look me in the face, and I got a good look at his green eyes. I didn't know who he was, but I knew then *what* he was. A faerie may look young, but his eyes will give his age away if one knows how to see it. Audra's new friend seemed like any other twenty-something in jeans and cowboy boots that night, but his eyes put his true age somewhere well north of that—not my peer, certainly, but not a spring chicken.

I started to get up, but before I did, Audra noticed me and dragged him over. "Miss Bonnie! This is Nick," she said, smiling at him. "He's visiting his cousin, and the cousin ran off with some girl and left him, so I'm showing him around."

He held out his hand, staring me down, *daring* me to say anything.

I shook it. "Y'all have a good time. Audra, honey, I'll be around if you need me," I said, meeting his stare. "Be careful."

We parted, and I heard his voice in my mind as they walked away: *She's yours?*

She's her own, I replied. *I don't want trouble.*

Neither do I.

Then don't hurt her.

I could feel the mirth in his thought. *I intend nothing of the sort.*

That had been that. Audra was young and infatuated by a handsome stranger, and I had no right to intervene in her love life. Moreover, I couldn't afford to cause a fuss—I didn't know which court he belonged to, and I didn't want to find myself attracting the wrong sort of attention. So I said nothing, and Audra looked wistful over the following week, as he'd left town the morning after their tryst.

Early the next August, she gave birth to a boy with auburn hair, a darker echo of his father's, and hazel eyes like hers. She named him Sam for his grandfather, and I crossed my fingers and prayed the baby was a slow learner.

That the child had fae blood was a given. His father, whoever he was, had to have been at least half fae, and I suspected he was full blooded. I'd heard of half-fae children raised in the mortal realm who didn't discover their talent until adolescence—or even adulthood, in rare cases—and I hoped that little Sam would be among their number. A child old enough to speak and understand can be reasoned with; an infant with talent is unpredictable and uncontrollable.

All was quiet for the first few months, and then *incidents*, as Audra called them, began to happen around her baby. When he was angry, objects fell off the shelves. When he wanted a toy from across the room, Audra might turn around and find it in his hands. The breaking point for her came when he was a year old and crying for milk. As she prepared a bottle, she turned at the sound of the refrigerator opening and watched, slack-jawed, as the backup gallon jug of whole milk flew across the kitchen and landed on Sam's high chair tray. He giggled and clapped in delight, but Audra scooped him up and run through the dark to my house, frightened out of her mind that her old family home might have picked up a poltergeist.

As Sam sat in her lap, sucking down milk and oblivious to his mother's distress, I told Audra the truth about myself and Sam's father. She listened with wide eyes, worrying her lip, and when I fell silent, she said, "Why didn't you warn me before I went off with Nick?"

"Who you take to bed is none of my business," I replied, "and anyway, I didn't know you intended to *sleep* with him."

"I didn't intend anything. It just...happened," she said lamely. "He was cute, and I was having a good time, and..." She sighed. "*Shit*."

I let her stew for a moment, regretting once more that I hadn't said anything to caution her away from him. "Sam's talented. I can't do anything about that," I finally told her, "but when he's a little older, I can teach him to control it."

"And for now?" Audra asked. "You didn't see it, you didn't see that jug flying straight at him—"

Her thought ended in a little squeak as a yellow fireball appeared in my open palm. "Honey, I've seen so much worse. The good news is that he should be a fast healer."

The fear didn't leave her eyes, even after I extinguished the flame. "If you don't think you can handle Sammy, or if you just don't want to, I'll take of him," I offered. "My mother didn't want anything to do with me. It's not fair to ask you to wrangle a faerie if you're not up to it."

Her expression softened. "Your own *mother* didn't want you?"

I shrugged. "She wasn't in the realm by choice, nor did she make the decision to let my father get a child on her. I was raised by a half-fae nursemaid, and my mother was sent home when I was four. She never looked back when she went through the gate." I cleared my throat, which had begun to tighten in warning. "But enough of that. You didn't sign up for this, and if you want out, I promise I'll raise him up right."

To my relief, Audra's arms tightened around her boy, and she shook her head. "Just tell me how to help him. Please."

I nodded and rose, then returned to the table with two bottles of beer. "You're good people, Audra. Sammy's lucky."

She popped the cap off her beer and took a long swig. "Will you do me a favor?"

"Probably."

"Show me your real face."

I made sure that the curtains were drawn, and then I obliged, letting my wrinkles melt away and my gray hair fall in a chestnut curtain down my back. "This is how your grandparents knew me," I said. "You see why I've had to make a few modifications."

Audra stared for a long, silent moment, then nodded. "You look real pretty, Miss Bonnie."

"You're a dear," I replied, and glamoured up again.

I didn't know the boy's court affiliation, and I didn't know how to find out. Instead, I figured I'd tell someone in the Fringe about him, just to keep everyone apprised in case they got word of weird happenings around a little boy in Texas. The Fringers I'd kept tabs on over the years were nowhere to be found, however, and not until Sam was nearly two did I learn why, when Badger Parsons accidentally woke me into a shared dream. Knowing that the Arcanum had lost its collective mind, I spent as much time as I could with Sammy, trying to impress on him even then how important it was to control himself, to be a good boy.

He learned slowly, but he showed progress. Unfortunately, a faerie's talent grows with his age, and Sammy wasn't getting any weaker. As he ran headlong into the terrible twos, I suspected that it was a matter of time before he slipped.

Which brings me back to the St. Andrew's nursery, where I did my weekly penance by looking after a room full of babies and toddlers for a couple of hours. Sammy was about four months shy of his third birthday that Sunday, and I kept an eye on him as he ran around with a dozen other squealing little ones in a convoluted game of tag. I had a pair of assistants with me that day, two young mothers taking their well-deserved turn as the congregation's babysitters, and I thank whatever deity might be listening that both were doing diaper changes when the fire broke out.

I saw it almost in slow motion. A four-year-old boy named Dylan had shoved Sammy—intentionally or not, I couldn't tell—and Sammy fell on his face. As his head rose, he scrunched his eyes up, preparing to wail, but before he could let out a howl of pain, a small fire erupted on the carpet in front of the culprit. Dylan cried out and backpedaled, but the flames seemed to track him...and their progress was speeding up.

I waved the fire out of existence, then yanked Sammy off the floor and out of the room as the other minders tended to Dylan's tears. I carried Sammy into the empty bride's room, locked the door, and plopped him onto the sofa. "*No, sir*," I barked, staring down at him. "We don't *do* that."

He looked at me sullenly, then lowered his gaze.

"Do you want the bad men to find you?"

Sammy started to tear up, and I sighed and sat beside him, letting him burrow against me as I stroked his hair. "You have to be a good boy, honey. Okay? No more fires."

"Dylan *pushed* me," he protested.

"It was an accident. You have accidents, right?"

His head bobbed.

"Wouldn't it be bad if someone set you on fire every time you had an accident? Wouldn't that hurt?"

"Sorry," he mumbled into my dress.

"I know, baby, I know," I soothed. "We're not going to let that happen again, are we?" I pressed, suspecting that whatever Sammy said, there would be fires in his future.

I took him back to the nursery, where I "cleaned" the scorched carpet with a combination of stain remover and magic. By the time the parents arrived, there was no sign of Sammy's conflagration, and Dylan seemed to have gotten past his brush with the flames. When Audra arrived, Sammy ran into her arms, and I murmured that we needed to have a little chat while he napped after lunch.

Late that evening, Audra asked me to come over. I entered quietly, assuming rightly that Sammy was asleep, and found his mother waiting in the kitchen beside a vase of the strangest flowers I'd ever seen—giant heads of fat purple petals that bobbed on impossibly thin stalks, like a child's drawing of sunflowers done with the wrong crayons.

"Sammy wanted to say he was sorry," said Audra, gesturing to the bouquet. "I told him he should draw you some flowers, but he decided to make his own."

"Tell him they're beautiful," I replied, giving the mutant blossoms a better look. The boy had obviously tried his best, but we had work to do.

"He made me some, too." She pointed to a vase of rose-ish flowers on the windowsill and laughed softly. "What am I going to do with him, Miss Bonnie?"

I pulled out the chair beside hers and took her hands in mine, remembering a time when they were small enough to curl up inside my fists. "You do the best you can, my darling. That's all I've ever done."

Audra smiled, then fell into a coughing fit and grimaced at the pain. I numbed it, and relief swept across her face. "If something happens to me," she said hoarsely, "you'll take care of my Sammy, right?"

"I promise."

She hesitated. "Will you help him find his daddy someday? If he wants to know, I mean."

I squeezed her hands. "Whatever Sammy needs. We'll get him grown, just you wait."

Though she coughed again, she smiled as I let myself out with my apology flowers. I waited until the door closed and the porch light went off, then glanced back at the ranch house.

They burn like candles, mortals. Some far too quickly.

"Don't you worry about your boy, my sweet girl," I whispered to the night, and made my lonely way home.

MAY: GEORGIE

I flew alone in those days.

My Joey had changed so much in two years. There was the issue of his newfound ability with magic, yes, but his personality had shifted, too. The Joey I first knew was quick to laugh and almost always up for a flight. This Joey seldom smiled, and while he sounded like himself, his mind was a darker place than it had been.

Joey dreamed of blood and fire.

I wanted to make it better, but there was nothing I could do. I wasn't allowed to go on a rampage in the mortal realm, as satisfying as that would have been, and I certainly didn't know how to break Helen out of her bonds. Dragons aren't magical beings, I had no special training in the subject, and so Joey's discussions of strategy with Toula and Aiden went past me like a headwind. The marrow of the matter was that Joey wanted his mate back, and their child as well, and for that, I was useless.

But I could keep him company at the house.

One evening during the previous winter, I was digesting dinner in the barn while Joey spread straw. He did it by hand—he was fidgety then, always needing to move, and I suppose the rhythmic process of creating bales, untying them, and dragging them around took his mind off of Helen and the hatchling. When he was finished and my bed was once again fluffy, he stepped back, brushed off his gloves, and glanced up at his apartment in the loft. "Helen will be home soon," he said.

I wasn't sure whether he was talking to himself, but I answered anyway. *You think so?*

"I feel it. Badger's going to find the Fringers any day now, and then we'll get her back."

I thought his optimism might be misplaced, given the snatches of conversation I'd heard, but I wasn't about to contradict him.

"She's not a fan of the loft," he continued, folding his arms. "She needs a real house to come home to. And we'll need a nursery."

What sort of house? I asked with suspicion. Sure, I was nearly grown, but I still disliked the nights when Joey slept elsewhere. As long as he was in the loft, I could sense him, even if I couldn't see him. The nights he'd spent away with Helen had left the barn feeling too big.

"A nice house. We can move the barn," he added before I could argue. I felt his mind reach for mine, and he smiled reassurance as he jogged over to pat my leg. "I wouldn't leave you, Georgie. We just need to do this for Helen, okay?"

Helen wasn't there, but I knew better than to point out *that* irritating fact.

Joey didn't sleep that night. He made camp near me, creating a table for his computer and generator, then lengthened it to make room for drawing paper. All through the dark hours, while I curled up nearby, he studied the screen and sketched, occasionally making color copies of the computer images appear on the paper. When morning came, he seemed exhausted, but he rolled up his paper and headed for the door. "Going to talk to the boss about a homestead. Back in a bit, sweetie."

The two of them returned shortly thereafter, Joey animated despite his sleepless night and Coileán decidedly more cautious. "If this is what you want," Coileán told him, looking at Joey's unrolled plans, "I'll give you your pick of the open land. You know it better than I do," he added with a little chuckle. "But are you sure you want to do this now? It's no trouble having the barn here, really."

"Helen's going to want our own house," Joey replied, tapping the paper. "I think she'll like this one."

Coileán shrugged at that. "Well, then, come inside, at least get some coffee down you, and we'll find a place. Do you feel comfortable building it, or would you like me to do it for you?" he asked, again eyeing Joey's drawings. "If you're there to tell me where I screw up, we could have this done by sundown."

But Joey shook his head. "I'll be fine, thanks. Just show me where I can put it."

Around lunchtime, I gave Joey a ride to his new estate, a wide swath of gently undulating meadow dotted with large trees. I circled as he consulted the maps, and then a white picket fence appeared around the borders of his land. *Now we know what we're working with*, he said to my mind, and I landed near the center. From the ground, I could barely see the fence line in the distance, and Joey turned in place, studying the land with satisfaction. A wave of his hand erased several nearby trees, and with that accomplished, he climbed onto my back again. *Want to go see Dad?*

The answer to that question was always yes—Peter had become one of my favorites, and not just because he was Joey's father. He reminded me of how Joey used to be, quick to laugh and excited about anything novel. Even after almost two years in the realm, he hadn't lost his fascination with flight, and I enjoyed taking him up. If nothing else, it was nice to be appreciated.

Peter and Rebecca lived in the Fringe settlement, but on the edge of town, next to the border wall. While I wasn't exactly welcome in town, there was no rule saying that I couldn't stick my nose into their back garden, especially when Peter was grilling.

"Hey, y'all!" he called, waving a spatula as Joey dismounted and vaulted the wall.

Rebecca, who was drifting around their backyard pool

on a yellow raft, lifted a dripping hand in greeting and beckoned Joey closer. "Hey, JoJo. You hungry? Dad's making cheeseburgers."

"I can smell that," he replied.

Any extra?

Peter scraped a patty off the grill and held it aloft. "Just a taste, big girl. Ready?" He flipped the burger into the air, and I darted my neck across the yard and snatched it near the top of its arc. True, it was barely a morsel, but it was a *good* morsel.

"You busy, Dad?" Joey asked, joining him at the grill.

"Not after lunch. What'd you have in mind?"

Joey smiled. "Got a little project. Wouldn't mind a hand, if you're bored."

The "little project" was anything but. Joey had made up his mind to build a house for Helen, and that was what he was going to do: build it.

Normally, when I saw a faerie make something, it came fully formed. Joey probably could have designed that house in his mind and given it form—or if not, Val or Coileán could have done it for him. Instead, Joey produced long wooden boards and bags of dry concrete and an endless stash of nails, and he and Peter got to work.

I soon learned that neither father nor son had any experience in construction on that scale. Peter had been a smith once—he'd shown me his home-forged weapons and explained how they were made—but that didn't translate to erecting a house. The two frequently consulted Joey's computer, reading instructions and watching videos made by smiling, competent builders, then trying to duplicate the results. Sometimes, they got it right. Others, they'd shake their heads and start over, or else Joey would enchant the problems away. I kept reminding them that the house could be finished at any time if they'd just ask Coileán for help, but Joey was stubborn, and Peter stayed the course. As for me, when I grew bored of watching them try and fail to make their beams perfectly straight, I'd go for long flights, missing Joey's presence. He was fidgeting on a grand scale, I could see that much—and Peter seemed to see it, too. When I dropped him back at his home one evening, he told me, "I know it's taking a while, but it's keeping JoJo busy. That's a good thing, yeah?"

Peter had a point, but still, I wearied of the sound of hammers.

By May, the bones of the house had long been set, and Joey and Peter had fleshed them out with floors and interior walls. Joey had added glass to the window sockets, and he raised the windows while he worked inside, giving me a view unhampered by glare.

One afternoon, Peter was downstairs, installing knobs to the kitchen cabinetry, while Joey had gone to the unfinished second floor to paint. There were three bedrooms upstairs, he'd explained, pointing them out to me on his plans. The master suite was relatively big, with generous closets and a tub almost large enough for him to float in—or so he said. Everything about the house seemed tiny to me, and I tried to remember how things had looked at human size during my awkward two months transformed. At the other end of the floor from the master bedroom was a pair of smaller bedrooms with a bath between them. The one on the right was the guest room, Joey said, but the other was for the baby.

I angled my head to keep one eye trained through a window into the nursery while Joey stared at the unfinished white walls and stroked his beard in thought. *Problem?* I asked.

"Paint color. What do you think?"

You want me to guess what color the hatchling would prefer?

"Yeah, good point. Baby doesn't really get a vote yet— I'm sure she'll have opinions in a few years, but she's only about a year and a half now."

Still floppy.

"Less floppy than you're thinking, but not yet to be trusted with interior design. What about this color?" A can of paint and a brush appeared at his feet, and he spread a rosy streak along one wall. "Too dark? Too light? Too princessy?"

It's…pink, I thought, perplexed by his indecisiveness. *I don't hate it.*

"But do you like it?"

Sure.

"Are you saying that to be nice, or do you mean it?"

I snorted. *It's wall color. What does it matter? Paint what you like, and if you need to change it when Helen comes back, do it then. This can't be difficult for you.*

"Well…no," he admitted, growing more agitated as he studied the smear of pink paint, "but…"

His voice trailed off, and he didn't fight me when I looked at his troubled thoughts. When I withdrew, I briefly wished for human hands so I could grab him by the shoulders and give him a good shake. *Your thinking is crazy.*

"What do you—"

Building the house isn't going to free her any faster, Joey. Choosing the right paint and flooring isn't going to speed this along. Is this what the project's been about?

He seemed stricken to be confronted with his personal insanity. "If I build it all for her, if I work and do it just right—"

Then you'll have a nice house. Unless my grasp of magic is worse than I realize, Helen isn't going to appear on the porch if you put up the correct curtains.

"You don't *know* that," he snapped.

It's a solid guess. I paused, sensing the brittleness below his anger, and tried again. *It's a nice pink. If you like it, use it. You can try to guess what Helen would choose from now until the day she comes home, or you can wait, do your best, and change it up when she gets here. But if there's not a way to break a spell by building a house, then torturing yourself is silly.*

Joey said nothing for a moment, just hugged himself and gazed through the marked wall. Finally, he murmured, "You can't understand."

I understand that you're hurting. If it were you stuck in the silo, I'd be upset, too. But since I'm thinking more clearly than you are right now, it's my responsibility to guide you back toward making sense. I maneuvered my head until my eye covered the entire window. *I love you, Joey. Please don't do this. You're only going to be disappointed if you put your hope for Helen in paint.*

He didn't look at me. "Then what am I supposed to do?" he replied, almost whispering. "Pretend like everything's okay? Go back to mapping like she's waiting at home for me? Play Wii with Aiden until I'm ninety?"

I don't know, but do you think Helen would want you to get worked up over wall color?

"Helen would want to be rescued. And I can't even do that."

When Joey sank to the floor and tucked his knees to his chest, I realized that I wasn't helping, so I told Peter to come upstairs. He entered the room and found his son rocking with his head down, then knelt beside him and rubbed his back. "It's okay, JoJo. It's going to be okay," he said softly. "Come on, buddy, let's get up."

But Joey only raised his face, revealing his wet eyes. "What if they never come home, Dad?"

Poor Peter. I hated to put him in that position, as he seemed to flounder with the question, but he managed to say, "You've got to have faith, son. That's all we can do right now." He glanced at the paint-streaked wall and added, "That's a nice color. Good for a nursery. I think Helen will like that a lot. You want some help in here? Tarps are still in the den."

Joey shook his head and stood, then closed his eyes and slowly exhaled. In an instant, the walls were a sandy brown, the floor partly covered with a patterned carpet, and the room filled with furniture—a bed, a dresser and mirror, a pair of nightstands, a rocking chair beneath a standing lamp. A utilitarian ceiling fan hung overhead.

Peter took a look at the new furnishings and shoved his hands into his pockets. "Change your mind about the nursery placement?"

"No point in making one. The baby's a year and a half old," Joey muttered. "What good's a crib if she's thirty the first time she sees it?"

"Come on, now, chin up," said Peter, clapping him on his tense shoulder. "They could be free tomorrow."

"Or a hundred years from now," he replied, shrugging his father's hand off. "Sorry. I'm going for a walk."

"You want company?" Peter called as Joey left the room.

Probably not, I told him.

He and I waited until the front door slammed, and we watched in silence as Joey stalked off across the meadow, heading for the fence and the woods beyond it. With a sigh, Peter came to my window and slid his head out, and I stepped back to avoid being poked in the eye. "You going to go after him?" he asked.

I can't fit through the trees. Let him go.

He studied Joey's shrinking figure for a few seconds, then muttered, "Nope. Hon, do you mind?"

I ducked until he could climb out onto my head, then lowered him to the grass and let him slide off. *He'll be back, really*, I thought. *I'm sure of it.*

"You've probably got the right of it," said Peter, straightening his T-shirt, "but that's my boy."

I curled up beside the unfinished house, watching Peter jog through the grass to catch up. If they spoke, I couldn't hear it, and it wasn't my place to pry. Together, they trudged on toward the trees, not touching but walking in tandem.

Shortly after they disappeared into the distance, a gate opened, and I turned to see Coileán come through. "Hey, Georgie. Are they in there?" he asked, pointing to the house.

Gone for a walk. Might want to leave them alone.

"Mm. Noted. Did you see where Joey put the plans?"

After a few minutes of rummaging in the house, Coileán rejoined me with the rolled paper in his arms. "He wants the barn to open into the kitchen," he said, showing me the sketch. "Not what I would do, but hey, it's his place. Might as well deliver it now."

With a wave of his hand, my barn materialized beside the house, and Coileán slid it into place and opened a doorway between them. The barn was considerably larger than the house, but that couldn't be helped—I'm not exactly petite.

Coileán surveyed his work, then nodded and looked up at me again. "Joey went for a walk, you said?"

With Peter. They went that way, I added, pointing a claw toward the woods.

His expression didn't change, but he continued to stare at the empty meadow for a long moment before saying, "Keep him company, will you? I'd prefer that he not be alone right now."

Joey slept in the barn that night—not in his loft, but in a sleeping bag plopped in the middle of my bedding. I coiled myself around him and closed my eyes while he settled in.

Helen's going to love the house, I told him. *Are you going to paint the rest tomorrow?*

"Maybe," he said, rustling the straw as he burrowed. "I don't suppose there's a rush."

Joey—

"Good night, Georgie."

I stayed awake until his breathing slowed, wishing I had the words to ease his mind.

JULY: SEAMUS MALONE

At forty-nine, I'd made my peace with the fact that I'd probably never have a son, barring a miracle with Badger. The situation was my fault—had I not run out on my fiancée twenty-four years before, we might have had a family and a semi with a tidy garden somewhere around Durham. Then again, given the Arcanum situation, we might all be dead in that scenario, particularly as our hypothetical children would have been witch-bloods. Considering the politics, maybe it was for the best that I'd never been a father.

I suppose the universe has a sense of humor, then, as around the time I finally reconnected with Badger, I found myself serving as a de facto responsible adult to a pair of orphaned teenagers. Two years later, Kip wasn't a teenager any longer. He'd chosen an arbitrary birthdate, doing the best he could to mesh our calendar with the passage of time as he'd marked it in the Gray Lands, and thus was three days away from his twenty-first birthday (at least according to his forged ID) when I took him on a pickup run to Gatlinburg.

I'd worked with both kids to get them competent behind the wheel. Our only vehicle on arrival in Rigby had been our secondhand SUV, and we'd since added an old Volvo sedan to the mix, one with a manual transmission. Amy had been halfway to a full driving license when she went on the run, and so all I'd had to do to bring her up to speed was coach her through the mechanics of the clutch over a week of jerky car park practices. As we'd expected, Kip had taken more work, but by the summer, I had them both to an acceptable level—and that meant adequate proficiency in certain driving techniques that weren't tested by the Virginia DMV. Sure, *I* could open a gate to safety at a moment's notice, but our eager young wards didn't have the knack, and Badger and I decided that tactical driving techniques weren't a bad thing to have in the arsenal.

In any case, Kip had grown into a reasonably proficient driver, and so I took him with me in the SUV to collect a trio of Fringers who'd spent the last two years hiding in a dilapidated mountain cabin on the edge of a tourist area— close enough to civilization to find provisions, but sufficiently remote as to go unnoticed. Badger had located them a few weeks before, and over the course of several nights' sleepwalks, she'd coaxed them into agreeing to trust us to evacuate them. It hadn't been easy for her. Our targets were barely more than kids, two fifteen-year-old boys and their eleven-year-old sister, and they'd escaped through a storm cellar when the Arcanum broke down their door and began shooting. Of a family of seven, they were all that remained, so I couldn't blame them for being wary of strangers. My first thought had been to bring Amy on the pickup, as she had a natural ability to put smaller kids at ease, but Kip needed the Interstate practice, and someone had to keep the shop running.

"Mind your speed," I said for the twentieth time that morning as he drove us southwest along I-85. "It's seventy, not ninety."

"Badger drives ninety," he pointed out.

"And when you've been at this as long as Badger has, I'll stop complaining. Let's not get ticketed, eh?"

I didn't worry about his license passing inspection, and if it came down it, I could have messed with the officer's mind and sent him on his way. Val had shown me that much. But I didn't want to—it felt like an affront to the badge I'd carried to screw with the local police, and any traffic stop would have inevitably forced my hand. Bad enough that I sounded exotic to the Virginian ear—and yeah, two decades in Belfast hadn't helped—but Kip's accent was in a state of flux, a developing amalgamation of at least a couple of British variants competing with Amy's drawl on top of his native tongue. He cut a striking figure, too, nearly a head taller than me, with a naturally red ponytail and a deep bronze complexion. In other words, he was the sort of individual that stuck in one's memory, and the last thing we wanted was scrutiny, particularly once we picked up the kids.

I cut my eyes toward Kip, wondering if the seeming convoy of articulated lorries was making him nervous. His shoulders were tense, and his mouth twitched as if he were fighting to hold back a confession. "Something on your mind, boyo?" I asked, keeping my tone light.

His gaze flicked in my direction, then hastily switched back to the road. "Maybe."

"Do you want to tell me, or should I start guessing? Animal, vegetable, mineral?"

He cracked the slightest of smiles at my poor attempt at humor. "Amy."

"Ah." I shifted in my seat, stretching my legs. "Have you fought?"

"No."

I waited, letting the silence blossom between us, until Kip grew uncomfortable enough to speak again. "She's eighteen now, you know?"

"Right…" I said, suddenly fearing where the conversation was going.

Badger and I had no room to talk—we'd been close all our lives—but Amy and Kip had decided quite young that they were off the market. It'd been nearly a year since she'd accepted his halting proposal, and since then, as far as I knew, they'd kept things tame—hand holding, pecked kisses, the occasional hug that lasted too long to be platonic. Remembering my own sordid youth, I didn't want to police their fun, but I'd taken Kip aside and stressed to him that in the eyes of the law, Amy was still a child. I'd also left him with an open invitation if he had questions, though I'd hoped to avoid discussing the birds and bees.

To my relief, Kip's troubles were of a different bent. "She might want us to become mates now. Marry," he said, correcting himself.

"She's legal," I replied, and chuckled. "Not getting cold feet, are you?" When Kip frowned, I realized my mistake. "Just an expression. Are you having second thoughts?"

He was quiet again for a time, but I caught him licking his lip as he stared at the motorway. "Maybe we shouldn't," he said, his voice barely audible over the hum of the road.

"Is there someone else?"

"No," he said quickly, "no one. But…"

"But she's witch-blooded?" I guessed.

"*No.* I don't care about that. I…" He struggled briefly, then said, "What if I can't give her sons?"

"Come again?" I said, taken aback by the question.

"That's the purpose of a mate, is it not? I'm meant to give her sons, she's meant to give me daughters. What if I can't?" he asked with a note of panic in his voice.

"*Loads* of people don't have children," I replied with practiced calm. "Have you asked Amy if she wants any?"

Kip briefly looked at me like I'd gone mad. "Why wouldn't she?"

"Not everyone does. And there's that witch-blood thing to consider, yeah? She might not want to pass those genes on." I shrugged. "If you can't have one naturally, maybe you can adopt. Think about how many orphans we've sent into Faerie." I paused to consider his profile—shocked or not, at least he knew to keep his eyes on the road—then said, "Is that a deal-breaker for you? If she doesn't want kids, that's it?"

"No," he mumbled after a time, "but…if she wants them, and I can't provide them—"

"You probably can't," I interrupted. "I mean, you've got some human genes deep down in there, but I don't think you're compatible. Could be wrong, but I wouldn't put money on it. And I'm sure Amy has thought of that already," I said before he could cut in. "If she wanted to fall pregnant, she could have gone after the boys here in town. I think it's obvious that she'd prefer to have you." I reached over and squeezed his shoulder. "*Talk* to her, Kip. You're stewing about something that could be a non-issue."

Releasing him, I settled back, satisfied with my handling of the situation. I was congratulating myself when Kip said, "Assuming we *are* compatible, I have, uh…questions."

The morning was young, and we had at least another six hours to Gatlinburg. Trapped, I stared straight ahead and nodded. "Never got the talk, eh?"

"Oh, I did. My father and brother were…um…informative. But considering the…the *mechanics*…"

If he could have overheard us from Faerie, I mused, my old man—himself an adopted father—would have howled and slapped his leg at my predicament.

"Turn on the cruise control," I told Kip, "then listen to me closely. I'm only going to say this once."

OCTOBER: TOULA PAVLI

"Thank you for coming," said Eleanor as one of her aides showed me into her office and closed the door. "I'm sorry to bother you so early, but I'm in a bit of a situation, and…well, honestly," she said, sounding embarrassed, "I could do with a wizard."

The queen didn't look distressed, but her mouth pursed in annoyance.

I did a quick scan of my surroundings: no aides, no visible recording devices or enchantments, and Eleanor had dressed in khakis and a light gray sweater. Faerie's idea of seasons was more like suggestions, but the morning was cool enough for sleeves. "What's up?" I asked. "Need aural comparison? I've almost got your end of the database up and running."

"I wish. It's my idiot brothers again."

"You're going to have to be more specific." At last count, Eleanor had almost two hundred younger half siblings. Family feuds were inevitable, especially given how many of them were fully fae.

"Hugo and Karl." She leaned against her desk and folded her arms. "They've been poking each other with sticks ever since they got here."

"Bad blood?"

She grunted. "From what I've been told, they were born two months apart, and they've squabbled from the time they could crawl. Now they've stomped all over my last nerve."

"Dare I ask?"

She grimaced. "Let me show you."

A twitch of her finger opened a gate beside me, and I took a look through the lightning-rimmed hole. The brick manor house in the near distance was appropriately grand, the trees all of a height and heavy with apples, and the ornamental lake glinted in the sun. Really, it would have been lovely had the ground not been covered in a thick layer of what appeared to be decaying flesh.

"*Shit*," I hissed, yanking my shirt over my nose to block the stench.

"No, that's dead animals. The shit-covered yard is at Hugo's," said Eleanor, quickly closing the gate. "Sorry about the smell. I've warned those two to leave each other alone, but they ignore me. That business happened during the night, and both claim the other struck first. As the realm won't provide the evidence, I need you to show me the truth of the matter. *Please*," she added, making a face at the place the gate had been. "I'll provide nose plugs."

There are highly technical forms of spellcraft that allow one to see anywhere, any*when* in time. The reason why I still don't know for sure who shot JFK is that the power needed to pull off a spell like that is astronomical, and it's the sort of project that can't be safely done without at least a couple dozen well-trained wizards. Having spent some quality time in the Archives after Greg Harrison slipped me credentials, I'd read about the one time the spell was successfully managed: it had taken thirty-five magi, but after three days of work, they'd managed to look back to the moment that Simon Magus disposed of his ensorcelled diary. The magi had been hoping that he'd buried it, only to learn that he'd given it to a wandering friar and asked him to carry it far away. Tracking the diary from that point could have taken lifetimes of viewing, and so the magi had given up.

I'd mastered a simplified version of that spell, albeit one far less powerful. Cast properly, it allowed me to look back in time, but only at a given location, and only within a limited window. I could rewind three days with acceptable difficulty, though a week pushed me to my limit. Fortunately, Eleanor had come to me within hours of the target time.

The paper masks over our noses and mouths somewhat muffled our voices, but it was either that or the nauseating effluvium. "Here's how this works," I told her as we squelched across the bloodstained grass—at least Eleanor had cleared a path through the carcasses. "Point me toward the direction from which Hugo came. Once I get this going, you'll see a ball of mist between my hands, and the picture will play in there. Spin it counter-clockwise to go back, clockwise to go forward. Got it?"

"I'll do my best," she replied, and angled me away from the house. "Right, Hugo's place is that way. Let's see what we have."

I held my hands a few inches apart and envisioned a sphere between them, concentrating as the ambient magic around me formed into focusing channels and brought the mist forth. I had to grit my teeth to hold it steady—even the pared-down form of the spell wasn't a picnic—but after a few moments, a live view of the meat-covered lawn came into view. "Go for it," I told Eleanor, trying not to shake with the strain.

She spun the ball like a globe, rewinding the picture through dawn and back into the blackness of night. Suddenly, I saw the white light of a floating orb appear in the image—Hugo, I assumed—and Eleanor slowly turned the ball until she reached the moment of its appearance. "Any chance of a time stamp?"

A whisper brought it forth. "Seven hours and forty-three minutes ago."

"Thank you. You can drop it," she replied, and I let the spell fall apart with relief. "Have you got it in you to do the same at Hugo's house?"

"Lead the way."

Eleanor opened a gate onto a feces-strewn hellscape

decorated with a lovely ivy-covered gazebo. "Told you," she muttered, waving a path clean for us. "I apologize, I should have tidied this, but I didn't want it to affect your casting—"

"Yeah, well, live and learn," I said, and produced the viewing mist again. "Typically, I work better in places that don't smell like latrines, but it's okay this once."

"Noted. And to be clear, I didn't imagine that I was signing up for *this* when I took the throne—oh, there's the picture. One moment…"

When Eleanor asked for a timestamp, the glowing numbers showed that we were looking back only six and a half hours. "And that's that," she said, stepping back from the mist. I let the spell break again as Eleanor, with a sharp wave, send Karl's apparent retaliation back into the ether. She opened a fresh gate to her office, and I followed her through, grateful to be able to take off the mask.

"What now?" I asked, flexing my stiff fingers. "Probation? Stint in the pokey?"

"I've got another idea. Will you join me for breakfast? It's the least I can do."

With the stench out of my nose, my appetite was returning, and I settled in with Eleanor at her smallest dining table, which could have comfortably seated eight. Once the kitchen aides left laden platters and a tea set, she sealed the door and did the honors with the teapot. "Here's the problem. Everything supposedly comes down to ego with us, yes? One can't afford to lose face."

"So I'd gathered. Are those baked beans?" I asked, pointing to a suspicious bowl set apart from the eggs and bacon.

"They're lovely on toast. I don't know why the rest of you can't see that. But back to Hugo," she said while I helped myself to the actual breakfast food. "If I lock him away, he's out of the public eye, and it's not as effective a punishment as I'd like. Plus, making cells like the ones Titania worked out would take time, and I'd rather get this underway while the offense is fresh."

"Understood. So, what about some version of the stocks? Uncomfortable but not too painful, public humiliation…"

"I'd thought of that, but you can't leave someone in the stocks for as long as I'd like to punish him. I was thinking a month at least, longer if he gives me any trouble."

I nodded and accepted the teacup she nudged my way. "And you wouldn't want to brand him or cut off a hand or anything, right?"

"No, that would be unnecessarily gruesome," she replied, stirring sugar into her tea. "I don't want to maim him, just drive home the fact that I can make his life exceedingly unpleasant if he keeps up this nonsense with Karl. Make an example of him to the others."

The ghost of a smile played on her lips.

"What did you have in mind?" I asked, glad at that moment that I wasn't Hugo.

Eleanor's smile widened. "I'm so glad you asked, dear."

As she drank her tea, she told me what she had planned.

It was an odd idea, but since she only intended to keep it up for a month, I figured it couldn't hurt anything.

Hell, I offered to help in the execution.

I stood against the wall of the massive marble throne room that afternoon while Karl and Hugo were escorted in. Eleanor, still wearing her sweater and khakis, had donned a tiara for the occasion, and she watched from her throne as her brothers twitched. For a moment, the only sound in the room was the waterfall behind the dais, but Eleanor muted it with a careless wave.

"I believe I ordered you to leave each other alone," she said, drumming her fingers on an armrest. "What say you?"

Karl hurried forward, though he stopped a few feet away from the bridge to the dais. "I defended myself. I woke in the night to the stink of…of *death*," he said with revulsion, "and I knew *him* to be the culprit."

"On the contrary," Hugo interrupted, "*I* woke to find my land befouled and retaliated. I was defending myself, sister, you must believe me."

The two men glared at each other, and Eleanor rolled her eyes. "You'll be thrilled to know that it's possible to look back in time with the proper application of spellcraft," she said, glancing at me over their heads. "I saw the whole thing. Thank you again, Ms. Pavli." She held up her hand before her brothers could speak. "Karl, you're disgusting, but you *were* retaliating. Consider this your warning."

His shoulders slumped with relief.

"As for you, Hugo," she continued, staring down at him from her artificial island, "you flouted my orders and lied to my face. What am I to do with you? What would *you* do with you?"

Hugo retreated a pace. "It won't happen again, I swear it—"

"No, it won't, because you're going to learn that actions carry consequences. Ms. Pavli, if you would be so kind?"

Eleanor and I had worked hard that morning, and our finished product deserved a proper entrance. I motioned open her office door and levitated out an object covered by a red drape. Eleanor nodded a wheeled stand into existence, and I sat my burden atop it.

Hugo backed away from the display, which, granted, could have been taken as a covered coffin by the paranoid imagination. It was far taller, though, larger than an Egyptian sarcophagus. With a flourish like a magician's assistant, I whipped off the drape, revealing the giant terrarium we'd made.

We'd put a lot of planning into the setup. A third of the terrarium was full of water, a tiny minnow-stocked lake that abutted a sloping sandy beach. Past the beach, the land turned into a miniature tropical forest. I'd shrunk a dozen coconut palms and banana trees down to bonsai size, and Eleanor had filled in the rest with proportionally small berry bushes and patches of tough grasses. We'd even added deadfalls to our little forest and sprinkled the beach with teeny seashells for a touch of realism.

Hugo regarded the terrarium with bemusement, then panic as he realized what Eleanor intended. "No," he said, holding up his hands as if warding her off, "no, you can't be—"

"This will hurt me much more than it will you," she said, going to her feet. "Binds can be so annoying like that. I'd advise you not to resist."

He tried to run—I'll give him credit for his dash for the door—but Eleanor, backed by the realm, was faster and stronger, and I watched as the bind shot after him and coalesced. As Hugo ran, he shrank, tripping on his clothes and then falling beneath their weight. With a smirk for me, Eleanor strolled across the room, riffled through the cloth, and freed her squirming brother, who was suddenly all of three inches high—barely half the size of a piq. She held him in her cupped palms and clucked her tongue. "Honestly, did you think that would work? Silly boy," she said, carrying him toward the terrarium. "And don't bother trying to enchant your way out of this—I assure you, my binding work is solid. I've been practicing," she said, lifting the mesh lid out of the way. "Right, then, down you go."

A little surge of magic deposited Hugo on the beach, and he simultaneously tried to find his feet and cover himself, much to Eleanor's amusement. "I'm sure you'll think of something," she told him, locking the lid back on. "The water's fresh, so you won't die of thirst, and I'll see that you get kitchen scraps to supplement. Do be careful where you relieve yourself—I'd hate for you to befoul your water. Oh, and here." A bronze knife half the length of my pinkie nail appeared on the sand at his feet. "Might come in handy. Make yourself comfortable—you'll be enjoying your little vacation for at least the next month."

Hugo squeaked from inside his glass prison, but Eleanor just shrugged. "Sorry, terribly hard to understand you. No matter. Come, let's set you up over here," she said, pushing the cart until it was in full view of the throne and bug-eyed Karl, who seemed barely able to restrain his laughter. "You'll have a few more hours of sunlight to get acquainted with your new home," she told Hugo. "Might want to explore. Maybe work on shelter. You know how fickle tropical weather can be."

While Hugo beat on the wall of his terrarium and squeaked at her, she turned to Karl and folded her arms. "It would be no trouble at all for me to make a second one. Go. You're welcome to visit tomorrow, but I have other appointments before dinner."

Karl ran out of the throne room, and Eleanor and I grinned at each other as his laughter echoed from the hallway. "How's the bind?" I asked her.

She wrinkled her nose. "Not bad. I can feel it, he's fighting me, but he won't be breaking out any time soon. So my little castaway had best get on with it," she added, tapping the glass above Hugo's head. "Once word gets around, I'm sure you'll have an audience to impress."

Hugo covered his face and emitted a high-pitched groan, then seemed to remember what he'd left uncovered and rapidly adjusted his hands.

"Going to give him a pair of pants?" I asked.

"Remember our time in the shit and corpse fields this morning?"

"Yeah, good point." I took a closer look at the terrarium and rubbed my chin. "One last thing. May I?"

Eleanor swept her hand toward the box in invitation, and I cast a miniature campfire into being on the beach. "You're welcome," I told Hugo. "It's your job to figure out how to keep it going."

"I mean, he's five hundred years old," said his sister, "he should know how to tend a fire by now."

"*Without* magic?"

"Mm. Good point. Well, when you see Coileán, tell him he's welcome to come over and have a peek at my new pet."

"Will do."

I nodded to the queen and took my leave, Hugo's squeaks barely audible over the sound of my footsteps on the marble floor.

As expected, I found Coileán in his office, reading petitions with a glass of scotch at hand. "Hey," he said, brightening as I slipped past his guards. "Where've you been? Astrid said you got a call at breakfast…"

"Eleanor wanted a hand."

"Everything okay?"

"Well, she shrank one of her brothers and locked him in an oversized terrarium, but other than that, sure." I flopped onto one of the couches and whispered a bottle of chardonnay out of the fridge behind his office bar. "How're you?"

"Uh…fine." Coileán waited while I poured myself a glass from across the room, then asked, "Did he deserve it?"

"*Oh* yeah."

He snorted and made a few notes on his laptop while I sipped my wine and kicked off my shoes—which, thanks to a judicious use of magic, had neither gore nor excrement stuck in the treads. "Do you have dinner plans?" he asked.

"Not yet."

"Want to join me? Maybe tell me about Eleanor's fun and games?"

I smiled. "Think I could clear my schedule. Just promise me one thing."

Coileán cocked an eyebrow.

"None of what I tell you gets used against me."

"Toula," he replied, bending back to his work, "I assume that if I tried to imprison you, either you or Val would kill me. You have my word."

"Just as long as we're clear on that, Gramps." I drained my glass and crossed my ankles on the throw pillow. "So, what's for dinner?"

NOVEMBER: ELEANOR

My dearest,

Little Amy finally came to tea today. I do hope I haven't traumatized the child.

It took a fair bit of encouragement to coax her across the border. The poor girl was skittish around me the last time we saw each other, though I can't blame her. Toula had just delivered the news that she could add Oberon to her largely unlabeled family tree, and I'd arrived while she was still digesting *that* bit of happiness. My father was a bastard of the first order, you know, and I've found no use for most of his children. Maybe Amy is glad to have some answers, but I understand why she hasn't been eager to become bosom friends with her kin.

Still, I like what I've seen of her—you would, too, I'm sure. Apparently, her talent as a crafter is unmatched in the Fringe, and she's been doing dangerous work in the mortal realm—a risky job for anyone, let alone a teenager. Yes, she has Badger and Seamus and Badger's magus cousin to guide her along, and she's deeply fond of the Gray Lander in their camp, but I want her to have *some* relative to whom she can reach out in time of need. I ran from my family at sixteen, after all, and I know what it is to be on one's own far too young.

So I got Amy's number from Aiden and sent her an invitation—nothing formal, just an offer to chat whenever she had a free moment. Amy politely found excuses at first, saying that I was busy and she didn't want to take up my time, but after a few insistences from me that I'd love to talk, she finally agreed. We chose a Sunday afternoon, when her shop would be closed. Lucian, my chef—I do so wish you could enjoy one of his dinners, the man's a genius—planned a light tea menu, and the preparations were going along perfectly until I had a terrible thought last night.

As I've mentioned, Toula has been kind enough to prepare a database of my court's aural signatures. Recalling that she'd done Amy's aural analysis, I rang her up and asked if she'd found matches for Amy's missing grandfathers. The unrelated one is still a blank, but unfortunately, she was able to identify one of my brothers.

I'll give you three guesses.

Anyway, Coileán dropped Amy off right on time today. The Fringe recovery group is living in his old building in Virginia now, you'll recall, and there's a tiny gate between there and his office that we can widen briefly without risking detection. She looked quite grown up in a green, knee-length cashmere dress and a pair of tall brown boots, very polished. Her experience has made her somewhat older than her years, I suppose, but she wears it well. I gave her a tour of the mansion, hoping it would help her relax. She was polite and inquisitive as I showed her around, stopping to examine the artwork and ask about various pieces of furniture, and though she nearly took a tumble on the marble floor, she caught herself and laughed it off.

It felt so *good* having her there, Walt. As busy as I've been with the court, I believe I'd almost forgotten how much I miss being around young people. Amy reminded me of some of my favorite freshers from years past—you know the type, slightly wide-eyed and awkward but eager to please. And since some of my furnishings are reproductions from our house, I thoroughly enjoyed telling her about them and where we found the originals.

In my preparation for her arrival, however, I made the first of several mistakes: I neglected to move Hugo out of the hallway.

We came around a corner, and Amy stopped in her tracks when she noticed what was in the terrarium. She asked me about it—the child sounded shocked—and I explained that Hugo was in extended time-out. He'd had a steady stream of visitors that day, and he was in a foul mood. But she crept closer for a better look, just the same.

I suppose I don't often speak of the island, do I? Given the constant tug of the bind on me, I try not to dwell on it—I do so enjoy talking of other matters with you, my darling. Permit me to set the scene.

Hugo has been a busy boy during his captivity, but then I suppose he's terribly bored. He's proven more resourceful than I anticipated. By the time I rolled him into an unused parlor for his first night, he'd cut a banana leaf, braided a crude rope from the tough grass dotting his little island, and fashioned a rough loincloth. He'd assembled a basic lean-to in the forest by the time I gave him his first afternoon rain shower, and within the week, he'd made a tiny raft and a paddle. I drop in scraps of bread and vegetables once a day when I clean his cage, but Hugo has taken to fishing for minnows. His early failures there were amusing—he couldn't make a proper hook, and the fish weren't interested in soggy bread—but then he carved half a dozen sharp sticks and went to sea with them, and he's actually become decently skilled at spear fishing.

When Amy took a look today, he was sitting on the beach with a beheaded minnow nearly his size, filleting it. His fire from Toula was still going in its little ring—I watched him scramble for two hours one morning when he woke to find it nearly dead—and he'd placed flat rocks around the edge to provide a cooking surface. As I said, resourceful. She asked what he'd done, and I explained that he'd been provoking another of our brothers, leaving out the nastier details—we were about to take tea, after all, and I didn't want to disgust her.

Hugo certainly wasn't pleased to have an audience. Amy waved at him when he looked up from his work, and he made a small, yet unmistakably rude gesture. But she seems to be possessed of a rather un-fae capacity for pity. Musing that it couldn't be easy to live in a fishbowl—her word, not mine—she asked if she could give him a care package and pulled a little blue microfiber cloth from her purse, the sort of thing one might keep on hand to clean sunglasses. I allowed it, she dropped it onto the beach, and Hugo began squeaking at us in bewilderment, charity being a mystery to my people. Amy expressed that she hoped he'd made good use of it—we concurred that the leaf loincloth he was then sporting had seen better days.

As I escorted her to our parlor and began pouring tea, Amy asked me more about my plans for Hugo. To be frank, they're still up in the air. He's spent a month in my custody already, and I've tacked on a second to his sentence for continuing to fight his bind. If he's a good boy, his stint as Robinson Crusoe will end by Christmas.

Fortunately, Amy wasn't put off her appetite by my unorthodox penal system—that would have been a pity, considering Lucian's spread. With a little prodding, she told me about herself—her childhood in South Carolina, her plan to run a half-marathon in the spring, her long engagement to Kip (that's the Gray Lander), and her aborted education. As for the last, she's begun online courses to test out of secondary school, and we discussed the possibility of university. Amy believes it would be too risky for her to enroll in an on-campus program, beyond the fact that it would cut into her time for crafting and Fringer retrieval, but I suggested several reputable distance-learning courses and offered to assist with admissions essays. (You and I certainly read our share of terrible fresher papers, and I'm sure I could help her avoid some of the more common pitfalls.) She seemed grateful for the offer, but before I could ask her more about her testing schedule, Karl stormed in.

I don't know how he had the nerve to interrupt me—I saw my poor aide standing in the doorway, flustered and trying to stop him. He marched across the parlor, red-faced and scowling, and demanded to know who had put a handkerchief in Hugo's cage.

You see, Karl has been coming by daily to gloat at our brother's condition. He's not the only gawker, but he's certainly the most faithful in his visitation.

Amy—who was perhaps too serene in proximity to an angry faerie—interrupted to tell him that I'd given her permission. He asked me who the devil *she* was and how I could allow her to do that after what Hugo did to his property. Again, Amy interjected, giving Karl her name and explaining that we'd all be better off if Hugo's wardrobe didn't disintegrate. I reminded Karl that a little kindness seldom hurts, but I might as well have been talking to a wall for all the good that did.

As he continued to rail against the unfairness of my benevolence, I cut my eyes to Amy, intending to reassure her before I shouted Karl out of the house. But the look of growing horror on the little thing's face killed my planned rebuke.

She knew. My God, the poor thing *knew*.

I should have prepared her. Had I anticipated that they would cross paths, I'd have warned her. The fault here is mine. But I tried to salvage what I could of the afternoon, ordering Karl out and warning him that I would deal with him later.

He couldn't take a hint. As Amy sat there on the verge of tears, he pointed to her and asked if "that lowborn wretch" was more important to me than my own brother.

My temper, as you know too well, can be a terrible thing, but I did my best to control it for the child's sake and restrained myself from throttling Karl. Instead, I calmly informed him that Amy was his granddaughter.

He took the news like a slap in the face, but at least his surprise shut him up long enough for me to get a word in. I started to apologize to Amy for letting her find out like that, but Karl interrupted, asking her which of his children had spawned her.

I swear it, Walt, what he said translates as *spawned*. My people aren't known for our deep parental affection.

Poor Amy had gone pink in the face by then, and I saw the tremor in her jaw, but she held his stare and asked why Karl had to look like her father. She managed to add only that her daddy was wonderful before she fell apart.

I held her while she sobbed and quietly told Karl that her parents were witch-blooded, and her aural signature proved her relation to him. Then I asked him to explain himself.

Karl was horrified—not for the fact that his little granddaughter was weeping on my shoulder, but rather because he'd sired a witch-blood, and I'd had the gall to bring its offspring into the realm. While he whinged about being confronted with a mongrel, I again demanded to know what he had done. He insisted it had just been a little fun…

…and then I saw the faerie in Amy come out. She stiffened, sat up, and wiped her napkin across her eyes, then glared at him with smeared mascara and shouted at him for raping her grandmother and walking around with her father's face like it was no big deal. I remember what she said as her fists balled: "He's *dead*. He didn't do anything wrong, and he's dead. And you're still here. Son of a bitch, you're still *here*."

Karl didn't say a word before he shot a bolt at her. Had I not shielded the child, she'd have died where she sat.

As I've said before, dearest, my family is a nightmare.

Still, I tried to maintain control of myself, reminding Karl that Amy was my guest, let alone family, and that I was still waiting for a proper explanation.

He huffed and rolled his eyes, but he confessed, blaming the affair on our brother Sven. Allegedly, Sven dared him to take one of the wizards, and so Karl waited outside the silo one night, followed a girl in a car to a restaurant in another town, and got into her vehicle with a touch of suggestion.

She wasn't strong enough to block him from her mind, and he had his way with her in the back. Walt, he *smiled* as he spoke of that night, and then he had the nerve to ask why it mattered—it was a stupid wizard decades ago.

Amy stared daggers at him. It was forty-five years, she snapped, and the woman's name was Fran Levey. She was nineteen at the time, and she named her son Jonas—not that Karl would care.

Karl asked her why he should give a damn about a dead mongrel.

To her credit, she kept calm and quietly told him about her father: how he was clever and ran tech support for a large law firm, how he could hunt with guns and bows alike, how he loved his wife and daughter, even taking time off work to serve as a chaperone for the boys when her cross-country team had a meet out of town. She told Karl that she loved her father dearly, that she missed him and her mother so hard that it ached, and that they had been her only family.

He failed to see the point in this information. Amy clarified: she just wanted whatever small part of him capable of comprehending to understand what he'd missed by never knowing his son, and otherwise, he could go straight to hell.

One attempted death bolt was bad, but two was too much even for my practiced patience. I shielded Amy with one hand and threw Karl across the room with the other. Fortunately for him, he hit a tapestry and not just the bare marble, but the blow still knocked him cold.

I apologized profusely to Amy—for Karl's behavior, for the lack of warning, for her ruined visit. She was gracious and suggested that she leave before Karl woke with a headache. Seeing the sadness in her eyes, I offered my condolences for what had befallen her grandmother. To my surprise, however, Amy merely shrugged. According to her father, her grandmother had sneaked out of the silo that night to meet a man fifteen years her senior. He'd pretended she didn't exist once she fell pregnant, and her parents had made her have the baby to teach her a lesson. But then she'd married a few years later and had another son and a daughter. Amy had never met them, and the only time she recalled seeing her grandmother, the woman called her an abomination. Apparently, Fran had little use for her tainted son and granddaughter.

I reminded her that you were a witch, my dear, and told her she could call on me at any time before I returned her to Coileán. She seemed pleased by that, I think. I do so hope she'll take me up on it.

As for Karl...well, he was distressed to wake up in a terrarium beside Hugo's. By then, Hugo had fashioned Amy's gift into a crude pair of trousers, held together at the seams with thin laces. I heard him laugh as Karl woke naked next door, and I told Karl to make himself comfortable—he'd be there for a while. To Hugo, I explained that the little dear who'd given him that cloth was Karl's witch-blooded granddaughter, which sent Hugo into another fit of laughter. I couldn't make out what Karl squeaked as he ran into the trees, but I'm sure it was obscene. I gave Hugo one of Lucian's perfect scones—it was a pity to waste them—and told him that he'd be free soon if he behaved himself. Maintaining two binds is a bit of a juggling act, but I'm sure I can manage it.

I miss you, my dearest. Like Jonas, you didn't do anything wrong, and you're dead, and my idiot brothers are still here, and there's no justice in it.

But I will have peace in my court. I swear this to you.

> Much love,
> Your Ellie

DECEMBER: GREG HARRISON

Christmas in New Orleans isn't what I'd call ideal. Decades of silo life had spoiled me with white Christmases, and even a few of my childhood holidays in Nashville had a festive dusting, just enough to make the day fun and the relatives visiting from more southerly climes step outside, consider the frosted view, and retreat to the warm kitchen. But my girls had made lives for themselves far beyond both the silo and seasons—Cindy in New Orleans, Abby in Los Angeles—and so Missy and I had taken to alternating holidays with them, weather be damned.

We used to spend Christmases together in Montana as a family, Missy and me, our daughters and their mundane husbands, the grandkids, and then the great-grandbabies, all four of them duds.

I hate that term. Three of our five grandchildren were slapped with the label before they were even ten. I couldn't bring myself to have them tested publicly, so I asked June Matherson, one of the few magi I trusted to keep my confidence, to do the honors in my apartment. When Micah, Ashleigh, and Katherine couldn't so much as make a paperclip twitch, she was gentle and reassuring; when Cora and Melissa managed to move a small cube with a dragonscale wand, she was encouraging and never mentioned how weak they were as young witches. Then again, her own boy was witch-blooded, a crafter par excellence but hopeless with a wand. I knew she would tell the kids the right things while I tried to hide my disappointment.

June was, as my mother would say, good people. I'd repaid her with nothing but grief. As far as she knew, her boy was dead, one of Coileán's many victims from the brief faerie uprising that had killed our poor grand magus and driven us into the installations for safety. Bullshit, all of it. Rick Matherson—Slim to the Fringe—was alive, if perhaps not well, and still crafting wands for the Arcanum. Exactly how James Mulligan had convinced him to do so was a mystery to me, but James kept the details to himself, and frankly, I didn't want to know.

There was so much blood on my hands already that ignorance came as a relief. I couldn't have told June exactly where James had stashed her boy any more than I could have led her to Helen's holding cell. That they were hidden somewhere within the silo was understood, but James never offered that information to me. I couldn't be trusted.

The man was evil, but he was strong, and he wasn't an idiot. Had he acted alone, I probably could have killed him—God knew I wanted to. But James had seduced far too many magi to his cause, and he'd made clear to me that the price of my family's peace and safety was my quiet compliance.

We like to think that when faced with difficult situations, we'd make the right choices, the honorable decisions, no matter the cost. I could have blown the whistle on James in the beginning and maybe shown the Arcanum that his story of faerie attack was mere fabrication, possibly even wrestled control of the assassin corps from him before James sent them out to slaughter the Fringe. At least I could have spirited Helen out of the silo that morning. But I'd been cornered by half a dozen of the strongest magi, who'd explained in graphic terms that if I put a toe out of line, my children were dead. They had photos, addresses, work locations, school names—hell, they'd mapped the route that Ashleigh took when walking Lilly and Emma to the playground. I looked at those photos they spread across my coffee table: Cindy and Jermaine at their anniversary dinner at Arnaud's, Abby and Tyler at one of their many award shows, Micah unlocking his new Volvo, Ashley and Hudson on a streetcar with the girls, Cora and Chris walking out of church with Hunter by the hand and little Annabeth in her car seat, Melissa running between hospital wings in her scrubs, and Katherine bent over her drafter's table in her firm's glass-walled office. If I wanted them to live, then other people's children would die. *Hundreds* of other people's children.

I made that choice. I made it even though Cora and Melissa could have been Fringers, even though the other three and the great-grands would have been executed as pollutants in the gene pool. I made my decision, and I told Missy what I'd done, and her alone. Missy didn't like it, either, but we knew damn well that our daughters could never know what we'd done. Cindy and Abby, who'd sworn to never speak to me again if I didn't let Helen marry Joey. Romantics, my daughters, Arcanum-reared wizards who'd run off to Howard University and met the mundane loves of their lives. My sons-in-law were good men, hard workers, the sort that almost any father would be proud to have for his little girl—Jermaine was a doctor, and though what Tyler did was always something of a mystery to me, his name appeared in TV and movie credits almost as often as Abby's did. But neither of them had a drop of magical talent, and there I was, the grand magus, losing my gifted daughters to the lives they'd chosen in the mundane world.

I was pathetic, James told me soon after his coup. How could I be trusted to run the Arcanum if I couldn't even control my own family?

I could have told him a few choice things in turn, but I bit my tongue and let the abuse go unanswered as I thought of Cindy's art shows and baby Annabeth, who looked so much like Abby had at her age, with dark eyes too big for her face and pinchable cheeks.

We said nothing, Missy and me, and so life went on for our scattered family. James never forced the girls to move into the silo—he never so much as contacted them, and their mother and I pretended that nothing was amiss. We made up vague, pleasant stories about retirement when we visited and tried to keep the conversation focused on the little ones.

At least Ashleigh brought her babies to her grandmother's house to open presents. Missy and I sat on Cindy's floral sofa that morning and watched as Lilly and Emma tore through their presents. Eight and six they were, my great-granddaughters, wearing matching snowflake-print nightgowns and red and green barrettes at the ends of their braids, and while Lilly wasn't entirely sure that Santa was real, Emma still found the toy bonanza magical.

They'd have been dead, had I said anything. I reminded myself of that when they ran up to hug me and pass me presents and show off their new dolls, both of them excited and chattering and eager to play with their uncle and aunt when Micah and Melissa rolled up with jackets thrown on over their pajamas. Jermaine made chicory coffee, strong and fragrant, and Cindy produced a delicious breakfast heavy on the andouille sausage. The house was full and raucous and *alive*: drifts of ripped wrapping paper, the running patter of barefoot children over the wooden floors, the smells of pine and Cajun spices, Melissa's laughter as she called her friends from the laundry room to wish them a merry Christmas.

I wanted to scream. Confess. Lock myself in the bathroom and puke my guts up until I was purged of my guilt.

Instead, I hugged Cindy a little too tightly, blamed it on the festive day, and tried not to think about June, all alone in her too-quiet silo apartment, hanging a stocking for her son.

—YEAR FOUR—

JUNE: POPPY KANE

There's a popular misconception about shifters, particularly those of us of the lupine variety, that we're bloodthirsty beasts barely contained within human skin, prone to show our true selves and go on a rampage when the moon is right.

That's absolute bullshit.

Despite what the idiots in the pack movement said, we are, first and above all, human—or close, I guess, if you want to get technical about it. Human-plus, maybe. We can't use any kind of magic, we're not complete psychos, we're not attached at the hip to carved sticks, and we don't erupt in weeping sores if we pick up silverware. Unless someone happens to have mental talent and realizes that he can't get into our heads, we fly under the mundane radar.

It's just that every so often, the wolf needs to run.

She's a part of me, the wolf. She *is* me, I guess, but I didn't meet her until I was thirteen. Puberty is miserable for mundanes, but boy, can it be hell for shifters. At least I grew up around my own kind in the Dark Company's New York barracks, so we were all going through our first changes together. I knew what was in store for me—both of my parents are lupine shifters, and my grandparents and great-grandparents before them, so unless someone had been sneaking around, there was almost no chance that I'd be anything else. A few of my classmates weren't so lucky. One girl was the product of ursine and feline parents, and she lived in fear that she'd take after her mother, lose control in a car, and wreck the thing when she went full bear. She did end up an ursine shifter, but since we lived out in the woods upstate, she had room to experiment until she got herself sorted out.

But even knowing what's ahead, it's *weird* the first time you shift. It doesn't hurt, and it's over in a matter of seconds, but there's so much adjustment that has to happen before you grow up and find your feet. I mean, your feet are literally the first problem—most shifters go into a quadrupedal form, and it takes practice to get all those legs coordinated enough to walk, much less run. While you're figuring out your balance, you're also inundated with new sensory impressions, and that can be a major distraction. The wolf has an excellent sense of smell, and suddenly, everything in the vicinity takes on a new level of significance.

For the record, I only tried *that* sort of sniffing once, at a slumber party when I was fifteen, and I learned far more about one of my friends than I had any desire to know.

Though I figured the wolf out eventually, I still remember how unsettling it was to see her looking back at me in a mirror for the first time. Most other shifters' secondary forms are passably normal—a shifted cat looks like a cat—but our wolves are twice the size of the standard model, like prehistoric monsters. We didn't have a good explanation for it beyond the tradition that our ancestors had spent time in the Gray Lands, and God only knew what could come out of *there*. But anyway, the wolf—*my* wolf— was huge, barely able to maneuver in my small bathroom. She had thick gray fur and golden eyes, a change from my usual brown-eyed brunette look, and she was slightly taller than me, even standing on all fours. Had she gone to her hind legs, she'd have grazed the ceiling.

I'd have grazed the ceiling.

It's difficult sometimes for a shifter to think of herself as equally both forms, especially as a teenager. You spend all that time and mental energy wrapped up in crafting an identity and carefully presenting yourself to the world, and then you have a bad day and turn into a fanged beast. When it happened in the classrooms in the Company barracks, no one minded too much—every adult in the building had gone through a similar phase—but it was embarrassing because many of us were stuck in our animal forms unless we'd thought ahead to bring a change of clothing. Some shifters go small—rodents, insects, amphibians—but when I shift, whatever I happen to be wearing gets *shredded.*

While I did get the wolf under control with a few years' practice, in times of stress, my instinct is to free her. My mind may still be weighed down, but the wolf doesn't care. The world is a sensory wonderland to her, and if I let her, she'll run until she's exhausted, too busy processing the myriad smells and sounds around her to bother with whatever was troubling me. It's escapism of the first order, I admit, but it works.

The problem is that when I'm particularly stressed, I eat my feelings, and the wolf doesn't stop with Doritos.

I hadn't freed the wolf often since coming to Faerie. Part of it was due to a lack of time and a load of responsibility, but in truth, I was hesitant to let her go around my half-fae boyfriend. Rufe had seen me wolf out—and as I'd been employed by the Company when we met, it wasn't a deep, dark secret that I could change form—but people like me always have a smidgen of unease when dealing with non-shifters. Someone might find you gorgeous and brilliant and hilarious, but will he look at you the same way when you're furry and can't speak?

Not that Rufe was any stranger to changing his appearance. He'd spent decades under increasingly heavy glamour, aging himself to match his years while working as a college professor. But while it was one thing to add wrinkles, it was quite another to add a tail. We joked about it—any time I left hair on the bathroom floor, we'd make reference to my shedding—but I never felt fully at ease shifted around him, even after several years together.

Then again, I seldom had time to even consider letting the wolf out. When the Arcanum upended itself, I'd been convalescing in Faerie, hanging out with Rufe at his parents' sprawling place. The Company had just fired me for fraternization and other offenses, and as I was suddenly homeless and unemployed, Rufe had offered to help me find a job at his school in Alaska—and thrown in a spare bedroom in his apartment. Moving in with a guy after a month might seem unwise, but Rufe and I had spent most of our time together in a shitty motel room on an extended stakeout, me transformed into a guy and bored out of my mind, and him stopping by with increasing frequency. He'd asked me out to dinner even when I was bound, slipped me into Faerie to give me a few hours back in my own body, and saved my life when I was hit with a bone-breaking bolt. By all appearances, Rufe had fallen *hard*, and I was right there with him. So what if he was almost ninety-three?

And then the self-appointed grand magus had given his ultimatum. Rufe couldn't leave Faerie, and I had nothing but humiliated parents to go back to. The decision to stay had been simple.

Of course, that led to another question: what could I do in the middle of the Fringe crisis? Instinct told me to hang back for a time and see how the chips were falling, but after about six weeks, I found a task. Rufe's sister Vivi—the lone Stowe sibling younger than me, and then only by a whopping three years—had tasked her brother with drawing up plans for a school for the Fringer kids. No one knew when we'd be able to leave, and so a school seemed like a logical addition to the new settlement, a way to keep the kids' education on track and give them a shred of normalcy. While Rufe tried to recruit teachers from among the refugees, I got a clipboard and went from house to house, noting ages, grade levels, and educational needs.

I'd expected that there would be problems, but I hadn't been prepared for the trauma.

The kids who still had at least one parent were coping,

but the ones who'd been passed out to fosters or stuck in the group home were barely treading water. Young ones had regressed, older ones were defiant, and those whose fosters had wearied of them and sent them to the home were dealing with a second round of loss. There weren't enough grief counselors to go around, and the therapists who had any background in child psychology were overwhelmed and overbooked. The adults who looked after the home on a rotating basis were doing their best, but so many of them were too traumatized to be effective or helpful.

While I didn't have any special training, at least I wasn't having flashbacks. I told Rufe what I had in mind, and we announced to Vivi that we were taking over the orphan dorm. She was too swamped herself to care about credentials, and the dismissed volunteers were just relieved.

On the first day, Rufe and I gathered the kids and laid down ground rules. There would be no more sneaking out, no more fistfights, no more stealing dessert from the little kids. Rufe disclosed what he was and what he could do in an effort to gain the upper hand, but a few of the older teenagers still tried to back-talk us. They'd almost made it to the door, declaring that the rules didn't apply to them, when I stopped them without saying a word.

A warning growl, deployed selectively, is an excellent tool.

The problem kids turned, saw me shifted and baring my fangs, and decided to stick around for the rest of the meeting.

I never had to shift after that. We survived the rest of the rocky summer, and then school kicked off, bringing with it a rhythm of classes and homework. I stepped in as a gym teacher with Hal, Vivi's all-too-mundane husband, organizing kickball games and a four-team soccer league. At night, while Rufe helped with homework and tried to remember how algebra worked, I held the little ones who just wanted to sit in a lap and be cuddled.

God, there were so many of those cuddles.

I got to know every children's book in the settlement by heart and downloaded more, flipping picture book pages on a tablet when I ran out of physical material. Rufe and I both got up in the middle of the night when someone woke crying—or worse, screaming—or wet the bed, but I was the one who was called in when a kid was caught cutting herself or standing in the bathroom with a noose around his neck. I didn't have the training for my job, but I could hold on if someone needed a hug or a dry shoulder.

Through it all, even when I was exhausted to the point of tears, Rufe never suggested stepping aside. I watched him with the kids—even the young ones, a demographic he'd never prepared to teach—and saw how gentle he could be. Rufe was patient and proactive, and he kept his sense of humor about our unanticipated career move as dorm parents, seeing as neither of us had children of our own. For almost three years, we worked and lived together, but while we officially kept separate bedrooms, one of us often sneaked into the other's room after lights-out in between making rounds to keep our charges from doing likewise. We became each other's anchor and sounding board, and I never felt safer than when I was spooned in bed beside him. When Rufe took me out to dinner at the settlement's little Italian restaurant on a chilly Valentine's Day evening and dropped to one knee, I barely blinked before accepting his proposal.

But that was February, and this was June, the day before our wedding. Vivi had organized substitute dorm parents for a week as a wedding present, and I was spending the night at her place while her eleven other brothers and Hal threw Rufe a low-key bachelor party at the settlement's tiny bar. By then, Vivi and I had become close friends—she was thrilled to have another woman around, no matter what else I might be—and Rohese, my soon-to-be mother-in-law, had warmed to me. Still, I was restless all afternoon, even after going over the final details with Father Paul, and I paced the length of Vivi's den as the sun sank. When I could take no more, I begged off from the planned rom-com viewing, put my engagement ring in the dish on the guestroom dresser, and let the wolf run into the night.

Late that evening, as I lay in a clearing in the woods and gorged myself on the buck I'd brought down, anxiety crept back into my mind like an obnoxious earworm. I loved Rufe—that was beyond question—but my thoughts circled around to the old point of insecurity: did he love *me*? All of me, the real me? Or did he love me in spite of myself? I told myself I was being stupid and tried to enjoy my messy dinner, but worry took firmer hold. I'd tried not to shift around him for fear of driving him away, but did I intend to stay in human form forever? Would my wolf eventually become such a turn-off that he'd give me the choice of her or him?

I knew what my mom would say: *It never works out with mundanes*. No one understood us but us—no one who's never felt the rush of the shift and the sudden unleashing of the senses could understand how integral the wolf was to my core self. Pretending she didn't exist would be tantamount to letting one arm dangle useless for the rest of my life. I could hear Mom's voice in my head, warning me of the dangers of looking outside the Company for love— but Mom didn't know Rufe. She wasn't here, was she?

I'd seen to that.

Though I saved every one of them, the messages I got from the mortal realm ripped me apart. First came the long e-mail from Mom: what was I thinking in ignoring my Company duties, what had gotten into me, how could I so embarrass the family, et cetera. Then, once they must have heard about the Arcanum and the evacuation, came the frantic texts. Was I alive? Safe? Was I with this Rufus person somewhere out of harm's way? As the days passed, they begged me to answer.

I never did. It wasn't that I was angry over the chiding

e-mail—oh, I was *furious*, but I would have sucked it up and shot off a few words of reassurance had I not feared the Arcanum. They'd used the Fringe's own network to find and slaughter them, and though I was almost positive it was my Company-instilled paranoia speaking, I was sure as hell not going to risk leading the Arcanum to my parents or the bunker if the wizards had somehow tapped my phone. Better to say nothing and keep them safe then drop a line and an electronic trail of breadcrumbs.

Gradually, their messages shifted in tenor. Tanner Adler, the fucking prick, had decided to forcibly retire most of the Company's lupine shifters in the wake of the "Alpha" scandal. It didn't matter that Bradley Knott and his pack buddies hadn't been working under Company orders—big wolves were seen as more of a liability than a resource, and for the good of the Company, they needed to step down. My parents told me that they'd been asked to move out of the bunker and into private housing. While the stipend had been generous, I knew the severance had to sting.

Though the messages had dropped off over time, Mom persisted. About once a month, I'd get a text: *Hi, baby. Please be okay. Let's talk. We forgive you.*

Always, infuriatingly, forgiveness was dangled at the end of her messages. As if I'd done something wrong. I did what Jeanine Nadel would have had the Company do, had Bradley and his buddies not eaten her alive. I did the right thing to help stop them *and* Moyna. And if I'd found love along the way, why was that a crime?

Unless Mom was right, and I'd be too much for him in the end.

And so I lay there in the woods, eating my feelings in spite of the fitted wedding dress I'd have to squeeze into in the morning…assuming, of course, that the groom didn't come to his senses first.

Suddenly, I smelled something familiar over the saliva-inducing aroma of warm blood: Rufe. A bit of alcohol, too, but that was unmistakably Rufe.

I raised my head and saw a small light in the distance—an orb, I assumed—and faintly heard him call my name. After a moment's indecision, I howled in reply, then returned to my deer while he stumbled his way toward me.

Rufe wasn't drunk—the scent of alcohol was more like a suggestion than a shout—but he'd come bearing a hip flask. He watched me cautiously from the edge of the clearing, then asked, "May I join you, or is this alone time?"

I lay low, averted my eyes, and flattened my ears, trying to put him at ease, but Rufe stayed put, gnawing his lip. After a time, I realized my error: as fae as he was, Rufe had probably never been around an animal that wasn't trying to escape or fight him. I attempted to make my meaning more overt and wagged my tail, hoping he'd catch my drift.

"Okay," he said, sliding down against a tree. "Don't mean to interrupt. If you'd rather I go, tell me. I won't be offended."

I kept eating, trying not to picture the scene from his perspective.

"Not in a talking mood tonight, eh?" he asked.

I glanced up, sighed, and lowered my innate mental defenses. Pointing one paw at him, I then pointed it at my head and waited, forming the answer in my thoughts.

"*Ah*," he muttered, and I felt him enter my mind.

Can't talk in this form, I thought. *If I shifted right now, I'd be naked and covered in blood, and Bambi here is delicious. Hope you don't mind*, I added, trying to color the thought with the nonchalance I wasn't feeling. This was me—raw, exposed *me*, bloody muzzle and all, and my poor fiancé looked like he was afraid I'd eat his face if he said the wrong thing.

"No, no, that…that's fine," said Rufe. "Sorry, uh…yes or no questions would be best?"

I nodded. *Want some venison?*

He considered his flask, then shrugged. "I had dinner with the boys, but you know what, fuck it. If you're willing to share…"

Coming up for air, I nudged the carcass toward him, and

Rufe severed the left haunch with a wave. Another touch of enchantment had the leg skinned, roasted, and on a platter, and he dug in with his bare hands. "Fresh," he said, his mouth full. "Did you bring this down?"

I didn't find him dead and waiting for me.

"Dumb question?"

I dignified that with a snort and ripped into the buck's side. *How'd you find me?*

"I'm not entirely sure. Vivi pointed me in the right direction, but I think the realm may have helped. Kind of got a feeling you'd be here."

With that said, we ate in silence for a few minutes, and then Rufe cleared his throat. "Are you nervous?"

Nervous? My stomach was flopping as I kept sneaking glances at him, trying to discern whether he was about to run away.

Yeah, I admitted.

"Me, too."

I huffed, then rested my chin on the deer. *Guess this isn't helping, is it?*

"Actually, this is great," he replied. "We had pizza earlier, and Luce made it, and he went frou-frou, as usual. You have pepperoni, you have sausage, or you have both. There's no reason to put goat cheese and arugula on a pie."

I don't know, sounds pretty good.

"This is better." He held the leg aloft with both hands and took a bite off the meaty end. "Manlier."

You look deranged doing that, sweetie.

"I know." He put it down and wiped his greasy hands on the grass.

Seeing his face working in the orb's light, I feared what he was about to tell me.

"Poppy," he began, then took a deep breath. "What I wanted to say…that is, uh, I mean…"

I closed my eyes and braced myself for the inevitable.

Rufe sighed. "If the age thing is too much…if you're having second thoughts…I totally understand. No hard feelings."

Surprised, I opened my eyes again and found him regarding me with a worried stare, as if he were preparing to be kicked. *It's not too much*, I thought, waiting for him to catch my response.

"Sixty-four years is a lot for us, I get it. If you're at all uncomfortable, I...I want you to be happy, whatever that means, and...well, if you're reconsidering, I don't blame you."

I wanted to laugh, but I couldn't quite manage in lupine form, and anyway, Rufe looked so serious. *Listen to me*, I insisted. *The age thing isn't a problem.*

"Oh. Okay," he mumbled, and cocked his head. "I just thought...you're nervous, too, and—"

Not about <u>that</u>. Jesus, Rufe, I'm lying here chomping down on a deer whose throat I ripped out with my own damn teeth, and you're worried that <u>I</u> might be having second thoughts about wanting to be with <u>you</u>?

He frowned, perplexed. "Is that what's bothering you? The shifter thing?"

It's not a <u>thing</u>. This is who I am, and I can't change it. I can keep the wolf on a leash most of the time, but—

"You're incredible," he softly interrupted. "Why would I want to change you?"

I stood, towering over him for a moment, and when Rufe got to his feet, I could still look him straight in the eye. He hesitated, and then, to my surprise, he hurried across the clearing and wrapped his arms around my neck. I stiffened, then relaxed in his embrace and rested my chin on his shoulder.

Seriously, I'm a messy eater, I thought as he ran his fingers through my fur. *I'm going to get your shirt bloody.*

"I might have mentioned that I'm fae," he murmured. "Stain removal isn't a problem."

I closed my eyes and enjoyed the moment, then realized what Rufe was doing and snorted. *Are you petting my neck?*

He froze. "Sorry, um...I didn't mean—"

You've never pet a dog before, have you?

"Sorry," he mumbled, releasing me.

I licked the side of his face, tasting venison drippings with a hint of beer. He backpedaled, laughing in surprise, then tripped on his feet and fell to the grass. I stood over him, pinning him where he lay, and licked him again before he could get his arms up to defend himself. *Behind the ears is a good starting place.*

"Got it," he said, his face glistening with saliva. "Oh, that feels *weird…*"

Less intense with a dog, I'm sure. I moved aside and stretched out next to him as he sat up. *Let's not tell your mom about this.*

"Agreed," he replied, and then, ever so tentatively, he reached out and rubbed the good spot behind my left ear. "Is that…"

Perfect.

There was relief in his exhalation. "Hey, Poppy?" he said after a moment's massage.

Yes?

"I can't wait until tomorrow."

Me, neither, I thought, and realized that I meant it.

I climbed to my feet and had a good shake, then nudged Rufe off the ground. *Come on, you, bedtime.*

"Yes, ma'am." He opened a gate onto Vivi's front yard and swept an arm toward the house. "May I offer you a lift?"

I padded through, and he followed me back to town. "One question," he asked as he closed the gate behind us.

Shoot.

Rufe pointed to Vivi's blue double doors. "How were you planning to sneak back in?"

Make sure the coast is clear, and I'll show you.

I waited until he was in the street, scanning for passersby, then loped to the door, shifted, and slipped inside before anyone caught me. When Rufe glanced back, I was standing behind the cracked door, and I stuck one hand out to wave goodnight. He chuckled and walked off, and I locked up and went to the guestroom.

I got a look at myself in the dresser mirror as I walked in: a little scratched, slightly sweaty, and as bloody in the face as if I'd shoved my nose into the deer's beating heart. It made for an odd juxtaposition with the lacy wedding gown hanging on the closet door behind me.

But my wolf was strong and fierce, and she deserved a little freedom.

Taking a last look at the evidence of my night out, I slipped my engagement ring back on and went to take a shower.

AUGUST: STUART PURCELL

The first weekend of the school year was sacred in that one needed a *damn* good reason to bother one's colleagues as they caught up on rest and patched any holes in their lesson plans. That was fine by me. I had work to do, and with the social calendar empty, I wouldn't have to make excuses.

A package had arrived from New Mexico midweek, an unassuming box held together with a copious amount of strapping tape. Had anyone looked inside, they'd have found adobe roofing tiles nestled in straw—material for one of my experimental mixed-media pieces, or perhaps something to grind down and work into my pottery. But at the heart of the box, cocooned in several layers of bubble wrap and brown paper, was the real prize.

Aiden had been a busy boy.

I'd carefully unwrapped the delivery, only to reveal what appeared to be a dead black beetle. When I touched it, however, I could tell that its body was made of metal…and then the damn thing twitched, scaring me half to death. It took a few experimental steps on my kitchen counter, antennae waving, then settled down and looked at me.

I put it in a mason jar, poked holes in the lid, and hid it in my mudroom.

"I was expecting a bug," I said when I called him that evening to confirm receipt, "not a *bug*."

Aiden snickered at my annoyance. "Camouflage. Just get it as close as you can, and it'll do the rest. Leave the program running before you head out so it'll sync right away, okay?"

I was no expert in bugs, entomological or techno-magical. My role was to be a relay station: the bug would pick up what it could from Arc 1 and report it to my computer—now running software Aiden had sent over disguised as a photo editor—and then my computer would automatically forward the data to Aiden's servers. I knew that he and Vivi would be using the bug to listen in on Arcanum chatter, but that was the extent of my knowledge. In situations where mental eavesdropping is a possibility, ignorance is safest.

Having been in Wright's Mill for three years, I'd become, if not accepted, at least tolerated, a harmless eccentric who had a penchant for taking long walks in the woods and setting up his easel in prime hunting territory. My living quarters shared space with my studio in my rented house, and I decorated accordingly. Bobby, my boss and landlord, didn't care what color I painted the place so long as I didn't give the police a reason to come out. The townsfolk had a libertarian streak and little use for any non-local government—the county commission was pushing it—and as far as most were concerned, I was a free spirit who gladly donated pieces to the annual library auction and hosted the occasional paint-and-sip night. My farmer neighbors might not have approved of Quentin's caftan collection, but by comparison to the feds on the other side of town, I was a golden boy.

The "feds" in question were the Arcanum, but they seemed to have the town fooled. Then again, which is easier for the average citizen to believe: the military is building a top-secret base on some empty land in a sparsely populated corner of Montana, or the local organization of murderous wizards is throwing together a decoy?

From casual conversations I'd had with my new colleagues at the school, I'd gleaned that everyone in town knew about the abandoned missile silo, buried somewhere deep beneath a farm or a patch of woods. The military had bought up a vast expanse of land back in the 1940s, and in the early 1960s, folks had witnessed all sorts of earth movers and concrete mixers being driven in. The project was massive but confidential, yet there were only so many ways for the builders to dissemble when anyone with a crop duster could see the giant hole. Work seemed to have finished in 1964, and Wright's Mill anticipated an uncomfortable existence with the incoming base personnel.

They never arrived.

Bad concrete was the word from the old-timers, a poorly chosen mixture coupled with a weak support system and an unforgiving water table. Some thought the military had hit an aquifer. In any case, the project was a bust, and the town breathed a sigh of relief when the last of the Jeeps rolled out. The government sealed up whatever entrances it had made, then sold off the land to a developer and a smattering of outsiders, people content to either run a few dozen head of cattle or regrow the woods for hunting purposes. The developer established a trailer park and a few small apartment buildings. The park wasn't well kept, and neither were the apartments, but somehow, there never seemed to be a vacancy. New people came to town and put their kids in the county-run school, but they mostly kept to themselves. Once the locals understood that no one was planning to change the character of their little town, they went back to business, minding their farms and pretending that the new neighbors didn't exist.

Thanks to Aiden, I knew the truth of the matter. Around the time that the silo was completed, the grand magus organized a team to hex the hell out of the place, then bought the abandoned silo and the surrounding land through a dozen shell companies. The Arcanum's North American outpost moved down from British Columbia, refurbished the silo, and built complex wards around the property—wards that, for instance, might make outsiders more amenable to believing that the surge in children at the local school could be explained by the few new trailers and apartments and farmhouses. In fact, the trailers were entirely decoys, while only a few of the other buildings were inhabited, and then only by security.

Shortly after I moved to town, the "military" returned, buying back some of the farmland and beginning rapid construction on a base behind a thick, wire-topped wall. The new facility had no characteristics visible from the road that gave away its purpose—and anyone who tried to fly over found himself in need of a new plane. No one knew what sort of technology was being employed to prevent aerial investigation, but the armed guards around the perimeter weren't the talkative sort. To the school's surprise, the facility apparently housed families, as there was an influx of new students as soon as construction ceased. The school board wasn't happy, but the large, official-looking check that arrived every August ended the complaints.

Like many of the locals, I'd taken to creeping close to the base for a peek, but I'd snapped photos and e-mailed them to Aiden for analysis. Midway through construction, he'd sent me a package via the Minor Arcanum containing a pair of unremarkable mirrored sunglasses. "They're enchanted to show the wearer traces of active magic," he'd explained over the phone. "Designed them myself. I made Coileán try a pair, but I think it hurt his pride."

The next Saturday, I'd gone for a walk near the unfinished installation. The sunglasses had proven effective against the glare of the sun on the hardpacked snow, but when I'd glanced at the construction site, I'd seen a mesh of glowing green lines covering the place like a net. Making what mental notes I could without staring for too long, I'd hurried home, printed one of my photos, and added the spell channels atop it. Once I'd scanned my work and sent a copy to Aiden, he'd run it by Arnold, Badger's magus cousin, for analysis. An illusion spell, Arnold had reported, nothing but spellcraft over a field. He'd cautioned, however, that the guns the guards were holding were presumably real, as were the wands they had to be hiding in their uniforms.

"Be careful," Aiden had cautioned me. "And if I were you, I wouldn't wear those glasses anymore. Might want to break them to be sure."

I wasn't a master spy, but I wasn't stupid. I'd smashed the glasses with a hammer and buried the pieces in the garbage.

A wizard doesn't run, but a *clever* wizard knows when to lie low.

The new facility was just another decoy, a way to explain the surge in children at my school. I'd sent the numbers from the previous few years to Aiden, who'd cross-checked with Badger and surmised that the vast majority of the North American Arcanum membership was now crammed into the silo. Through some strange means, Badger had confirmed that James Mulligan was in residence, so we could assume that the Arcanum executive cabal was still in the installation. And *that* meant ample opportunity to intercept the official chatter going to and from the silo— that is, if we could get a bug in place.

The Fringe had a history of technical espionage, and that knowledge base, coupled with Aiden's facility with robotics and magical talent, had finally borne fruit.

On Saturday morning, I packed my plein air kit and headed off into the woods. I sketched a duck pond and added reference dots of color, then moved on to a mature grove in which a coyote skull had been bleached and picked clean over the summer, and finally, fighting the hammering in my heart, I set up my easel next to the trailer park. It wasn't easy to play dumb. I'd been told how many cameras the Arcanum had installed around the trailer park, and I had a rough idea of where the wards ended, based on the strength of my inexplicable certainty that I needed to get out of the area. Sweat trickled down my spine as I pictured a pair of black-clad assassins creeping through the woods. Keeping my eyes trained on the pasture across the road, I drew cows and trees and distant hills, then knelt and rummaged through my knapsack for my paints.

When I was sure that no one was watching me, I unscrewed the jar lid and shook the metal beetle into my palm. It woke, turned in a circle, then twitched its antennae at me as if in greeting.

"Godspeed," I whispered, and laid it in the tall weeds.

I didn't watch it depart. Pulling my palette and paints out, I began to give color to my sketch, trying to capture the play of sunlight on the waving grass and the plodding motion of the cattle without allowing my hand to shake too badly. The exercise was frustrating—even though I wasn't standing beside the wards, I was the sort of person they'd been built to keep away, and so I couldn't get into my usual mental zone while I worked. With the painting half-finished, I packed up and set off for home, cursing myself for being so *weak*. I was a wizard, damn it; I should have been able to come up with a counter-spell to work against the wards…

Shut up, Stuart, Quentin ordered. *Play your part.*

He had a point, I mused. The folks stuck in Faerie could create wonders, and Badger could send her consciousness out into the universe, but I alone had survived three years at ground zero. Surviving without magic or magick—that had to count for something, right?

My feet ached by the time I climbed the front stairs and unlocked the door, and I set my unfinished work aside for the morning. While I microwaved a Lean Cuisine, I went to my laptop and wiggled my mouse, hoping that the bug was on track to its destination.

As instructed, I'd left the software running, and an alert box had popped up in the middle of my screen while I'd been out.

NEW AUDIO RECEIVED. PLAY?

I knew I couldn't listen to it, not with the possibility of mental prying in my life, but I picked up the phone and called Faerie. "Aiden?" I said as the line clicked open. "Check your inbox."

NOVEMBER: AIDEN CARVER

The espionage program—the first test bug, and the five friends I sent after it, with Stuart's help—was a smashing success. My tiny, highly shielded surveillance devices had dug deep into the ground around Arc 1, following the active magic, and attached themselves to the outside of the silo. No ear could have heard through that many tons of concrete, but the bugs weren't listening for sound. Instead, I'd designed them to tunnel around the structure until they sensed both strong concentrations of magic and electricity, then burrow into the thick walls. The bugs were set to hunt for the silo's antiquated telephone lines…and I'd instructed them to dig to approximately the level of the grand magus's suite. As I'd expected, no one had bothered to set up Wi-Fi in the silo since my departure, and now I had ears on three computers and three of the executive suite's phone lines.

A month and a half into the program, there was no indication that anyone suspected the security breach. Sure, the silo was home to some of the top wizards in the world, but technomancy was a nascent discipline that precious few ever studied. I'd grown up with nothing *but* tech, however, and with Coileán back at the helm, I had time to play.

The data coming in from Stuart's computer were largely quotidian—e-mails about meeting agendas and notes to aides, for the most part. But for the first time in years, we had access to Council matters, no matter how insignificant. It was only a matter of waiting until something juicy came through. Unfortunately, sorting through the data was a user task, not something I could trust to a program, which meant long nights for me playing catch-up alone in my suite. Coileán didn't have time to help me—which was okay, in all honesty, as I didn't trust him around my machines—and while I'd considered drafting Joey, I didn't want to add the stress to his mind. It wasn't as if Mulligan and his buddies were chatting back and forth about where they were hiding the Fringers, after all.

I was scrolling through e-mails about the upcoming Thanksgiving dinner in the silo late one night when I heard the unmistakable crackle of a gate opening behind me. I spun my chair around, ready to tell off the intruder—everyone in the palace had been made *very* well aware of my feelings regarding gates in the proximity of my servers and other fryable electronics—but there was no one on the other side of the small hole in my wall. The gate itself seemed strange, maybe only four feet tall and uneven around the edges, and I saw nothing but a diffuse, dim glow in the other room. Curious, I rose and peeked through the gate, and I realized that the glow I was seeing was coming from a nightlight in the shape of a smiling flower.

"The heck?" I muttered, trying to pick details out of the dark room, but before I could investigate further, I heard a command in my mind: *She did it in her sleep. Convince her this is a dream.*

"Convince *who*?" I asked, recognizing the realm's familiar voice. She'd left me alone for several years, but I couldn't forget the sound of her thoughts in the back of my head.

Stand aside.

Faerie sounded disquieted, which was unnerving enough on its own, and so I did as she ordered, returning to my swivel chair and watching the gate. "Are you going to tell me what's going on?" I asked.

Before the realm could reply, a little face appeared in the gate's opening, bathed in the bluish-white light of my monitors. A toddler—a kneeling girl wearing a long green nightgown with a pair of bunnies on the chest and clutching the paw of a pink stuffed dog. Her blonde hair had snarled with sleep, and her dark eyes widened in shock when she noticed me, an expression that I'm sure I mirrored well.

I didn't need to ask who she was. Chubby cheeks and baby teeth aside, she was the spitting image of her father.

Her surprise quickly melted into joy, and she crawled off her bed and ran through the gate into my room. "*Daddy!*" she cried, and sprang for my lap.

That word would have been scary for any twenty-one-year-old guy, but I had to think quickly. I caught my niece and lifted her up to hug her, smelling her baby shampoo and the Ivory bars Mom had always favored, and prayed to anyone listening for guidance. "No, sweetheart," I murmured as her arms tightened around my neck, "no, I'm sorry, I'm not your daddy."

She pulled back, confused, and then her face began to fall.

"I'm a friend," I told her. "You're having a very special dream, and I'd like to be your friend. Could we be friends? Would that be okay?"

I repositioned her in my lap and gave her another hug, but even that wasn't enough to overcome her disappointment. "Do you know where my daddy is?" she asked, staring at me with Joey's sad eyes. "Or my mommy?"

"No, I don't," I lied.

Her little shoulders slumped. "I don't have a mommy and daddy. Just a grandma and grandpa. My friends at daycare, they have mommies and daddies."

My heart broke, but I tried not to let on. "I bet you'll find them someday. But not tonight," I said, and carried her back to the gate. "Too much dreaming will make you sleepy tomorrow. Better get back to real sleep."

"Okay," she said as I put her down, then gave me a searching look. "This is *really* a dream?"

"A special, secret dream. Can you keep a secret?" I asked, cringing inside at how creepy that sounded.

But my niece was too young to fully comprehend the

nuances of stranger danger, and she just smiled and nodded.

"Good girl. By the way, what's your name?"

"Roslyn," she replied, then slipped between the realms and climbed onto her bed.

As soon as she was beneath the covers, I closed the gate, then leaned against the wall, focusing on the cool stone against my forehead while I waited for my heart to stop hammering.

Roslyn. I'd held my niece and lied to her face, and I'd sent her right back into that snake pit...

"What the *hell*?" I snapped to the empty room. "*How?*"

The realm sounded tired but relieved. *The child has talent. As I said, she opened a gate in her sleep.*

"But how? Nothing gets through those wards—"

Toula left an exception built in for Helen and Joey together, did she not?

I paused and frowned into space—as per usual, the realm wasn't in a mood to materialize. "Been listening to Toula try to sort through this mess, huh?

It is unavoidable, she replied. *But my understanding of the ward system is that this exception remains open. What is Roslyn if not the combination of her parents?*

"Holy shit," I whispered, letting that sink in. The baby could get through the wards. *By herself.*

I'd panicked just then, but surely she would do it again. Next time, I'd stop her from returning, just slam the gate and keep her safe in Faerie—

No. No, I couldn't do that.

A three-year-old, disappearing from her bed in the middle of the night, taken from an underground facility? That was virtually impossible without magic. Mulligan would blame us, and what would he do to his hostages in return? If I kept Roslyn, would he kill Hel? Or no—maybe Hel was Mulligan's best prize, and instead, he'd kill a handful of Fringers.

I sent her to you, said Faerie, *because I believed you could do the right thing.*

"Yeah, well, this is way above my pay grade," I muttered, and hurried off to find my brother.

Coileán regarded me with disbelief when I told him what had happened, and he asked me to repeat myself, only at half the speed. I did so with the help of a double of scotch from his office bar, which I poured with difficulty due to the tremor in my hand. Once I'd finished and he'd taken a moment to mull it over, he said, "None of this leaves my office, understood? Let me tell the parties who need to be consulted."

I slugged back the rest of my drink, grimacing at the burn. "Got it."

"And not a word to Joey."

My glass was empty, and I suddenly wished for another scotch, if only to help with the sick knot in my stomach. Coileán didn't need to explain himself—I saw the situation as clearly as he did.

If Joey found out about Roslyn's visit, he'd be furious with me for sending her away, but then he'd demand that she be brought to him the next time she made the crossing. That would be bad, but what if he then took advantage of the open gate, stormed into my parents' apartment, and demanded Hel's return? One undertrained faerie against the Arcanum—how well would *that* work? Even if we invaded en masse through Roslyn's bedroom, maybe Mulligan had a kill switch—maybe he'd murder Hel and the Fringers before giving them up. And while Badger had found Hel within Arc 1, she still hadn't spotted the Fringers. What if Joey, in his rage, killed everyone who knew where they'd been hidden before we located them?

Still…

Coileán must have seen me waffling, as he doubled down. "You *can't* tell him, Aid. Not even her name."

"I know, I *know*," I said, and scowled at the coffee table between us. "I get it. It's just…"

"It's Joey," he finished, and sighed. "Moon and stars."

Whether we kept this under wraps for an hour or a decade, when Joey found out, it would come as a knife in the back. He was my best friend, not to mention my brother-in-law, and he was certainly more than just our distant nephew to Coileán. He'd been a wreck for the last three and a half years, worried sick over Hel and their baby. I couldn't, in good conscience, keep news of his daughter from him.

But I had to consider the scales. And when I weighed Joey's feelings against Hel's safety, there was no contest.

"Not a word," I told Coileán. "I swear. This conversation never happened." I put my glass aside and pushed myself from the couch. "But if, hypothetically, she were to return..."

"Can you keep up the charade?"

"If I have to."

There was pity in his eyes when he looked up at me. "I'm sorry to ask it of you, but..."

"Secret's safe," I said, and left him.

I took the long way back to my apartment in the palace, then turned off my monitors and lay on my bed, staring at the ceiling in the dark and trying not to think of the disappointment on Roslyn's face.

I'd sent her back to the silo. I still had nightmares about the fucking place, and yet, I'd pushed her on her way home to that hellhole. She was helpless, just a little blonde kid who took after her daddy...

Who, like me, bore a certain strong resemblance to Titania.

Never mind Mulligan. God, I'd sent her back to my *father*.

"I'm so sorry," I whispered, and lay there unsleeping until dawn lit the sky.

NOVEMBER: FAERIE

I'd known she would be strong—I'd made her that way. And yes, I'd called to her, ever so softly, from the day she drew breath, my attempt to plant within her a longing for her true home. But never had I anticipated that she would come to me so *soon*.

She'd grown old enough to understand that she lacked the parents her peers enjoyed, a mother and father to hold her and dote upon her, but she was still too young to fully comprehend her grandparents' lies. The Carvers had told her that her parents were dead, but what is death to a child barely three years of age? Her mother and father weren't with her, so logically, they were missing and could be found. And her deepest mind, having heard me all her life, made a way for her to search.

I almost directed her gate to Joey. Had she been older and more secure in her abilities, or at least more focused upon her target, she would have found him. Fortunately, her gate was the result of a subconscious act, and I diverted it to Aiden before she woke to find a glowing hole in the wall beside her bed. Seeing her confusion as to his identity, I resolved to send her dreams of her parents in the future— scenes plucked from my memory and Joey's, and replayed for her until she knew whose she was and where she belonged.

When she woke the next morning, she rolled over and sat up, hugging her toy as she frowned at the subterranean darkness. Surely she remembered what had transpired during the night—surely she was attempting to make sense of the unfamiliar.

But then, so much is unfamiliar to small children. I had a chance.

A dream, I whispered to her deepest mind. *Only a dream. Tell no one.*

I repeated it in a calming loop until her door opened and her grandmother lit the overhead light. "Good morning, sweetie," said Rachel, tightening her bathrobe sash. "Are you hungry?"

Roslyn nodded and clambered out of bed.

"Let's go potty first, okay?" Rachel continued, reaching for her hand. She steered Roslyn into the small bathroom down the hall and leaned against the sink as the child tended to herself. "Did you sleep well?" she asked, covering a yawn.

Tell no one.

"Uh-huh," said Roslyn.

"Good." Rachel helped her clean up and ushered her into the kitchen. "Pancakes? It's Tuesday, so you're going to daycare today."

She helped the child into a chair, and Roslyn played with the salt and pepper shakers until a cut-up pancake on a plastic plate was put before her. "Eat while it's hot," Rachel instructed, and straightened as Howard entered the kitchen, already dressed for the day. "Morning, Grandpa. Your breakfast is by the stove."

He grunted, poured coffee, and sat across from Roslyn, who studied his dark green ceremonial robe as if she'd never seen one before. "Why do you wear pajamas to work?" she asked, tilting her head.

"Eat your food," said Howard.

"But why—"

"*Eat*, Roslyn."

"Grandma," she said, glancing toward the sink, "can *I* wear my pajamas to daycare?"

Howard slapped the table, and Roslyn jumped as she turned to see his scowl. "One more word," he warned, "and you'll be excused from the table."

Rachel continued to wash the pan, and finding no help there, Roslyn picked up her next bite and ate in silence.

Another ordinary morning in the Carver home. I breathed a sigh of relief—metaphorically speaking—and turned my attention to the most pressing matter within the realm.

One of Oberon's elder daughters had hosted a large gala during the night, a masque. She'd neglected to invite several of her siblings, which seemed reasonable to me, as they'd been feuding for four months. But the silly children had taken the lack of invitation as a personal affront, and they'd come disguised with the other revelers, intending to do mischief to the hostess at the gala's height. Someone had revealed their presence to her, and she'd confronted them with several more of their siblings. The masque had turned into a brawl in short order, and all that remained of the lakeside manor was smoldering ashes.

Eleanor had called upon Coileán to borrow one of his secure cells overnight while Toula showed her the sequence of events. Her prisoners had been cramped—most of his cells were still being used to house the captives they'd taken from the remains of Mab's court—but I suspected that their situation would soon change. While Eleanor had yet to pass sentence on any of the incarcerated, she had been *quite* busy for hours.

I couldn't say that I approved of her plan, but the court was hers to rule, after all. Nothing she'd done warranted my intervention.

Anyway, the miniature seagulls were an interesting touch.

DECEMBER: RUFUS STOWE

The aide eyed me suspiciously, but then I wasn't exactly a familiar face around the mansion. I had work enough in the settlement to keep me busy from dawn until late in the night, and now a wife on top of that. Granted, marriage had only formalized the reality of our relationship, and we no longer had to sneak about the dorm like students out after curfew, but still, it was crucial that I make time for Poppy, and not only around the big dining room with our young charges. I'd almost declined the invitation that afternoon in favor of a quiet night in with my bride, but she'd insisted that I go. "She's your friend, Rufe," she'd said, and kissed me. "She needs you more than I do tonight. Go pour one out."

"Wait here," the aide told me, stopping in the vestibule to the inner office. While I considered the rippling koi pond set into the white marble floor, the aide rapped twice at the door and cracked it open. "My lady? A *Rufus* to see you?"

He pronounced my name with evident distaste, but I held my tongue.

"Show him in," she called from the office, and the aide beckoned for me to enter.

I paused at the threshold and dipped my head. "My lady."

"Dr. Stowe," she replied with due formality, regarding me from her cluttered wooden desk, then glanced at the aide. "Thank you, you may go."

Once we heard the echo of the outer office door closing, we relaxed. "Hello, Rufus," she said, standing. "Thank you for coming."

I smiled. "How's it going, Ellie?"

"*Eh*. You know." She shrugged and softly laughed, letting one arm flop toward her desk. "I'm seldom bored. Missed you."

There was no one present to see us hug, which was for the best. I knew without question that I was one of my queen's favorites—I could have asked for a hundred acres and a hunting park, and she'd have gladly given it. But the last thing I wanted was to be sucked into court politics, even if my place near the top of the heap was secure, and so Ellie and I maintained our distance. Oh, now, we *spoke*—we'd been chatting by e-mail for years, and our new jobs hadn't changed that—but in-person meetings were infrequent, and usually private matters. Had Poppy not understood, she might well have imagined that we were carrying on an affair.

Nothing could have been further from the truth. I'd met Ellie and Walt in 1975 at a historians' conference in New York. I was a tenured, respected professor with twenty-five years' experience, and they were the young wunderkinds from the University of Durham, only two years married and decades away from conquering their department as a power couple. I liked them immediately. Walt had an easy laugh and a preference for tweed and bowties, but Ellie had a mischievous sparkle in her green eyes, a ready wit, and an impressive command of her field, particularly for a young woman. I'd offered them my assistance in their professional development, seeing myself as both a friend and mentor.

And then, after thirty years' acquaintance, Ellie and I had learned, quite by chance, just how much glamour we'd been using. I was nearing the end of what would have been my mortal lifespan, having lived and worked under a single identity for nine decades and change. My supposedly young protégée was more than seven times my age—and my new queen. She was also recently bereaved, as Walt, a witch, had been murdered about two weeks before.

Exactly *when* in those two weeks he'd died was a subject

of contention with Ellie every time December rolled around. I reminded her that he'd been kidnapped on the thirteenth and presumably beheaded soon thereafter. (I'd made the mistake of asking Badger about it once and received enough details to turn my stomach.) But Walt's enchanted, still-living head had been delivered to Ellie on the sixteenth, and she, not realizing that all spells and enchantments on living things break when crossing the border into Faerie, had carried him over for safekeeping. What was left of her beloved husband had died instantly in her arms.

Ellie blamed herself for Walt's death—there was no getting around that, no matter how much I tried to convince her otherwise. In her mind, it came down to her poor timing. She'd known she was her father's heir for more than a year before Walt was snatched, but she'd ignored it and gone on with life as usual. Had she accepted the responsibility, come clean with Walt about her inheritance, and brought him with her, he'd probably be alive. Instead, unwilling to give up her life to run the court or admit to Walt that she'd been born a high lady, she had done nothing until Coileán and Aiden paid her a visit. Walt had been understanding and willing to accompany her, but he'd asked to go to one last conference—and that had been the end of that. Walt's death had been gruesome and senseless, a horsehead in the bed from Coileán's hellion of a daughter, and Ellie was left to pick up and carry on without him.

"I still write him letters," she'd confessed to me the previous December, once we had a few drinks in us. "Of course, he's not written back, but...part of me hopes, you know?"

That afternoon was the fourth anniversary. Ellie wore a black sweater over slim black trousers, a professional sort of ensemble unless one knew how to view it, and jewelry of jet set in gold. We sat together in one of her small, well-appointed parlors, drinking brandy and snacking on a platter of nachos as the light outside shifted toward golden, talking about everything and nothing. Wait certainly came up, but the conversation veered in other directions. Ellie just didn't want to be alone with his ghost.

"Six months is an accomplishment, especially under these conditions, and I'm thrilled for the both of you," she was saying, when someone knocked at the parlor door. Frowning, she called the intruder into the room, and the door opened to reveal my brother, still in his chef's whites. "My lady," said Luce, "sorry to bother you. If you still don't want dinner, I thought I'd go see my mum and dad unless there's something…" He spotted me in the shadows and grinned. "Rufe! What the devil are you doing here, boy?"

"I was *invited*," I replied, standing to give him a brief hug. "You're interrupting."

"And everything's sorted here," said Ellie, gesturing toward the nachos. "Say hello to your family for me, Lucian."

He and I smiled at each other. "Uh-oh," I said, "*Lucian*. Someone's in trouble."

Luce snorted, plucked my glass from the table, and drained it. "Mind yourself, little brother. My lady, if this scoundrel proves to be a bother, let me know, and I'll deal with him."

"That won't be necessary," she replied, but barely hid her amusement. "Have a good evening."

"And you. Rufe," he added with a quick nod of acknowledgement, then turned to go. Before he reached the door, however, he paused and looked back at us. "Have you seen Lilliput?" he asked me.

"Lilliput?" I echoed, bemused.

Luce chuckled. "You've got to get out of the settlement more often. It's…*impressive*," he said, then nodded to Ellie again and slipped out.

I refilled my glass and gave her a questioning look. "Dare I ask?"

She topped hers off as well and took a deep sip. "A penal project of mine. Somewhat unusual. Promise you won't be horrified?"

In a former life, perhaps the space had been a large parlor. It offered a lovely view of the ornamental lake and Ellie's flock of swans, and the walls were made of the carved marble she'd used in the more public rooms of the mansion. But the entrance was blocked by a piece of what appeared to be Plexiglas rising a yard above the floor—the *hallway* floor, at least. The room's floor seemed to be much deeper, from what I could see through the water, though it was difficult to judge distance with the waning sunlight. Really, it was like opening an unassuming bedroom door and finding oneself confronted by an indoor swimming pool.

The Plexiglas wall continued around the room, a sleek protective surface between the marble and the little sea. And it *was* a sea of sorts—tiny waves splashed against the wall, some with even tinier whitecaps. Glancing up, I saw the cause: the room had self-contained weather, puffy clouds drifting and dissipating between the sea and the ceiling, both of which were beginning to streak with the colors of the sunset. A sourceless warm breeze blew against my face, as though I'd wandered into a tropical spring.

"This way," said Ellie, gesturing a ladder into being, and brightened the light of the room to midday with a wave of her hand.

I followed her up onto the almost transparent catwalk network crisscrossing the room. Below us, I could make out perhaps four score little islands of a variety of shapes and sizes, some barren hillocks of volcanic rock, others sandy mounds topped with miniature forests of palms and grasses. The gentle waves broke against the beaches with an arrhythmic swish and sizzle. I was about to ask Ellie why she'd built a dollhouse version of the tropics when I noticed movement on one of the larger islands.

The figure was male, I surmised, seeing as it was wearing only a loincloth of leaves. Its skin had burned, and its hair, almost as pale as dandelion fluff, hung down its back in a ratty ponytail. Leaning closer, I could make out its sullen face. It was indeed a tiny man, but not a piq like six-inch Kuni—it was smaller and wingless, and it appeared to be nocking a tiny bow.

I blocked the arrow he shot at my face with a weak shield, and the sliver dropped harmlessly into the sea.

As I walked over the room and looked more closely, I saw similar figures on many of the islands, men and women sporting makeshift clothes of leaves and bits of rags. Some had built lean-tos on their islands. Most had campfires on the beach, though one ash-covered island suggested that fire safety wasn't everyone's priority. A few had built little rafts—two with sails—which bobbed on the waves like bath toys.

When I made my way back to Ellie, she looked almost guilty. "May I be frank?" I whispered.

"Please."

"What the hell, Ellie?"

She chuckled and gazed over the side at one of the primitive sailboats. "A few of my siblings failed to take to heart my rules against rioting, brawling, and arson. I'm giving them a chance to think about their actions, work out their differences."

"By dropping them on Alcatraz Archipelago? How are you even keeping them in there?"

"Binds," she replied, arching an eyebrow at my undisguised shock. "It's simpler than I'd anticipated, and it's become easier with practice."

"You've got *how* many of them bound?"

"Twenty-three. Keeps them small and unable to enchant, so they've got time now to worry about real problems instead of the petty bullshit they've been fighting about." She gestured at the intricate ward system around the room. "They can't drown, no matter how much they try. If they get close, they immediately appear on the nearest beach. They can't kill themselves or each other, though injury isn't out of the question. I've stocked a few of the islands with populations of miniaturized feral hogs and sheep, and they've got all the bananas, coconuts, and breadfruit they can eat. Plenty of minnows in the sea. The water is fresh, and the area scrubs itself of bodily waste once a day. If they'd work together, they could have an easy time of it."

"But."

She smirked. "Precisely. I scattered them randomly, hoping that their predicament would make them set aside their differences and cooperate once they learned to build boats. So far, only two of them are at all competent at sea." She squinted, then pointed out the rafts with sails. "The one fishing off to the right is Lianne—she's resourceful, that girl. The one that just beached is Karl. He's better at getting about, but then he's been in time-out since last November."

"A month sounds reasonable—"

"No, no, *last* November. He's been with me for a bit over a year."

"My God," I murmured, peering closer at Karl's island. He secured the raft, then scurried around the beach, taking advantage of the extended daylight to check the thin ropes he'd strung between trees and posts.

"An alarm tripwire," Ellie quietly explained. "It's hung with bits of seashell and bone. Should make a noise if someone stumbles into it."

That wasn't Karl's only defense. He'd built a treehouse deep in the little forest of his island, and though I couldn't get a clear view through the canopy, I saw the defensive wall he'd made of sharpened logs. "Clever," I murmured.

"He's learned. Every so often, I send a strong storm—not a hurricane," she assured me, "but something sufficiently wet and unpleasant. The treehouse has withstood them so far, and he needn't worry about flooding."

"And what if someone comes along and tries to burn the place down?"

"He's actually made buckets from hollow trees and sap. Keeps a few filled up there, plus his weapons. But he hasn't had to use them. As I said, only Lianne is at all competent at sea, and she's too busy harrying a few of our sisters to bother with Karl."

I watched Karl work for another few minutes. His skin had tanned to golden brown, and his blond hair ended in a jagged cut just north of his shoulders—a DIY job, I surmised. Unlike the others I'd seen, he wore pants made of yellow cloth, apparently the same material as his raft's sail. "The epitome of fashion," I said.

"You like those trousers, do you? That was a dinner napkin. I drop in bonus items every so often, and he made good use of one. A few of them have tried to use pigskin or sheepskin, but no one so far seems to have worked out hide preparation."

"I wouldn't know where to begin," I confessed.

"Patience, meticulous removal of flesh, and a good soak with some brains, for starters. Then again, so few of them have been able to hunt successfully. Either they haven't yet found the game or they're inept with their weapons. If only they worked together, they might have a chance. Ah, well. Seen enough?"

"Sure," I said, and followed her off the catwalk.

Ellie lowered the lights, resulting in a faint chorus of squeaked complaints, and false stars began to pop out in the ceiling. "I designed the sky to mirror the constellations visible in the South Pacific," she said, and gave the room one last look before closing and locking the door. "*So.* That would be Lilliput."

I accompanied Ellie back to our drinks and nachos, but I couldn't stop thinking of Karl, marooned in a tropical prison for the last year, and of his less well-acclimated fellow inmates. "How long do you intend to keep them there?" I asked as she poured a fresh round.

"I haven't decided. It's making my life easier, to be honest. I mean, managing the binds does tire me, but the deterrent effect has been better than I'd hoped. I dropped everyone but Karl in there last month, and since then, I've had only three complaints, all of them against Coileán's people. The loudest voices in the court have been oddly quiet," she said with a knowing smile. "Can't imagine why."

"People aren't lining up for a forced vacation in paradise, eh?"

"No. And I've made it slightly less enjoyable by opening the room to spectators. I suppose it's rather humiliating to have the court witness your punishment."

I drank my brandy, stalling while I thought of a polite form for my next question. "Aren't you at all concerned of what will happen once you *do* release them?"

Ellie smiled and crossed her legs. "What, you think I should fear assassins in the night?"

"Honestly?"

"My brother Hugo survived my first little terrarium, and he's been the better for it," she replied. "Comes by almost daily to mock the others, but I can live with that. As for would-be assassins, they'd best hope that they kill me." Her green eyes hardened. "I've made it abundantly clear that attempts on my life will be treated with the utmost severity."

"Probably not a bad idea," I said between sips.

We drank for a moment in silence. As I reached for a chip, Ellie quietly asked, "What do you suppose Walt would say? About the archipelago, I mean."

I'd never seen her look so uncertain, and in that moment, I was grateful that my mental defenses were decently strong.

"I think he'd have questions," I told her, and ate another perfect nacho.

In truth, I thought Walt would be appalled, but I didn't elaborate on my answer, and Ellie didn't press me.

"So," she said, scooping a bit of guacamole off the platter, "how's school these days?"

—YEAR FIVE—

APRIL: FATHER PAUL MCGILL

The wedding was, without question, the strangest I'd ever conducted.

Neither the bride nor the groom was Catholic, but that hadn't been a problem for me for some time. When you're the only priest in town and someone wants a church wedding, you do your part and trust God to overlook your failings. So far, all six couples I'd counseled and joined at the altar remained together, and three had little ones on the way. The settlement was growing, and if it could do so within the bonds of holy matrimony, so much the better.

But this wasn't to be a church wedding. Badger and Seamus wanted a priest who understood their situation and wouldn't bother with such trivialities as a marriage license, and I was the man for the job.

There was the small matter of getting everyone together, however. Badger wouldn't cross into Faerie, as no one was sure whether Nath would find out and mark that as the end of the ceasefire. I was reluctant to go the other way, however. I was nearly seventy-five, and at my age, I didn't want to experience the effect of my missing four years slamming into me at once. The solution, then, was to conduct the ceremony through a gate. Conveniently, there was a tiny gate already in existence between the wall of the Rigby apartment's den and Colin's office, which the Fringe extraction team had been using for years to shuttle refugees into Faerie. But there was a catch: in case someone from the Arcanum was monitoring the background magic around Rigby, the gate couldn't be widened for long.

We decided that five minutes would be sufficient for the basics.

Shortly before the appointed hour, well-wishers for the couple clustered around the bookshelves where the gate was hiding, some already holding flutes of champagne that Colin had put out for the occasion. Naturally, he was in attendance, as was Eleanor. Vivi and Hal had come on behalf of the Fringe, Aiden had slipped in with Joey, and all of Seamus's family had arrived together, as Val and Toula had stopped by town to pick up Tom and Mary Malone. Seeing the four of them standing together warmed my heart. I hadn't known what to expect when the Malones arrived, two of the few of us in town who were truly mundane, but they were a charming couple, albeit deeply concerned about the safety of their son and Badger in the other realm. The settlement was small enough that the good gossip inevitably reached me, and so I knew that Seamus's aunt and uncle had stopped in to meet his adopted parents and try to help them acclimate. There was, as far as I could tell, no tension among them—Seamus's parents loved him fiercely, and they were happy that he'd found other relatives who cared about him, too. Mary held a camera in one hand and a wad of tissues in the other, and she beamed at anyone who chanced to look her way.

Right on time, I heard a female voice call through the wall, "We're ready! Are y'all?"

"Ready and waiting," I replied, and stepped back a pace as the hole widened into a doorway of sorts.

The bride and groom were already in place, arms linked and grinning. Seamus had donned a good dark suit for the occasion, but Badger was resplendent in a cream-colored pantsuit and pale blue heels. She held a small bouquet of red roses tied with a white satin ribbon. Behind them, I saw the rest of the guests: Amy and Kip, and then Arnold, Badger's only expected family.

I heard the shutter click as Mary began snapping photos and sniffling with happiness.

"Dearly beloved," I said, stepping to the side so that those in both realms could have a decent view, "you know why we're here, and the clock is running." That earned a chuckle from the couple, and I pressed on. "Seamus Charles Malone?"

He nodded.

"Hannah Kathleen Parsons?"

"Present," she replied.

"Fantastic. Do each of you take the other to be your spouse, to have and to hold from this day forward, for better or for worse, for richer or for poorer, in sickness and in health, to love and to cherish, from this day forward until death do you part?"

"I do," they chorused, their smiles widening as they traded glances.

Amy stepped forward with a pair of gold rings, and they quickly slipped them on each other's hand.

"Any objections?" I asked, looking around for form's sake. After a few seconds' pause, I turned back to the couple and nodded. "Seems to be in order, then. What God has joined together, let no man put asunder. And with that, I pronounce you husband and wife. You may—oh, good, you beat me to it," I said as the two embraced to a round of applause.

"About time!" Tom called behind me, and the couple laughed when they came up for air.

Having fulfilled my role, I stood out of the way and let the others have a moment with the bride and groom. Colin passed around champagne through the gate and gave a brief toast, but everyone seemed to know when it was time to step back and let the Malones have a moment.

"*Finally*," said Tom, grinning from ear to ear. "Never thought I'd see the day. We're thrilled for you, we truly are."

Mary, whose mascara was already smudged, smiled at them and dabbed at her eyes. "Look at you. I'm so proud…" She honked into her tissues, then laughed helplessly at herself. "These are happy tears, I promise."

"Love you, too, Mary," said Badger, whose eyes seemed a bit misty by then as well.

"I love you both," she replied. "Hannah, I mean this sincerely, there's no one else I'd want for my boy. Kathy and Brian would be so pleased if they were here, you know that."

She nodded and blinked hard.

"You've always been family, you know, but it's official now," Mary told her. "Finally got my daughter, didn't I? And as for you," she said, turning to her son, "no more running off, eh?"

"Come on, Mam, it was just the once!" he protested, laughing.

"Oh, 'the once,' he says! We should have done this twenty-five years ago!"

"*Mam...*"

Badger took Seamus's hand and pulled him close. "He's stuck with me now. No worries, Mary."

"Yeah, she's a sleepwalker," Amy chimed in from behind them. "If he runs, she'll just hunt him down."

Badger grinned, then turned to her. "Here, love," she said, handing off her bouquet. "I believe this is yours. And with that," she said, turning around again, "we'll be off."

"We'll be on our glorious three-night honeymoon in Savannah if anyone needs us," said Seamus, "but unless there's an emergency—"

"There won't be," Eleanor interrupted, waving them on. "Congratulations. Now *shoo.*"

The newlyweds were still laughing as Colin shrank the gate, and once his bookshelves were back in order, he plucked another flute from the bar. "And they're hitched. This isn't going to drink itself, people."

I had a second glass, then a third, toasting along with anything and everything that came to the wedding guests' minds. As the party began to wind down, however, I caught Joey standing alone by the window and joined him for a quiet word. "Keep the faith, son," I murmured, squeezing his arm. "She's alive. You know that."

He sighed softly. "Do you think she hears Badger? When Badger tells her I love her, do you think she gets the message?"

I didn't know, but I didn't want to say as much. Instead, I wrapped my arm around his back, and we stood there together, staring out at the roses, until the others had gone on their way.

MAY: VALERIUS

There was one failsafe method of catching a moment with Paul, but it necessitated an awkward wait in the back pew of the settlement church.

The place disconcerted me. The building itself was innocuous, a high-ceilinged room studded with narrow windows of colorful glass, but the decoration at the front of the room made me squirm internally. Oh, I knew *why* it was there—Paul had explained his belief in a crucified god—but seeing it hanging over the altar in life-size proportions was deeply disturbing. I'd asked him after one such uncomfortable wait how his congregation remained unbothered by the sight. "Crucifixes are nothing new to cradle Catholics," he'd said. "Primary symbol of the faith, you know?"

Then again, no one else sitting in there had witnessed a live version of the execution frozen in wood in front of them—the *sanitized* version in wood, I should say. When I was ten, one of my father's friends was murdered by his slave. As usual, the other slaves in the household were crucified with him as a warning. My father took my elder brothers and me to see them: fifty-six men and women, some old, many young, all naked and bloodied. By the time we arrived, the weakest had died, and the legs of the strongest were being broken with heavy mallets to speed the process along. I'd vomited, and my brothers had laughed.

Looking away from the gruesome decoration, I found that the wriggling baby two pews in front of me had turned around over his mother's shoulder and was staring my way.

I waved. The baby grinned and turned his face into the safety of his mother's neck, then chanced a second look. Another wave made him giggle, and his father glanced back and smiled wearily. The child and I kept up our game for the duration of the service, much to his delight, and when the family stood for the final procession, his mother turned around and mouthed *Thank you.*

She hadn't recognized me as a stranger, for which I was grateful. It was understandable that the Fringers were nervous around the rest of us, but I hadn't gone to the settlement to cause offense.

A teenage boy led the procession out, followed by Paul, who sang lustily, if not well. The priest caught my eye in passing, and his brows raised in query. I nodded and spoke into his thoughts: *A word in private, if you have time.*

I waited where I sat for the others to file out—Paul stood at the door, shaking hands and greeting the children with all manner of hugs and hand slaps—and when the last had departed, he closed the heavy doors and beckoned for me to follow. "Sure, I've got time," he said. "Let me get this off, and we'll go to the house."

I stood outside his office while he disrobed and put his outer garments away. "Guessing you didn't stop by for the homily, huh?" he joked through the open door.

"I'm afraid I missed it."

"Well, you didn't miss *much.*" He smoothed his thinning gray hair in the wardrobe mirror, then removed his glasses and polished them with a handkerchief. "The Lectionary wasn't overly inspiring this week, so I pulled from my files and tweaked. Hard to believe we've been here long enough to cycle all the way through the readings," he added, and closed the door. Come on, let's get out of here before the Altar Guild catches me loitering."

"The what?"

"Susan Genovese," he replied, leading me outside toward the adjacent house, a modest affair of gray stone that seemed to have sprouted from the church's side. "Does the flowers and such. She's a lovely lady, but if you give her an ear and an opening, you'll lose at least an hour."

Paul had left his computer, books, and a notepad on his kitchen table, and he hurriedly swept the mess aside. "Have a seat," he offered. "Get you a beer?"

"If you're drinking…"

"Nah, just water for me," he said, and flipped the tap. "I overestimated the crowd today and consecrated *slightly* too much wine—"

"Which couldn't go to waste?" I finished.

"Which can't be poured down the drain. My crucifer today was thirteen, and my altar servers were barely sixteen—you saw those kids, yeah? Wouldn't do to send them home tipsy." Still, he pulled a beer from the refrigerator for me and popped off the cap.

I knew of refrigerators and other such appliances from my sister, who had fully stocked her apartment's kitchen and didn't mind explaining the machines' uses. They weren't truly like the versions she'd known in the mortal realm, she said—those had run on electricity, whereas her homemade appliances ran on magic—but they accomplished the same ends. Whichever of the Stowe boys had designed the Fringers' kitchens had done much the same for them.

"So," said Paul, sinking into the chair beside me with his glass of water, "what's on your mind, Val?"

I sampled the beer and was pleasantly surprised—whoever had taken to brewing in the settlement knew what he was doing. "Can you keep this in confidence?"

"To a point. I won't breathe a word of this if you don't want me to, but…" He tapped his temple with two fingers. "No defenses, remember? If confidentiality means life or death, then you probably shouldn't tell me."

His matter-of-factness and lack of obvious fear was refreshing. There was nothing imposing about him—Paul was about my height but softer, an elderly man with a wrinkled face and a paunch. In truth, he reminded me of my father's uncle when he smiled. There was kindness in his dark eyes, but there was confidence, too. Mundane though he was, Paul seemed to have made his peace with magic in a way that most Fringers had not.

"Nothing so serious," I told him, "but I'd prefer that it remain between us."

"You have my word. Fire when ready."

As I drank, I put my thoughts in order. "You know Coileán fairly well, yes?" I said.

Paul mulled that over, then nodded. "Probably as well as anyone. I've known him for, oh…fifty-one years, give or take a few months. Guess that doesn't sound like much to you, but—"

"No, you've known him far longer than I have. Coileán has always been something of a mystery to the court."

"I mean, he *did* stay gone for a few centuries," Paul replied. "You're not looking for dirt on him, are you?"

"I'd like to keep my head in its current location," I said, smirking back at him. "But…were you with him when he developed feelings for Meghan?"

Paul whistled low and nodded. "Tried to break that up before it started. He didn't take my advice."

"How long was it before he fell for her?"

He squinted at the ceiling. "Weeks, maybe. Could have been less. She moved in with him the day they met, you know. He gave her a job, she needed a place to live, and voila. She was engaged to someone else, so I suppose whatever he felt for her at first was unrequited, but when he skipped town, she was *desperate*. Poor kid," he muttered, shaking his head. "I screwed that up. Should have told her the truth about him as soon as he bailed, but…"

"You were afraid?" I ventured.

"No. He was my friend," said Paul. "My partner. He thought he was doing the right thing, and I wasn't going to betray his trust. And we know how well *that* worked out, but what can I say? I'm only human, right?"

"That's not actually a bad thing."

He chuckled. "Has its moments. But back to your

question—he fell hard and fast. We're talking meteor on a collision course. Now, dare I ask why you're traipsing down memory lane?" His expression veered toward pained. "*Please* tell me this has nothing to do with Eleanor."

"*No.* The gods have been merciful."

"Oh, good." He shuddered and took a sip of water. "Someone else?"

I hesitated. "It...seems that way."

"Mm. Something new and sudden?"

"No, which is why I asked about Meghan. This has been growing slowly, but these days, if he's not working, he's probably with her. I thought I saw it coming a year ago, but it's as if he's just now waking to the fact that his feelings for her are more than platonic."

"Colin's not a master of romance," said Paul, which was perhaps the understatement of the day.

"I get the sense that he...he's not *infatuated*, but he's realizing his own desires. I think it concerns him, in truth."

"Could be a little scary. The first blush of love can be a heady experience."

"Not to be rude," I replied, "but what would you know of that?"

Paul's smile was enigmatic. "I wasn't always a priest. So, who is she? Someone within at least a few centuries of his age?" he asked hopefully.

"Toula," I mumbled.

"*Toula?*" He leaned back in his chair and considered the matter, his hands clasped over his stomach. "I mean, she's not the worst girlfriend he could choose, but..."

"Exactly."

"So, then, are you worried about this as *his* friend or as *her* brother?"

"Both," I confessed.

He grunted. "Fair enough. Does she reciprocate?"

I could only shrug. "If she does, she hasn't told me. Has Coileán mentioned anything to you?"

"No, but that doesn't mean anything. I haven't seen him

since Badger and Seamus's wedding." He drained his glass and set it aside. "Well, now, did you come to me for a sounding board or for advice? I wouldn't want to presume."

I spread my hands. "You're the one who's been through this with him. If you have advice, I'll hear it."

He leaned forward and steepled his finger. "Then I suggest that you let it ride. Sorry, idiom," he said as my brow furrowed. "Don't do anything yet. Wait and see where this goes—he might snap out of it, or there might be something to this. No sense in confronting him now. He'd probably just get defensive and deny everything."

"That sounds reasonable," I replied, propping my head on my fingertips.

"But you don't like it, because Toula." He smiled when I glanced up. "Come on, man, I'm not *blind*. You don't want baby sister getting her feelings hurt."

"Would *you*?"

Paul laughed to himself. "Let me tell you a little story. I'm the youngest of seven. Three boys in a row, three girls, and then me. Once my brothers went off to college and joined the army, *someone* had to stick up for our sisters' honor. Unfortunately, the girls had a habit of dating football players." He rose to refill his glass at the sink. "My youngest older sister, Mary Ellen, was only a year older than me, and she was gorgeous. She took up with a boy on the defensive line. He went on to the NFL draft, so that should give you some idea of what a beast we're talking about."

It didn't, but I kept my ignorance to myself.

"Anyway, Mary Ellen came home crying one afternoon, and when I bugged her enough, she told me that the knuckle-dragger had been seeing another girl on the side. So I did what any good brother would do in 1961 in North Carolina: I called him out on it in public, and we had ourselves a good old-fashioned schoolyard brawl."

"And you…showed him the error of his ways?"

"With these?" he asked, flexing his doughy arms. "*Hell*, no. I'm not a fighter. I used to be able to throw a punch every so often and get lucky, but that guy had a head and a hundred pounds on me. He broke my left arm and three ribs before his coach got a leash on him, and I got to stay home from school for the rest of the week with two black eyes and a concussion." He returned to the table and winced as his knees bent. "If I'd been smart about it, I'd have stayed out of Mary Ellen's business, but that was my sister crying her heart out in the bathroom, you know? Sometimes a fellow sees red and pulls some *dumb* stunts. Now, that was me at sixteen. What happens when *you* blow your top?"

I took a long drink of beer. "Nothing pleasant."

"Figured. So if I were you, I'd sit back and see how this goes instead of running in like an enraged gorilla to break up something that might be nothing more than a crush."

"You say that," I retorted, "but if it were your sister—"

"Oh, I'd be antsy, too. Once it was just the girls and me at home, I got nervous every time a new date showed up at the front door—you know, is this some punk I'm going to have to try to fight? But all three of the girls ended up marrying boys they dated in high school, and they had three or four kids apiece, and I made it to graduation with my thick skull intact." He smiled faintly and shook his head. "Toula's not some lovesick teenager, and from what I've been told, she's not the naïve kid that Meg was. How old is she now, forty?"

"Forty-two."

"Then she probably knows what she's doing. You're in an awkward place, I get it, but I suggest butting out and letting them decide what, if anything, is going on between them."

"I suppose you're right," I mumbled after a moment, and finished my drink. "Thanks for your time."

"My door's open," said Paul, pushing himself from his chair as I stood. "And as I said, this stays between us." He hesitated, then added, "I, uh…I'd like to avoid a repeat of what happened last time. If you see something particularly troubling…"

"I'll be back," I assured him, and opened a gate to my quarters.

When I knocked on Toula's door a few minutes later, she was flushed but grinning, her hair droopy with sweat and her shirt damp in odd patches. "Hey!" she said, pulling me into the apartment. "Come see, come see."

She hurried me into her padded practice room and pointed to an intricate ward construction in the corner, a glowing lattice of gently pulsing channels. Beneath its dome was a second ward system, as complex as the first but more irregular, all rising over a replica of the Arcanum's decoy trailer park. "Watch," said Toula. "Any time, now…"

The inner wards collapsed in a soundless implosion, and Toula clenched her fist in victory. "*Yes!*" she cried. "Catastrophic ward failure in seventeen minutes!"

I puzzled over her project. "Congratulations?"

"Thank you! Still has a long way to go, but…" She noticed my bemusement and laughed. "Okay, that was a model of the silo's ward system. I built one over it that's strong enough to almost completely block magic from getting inside. Even here, with the higher magic concentration, the silo wards failed in under twenty minutes. First run-through was twenty-three minutes, so I'm making progress."

"So," I said, rubbing my chin, "the idea now is for you to return to the silo, throw this new ward system together, and wait for the Arcanum's to go down?"

She sobered. "In a perfect world, yeah. In practice, I've still got two problems: building my wards quickly enough to avoid detection, and draining the silo wards before someone gets smart and opens gates within the silo to keep them powered. Ideally, I need to work out wards that can take the silo's down in under a minute, and I need to be able to build them in Montana in about the same time frame. Nothing to it." She stared at the replica trailer park and sighed. "It needs a lot of work. But any progress is still progress, right?"

"If anyone can do it, little sister, it's you."

She smiled and shoved her shoulder into mine. "You and Coileán have been reading the same book of encouraging platitudes, huh?"

"I meant that!" I protested, and followed her out of the practice room. "What else has Coileán been saying?"

"Eh, the usual—we'll find a way, the Fringers are alive somewhere, he's totally going to kick my ass at Monopoly one of these nights. I'd settle for two of three."

"Monopoly?"

Her smile veered toward the evil end of the spectrum. "Oh, someone's never *played*. Are you on shift tonight?"

"No…"

"Come by after dinner, then. You can both lose to me. I mean, he's won several times to date," she admitted, "but his current losing streak is twenty-one games. Your odds are decent."

I considered the invitation, weighing it against the scheduling I'd put off for the last three days. "Coileán plays often, does he?"

"Few times a week. Guess you could say we've gotten into a habit."

The thought of Coileán sitting unsupervised with my sister shifted the balance, and I slung my arm around Toula's shoulders. "I'd be delighted to join you. Perhaps you should teach me the rules in advance."

AUGUST: STUART PURCELL

Kindergarten drop-off on the first day of school was always a madhouse at Wright's Mill. Parents trickled in with their little ones, clinging to hands or backpack straps and offering reassurance in the saccharine tones that only work on the very young. Some kids had screaming, kicking meltdowns in the lobby, while others took off running for their new classrooms, leaving their parents in need of tissue and a hug. I was among the few teachers who got to appreciate the circus from a distance—the music teacher, one of the two gym coaches, the librarian, and I were the only ones without homerooms of our own, and so tradition dictated that we take our coffee in the front lobby to watch the parade and ostensibly welcome the students.

But that year, I was on my own. The coaches were busy with last-minute maintenance on the football field, the music teacher had a flat tire, and the librarian was subbing with the sixth graders for the computer teacher, whose flight out of Cozumel had been delayed by weather. Bereft of my usual companions, I put my coffee in a thermos, collected a stack of the best of the previous year's artwork, and started redoing one of the lobby bulletin boards as the kids arrived. After a few minutes' work, I was roped into assisting with the traffic flow as well, as drop-off was a madhouse. The problem was the four-year-olds, who were unexpectedly down to a single teacher. Parents who'd come through earlier that month to meet Mrs. Egerton were concerned to find themselves directed to Ms. Roche, who was all of twenty-five and overwhelmed to be tasked with thirty charges who were barely more than toddlers. It couldn't be helped—Paula, the preschool veteran, had suffered a stroke two days before school started, and word from Billings was that they'd found a brain tumor. She wouldn't be back any time soon, and while the county scrambled to find a competent replacement, poor Janie was on her own.

Somewhere between guiding a fresh batch of confused parents to the right room and stapling a few more paintings to the board, I looked around and found a small girl slouching against the wall, hugging herself. She was a tiny thing, a chubby-cheeked kindergartener with a pink dress and pigtails, and as there wasn't an adult anywhere nearby to claim her, I did the responsible thing and put down my staple gun. "Hello, there," I said, squatting to be on her eye level. "I'm Mr. Galloway. What's your name, sweetheart?"

She sniffed, and it didn't take a genius to deduce that she was on the verge of tears. "Roslyn," she mumbled.

A blonde four-year-old named *Roslyn*.

My blood ran cold, but I tried not to show it. "Roslyn," I repeated with a plastered-on smile. "Isn't that pretty. Are you in Ms. Roche's class?"

She nodded, but her lip quivered. "I want to go home."

"But you're going to have so much fun today," I said. "And you have all those new friends to meet. Don't you want to come see your classroom?"

In reply, her dark eyes filled.

I glanced down the hall and spotted Janie, who was dealing with a knot of irate parents. "You know," I told Roslyn, "you don't have to go in there right now. Want to come help me in the art studio for a few minutes?" Sensing that a meltdown was imminent, I deployed my magic weapon: "I have cookies."

She swiped one little fist across her eyes. "What kind?"

"Oreos. Is that okay?"

Roslyn nodded, then took hold of the finger I offered her and followed me upstairs.

I hadn't intended to abscond with a new student, but I

decided I'd done no harm, as Roslyn seemed to cheer up once she had two cookies in front of her. She and I sat opposite each other at a paint-stained table, me eating the Oreos as nature intended and Roslyn busily twisting them apart and scraping the cream with her front teeth. "I'm sorry I don't have any milk," I told her, offering her another hit of chocolate from the package. "Just coffee creamer, and that would be yucky."

She considered me with curiosity, her mouth dotted with black crumbs. "Why are you wearing a dress?"

"It's not a dress. It's a caftan," I explained.

"It looks like a dress."

"Maybe," I allowed. "But it's very comfortable."

Apparently, she wasn't desperate to learn more about Moroccan fashion. "My dress is new, and it's *swishy*," she announced, then slid off her chair to twirl in circles as a demonstration.

I made the proper sounds of admiration as the first bell rang, then slipped her one more cookie for the road and convinced her to give her classroom a try. "If you don't like it," I said, walking her through the emptied hallway, "come find me."

She grinned when I dropped her off—the chocolate bits between her teeth were a dead giveaway that she'd had a second breakfast—and I waved to Janie as Roslyn wandered into the chaos of playtime. When the kids seemed occupied, I gave their overwhelmed teacher a questioning look and a thumbs-up. Janie nodded wearily, and I mouthed *Namaste* and slightly bowed before making my escape.

I'd assumed that would be the end of it—some kids were just a little shy on their first day—but the next afternoon, as I prepared to lecture the seniors about the Lascaux cave paintings, the studio door creaked opened, and I found Roslyn peering through the crack. "Hi, there," I said as the older kids tittered. "Couldn't take any more kindergarten, huh?"

She shook her head.

"Do you want to draw a picture?"

That evoked an excited nod, and I let her sit in the corner on a box of computer paper with an old lap desk and a basket of crayons. She eagerly scribbled at first, but as the period went on, I caught her watching the slideshow and smiled to myself. When the seniors filed out, I escorted Roslyn back to class, told frazzled Janie where she'd been, and assured her that it was no problem—if I could take a kid or two off her hands for a few minutes, I didn't mind.

Roslyn was back the next morning, then twice on Thursday. On Friday afternoon, she gave me her latest drawing, a stick figure with gray hair and a purple splotch over the crude limbs. "That's you," she said proudly, beaming up at me.

I knelt and gave her a quick hug. "That's the nicest portrait anyone's ever made of me," I said, which wasn't a lie, and promised to put it on my refrigerator at home. "Can you sign it for me?"

It took her a moment's concentration, but she managed to scrawl *ROS* in the corner. Sure, the S was backwards, but two out of three wasn't bad.

I kept my promise, and the picture went onto my fridge with a magnet from the Missoula Art Museum. I sat at my kitchen table for a time and stared at the drawing as if contemplating its artistic merit—there was little, but she got points for effort—and then I picked up my phone and asked the universe, as always, to never let my subterranean neighbors overhear my conversations.

Three days before, I had checked the kindergarten roster for full names. It was time to finally pass certain information on.

The call was answered quickly—it was dinnertime in Virginia—and Badger gave me the number I needed. "We're a touch off-sync," she added, "so you should be close to lining up, time-wise."

I thanked her and hung up, then dialed and waited through two rings, three, four. Just before the voicemail clicked on, I heard a man ask a cautious, "Hello?"

"It's Stuart, Joey," I said.

There was a sharp intake of breath on the other end. "Stuart, hi, I'm sorry, I didn't recognize your number—"

"No problem. I just, uh…" I paused, trying to think of the phrasing least likely to upset him. "School started back this week. There's a little girl in the 4K class named Roslyn Carver."

Silence.

And then I heard him murmur, "Do you think…"

I didn't think—I *knew*. Aiden had warned me about her and about what we weren't to tell Joey.

"She looks just like you," I told him. "I'm sorry, I haven't been able to snap a picture—it's sketchy for older male teachers to be taking covert photos of the little girls, you know? But I'll see what I can do."

His voice quavered. "Is she…is she okay?"

"Seems happy. She's adjusting to school. Sweet kid. Can't really draw for shit right now, but that's to be expected."

He emitted a strangled sound that might have been laughter.

"I'll look out for her, Joey," I promised. "And I'll call when I can. But we need to keep this short, you know…"

"Yeah, sorry. I'm sorry. *Thank you*," he said, and was gone.

NOVEMBER: COILEÁN

It didn't feel right to plop a chair in the grass beside Meggy's grave. Even a bench felt unearned. No matter what posture I took, I would inevitably be speaking down to her, but regardless, I didn't deserve a seat.

So as usual, I sat on the ground by the white rosebush that served as her headstone and kept vigil in the oak grove.

November twentieth was the one day a year when I insisted that my guards leave me. What I did with Meggy, I did in solitude, and I didn't need a guard or two standing by, clearing their throats and shuffling as I sat in silence. I didn't want an audience.

Meggy never spoke, naturally, and I seldom had more than a few words for her. I told her that our daughter was likely still alive and far away from me. I apologized again for losing my temper, for not seeing the signs in time, for killing her when I was trying to kill Moyna. *She was trying to kill you,* I insisted for a few years before accepting that Meggy wouldn't have cared. She'd loved her baby, even at the cost of her life.

Someday, I told myself, perhaps I'd think of the right thing to say, the words that would absolve me of my guilt and make things right between us.

And perhaps I'd learn that I'd actually killed Meggy's evil clone. The odds were similarly slim.

I was pulled from my admittedly melancholic reverie by the sound of footsteps on fallen leaves and looked up to find Toula nearing. I said nothing, hoping she would get the hint, but instead, she took a seat beside me. She kept a moment of respectful silence, then said, "You're needed inside."

"Can it wait?" I muttered.

"It shouldn't. Come on, you can mope later."

"I am not *moping*," I snapped back at her, sparing her a sidelong glare.

"Bullshit. Once Mina told me which direction you'd headed, I knew *exactly* what you were up to."

"Mina should learn to keep her mouth shut."

"Yeah, well, Mina and the rest of them were nervous about bothering you, but seeing as I don't work for you, I said I'd take the bullet."

My temper was flaring, and I struggled to keep it down. "Can I not have a little time to pay my respects? Is that so damn much to ask?"

Her blue eyes—pretty, though so much darker than Meggy's had been—softened a degree. "I get it."

"You don't."

"No? Who do you think keeps her grave clean?"

That took me by surprise. As if seeing it for the first time, I considered Meggy's gravesite: a perfect rosebush over manicured grass, a neat patch in the midst of a litter of gray, fallen leaves.

"I loved her, too," said Toula. "Not like you're thinking," she added before I could ask. "There was never romance between us. But Megs was the closest thing I had to a real friend for a long time—we were each other's family at holidays, you know? I didn't have anyone waiting for me in Montana, and she sure as hell wasn't going back to Arizona. And then I stood by and let her kill herself, so *yeah*, I get it."

"You didn't shoot her," I mumbled.

"No, but I didn't knock her out and lock her up for safekeeping, and I missed every goddamned sign along the way. Too busy with Greg to see how quickly things were deteriorating with Moyna. I should have checked in more often…"

"And done what? *Meggy* thought she was just being a teenager."

"Yeah, well, she had desperation blinders on, and so did you. I should have paid better attention." Toula sighed and scratched her arm. "But that's water under the bridge, and neither of us is going to make this any better by sitting out here, kicking ourselves."

The silence stretched between us for a time, broken only by a pair of squirrels chittering in the trees behind us.

"My last memory of her is her body in my arms," I said softly. "That look of surprise and anger on her face, and two holes blasted through her…"

"I fixed her up for burial," Toula murmured. "While you were having your come-apart. And then I got to stage her death back home."

"Huh?"

Toula barely smiled, and what little appeared was sad. "I didn't want her to be a missing person forever. Her mom…" She paused and swallowed hard. "Megs didn't have a great relationship with her family. Her brothers were okay but were busy doing their own thing, and Megs always resented her mom for choosing her husband's happiness over her daughter's. I don't think she ever told any of them about finding Moyna or moving to Rigby. And she kept her house, did you know that? Made the mortgage payments. Stored her old car in the garage. She didn't go around there—new life and all—but I think she wanted the old one in her back pocket."

"Can't blame her."

"Yeah. So I went out there a few days after she died and left a copy of her body at the top of the driveway. Made it look like she'd had a heart attack. I left a phone in her pocket and put myself in as the emergency contact, and I got a call from the police that afternoon."

Toula stared through the rosebush as if watching the memory play out like a film. "I went down to the morgue, and I identified her and said I'd handle the estranged family.

I'm the one who broke the news to her mom. They had the body shipped out to Phoenix and buried it somewhere there—I wasn't invited to the funeral, *if* they had one. I hope they did," she muttered. "And that was the last I saw of Megs—a fake version of her in a morgue drawer. Then I went back to Montana, and Greg made me go to therapy. And here we are now, seven years later," she said with a weak laugh. "Look how far we've come."

"You're right. At least I finally left my room," I said. She responded with an elbow jab, but her smile that time, though still small, seemed genuine. "Thank you again for…you know, for looking after her. When I couldn't."

"Of course." She contemplated the roses for a moment more, then stood and brushed herself off. "Lailu is waiting. You need to get your butt back inside."

"*Lailu?*" I asked, climbing off the grass. "I wasn't expecting her."

"She didn't look happy. And since your guards are wusses, here I am, come to fetch you. You're welcome."

I snorted and followed her through the trees toward the palace. "I'm going to tell Val you said that."

"*I'll* tell Val I said that. Come on," she said, and took my hand. "Deal with the living first. The dead can wait."

NOVEMBER: KUNI

Fortuitously, I was keeping Aiden company when the messenger arrived. Not so fortuitously, I was in the hot tub when he did, which was mildly embarrassing. One does wish to preserve one's dignity, even among the daig—the fae, to use their word—but this can be a vexation under the best of circumstances.

"My lord," the aide said, standing quite far from the door into Aiden's iron-laden workshop, "Lailu has arrived with an entourage."

Aiden looked down at me for an explanation, but all I could offer him was an exaggerated shrug.

It was, I'd discovered, best to slow and amplify all gestures when attempting communication with the daig. Their eyes seemed less keen than ours, their ears less sensitive—or perhaps that was a function of their incredible size. When one is a giant, I suppose it's possible that one sees and hears so much that one cannot notice details and minutiae for the sensory blast. By then, I'd lived among the daig for days—by their odd reckoning, approximately five years—and I was gradually acclimating to their customs and limitations. Among the first lessons I absorbed was the necessity of modulation in all things, particularly slower, lower speech, as my audience lacked the ability to discern the nuances of intonation. When in doubt, gesticulation covered for much—assuming, that is, that the daig could make sense of my flailing.

But they had treated me kindly, those daig I claimed. I had adopted Aiden in particular. Though the boy's days were few, he had demonstrated fortitude and the beginning of wisdom, and he had made an earnest effort to learn our tongue. Magic provided us the rudiments of each other's language, but the exercise had been dearly trying. He couldn't make sense of my words at my accustomed speed and pitch, while to me, his attempts at conversation were often hilariously wrong. I did try not to laugh so as not to insult him—he was a good boy, and intelligent in many aspects—but it took him several poor trials before he understood that his tonal shifts were grotesquely made. "Smaller," I told him, spreading my arms wide and bringing them close together. "You are speaking, not singing." I tried to model for him, but he couldn't hear the distinction when I spoke normally, and once I realized that I had to speak at a comically slow pace and deep tone to be understood, the lesson was lost. Aiden could make himself understood to piq ears, but even when he did his best, he sounded somewhat deranged.

Still, Aiden was a generous host. He seldom bade me leave when I sought out his company, and he tried to make my accommodations more comfortable, though sometimes he struggled to properly scale down his gifts. Had he never given me another moment's consideration, I would have thought well of him—he had saved my leg, my wing, and my life—but he had become a friend of sorts. Though the child had a talent with the potential for catastrophic destruction, he proved willing to employ it in the crafting of piq-sized furniture and beers, for which he had my gratitude.

The hot tub was his invention of the afternoon, a cube with molded seats and massage jets that felt blissful on my aching back. Having spent the previous day in the orchard and the woods beyond them for a change of scenery, I'd awoken with stiff flight muscles that twinged with every move. I'd limped to Aiden's apartment, and he'd provided the hot tub on the window ledge beside his computer desk. He'd even thought to provide towels.

Unfortunately, as the aide demonstrated, this scene produced a reaction I'd come to despise from the daig: a crumpling of their enormous faces, followed by some booming variant of, "Oh, how cute!"

It is humbling for a man of my days and days to be considered *cute*, but short of transformation, there was little I could do. Aiden's hand was longer than I was tall, and for some reason, something about my relatively diminutive size, coupled with my wings, made me adorable to the daig. Humiliating, yes, but expected.

That afternoon, at least, the aide was too concerned to fixate on me for long. "Should we send word to the king?" he asked Aiden.

Aiden grimaced. "I hate to bother him *today*. Did Lailu say what's on her mind?"

The aide shook his head. "She asked for him and the queen, and she will say nothing else."

Sighing, the boy rose. "Kuni…"

"On it," I told him, climbing out of the relaxing bath. It was best, I'd found, to keep my speech simple with the daig, given our respective limitations. After a brisk toweling, I dressed quickly, wrung out my ponytail, and flew to his shoulder. "Ready," I said, gripping his collar to steady my perch.

Aiden carried me through the palace and into the throne room, where my aunt waited with several of her best guards, a multicolored cluster of glowing forms spread over two chairs in the front row. "Allow me," I offered, patting Aiden's neck, then slipped off and flew to greet my people.

"My queen," I said on landing, and bowed low from habit. "Warmest greetings to you."

She cupped my face in her palms and lifted it, and I turned my eyes up to meet hers. My aunt was more than a head taller than me, which struck the daig as strange—why, they enquired, would a female be taller by a third than the males around her?

Why, I countered, were their king and queen *not* larger

than the rest of their people? My aunt was obviously a queen by her size; her daughters would grow taller as their days passed, then leave with their own bands in days to come. The daig are peculiar, however, and they puzzled over even our most sensible ways.

"Kuni," said my aunt, and kissed my forehead. "Be well. You are safe?"

"Safe from all except large feet," I replied in jest. "And you? What brings you here?" I gave her escort a calculating glance: six well-seasoned warriors, male and female in equal number, all unencumbered by clothing but for their sword belts and loincloths. I envied them their comfort, but the daig are overly modest, and I abided by their customs when I was around them.

My aunt released me and clasped her hands. "Nineteen children are missing. A hunting party—Nioti took them into the deep woods yesterday, but a daig surprised them and stunned them all. Nioti had taken point and was outside of the blast's reach, it seems, but the other were kidnapped."

"And Nioti?"

"Grief-stricken. She blames herself."

That news was hardly surprising—Nioti had served as a tutor for days and days and *days*, and her charges loved her. For nineteen to be taken before her eyes…

"She couldn't have stopped a daig," I said. "At least she returned to tell you of their fate."

"Which I would investigate further, and *now*," she replied, then looked over my shoulder toward the door. "Ah. Toula."

I turned and found Toula and Aiden in conversation, their rumbles echoing around the empty throne room. "Coileán is indisposed today," I explained. "I suspect that Toula will be sent to retrieve him."

"Sweet to disguise the bitter?" said my aunt, a knowing lilt in her voice.

"So suggest the rumors. Take your ease," I said, nodding to her guards. "I'll learn the truth from Aiden."

After a moment's persuasion from Coileán's guards, Toula left to fetch him, and Aiden and I saw to my people's comfort. He constructed proper chairs to sit atop the daig-sized seats, padded stools with the narrow backs we prefer to avoid wing constriction, and offered refreshments in his imperfect speech. One of the guards began to titter, but my aunt silenced him with a glare and accepted the boy's hospitality.

Soon enough, Coileán entered the room with Toula, and he proceeded to the row of chairs to greet my aunt. "Lailu," he said, taking a seat near her party, "my apologies for the wait. What brings you south?"

When she repeated herself in the daig tongue, his face grew dark. "My court has been warned that your territory is protected," he said, and reached into his pocket. "Let me get Ellie."

A quick conversation later, the daig queen appeared by gate, seemingly as concerned as the king. "*Nineteen*, you say?" she asked my aunt upon arrival. "What did the kidnapper look like?"

My aunt jumped onto Eleanor's outstretched hand, the better to be heard. "Nioti saw little. A dark cloth mask covered all but the eyes, and a hood covered the head."

"Male or female?"

She, too, had learned the utility of an exaggerated shrug. "Nioti could not say. It's difficult, you understand, for one unfamiliar with the daig to determine these things."

"Mm. But definitely daig?"

"Daig or daigul."

I doubted it had been the latter—the daig-sized creatures without magical ability tended to remain within their enclave—and as Eleanor and Coileán traded glances, they seemed to concur with my assessment. "A Fringer, do you think?" she asked him.

"Not if they were stunned. What non-magical equipment would do that, some sort of sonic cannon? Electric flyswatter?"

"Good point," she muttered.

Toula stepped closer. "Does your Nioti remember where this happened?" she asked my aunt. "If you can take me there, I can look back, maybe find a clue."

But my aunt shook her head. "It was dark. She remembers generally where they were, but in the chaos…"

Toula made a face. "I mean, I could *try*, but—"

"But it won't do much good if the thief was masked, anyway," Coileán interrupted. "Aiden, find out where Joey is. Maybe Georgie can spot them on a flyover."

I accompanied Aiden back to his apartment, disturbed and racking my brain for a lead. Who, I mused, pacing his long desk, would want nineteen of our children? What use were we to daig or daigul? If the kidnapping had been for ransom, surely terms would have been delivered…

Behind me, Aiden inhaled sharply and muttered.

I knew few phrases of the daigul tongue that Aiden occasionally employed, but *holy shit* was among them.

"What is it?" I asked, turning to see him staring down at me.

"Don't move," he replied, then reached over my head and lifted his pencil jar. I followed its flight with bemusement. The jar was ordinary among Aiden's possessions, one of the screw-lid type that he used to safely store metal components in his workshop. He had repurposed one for pencils and other detritus, which he hastily shook out onto the desk. "Okay," he said once the jar was empty, "could you hop in for a second?"

I eyed the jar with suspicion, but it was sufficiently wide-mouthed that I could slide inside without great difficulty. Once I'd braced myself, he tilted it upright, then carried me into the windowless bathroom and shut the door. Positioning us before the mirror, he asked, "Are you seeing what I'm seeing?"

I considered our reflection. He'd kept the lamps off, and so the only illumination in the room was my personal radiance, a golden corona amplified by the mirror and brilliant in the darkness.

"I…see myself," I said, my voice reverberating strangely from the bottom of the jar.

"Yeah," Aiden replied. "But I also see decoration."

"*What*?"

His face loomed large over the mouth of my temporary prison. "There's this thing some kids do in the mortal realm. Ever heard of catching fireflies in a jar?"

"No…"

"They're these little bugs that flash lights on their abdomen to communicate," he explained. "Harmless. You can catch them pretty easily and put them in a jar, and they'll flicker for a while. If you want a similar effect without, you know, snatching bugs, you could put some string lights in a jar."

The picture he was describing came into focus, and my jaw dropped. "Or a piq. You think the kidnapper was a child?"

"No. Mind staying in there a minute longer?" he asked, taking me out of the bathroom. "I need to make a point."

I acquiesced, bracing my palms against the glass to steady myself during his jostling jog back to the throne room. When he burst in, his brother, Eleanor, and Toula were still deep in conversation with my aunt, and all four—and my aunt's guards—looked up in alarm.

"Rustic, yet whimsical, votives," Aiden announced, holding the jar by the rim. "Who's having a party tonight?"

There were no large events scheduled among Eleanor's people for that evening, but Coileán received word that a garden party had been planned for sundown. We went as a group to the hostess's home, a turreted stone residence with expansive ornamental gardens—my aunt's entourage, my four daig, myself, and several of Coileán's guards for emphasis.

The hostess was pretty, a brunette with blue eyes and a

floor-sweeping gown of red silk. "My lord," she said in surprise, seeing her caller, then noticed the modest crowd behind him. "Lady Eleanor? What's the meaning of this?"

"Good afternoon, Odette," said Coileán. "This won't take long. Were you in the northern woods last night?"

"I…I don't know what you mean…"

"Aiden."

He stepped past her and headed through the house toward the back doors. I rode along on his shoulder, scanning our path for signs of life, but my search was brief. Once Aiden threw open the doors to the garden, I saw that he'd been prescient.

Dotting the wide stone patio were a series of round, cloth-draped tables set for six. Long rectangular tables lined one side, bearing empty stands and trivets marking the future location of foodstuffs. Positioned in the middle of each round table and at intervals along the apparent buffet were glass cannisters perhaps twice the size of Aiden's pencil jar, each with a decorative brass lid—and each containing a single child. Some sat and clutched their knees, some had curled onto their sides, but a few noticed us and began hammering their fists onto the walls of their prisons, the glass muting their cries for help.

"Coileán! They're here!" Aiden called back into the house, then quickly examined the first cannister and removed the lid. The girl within gasped and weakly tried to fly out, but Aiden stopped her with his palm. "Wait," he told her with his best intonation. "I will tilt it."

Once the jar was on its side and braced against a plate, I scrambled in to see to the captive. Walking across the slick, curved glass was something of a challenge, but I reached her quickly enough and pulled her to her feet. "Are you hurt?" I asked.

She shook her head but continued to breathe in deep gasps, and to my horror, I realized why. "Aiden!" I shouted. "The lids don't have air holes!"

He employed another word I had learned of the daigul

tongue—*fuck*—and dashed to the second table. After yanking the lid off the jar at its center, he sped on to the third, not stopping to tend to the captives.

By the time the others joined us—Odette, I noticed, was flanked by two of Coileán's guards—I had half-carried the girl out of the cannister and stretched her on the tablecloth. Her breathing had begun to calm, but her skin remained pale, her glow fainter than normal. "Rest," I said. "You're safe. I must assist the others."

Before I could take flight, I heard Coileán mutter, "Moon and stars."

Suddenly, with a pop and hiss, every lid on the patio broke free and clattered to the tables, leaving Aiden, cannister in hand, looking slightly abashed. Coileán barely nodded, and the vessels dissolved into sand, which began to blow away in the cool breeze.

My aunt's guards dispersed at once to the captives' aid, and as I looked around for those who had yet to be examined, my gaze fell on the buffet. A boy and girl stirred and crawled toward each other around a decorative platter, but a girl farther down the table had yet to move. With a twisting stomach, I landed at her side and knelt to feel her neck, though I sensed even then that it was futile. She had turned ashy and stiff, and most tellingly, she no longer glowed. Detecting no trace of life, I rolled her onto her back and tried to force air into her chest, but she was long past the point of potential response.

"Coileán!" I yelled, jumping to draw his attention.

He hurried to my table and stared down at the dead girl, one hand cupped over his mouth and chin.

"What'd you find?" Aiden began as he approached, then stopped and gawked. "Oh, no. *Shit*, no. Is she…"

"Dead," I confirmed.

A cry went up from one of the dining tables, and Aiden ran off to investigate. He returned a moment later, visibly shaken. "Little boy. He didn't make it, either."

As quickly as they could, my aunt's guards ferried the

children to the center table. Some could speak and move about. Others were barely strong enough to sit up. Perhaps some of the lids had sealed more tightly than others—I can only hypothesize. While the daig conversed with my aunt, I pulled Aiden away from their pack and pointed to the terrified children. "Water," I told him. "Warmth. I need your help."

Though badly disturbed, the boy followed my orders, starting a campfire in the middle of a saucer and producing piq-sized cups of water. He put a stack of flannel blankets near the fire, and a few of the children wrapped up and huddled with each other. As he attended to them, I saw that they were beginning to lose their fear of him—though daig, he was working for *me*.

With the children settled, I counted them…then recounted twice, added in their dead companions, and came up short. "Eighteen," I said, tugging on Aiden's cuff for his attention. "There's still one missing."

The girl we'd first freed stood and padded toward us. "I know where she is," she said softly.

Aiden placed his open palm on the table by her feet. "Can you show us?"

I climbed aboard and held out my hand, steading her as she tentatively shuffled toward the hollow at the center. When she was settled and murmuring directions, I amplified and clarified them for Aiden. "Center buffet table. Look beneath. She saw Odette hide a jar under the tablecloth."

He deposited us atop the table, then knelt and lifted the drape. Shortly thereafter, he once again muttered, "Fuck."

"Dead?" I called down.

"Yeah," he said tersely, then stood, holding the cannister out of our guide's sight. "I'm going to take her to Lailu. Be right back."

When he walked away, I explained to the girl what he'd discovered. "When did she die, did you notice?" I asked.

"Before noon," she mumbled, holding her blanket around her neck. "The sun was climbing. She stopped moving, then she stopped glowing, and the daig put her under the table and rearranged us." She sniffled, and her green eyes, large even by our standards, welled with tears. "Are they going to kill us now?"

"No. *No*," I soothed, pulling her against my side. I couldn't tell her that my daig would make the situation better—the child had lost three of her friends overnight and shook even as I held her, and no punishment to Odette would ameliorate her loss.

The children were in no condition to travel. Exhausted, dehydrated, famished, and deeply grieving, they made camp in my apartment that night.

In most regards, it's difficult to be piq in a space designed for the daig. When I moved into the palace, I did so with Aiden's assistance, as Coileán's ordinary guest suites were unsuitable for my needs. Aiden had taken a room and transformed it beyond recognition, removing the furniture and replacing it with trees, niches in the stone walls, and a generous pond with a small waterfall, perfect for bathing. He'd done anything I requested, from planting berry bushes to building a treetop bedroom fit for my aunt. That evening, he worked his magic once again, making beds for the children, my aunt, and her entourage, adjusting the temperature against drafts, and keeping the long table he'd made laden with food sized for our hands—pieces of meat, bowls of mashed potatoes and rice, broccoli minced into manageable chunks, rolls to be torn apart and dipped in butter. Astrid had stopped by, seen a table lined with hungry children, and created a variety of perfect cakes, which went a long way toward making her their new favorite person.

But as the children ate their fill and fell asleep, my aunt touched almost none of the food or drink. She sat near the warmth of the fire pit Aiden had set up by the pond, holding a cup of water and staring into space. Her guards and I were unable to temp her, and I had almost resolved to retire for the night when there came a knock at the door. Assuming it was Aiden, I flew to the latch release button on the wall to bid him enter.

It wasn't Aiden, but rather Coileán, who trod cautiously toward the pond. "Lailu," he said quietly, dropping to one knee, "may I have a word? And Kuni, would you come, too? I'd like a witness."

She nodded and stepped into his hand, and he carried her into the vestibule of the apartment and placed her on a decorative side table as I flew behind them. Kneeling again to look her in the eye, Coileán kept his voice low. "If Odette were one of yours, how would you punish her?"

My aunt folded her arms across the bosom of her ceremonial gown. "If she had killed one person intentionally, I would cut off her wings and banish her."

Coileán nodded. "A slow death."

"Depending on how quickly she could run."

"And if she killed again?"

"Wings and arms."

He grimaced. "Sensing a theme, here. But what about Odette, under these circumstances? Kidnapped nineteen. The first death might have been an accident, but she did nothing to prevent the next two."

"And who is to say how many more would have died, had we tarried?" my aunt replied. "Perhaps she did not intend the deaths, but her indifference toward the children's well-being is reprehensible."

"Agreed. So I ask you, how would you punish her?"

She didn't hesitate. "Death. No exile, just death. If one kills in anger or in revenge, that is comprehensible, if unfortunate. But she kidnapped and killed for no reason other than…than *party* decorations and apathy."

"Good to know."

My aunt cocked her head. "You intend to punish her?"

"Oh my, yes," he replied. "I just wanted to be sure that I wouldn't offend your sensibilities in so doing."

For the first time that evening, my aunt smiled. It was

neither a broad nor a warm smile, but nonetheless, she was pleased. "When?"

Again, Coileán held out his hand. "Madam, if you'd like to observe, you're most welcome."

She stepped aboard and arranged her skirts, and Coileán carried her out the door.

The fire was burning low when they returned. Coileán knelt and let her step onto the floor by the pond, then stood, nodded to me, and saw himself out. When the door closed, I approached my aunt and asked, "What did he do? Send her to Eleanor's archipelago?"

"He executed her," she replied. "An instantaneous death. Had I been Coileán, I would have suffocated her, but his method was effective."

The news surprised me. "Then what took you so long?"

Her queer smile flickered across her face. "Several of her friends came to the palace to demand her release. Coileán explained to them what happened to her and why."

"And how did that go over?"

"They protested, but he insisted that we are to be left unmolested. I believe the message was delivered tonight." She leapt and flew to her bed, and I followed her, landing on a nearby branch. "It's a positive turn, you know. Their predecessors never considered us people. You've done well, little nephew."

"I've done nothing but eat their food and annoy their dragon," I protested.

My aunt's smile that time was genuine, if brief. "Then continue to do so. Convince them that our lives are equal to theirs in worth and dignity. Tomorrow, I will take the survivors home with our dead, and you will remain here to remind the daig that this must never happen again."

I bowed my head. "My queen."

She patted my cheek. "Your parents were emissaries to the daig once, and they never fared as well as you have. You're a credit to my brother's memory, Kuni."

"I have always striven to be such."

"And succeeded. In future days, if you would return to us, I will understand, but for now…"

"My work is here," I finished, and flew to my own bed. But sleep evaded me, and after a time, I rose and let myself out via the piq-sized door.

As I'd expected, Aiden was awake when I buzzed at his suite, mussed but puffy-eyed. "Hey, man," he said as I landed on his shoulder. "Want a beer or something?"

"I'd join you."

He prepared two of different sizes and carried me onto a balcony across the hall, and there we sat, speaking little but saying much, until sunrise.

FEBRUARY: CAREY JONES

In 1989, when I was fifteen, my parents forced me to endure a summer in Arizona with my dad's aunt, Mabel Wheeler. This was a good thing, they told me—I showed promise as a young wizard, and Aunt Mabel had mastered the four great magics. She was willing to teach me to sleepwalk.

Looking back, it was a gift, but I was less than thrilled. Like a few of my more distant relatives, Aunt Mabel lived within the Naabeehó Bináhásdzo—the "Navajo Nation"—which meant spending the summer away from home. Granted, Albuquerque wasn't the most exciting spot in the universe, but at least all of my friends were there. Instead, I got Aunt Mabel, a sour-faced old woman with a perpetual expression of disapproval, long gray hair, and teeth gone various shades of yellow and brown from decades of smoking. Her voice was a rasping croak, and she frequently interrupted conversations to hack phlegm into a wadded tissue.

Of the four great magics—wandless casting, gate creation, transformation, and sleepwalking—the fourth is the least frequently mastered. Any idiot with sufficient power can work a spell without a stick or force a gate open, and while it takes finesse to pull off a decent transformation, it takes an entirely different and highly disciplined style of focus to sleepwalk. The Arcanum, which thinks itself so erudite in terms of wizardry, has forgotten the art altogether. Despite her prickly disposition, Aunt Mabel was a brilliant wizard, known and respected by the Minor Arcanum's members worldwide, and at my parents' request, she had generously agreed to teach me the most challenging of the great magics.

That didn't mean it was going to be fun for either of us.

She didn't like me—she didn't have much use for children in general, and she'd never entirely forgiven my grandfather for marrying a white woman and moving away with so many of their cousins. But her mind was as sharp as her tongue, as I learned whenever my thoughts wandered during our lessons that sweltering summer. For weeks, I lay on Aunt Mabel's plastic-covered couch beneath a wobbly ceiling fan, trying to push myself into a trance instead of focusing on the way my sweat was pooling beneath my sticky limbs. When I failed, she would snap at me. When I asked for a break, another reprimand. When I whined or mouthed off, she called me a lazy ingrate.

Honestly, I think I finally learned to sleepwalk just to get her off my back.

But once I made it into the dream space on my own, I decided that it was worth the layer of skin I lost every time I ripped my legs away from the couch covering. In trance, I hovered high above Aunt Mabel's house in a world of gray on gray, my skin glowing with a bright gold light. As I hung there, taking in the neighborhood and the terrain below, Aunt Mabel rose to join me, also glowing and unencumbered by her age and deteriorating lungs—and for once, she smiled with satisfaction. "I *thought* you had it in you," she said, and drifted toward the north. "Come on, I'll show you around."

I followed her, amazed at the ease of motion, but when I tried a magnification spell for a better look at the ground, the spell refused to coalesce. "Something's wrong," I said, pausing mid-float.

She turned, her eyebrows knitting. "Oh?"

"My casting's not working."

The look on her face had grown far too familiar to me that season. "Of course it isn't," she snapped. "Didn't your parents teach you *anything?*"

"Not about this," I mumbled. "Why can't I cast?"

Taking pity on me, Aunt Mabel flew closer and lowered her voice. "If I had a good answer for that, I'd give it to you, Carey. Just know that it's virtually impossible to cast in the dream space. Think of this a place of community. It's for talking, not fighting—a place where we can reach out around the world and speak with each other. You have the ability, and so you'll have the responsibility as well."

"What responsibility?"

She sighed at my ignorance. "When a message needs to go out across the Minor Arcanum, the fastest way to transmit it is between sleepwalkers. Try picking up the phone and calling a wizard in China," she added with a little smirk. "I assure you, this is *far* easier. And since you'll be tasked with the distribution of information, people will learn your face. They'll begin to look to you in time of need. It'll be up to you not to betray that trust."

But as she spoke, I picked up on a loophole. "So...it's *virtually* impossible to cast here, but not *completely* impossible?"

Aunt Mabel's eyes narrowed. "There's only ever been one person who could cast in the dream space, and he turned it into a place of slaughter." She waited, studying my face as I tried to remember my parents' occasional history lessons, then sighed again. "I'll explain later. For now, come along. No need to waste time."

Over the next weeks, Aunt Mabel introduced me to many of the other sleepwalkers: a Québécois pharmacist, a Nigerian banker, an East German grandmother, a Brazilian capoeira mestre, an Australian chef, a Chinese schoolteacher, a Haitian attorney, and my favorite of the bunch, an elderly rabbi from Miami who gave as good as he got from Aunt Mabel—all in fun, from the sound of their banter. Language was never an impediment within the dream space, and I was thrilled to be part of an exclusive international club. Once I was back in my body, however, sweating in Aunt Mabel's stuffy house, she gave me the history lessons I lacked, drilling the major figures and events of the Minor Arcanum's past until I could recite them to her satisfaction and explain why they mattered. When she taught me about the lone caster in the dream space, she turned and spat at his name. "Simon Magus, the Arcanum calls him. He conquered the Old World, then came after the parts he'd never set foot on. When the peoples of the Americas and Oceania didn't bow, he massacred them in their sleep. A one-man genocide—a preview of what mundanes did here centuries later. The Arcanum reveres him, you know," she said, pausing for a sip of lemonade. "But that's their way, isn't it? They do love their conquerors. And *that*, little girl, is why you must never trust an Arcanum wizard."

Aunt Mabel didn't limit her lessons to history that summer. As she introduced me to more and more wizards, old, young, and in between, she began to prepare me for my future. "Someday," she said over dinner, "you won't be Mabel's little grandniece. You'll be Carey, whoever she may be. People will come to you with their problems. They'll look to you for advice." I must have seemed incredulous, as she smirked and speared a forkful of salad. "You will master all four great magics—I feel it, and I'm seldom wrong about that. This puts you in a category beyond the average wizard. You'll be a leader, whether you like it or not." She leaned across the table and held my gaze. "We don't need fancy titles and robes and jewelry, all that Arcanum nonsense. You'll be a leader in time. And when that day comes, I hope you do your duty. Protect our people—not just wizards or Diné or even your family, but *all* of the Minor Arcanum. That's the price I ask of you for your education," she added, and hacked a fresh gob into her napkin. "Now eat your chicken, it's good for you."

Aunt Mabel was crotchety, but she knew what she was talking about. I learned the great magics, I was acknowledged as a reliable sort of wizard, and by the time I hit my forties, I'd quietly become a force of stability in my sphere of influence. Sure, I didn't know everything, but I did my best, and people seemed to respect that.

Which meant, of course, that the strange cases showed up on my doorstep.

In my mundane life, I was a large-animal veterinarian, a useful trade in an area heavy with ranchers. I wasn't a world-class expert, but I knew my way around the back end of a cow as well as anyone, and when medicine failed, sometimes magic could save the day. I'd earned a reputation as the sort of vet who'd drop everything and drive in case of emergency, which is why, one winter morning, I got a call from the sheriff's department.

Anita Hernandez, the dispatcher on duty, was the daughter of a local horse breeder, and so she'd given the deputy my number. "It's a cougar," he explained. "Looks like it's got a busted foot, maybe more. Ernie Dunlop found him on the edge of his property at sundown. Doesn't look like it's killed anything, so Ernie called us instead of shooting it. Would you take a look?"

I thought of telling him to call Game and Fish, but my calendar was clear, and my husband, Zeb, was hauling a horse to California. "Sure," I told the deputy, and grabbed my kit.

Half an hour later, I met a trio of deputies behind the county jail, where the patient waited inside a large dog cage. It was definitely a cougar—tawny, muscular, brown-eyed, and far too big to fit comfortably in a cage suited for a German Shepherd. The cougar watched me silently, its tail twitching against the bars. It continued to study me as I started calculating how much tranquilizer I would need to safely examine it, and I met its eyes, unnerved by its stare.

It winked.

I blanked my face before I could reveal my surprise to the deputies. Sending them off to get me a cup of coffee— and themselves a needed refill—I crouched beside the cage and murmured, "Do that again."

The cougar obliged.

With a whisper of spellcraft, I tried to examine the cougar's mind, only to come up against an impenetrable mental wall. "Hang tight," I told it as the deputies returned with my drink. "Guys, I can't treat it here," I said, and sampled the bitter office coffee. "Who wants to help me get the cat into my car?"

Back at the ranch, I offloaded the caged cougar with a flick of my wand and floated it into the bunkhouse we used to house evacuating Fringers. With the doors secured, I opened the cage with a whispered word as I stood back, praying I wasn't mistaken.

It worked its way out of the cramped cage, hissing as it put its weight on its back-left foot, and flopped onto the rug to stretch. Instead of curling up or licking its injury, however, the cougar seemed to dissolve over the space of seconds, and a naked man with curly blond hair appeared in its place.

"Was it really necessary to use the cage for the trip?" he asked, his voice deep and weary.

"In case I was wrong about you, I didn't want to get my face mauled off."

He considered that, then shrugged. "Fair. Any chance of borrowing pants? Mine are back in my car, about fifty miles away."

Zeb and I kept a stash of clothing around for our Fringe guests, never knowing what they'd need when they arrived, and so I soon had the shifter outfitted in jeans and a red sweatshirt. He hobbled to the couch and propped his foot at my direction, revealing a mess of lacerations and bruising. "Broken, do you suppose?" he asked.

I gently palpated his foot and ankle. "Maybe. I'll X-ray in a minute. What happened?"

He yelped as I hit a sore spot. "There's a male cougar

running around in the scrub. A real one, I mean. He didn't appreciate the perceived competition, and when I ran, I caught my foot in an old trap. I shifted long enough to get the trap open, then limped in this direction. That rancher found me first last night. At least he didn't take the *Old Yeller* approach to injured animals."

"I mean, you didn't have to stay in cougar form," I pointed out.

"True. But if there's one thing a rancher likes less than a large cat, it's a naked stranger prowling around the house. Or limping," he amended, scowling at his foot. "If you could give me a lift to my car and maybe a couple aspirin, I won't take up any more of your morning."

"Or you could do the smart thing and sit there until I've got a healing spell in place," I countered, standing. "But before I get my equipment, I'd like to know what the hell you're doing in my town, Mr. Adler."

One blond eyebrow rose. "The Virginians sent a BOLO, did they?"

"Maybe. So what have we done to merit a visit from the Dark Company?"

He smiled faintly. "Covering your ass, in fact. I'll tell you all about it if you'll fix the foot. And since I've been meaning to properly make your acquaintance for some time, it's Tanner, Dr. Jones."

Half an hour later, once I'd confirmed the break and was weaving a combination healing and numbing spell around his injuries, Tanner kept his end of the bargain. "I'm still in the Arcanum's employ, you understand," he began. "Or James Mulligan's, more precisely. He retained our services to locate Badger Parsons and Arnold Lowe. I decided that the greater good was better served with the two of them unfound, but I still have to keep up appearances. Mulligan puts a tail on me every so often—he thinks he's sneaky, but his assassins aren't the stealthy type."

I stopped casting and glared at him. "You were leading them to *us* instead?"

"No, of course not," he replied, appalled at the accusation. "I was making a show of searching this area, only to come up emptyhanded. Nothing to see here, Jimmy, better send your goons in black to bother someone else." He leaned toward me as I resumed my work. "I know what happened with Nath, and I know what you and your husband have done for the Fringe. I *respect* that. You're crazy, now, but I commend you for fundamental decency."

"Likewise," I murmured, and finished the spell. "Sit still and don't try to walk on that yet. I'll get you some crutches."

I'd almost made it to the door when Tanner asked, "Why get involved?"

"As you said, fundamental decency," I replied, turning around. "I'm not a fan of murder in general."

"But you're exposing yourself to danger," he pressed. "You, your family, the Minor Arcanum...why take that chance? What's the Fringe to you?"

What, indeed? Tanner wasn't the first to ask—that had come from four sleepwalkers, who'd cornered me one night shortly after Badger struck her bargain with Nath and demanded to know why I continued to stick my neck out for them. *She's dangerous,* they'd insisted. *Could turn into Simon Magus reborn. She's his blood, isn't she?*

And then the kicker: *You were right to throw them out.*

It'd been three and a half years, and I still cringed when I thought of that morning. Badger had cast in the dream space—an innocuous spell, pulling food and a blanket from the ether for a sick, hungry child, the sort of thing that would be applauded under other circumstances. Instead, seeing her accident as a threat to us all, I'd forced her to leave the ranch and suggested that she leave the realm while she was at it.

I wasn't *wrong.* Badger was the first wizard since Simon Magus strong enough to cast while sleepwalking, which meant that she could attack us in the dream space. She'd used that skill to great effect on Nath, after all. But once I had time to analyze my knee-jerk reaction, I'd realized that

I had little reason to fear her. Badger was a cop, not a conqueror, and she'd demonstrated her readiness to help us. Still, the fact remained that I was the only sleepwalker willing to meet up with her in the dream space.

Aunt Mabel had told me that I had a responsibility to my people. I suppose my circle was just a little wider than the one she'd drawn.

"They're with us," I told Tanner, "and they need help. That's enough for me." I paused, considering the shifter in his oversized borrowed clothing, then said, "You want breakfast? Zeb left me with huevos rancheros."

A little smile played at the corner of his mouth. "Inviting a member of the Company into your inner sanctum? Is that wise, Dr. Jones?"

It wasn't, but then again, he'd broken his foot on our behalf.

"I trust that you won't make me regret this," I said, and opened the door. "Wait until I come back with crutches. And it's Carey."

—YEAR SIX—

MARCH: VIVI STOWE PERRYMAN

"Honey?"

I looked up from my laptop when my home office door creaked open, spilling hallway light through the crack. Hal, disheveled with sleep, squinted in at me as I worked by the glow of my screen. "Hey, babe, what're you doing up?" he said, his Virginia drawl more pronounced with the late hour—or early, maybe. Telling time was an iffy proposition in Faerie.

"Tweaking," I replied, stifling a yawn. "Couldn't sleep."

He let himself in and picked his way around my cardboard boxes and computer bits to rub my shoulders. "You're going to be great," he said, working on the knot in my neck. "Just picture them all naked, yeah? Hell," he said, leaning closer to my ear, "if it gets *really* bad, give me the signal, and I'll get Rufe to make the clothes disappear for real."

I laughed, then hissed as his thumb ground into the worst of the knot. "He wouldn't."

"All right, then I'll have Harry on standby. Maybe James. Ned might get picky about it, but at least one of the guys would come to Baby Sis's aid."

"Please don't give them ideas."

"Spoken like your mom."

I awkwardly swatted at Hal, who chuckled and continued his massage. Hal had been a high school lineman before we met, but whatever strength he had lost since hanging up his jersey seemed to have migrated into his fingers. His neck rubs were the nearest thing to magic that my mundane husband could manage, and I adored them.

"Scroll up," he said. "Let's see what you have."

I returned to the start of my speech and let Hal read it over my shoulder as he worked. "Very nice," he said after a few minutes of silence. "You ended on a good note."

"I've got to give them *something*," I said, staring at the black text. "Five years, Hal. Every year, there's talk that maybe this will be the last one, and then we're right back around to March."

He squeezed my arms, then rested his chin on my shoulder and held me from behind. "There's not a damn thing you can do to end this any sooner, and you've done much more than most for the Fringe. Don't try to carry this, babe, it's not your burden."

"I know," I said, sighing, "but if I could give them hope…"

"There *is* hope. We're safe here. People smile at you on the street. I coached a soccer match last night in the park—"

"All the players were above average?" I teased.

"Uh…negative. *Firm* negative on that one. I'm surprised that some of those kids can walk and chew gum. But people were cheering in the stands, and no one cussed out the ref or the coaches."

"Would *you* cuss out Poppy?"

"Hell, no, but that's beside the point. People were happy," Hal said, his breath warm on the side of my face. "Life's happening, Vivi. Folks aren't sitting around in a holding pattern, waiting for the gates to open again. I mean, this place ain't perfect, but it ain't too shabby, either."

I grinned. "Robbie will be thrilled to hear such high praise."

"I keep telling him that things would be so much better with a waterpark, but he won't listen to me." Hal kissed my neck and straightened. "Come back to bed, honey. Big day tomorrow."

"Which is why I'm prepping now," I told him. "Get

some sleep. I'll crash eventually."

Though he seemed reluctant, he left me to my work. I pulled off my glasses and polished the lenses on my T-shirt, then got up to make coffee.

Like every other appliance in the house, the coffeemaker was the product of enchantment—one of the few touches in town that wasn't Robbie's doing. Our brother James had been the designer behind them, and ever since, I'd leaned on him to keep the place running. Robbie could plan and build and create, but James was more pragmatic, a former financier in need of a task. So many of our brothers had been set adrift, cut off from whatever iteration of their lives they'd been leading on the day of the coup. Our parents hadn't raised us to lie about, and suddenly, we were trapped in a realm in which the most serious decision anyone made on a regular basis was crafting guest lists. That had settled well with none of us, which was how I'd found myself with a willing cadre of assistants—a great development for me, as I'd become the town's de facto mayor.

I didn't know jack shit about running a community—I'd been lucky to keep my Fringe work from interfering with my paranormal investigations and occasionally find time to make a fancy dinner for Hal. But people knew me, they knew that I was on decent terms with the king and queen…and then it came to light that I had twelve brothers willing to pitch in. At twenty-five and change, I'd been put in charge and left to tread water.

They'd come through for me, my big brothers. Five years on, Ned still headed up security, keeping unauthorized faeries out and strongly discouraging the Fringers from wandering beyond the low demarcation wall. Matthew, who'd worked on and off with Ned after spending a couple hundred years in the navy, served as his right hand on the security front. Harry rounded out their trio, though having grown up running fishing charters in Alaska, he slipped off to sea with regularity. Robbie, of course, had built the town from the ground up and continued to add and redesign as families grew or Badger's team sent stragglers across the border. Adam, who'd always been something of a jack of all trades, had owned taverns and bars for years, and when a few folks had expressed interest, he'd turned one of Robbie's parks into a brewery and taught the fine art of craft beer production, much to Robbie's chagrin. Luce came around on occasion, particularly when I needed catering, though he had his hands full running Eleanor's kitchen. Peter had always been a wanderer, but when he wasn't exploring the wilds of Faerie, he was happy to lead short expeditions for Fringers with a desperate need to get out of town. Rufe had thrown himself into the school project, and with the first few years under his belt, he'd worked out the worst of the kinks and even prevailed upon our brothers to fill teaching needs—Charles, a literary dabbler, was happy to talk symbolism with the high schoolers, while Stephen, who'd never been anything but a lawyer, reluctantly agreed to teach debate and soon discovered that he enjoyed it. Leo, a talented painter, couldn't be convinced to teach art, but he had a gallery in town and had recently begun offering private lessons to interested kids. And then there was James, who made sure that the grocery store's shelves stayed stocked, the taps ran, and the waste disappeared.

I was so lucky. We all were.

And the town wasn't a bad place. For the first time in our lives, we didn't have to worry about accidental displays of magic. The lesser bloods could be trained in safety, and Toula came out once a week to work with the young witches. No one *had* to hold down a job (though most helped out somewhere around town at least part-time), there was no money (or taxes), and crime was virtually nil. People had time to tinker, to invent, to work on the books in the back of their drawers or take up pottery. Our little civic orchestra had improved with practice, and while our theater troupe wasn't ready for Broadway, they gave it their all. Sunday afternoon in the main park was dedicated to the weekly pickup soccer game, the movie theater and its more artistic rival across the street traded friendly jabs on their marquees, and some of the parents had banded together to make their own scouting group, reaching out especially to the orphaned kids in the dorm. Late in the evening, I'd hear laughter and see the wobbly headlamps of packs of kids biking up and down the streets in the darkness, especially during the summer holiday.

And then there was the other matter, the one that weighed so heavily on the senior Fringers' minds: no one was getting older. Sure, the kids were growing up, but thanks to Faerie's quirky makeup, no one older than her mid-twenties was aging. We were safe, protected, and provided for, and no one had to die…provided that we never left. Crossing the border, no matter how briefly, would throw on the missing years all at once.

There was quiet talk in some circles about finding a way to stay even after the Arcanum mess was behind us. I couldn't answer that—I was just the thirty-year-old mayor, still wet behind the ears in many of my compatriots' estimation, a baby to everyone in my family but my husband and sister-in-law.

Still, someone had decided for the third year in a row that I should say a few poignant words at the anniversary commemoration. I'd written a decent speech, but the more I read over it, the cheaper it sounded. I was psyching myself out, I knew that, but there's not much room for rational thought between midnight and dawn.

The coffee finished its drip, and I tasted it. Not awful, but not my favorite. Hal had picked up the dark roast again.

I carried the mug back into my office, found my phone on the desk, and sent a brief message: *U up?*

Yes, came the quick reply. *Problem?*

Got whisky?

A gate opened between my desk and the door, and I slipped through into Coileán's office. "Morning, Chief," I said, heading for his bar. "You too, huh?"

He spread one hand over the papers on his desk as if

showing off a prize. "What's keeping you awake this time?"

I dumped a liberal splash of booze into my coffee, swirled, and took a test sip. Better.

"Got to give a speech tomorrow," I said, cradling my mug. "I *hate* public speaking."

He nodded while I drank. "There are drawbacks to every job, Vivi. Just...try to imagine everyone naked. You'll be amused, aroused, or disgusted, but you won't be nervous."

"You sound like Hal." I leaned against the bar and lifted my spiked coffee in salute. "Five years, man.

Coileán raised his own tumbler in reply. "To survival."

"Cheers." I sipped, twitched at the burn, and suppressed a cough. "You coming out tomorrow for the festivities?"

"Hadn't planned on it," he said, bending back to his work. "Get some sleep, kid. Let the whisky help."

"Thanks," I said, turning for home, but paused at the edge of the gate. "I mean it. Thank you for everything. You and Eleanor. I don't know where we'd be otherwise."

He glanced up again and smiled faintly. "Want to thank us in deed?"

I frowned. "What'd you have in mind?"

"Have a word with whomever is in charge of the bell tolling and see that it's over in an hour or so, would you?"

"You've got it. Least I can do," I replied, and slipped home to drink myself into a few more uneasy hours of sleep.

JUNE: JOEY BOLIN

Georgie and I were flying low over a remote cluster of islands in the great western sea, getting better images for Aiden, when I felt her slow. *Is that who I think it is?* she asked, banking to the right to circle a sandy disc perhaps a block wide.

I peered over the side of her neck, then switched my helmet's view to one of the many cameras in Georgie's rig. The pale legs were otherwise nondescript, but as the camera picked up the details of the woman's face, recognition flared.

Ilunna.

I'd have known her face anywhere, and with good reason: I'd known her in the Biblical sense, my first dalliance since I started seriously contemplating whether I was being called to the priesthood. A few days after our night in the sand, I'd dropped out of seminary. It wasn't Ilunna's fault— those strange days just confirmed what I'd suspected about my unfitness for a life in the Church—but still, I hadn't gone on spring break intending to bed a merrow.

At least she'd decided to get freaky in human guise. Thank God for small mercies, as I've never had a deep desire to witness exactly how baby mermaids are made.

Ilunna, I told Georgie, *or her twin.*

Go in?

Sure.

Georgie continued to bank in a lazy spiral around the island. Before Ilunna could flee, I thought to her, *It's Joey. Nothing to fear.*

She stood and brushed the sand off her *painfully* naked body, all taut muscles and pleasing curves topped with long black hair and a perfectly friendly smile. She raised a hand in greeting as Georgie executed a two-point landing in the shallows. By the time the dragon's front feet had reached the shore, I was sliding out of the saddle and onto the beach.

"Hey," I said, yanking off my helmet. "Long time no see."

Ilunna's grin spread at the sight of my sweat-plastered hair. With the riding duster and boots, I was overdressed for the warm weather and pink in the face from the helmet. "Joey!" she said, stumbling over the distance between us, and I ran forward to catch her before she could take a tumble. She smiled gratefully and righted herself by bracing against my arms. "These useless things," she muttered, glancing at her legs. "I came up for the sun, not for speed."

She tried to kiss me in greeting, but I turned my head, and her lips caught my stubble. "Married," I told her.

"Yes, *right*," she said, her dark eyes widening in comprehension. "I'd heard as much from Father. You and Helen?"

I nodded, trying to ignore the pang in my chest at her name.

"Well…if that's your people's custom, then…should I congratulate you?"

"Appreciated." When she was steady on her feet, I released her and stepped back. "You remember Georgie?"

Ilunna looked over my shoulder at the massive black dragon behind me and broke into a wide smile. "Georgie, hello!" she cried, slipping past me and staggering toward the water. "This is your true form?"

Indeed.

"You're *beautiful*. I'd have been upset to be transformed, too, if I were you."

I sensed more than heard Georgie's pleasure at the compliment. Merrow or not, Ilunna knew her way to my companion's heart.

"You're a long way from home," I said. "Trouble in the Keys?"

"No, things are fine. Quiet," she replied. "I wanted a few days away from the family, and the hunting is good around here. There's a reef," she added, pointing to the shallows, then paused and cocked her head. "How did you speak to my mind?"

"Long story," I muttered. "Short version, I have talent."

"Ah." She took a seat on a small sand dune. "How is your Helen, anyway? Am I ever going to meet her?"

I blinked hard, trying to control my face, then managed, "Your father didn't tell you?"

"Tell me what?"

"Helen's been imprisoned in Montana for more than five years."

Her jaw dropped, and Ilunna rushed to cover her gaping mouth. "I'm sorry," she said, "I didn't realize...Father said there had been hostages taken, but he didn't say—"

"It's okay."

"No, it isn't. I...I didn't intend to cause you pain. Five years, you said? How many moons?"

"Uh..." I thought through the math. "About sixty-eight, I think."

Ilunna's face fell. "Joey, I *am* sorry," she said, pushing herself to her feet again, then returned to my side and hugged me. "Is there anything I can do?"

I shook my head. "She's being held in the Arcanum's facility in Montana. Landlocked and underground."

"Tricky. If they ever move her to a coastal area, or near a major river..."

"I appreciate it," I said, and reached into my inner coat pocket for my leather wallet. I wasn't carrying ID or cash those days, but the wallet was old enough to have plastic sleeves for pictures in the middle. "This is Helen," I told Ilunna, showing her a snapshot I'd trimmed to fit. "And this one—that was her magus ceremony. That next one was us on our wedding day."

She flipped through the few pictures I carried, then paused at the last, a black and white headshot. "Who…"

"That's our daughter. Roslyn," I said, flipping the wallet around to look at her little face. The school yearbooks weren't printed in color, but Stuart had done his best to send me a photo. She did look like me—he was absolutely right about that—but I saw traces of Helen in her smile.

Ilunna cut her eyes to Georgie, then back to me. "You didn't bring her with you today?"

"I've never met her. She's a prisoner there, too. This…" I paused and swallowed hard. "That's the only picture of her I've ever seen. She's almost five. But," I continued, willing myself not to cry in front of Ilunna, "I can't do anything for it right now. We're stuck playing this damn waiting game, and so I'm out with Georgie, taking pictures."

We're making maps, Georgie explained.

Ilunna stared at me for a long moment, as if stunned, then squared her shoulders and gestured toward Georgie. "Tell me about these maps."

I recognized a distraction when I heard one, but I went along with it. Escorting her to Georgie, I walked her through the camera rig, then put my helmet on her and let her see the mapping overlay on the visor. She clapped in delight, and when I took the helmet back, her eyes sparkled. "What's it like up there? How far can you see?"

Want a ride? Georgie offered.

"Yeah, how about a spin?" I suggested. "It's very safe—Georgie won't pull any stunts with you on there."

Or so he thinks. She showed her teeth, a draconic quasi-grin, when I glared in her direction.

The merrow nibbled her lip as she thought it over, then nodded excitedly. "How do you climb on?"

"Hold it," I said, catching her shoulder before she could get far. "You're underdressed for this."

She glanced back at me in annoyance. "Clothing is unnecessary—"

"Maybe, but it's cold and breezy at altitude. I don't want

you to freeze."

Though she regarded me with skepticism, she gave in when Georgie emphatically nodded. "If you must."

I thought for a moment, then came up with a version of my own riding gear, including a duster, gloves, and protective goggles. Ilunna tugged at the unfamiliar layers and turned to see the coat swish, and I helped her adjust the goggles. "Debris and wind," I said. "Georgie has yet to hit a bird, but if she did—"

There's always a chance of bone shrapnel.

Ilunna grimaced but let me help her across the beach and up onto the saddle. "Sit forward," I said, "one leg on either side. I'll sit behind and keep you steady. Going to guess you've never ridden before, huh?"

"Was it obvious?" she joked.

I slid my feet into the stirrups, shoved my helmet on, hooked her around the waist, then gave Georgie's neck a pat. *We're set.*

You want loops, right?

Very funny.

Ilunna gasped, then shrieked as Georgie ran and leapt, but her cries turned to excited laughter as she looked down on the receding waves. Her words were lost to the wind, and I told her, *Think. I can pick up on it.*

This is incredible! was what I found at the top of her mind.

She wedged herself against the saddle, and I held on as she leaned from side to side, staring at the shrinking islands.

I remembered how it felt the first time I rode with Helen. Georgie had been maybe half her full size back then, and Helen had been soaked and pissed with Coileán for letting Aiden play peacemaker with Moyna and her giant sea serpent. She hadn't been happy to climb aboard, but I'd held her in front of me like I was holding Ilunna, and Georgie had made the short flight back to shore. Then I'd taken her out a second time—a real flight—and she'd insisted on riding behind me. But she'd laughed and tightened her hold on my stomach every time Georgie so much as banked, and when I'd helped her off, she'd been practically glowing.

She should have been there instead of Ilunna. We'd had far too few flights together, and even if my body was excited to be in proximity to Ilunna, I wanted my wife in my arms.

And Roslyn—surely she wouldn't be scared of Georgie, not if we'd raised her around the barn. My parents had put me on horseback as a little kid, so I'd have taken her up by then, holding on tightly and showing her the contours of the land. Even if she'd gone to school in Montana, even if my genes screwed up the talent she should have had from Helen, she'd have damn well been the only kid in her class who knew what it felt like to ride the wind. Maybe that would have been enough to make up for the fact that she'd been born witch-blooded. Maybe not. But I'd have protected her. God, I'd have given her anything.

Georgie only stayed up a few minutes, long enough to give Ilunna a thrill but not so long that her legs would cramp, and splashed down back at the island. I dismounted and helped Ilunna make a less than graceful slide off, and she hugged me again. "That was wonderful. Thank you both," she said, leaving me to fling her arms as far as she could across Georgie's neck.

As Georgie and I departed, Ilunna was busy removing her outerwear and spreading it across the sand as a makeshift beach towel. I didn't have to keep watching her— my memory could provide me excellent details about Ilunna's attributes, a fact that I tried to never bring up around Helen.

She's nice, Georgie thought. *Too physical, but nice.*

She said you're beautiful, I reminded her.

And so I am.

Modest, too.

I never claimed that. What's my heading?

I checked Aiden's requests and gave her the coordinates, and off we went, heading for distant islands while I tried not to remember the feeling of Helen's body pressed against mine.

OCTOBER: HELEN CARVER

I wasn't raised religious. It's not an Arcanum thing, necessarily, though we tend to produce more agnostics than anything else. I mean, we know so much more than the average mundane about what's lurking out there, so who's to say there aren't things we've yet to discover?

My husband was raised a good Catholic boy—that stint at seminary was a giveaway about his thoughts on the matter—but he was never pushy about it. He was happy to answer my questions and take me with him to Mass on occasion, even engage in light theological debate, but he understood that I was probably never going to convert.

I'd asked him about Purgatory—where it allegedly is, what happens there, how long it lasts, and whether one can really get a reduction in sentence if the right people pray on one's behalf. He'd answered as best he could, leaving me with competing visions from throughout the ages and more questions than answers.

After years in my particular prison, however, I had a better idea of the concept.

I felt Russell Mulligan slap me across the face. I knew it was him—his father seldom laid a hand on me, and never like that, but Russell took his pleasure where he could get it.

"Dad said your little mongrel spawn is starting to cast," he said, his spittle falling on my burning cheek like rain. "Or so Howard reports. That's good, you know. We'll raise it up right, make a decent wizard out of it. And then we'll send it to Faerie to avenge you. Won't that be nice?"

I said nothing, of course. I couldn't, though I longed to

sit up and throttle the bastard.

"Better hope the brat doesn't take after Daddy," Russell continued, leaning closer to my face. "If it starts enchanting, well....accidents happen, you know? Kids don't always bounce."

I wanted to drop him out a tenth-story window and see for myself, but the bind didn't care.

He patted the cheek he'd just struck in mocking consolation. "Then again, if it starts enchanting, maybe Howard will knock some sense into it first. You never know."

What I knew was that I didn't want my monstrous parents anywhere near my baby, but I didn't have a choice.

"Sweet dreams, bitch," said Russell.

I heard the door slam behind him and drifted back into darkness until Badger's voice broke through like a trumpet: "Hello, Helen. How're we doing?"

Oh, peachy, I thought to myself, filling in the gaps in our conversations as per usual. Badger couldn't hear me—as far as I knew, she wasn't even sure that I could hear her—but the farce made my torture ever so slightly more bearable.

"It's the first of October," she said gently. "Roslyn is five today."

Five. I'd missed her first five years. If I could have wept, I'd have been bawling.

"I'm sorry, love, I know that's painful," she hastily added, "but the good news is that she's healthy and still very much alive. Stuart sent us a copy of her yearbook picture— she's Joey's little twin. *Cute* kid. Oh, and he says she's going by Ros now, since she's such a grown-up kindergartener. Could be worse, you know. I mean, I *did* start answering to Badger, and my mum was less than thrilled. Then again, she was Texan, and the fact that I never went by Hannah Kathleen was one of the great tragedies of her life."

I couldn't laugh, but I appreciated Badger's effort.

"Anyway, Stuart said that Ros brought cupcakes today for the occasion."

Vanilla or chocolate?

"He didn't give me many specifics other than the fact that they were grossly pink. She saved one for him. They're still chummy, those two. Might not be the best news as far as cultivating Ros's taste in friends goes, but it's certainly convenient for us. And I'm not being fair to him," she said with a note of self-reproach. "He's doing yeoman's work—he's the lone art teacher for that school."

But is he still trying to cast spells?

"At least he didn't go for chemistry," Badger muttered. "I'd hate to see what his potions looked like if he had access to a proper lab."

You and me both, sister.

"And with that disturbing image, I'd best be going. Just remember: your daughter is alive and well, and the experts in Faerie are still working on a solution. We're going to get you out of here, Helen, I promise. In the meantime, Joey sends his love."

Tell him I love him, I thought, but Badger was gone, and she hadn't heard me.

No one ever heard me.

God, I begged as I slipped under again, *if you exist, don't let me die alone in here.*

OCTOBER: FAERIE

Every visit was tantamount to reopening a fresh wound. I knew that, and I hated to do it to the child—I'd asked much of him already. But Roslyn continued to make gates in her sleep, and she had to be directed *somewhere*.

Aiden had written his own fictions to explain to her where she was and why. The stories didn't seem ultimately convincing to me, but then Roslyn was barely more than a babe, willing to take instruction in the ways of the world. Aiden was never less than kind to her, but he kept their visits brief, allowing her to tell him whatever was on her mind before ushering her back to "sleep" through the hole in the wall.

That night, she was excited to see him, and he greeted her with a wide smile. "Happy birthday, Ros," he said as she scrambled through the gate. "You're a big girl now, huh?"

She nodded. "Grandma made me cupcakes for school, even though they're full of fat and sugar."

She sounded as if she were parroting words in another tongue, the syllables known but the meaning unfamiliar, and I assumed she'd heard the refrain from someone older.

"Mm. Grandma's trying to make everyone eat healthy again?" asked Aiden.

The girl looked glum at the reminder. "Yeah. I don't like spaghetti squash as much as the real thing."

"You're not alone, sweetie," he replied, and tousled her hair. "Get any good birthday presents?"

"Yeah!" she said, perking again. "I got *two* horses, a bay and a...um..." She spoke slowly, fighting to produce the term. "An Appa...Appaloo..."

"Appaloosa?"

"That's it!" She paused, tilting her head. "Do you think Grandma and Grandpa would ever let me have a real one?"

"An *Appaloosa*? Those are pretty big, you know."

"Not a big horse—there's little ones, I saw them on TV, and, like, they can lead you around if you can't see, and they're really cute, and I'd walk it and everything."

"But do you think a horse would want to live underground?" he replied. "Can you see a horse in the elevator?"

She giggled at the notion. "Like, we're riding up, and it stops, and the Council wants to get on, but there's a *horse*..."

"It might get scared and poop."

"*Eww!*" she cried, and laughed anew.

Aiden hoisted her into his chair, and she wrapped her arms around his neck as he hugged her. "Time to go back to deep sleep," he said, standing to carry her to the gate. "Dream of your little horse." He put her down beside the hole, then knelt and gave her a pat on the shoulder to hurry her along. "This is going to be the best year yet, Ros. I know it."

She burrowed beneath her blankets and waved, and he closed the gate. Sighing, he pushed himself off the floor, but instead of returning to his chair and his interrupted data compilation, he sat on the window ledge and stared out at the night. "All clear," he muttered.

Kuni slipped out from a chink in the stone wall. "Close call."

"She's getting faster."

"I meant my offer," he said, landing on the ledge beside Aiden. "Let me speak with my aunt. She would send someone to watch Ros if asked."

"And I appreciate that," he replied, leaning against the glass, "but Coileán said no. Too risky."

"Hiding isn't difficult."

"But think of the worst-case scenario. A piq is found in

Ros's room…what does Mulligan do then?"

"He's made no prohibition against *us*," Kuni pointed out.

"True, but do you really want to split hairs with him?" His exhalation fogged the window. "Probably best to let Stuart keep doing his thing for now."

Kuni leapt and landed on the window handle, the better to look down at Aiden. "This is the Stuart who thinks he is…" He frowned. "Not daig…"

"A wizard," Aiden offered. "And yeah, that's the one. But I've got to give him credit—he's been hiding in plain sight in Montana for five years. He's done more for the cause than any Fringer, with the exception of the Virginia crew. The guy's no wizard, but he's got *balls*."

Kuni nodded. "Granted. But what happens when Ros makes a gate and isn't sleeping? What if she accidentally makes one to you?"

Aiden sat up and stared back at him. "Let's just hope that never happens."

Through the myriad fine holes between the realms, I could see the child sleeping, breathing softly as she snuggled with her increasingly shabby toy dog. The day would come, I mused, that she would cross through with full awareness of her power. But that night, she was five and tired from the excitement of the day, and deeply asleep.

I had yet to give her a gift, and so I sent her a dream of her parents, Helen barely pregnant, Joey feeling Helen's belly and speaking to their unborn daughter. The child's lips twitched toward a smile in her sleep, and I left her to her rest.

FEBRUARY: ELEANOR

My dearest,

The problem with gossip is that upon hearing it, one is often struck with the urge to spread it around. There being no one I can trust with this information at the moment, I'll tell you instead.

Toula invited me to a board game night in her suite this evening. It seems that she, her brother, and Coileán have a regular Monopoly schedule, but as neither of her opponents is particularly gifted at the game, Toula is in search of a challenge. I assured her that I was *quite* familiar with Monopoly—those game nights in our last years in Durham finally came in handy, eh?—and I suggested a different game to make things more interesting.

Toula knew the rules and mechanics of Settlers of Catan. The boys, predictably, did not, and so she and I wiped the floor with them before my ultimate victory. We played three more rounds and drank several bottles of wine, and while I didn't win every game—the binds do take their toll, you know, and sometimes my mind wanders these days—I put up a good fight.

And then, as the night progressed, I saw it.

They were *flirting*.

Toula and Coileán have teased each other as long as I've known them, but this…well, this was something different. The secret little smiles, the jabs, his willingness to make poor trades with her when she pouted—either there is more going on between them than anyone cares to make public, or I've lost my mind.

And if I've gone mad, I'm not the only one. I asked Val during one round if he was seeing what I was, and he confirmed it. Small wonder, then, that he seemed so pleased when I showed up tonight. The poor man's been chaperoning his king and his sister all alone. He sounded resigned to it, and I couldn't help but think of Archie Willoughby that spring when his secretary and his postgrad began their not-so-secret courtship. I should hope that if these two progress beyond what I witnessed this evening, they'll carry on somewhere that isn't a broom closet.

I never knew Mab or Titania, but from what I've been told, they despised each other. I smile now thinking of what they would say if they knew what their children were up to in their absence. Should you meet them somewhere in the Great Beyond, do send my regards, darling.

By the way, the archipelago is working beautifully. Fifty-two inhabitants now, and the court has been calm for three weeks. I believe the others are getting the message, I truly do. Though it's taxing keeping that many people bound, I'm managing. I haven't got a firm timetable for returning my little castaways to their former lives, but I can't help but wonder how much good it would do to keep them isolated for a few years. Remove the rebellious element from the general population, you know, and watch the others fall in line. I don't suppose you'd approve of long-term incarceration—you always had a soft heart, my dearest—but I can't say this has been anything less than a success. While I'd aspire to be my court's beloved queen, given my druthers, I realize that so many of my people *cannot* love me, and so I must be content with their fear. Love or fear, the result will be the same: I will have peace if it kills me.

Much love,
Your Ellie

—YEAR SEVEN—

JUNE: KIP

On the night before my wedding, I was summoned to my ancestors.

Everyone knew of the dreams, the unexpected glimpses into the far land, but no one spoke of them in detail. A man's father and grandfathers might caution him before making a risky decision or offer guidance in time of need, but such dreams were infrequent. If a man dreamed of his ancestors once, he was fortunate; twice, highly favored.

I didn't feel anything but nervous as I crossed the wide plain toward the bonfire in the distance. I was back in my unbound body—*that*, I'd noticed immediately—and I was still adjusting to the different balance when Hib ran up to join me. "Little brother," he said with a grin, and clasped my shoulder. "Welcome. You're expected."

He escorted me the rest of the way, and I'd started to imagine that this might be a pleasant experience until I saw my father's scowl and folded arms. "Father," I began, thrilled to see him again, but I stopped before approaching. "You're angry?"

"What do you think you're doing, Kippet?" he said, employing the warning voice I knew well from childhood.

"I...dreaming, I suppose..."

By then, other men had drawn closer—my father's father, my mother's father, and more I couldn't name but whose features reminded me of my known family. Hib had stepped back, leaving me to face a semicircle of displeased ancestors on my own.

"That woman," Father continued, glaring at me. "The

one you intend to take to mate."

The hair on the back of my neck and down my mane began to rise. "You don't know Amy."

"She's not of our people."

"I love her," I replied through gritted teeth.

"She can't give you daughters, you know," said my mother's father. "And you can't give her sons. You've laid with her, and yet you haven't gotten a child on her."

"What…that…damn it, are you *spying* on me?" I managed, flustered to the point of blushing.

My unbothered ancestors merely stared until I brought myself under control.

"For your information," I said stiffly, "and not that it is *any* business of yours, we've as yet taken measures to prevent children. Our circumstances aren't ideal."

"Come, now," said my father's father, "be reasonable, boy. You know she'll never bear your children."

"You are all that remains of this family," said Father, and swept his arm toward the multitude around the fire. "Our sole hope against extinction. And you would be so selfish?" He stepped closer to me, his tail twitching in agitation. "What is she to you, anyway? A half-formed creature—"

"Stop it," I muttered.

"—and a *mistake*. She knows she should never have been born. Why would you take *that* to mate?" He shook his head and sighed. "I taught you better, Kippet. I raised you to respect our people, our traditions, our heritage…and this is what you think of us? You spit in our faces? Look at you," he said with a sneer of disgust, "stumbling over your own feet like you've never seen them before. You've forgotten who you are."

His words pounded against me like a sledgehammer, striking my weakest parts, but I refused to back down. "I've forgotten nothing," I retorted. "I've *survived*. And I know more about our people than you ever did, so don't tell me what I should and shouldn't want."

"That useless piece of half-bred filth—"

"*Stop it!*" I bellowed, and before I knew what I was doing, I punched my father squarely in the torso. He doubled over with the blow, and I darted back, breathing heavily and raising my fists as protection against the rest of my kin. "Stop," I said. "Say what you will about me, but leave Amy out of this."

Father raised his head, and his expression spoke of disbelief and betrayal. "You would *strike* me?"

"If that's what it takes to defend my mate."

"Your *mate?*" he echoed. "You still intend to take her, even though your ancestors are standing before you, telling you how strongly they disapprove?"

At that, I lowered my fists and looked him in the face. "My life will not be ruled from the far land. I love Amy. I'm marrying her in the morning. And I don't give a shit how you feel about that."

A hush fell over the camp, broken only by the crackling of the bonfire.

And then, to my surprise, Father smiled.

"Good. *Good,*" he said—and confusingly enough, he seemed to regard me with pride.

"You passed," said Hib, coming up on my left, and slung his arm around my neck. "I got the same treatment before Kanu and I agreed, only from those two," he said, pointing to our chuckling grandfathers. "It's tradition."

"*What* tradition?" I said, thoroughly perplexed. "No one ever told me—"

"Because then the effect would be lost," Father explained, and pointed to a man standing near the edge of the semicircle. "My mother's father's father did it to me."

"The point is to see whether you're certain about your mate," Hib continued. "If you back down, you're not ready. Nicely done."

Father approached and held me by the shoulders, then hugged me tightly. "Be happy with her," he said. "For what it's worth, you have my blessing."

"Sorry about the punch," I mumbled.

"There is no pain in the far land," he assured me, and grinned as he withdrew. "But I faked it well, didn't I?"

I couldn't help it—my eyes began to prick. "I'm sorry. I'm so sorry about—"

"The etalre? There was nothing you could have done, son. You lived. I'm grateful for that. Don't blame yourself for surviving."

"I didn't even avenge you, Badger and Seamus and Jim—"

"*Kippet.*" Father gripped my shoulders again and squeezed. "My son is a good man. I'm satisfied." He smiled while I swiped my hands against my eyes. "Your mother and sisters couldn't be here—this testing is between a man and his fathers, a woman and her mothers. But they're proud of you. Go, be happy. Be good to her." He retreated a pace, and the corner of his mouth ticked. "And should she bear a son for you…know that his ancestors will be waiting when he decides to take a mate."

"This is cruel."

"It works. Listen to your elders."

"Still seems unnecessary," I replied, but laughed. "And you're really not upset about Amy?"

Father glanced behind him at motion in the crowd. "You realize this place is for your fathers, yes? *All* of them?"

He stepped to the side, and a dark-haired man—an unmistakably *human* man—moved to the fore and smiled up at me.

"There are few secrets in the far land," said Father. "And this is not goodbye forever. Live your life, and when you reach this place in truth, we'll be waiting."

I don't remember leaving him—all I know is that I bolted upright in bed, felt for my bare legs to see whether I had four or two, then collapsed back onto the mattress, staring at the darkness until I could take it no longer. I rose, felt my way to the door, then slipped into Amy's room, guided by the dim pink glow of her salt lamp.

She, too, was awake, sitting on the edge of her bed, and

she moved over when I sat beside her. "Couldn't sleep?" I asked as she rested her head against my chest.

"No, I was asleep…I just had the weirdest dream," she replied.

"Oh?"

"Yeah." She hesitated, then asked, "Would it sound weird if I said I met your mom?"

I pulled her closer and rubbed her arm. "What did she say?"

"'Welcome to the family,' more or less."

I tried to be subtle when I sniffed, but Amy noticed and reached for my face in the dim light. "Kip? Oh, honey, I'm sorry, I shouldn't have mentioned—"

"No," I said, catching her hand as it brushed against my wet cheek. "I'm not upset."

"Then why—"

"Because," I said, kissing her fingers, "I saw the far land, too. And she meant it."

SEPTEMBER: STUART PURCELL

The one piece of nice furniture in Bobby's office was an old oak desk, which he'd lovingly refinished the year before in my garage. Everything else was utilitarian Cold War–era metal, cheap particleboard, or salvage. The county had a budget, after all, and Wright's Mill's principal's office décor wasn't high on the priority list. He'd done his best with fresh paint, a knockoff oriental rug, standing lamps, and framed landscapes, but the office still wasn't the sort of place that inspired people to come in for a nice chat.

Maybe that was the point.

Bobby sat behind his desk in his squeaky swivel chair, his hands folded on the scuffed pleather blotter. Across from him, in an assortment of chairs dragged in from other offices, sat three sets of parents and their first-graders. There simply wasn't enough room for another chair, and so I leaned against the wall, conscious of the adults' baleful glances and trying to keep my outward cool. Bobby might have been unaware, but I knew damn well that there were six trained wizards in that enclosed space, and none of them liked me that morning.

To be fair, I didn't like their kids. The three boys had been running as a pack since 4K—I'd watched them when I subbed as playground monitor or took my lunch in the cafeteria—and they were rambunctious unless physically restrained. The kindergarten teachers had kept a firm hand on them—even Janie Roche, once she'd found her feet— but the boys' first-grade teacher was letting them get away with murder.

Then again, she was Arcanum, and I suppose that at the end of the day, Beverly had to look out for number one.

By then, the beginning of my seventh year of teaching, I could spot a silo dweller at fifty yards. There were different tells, but the easiest was peer group. Like the students, the faculty tended to congregate in two groups, "military" and mundane. Those who had made it known that they had ties to the installation were tight-lipped about their home life or what their alleged spouses did, and while they were never antagonistic to the rest of us, neither were they chummy. Beyond that, I'd picked up a few tips from Aiden. There was, to be kind, an Arcanum "look," especially in the families with the purest bloodlines, and it wasn't exactly a thing of beauty. Others occasionally displayed a tic in times of stress, reaching toward the waistband for a wand that wasn't there. And then there were the necklaces: thin gold chains without ornamentation or any sort of pendant, worn by a few teachers and more than a handful of students. They might have been mistaken for half-covered saint medallions if one didn't know to look closely. Aiden told me the chain was a symbol that the wearer was either a magus or close kin to one, usually a spouse or a child (or, more rarely, a sibling, niece, nephew, or grandchild).

Though her mother had been grand magus, albeit briefly, Ros never wore a necklace. The boys I'd condemned to Bobby's office—Silas Morse, Lyle Conrad, and Antony Copeland—were a different story. Their necklaces were on full display that morning, as were the identical chains around the necks of both elder Morses, both Conrads, and Mrs. Copeland. I surmised that at least two of the adults in the room were magi, which did nothing to ease my queasiness.

"Thank you for coming," Bobby began once the parents and their sullen sons were seated. "We'll keep this brief. Quentin, could you fill everyone in on why we're here?"

"Certainly." I straightened, affecting as much dignity as I could in my blue-striped caftan. "Yesterday morning, during the first lunch period, I went to my supply closet to prep for the afternoon classes and found Ros Carver hiding in the corner, crying. I pulled her out of there and sat her down, and she gradually told me that these three had stolen her lunch, run away with it, and dumped it in the trash before she could catch them. When she tried to tell Beverly Tifton, one of them smeared a glob of peanut butter in her hair—"

"Peanut butter isn't allowed in the school," Mrs. Conrad interrupted, smirking as though she'd played a straight flush.

"It was a nut butter of some kind," I replied, resisting the urge to smirk back at her. "I spent the rest of the period washing it out and drying her hair with paper towels. So I walked her back to the cafeteria as her class was finishing, and then I had those kids at two for art. We were using tempera paint—washable, thank goodness. I was helping another table, and I turned around in time to see those three come up behind Ros and squirt paint all over the back of her shirt." I crossed my arms and stared down at the seemingly unabashed parents. "That's when I dragged them to the office."

"For a little paint?" Mr. Morse asked, arching a brow. "Kids will be kids, Mr....uh..."

"Galloway," I said. "Accidents happen—the state of the studio tables is testament to that. And sure, kids goof off and get themselves messy. But your children ganged up on a classmate twice in one day, and that's not the sort of behavior we can tolerate."

"Don't you think we should leave that question to your boss?" Mrs. Conrad interjected with faux sweetness. "What do you think, Bobby—was it really worth disrupting our sons' education over a little roughhousing?"

"That wasn't *roughhousing*," I protested, "that was straight-up bullying. That kid was in tears—"

"They're first-graders," said Mrs. Copeland. "Little things set them off."

Mr. Morse gave me a long once-over. "I'm sure that

school wasn't easy for you, Mr. Gault—"

"*Galloway.*"

"—but don't you think you might be…I don't know, projecting?"

As much as I wanted to snap at the bastard and his fidgeting offspring, I kept my composure and did the mature thing. "Mr. Gillespie," I said, turning to Bobby, "I stand by my decision. I think it would be appropriate for the boys to write their classmate apology letters, and then we can all move past this."

Bobby looked at me, and then he gave the parents a long, hard stare. "I believe," he said slowly, "that the boys have been punished enough. They've already had what amounted to a two-hour in-school suspension, between yesterday afternoon and this morning. That seems more than sufficient for…roughhousing."

He pronounced the last word with distaste, but the glance he shot me begged me not to quibble.

As the parents stood to take their sons back to class, Mr. Morse asked Bobby, "This won't happen again, then? We won't be pulled away from our work over nonsense like this?"

"We'll handle it," Bobby assured him.

I said nothing until I heard the distant stairwell door close, and then I wheeled on my boss. "You didn't see her," I said, slapping the desk. "They were *attacking* that kid, and—"

"I know, Quentin, I know," he said, and sighed as he massaged his temples. "You realize that this school will go under if we don't get those nice, big, *voluntary* checks from the base folks, yeah?"

"Yeah," I muttered.

"I understand from Beverly that two of those parents are pretty high up the food chain out there. Marcie Conrad and Alan Morse."

"Lovely people."

"You said it, not me. We can't afford to antagonize

them. And you…look, I don't mean this as a threat, but if they come snooping after you, asking about credentials and such, I'm going to have no choice but to cut you loose. You've been great, and I don't want to lose you, but if it's one teacher or half our funding…"

"I understand. But what do I do the next time Ros or some other kid is hiding in my closet, huh? Look the other way?"

Bobby paused, and when he spoke again, he looked as if there were something bitter in his mouth. "I'd suggest you clean them up as well as you can and remind them that it gets better. Can you do that?"

I looked him square in the eye. "Do I have a choice?"

"Not if you want to stay here."

There were many things I wanted to say to Bobby in that moment: *Grow a spine. Take a stand. I thought you were better than this.*

But giving voice to those thoughts would have meant submitting my resignation, and a wizard doesn't run.

"Guess I'll be stocking up on therapy Oreos, then," I said, and let the door slam behind me.

OCTOBER: SEAMUS MALONE

It took Badger eight long months to gain the Varga children's trust. Well, they weren't children in the technical sense—Iris and Andy were twenty-three and twenty-one, respectively—but they'd been on their own since the coup, sister and brother against the world. Vivi had pulled information for us from the old database: their parents were Hungarian nationals who'd immigrated to Canada as young children, where they'd met, married, and started a family. Both were witches, but there was nothing in the system about their kids other than their names and ages. Eventually, Iris told Badger how she and her brother had come home from school to discover the door broken down, the house empty. With no bodies to be found and warnings plastered all over the Fringe network, they'd assumed their parents had been snatched and ran.

Badger found them in a remote corner of the Alaskan backcountry, their glow in the dream space so faint that she'd overlooked them for years. When she finally investigated, what she found so shook her that she barely spoke the following morning. I caught her on the fire escape at dawn with a cold, over-brewed cup of Earl Grey, staring out to sea. Not until I coaxed her back inside and convinced her to pick at a piece of toast did she tell me what she had seen.

The Vargas had lived in a leafy neighborhood in Vancouver, a place not ridiculously posh but more than merely comfortable. Somehow, their unaccompanied, untrained children had run more than three thousand miles to the northwest, where they were subsisting in an abandoned miner's cabin. As Badger described it, the place was little more than a shack, leaning and uninsulated by any conventional means. But the kids had done their best, salvaging corrugated metal to repair the leaky roof and stuffing the chinks between the rough-hewn boards with mud. The first cabin in which they'd squatted had burned down due to a mishap with their cooking fire, but they'd learned in the intervening years, and they slept near their makeshift stove, a metal wash basin elevated by a hard mudpack. Most of the smoke escaped through a hole in the ceiling, but not all. Badger hadn't been able to make out fine details in her sleepwalks, but she could well imagine how soot-stained the interior of the cabin had to be.

The kids had the hard, pinched look of the long-hungry, compounded by years of rough Alaskan winters. When they finally trusted Badger enough to answer her questions, they told her how they'd learned by trial and error to fish and hunt and forage. Their neighbors, if one could call them that—no one lived closer than two miles—had been suspicious of the pair but were willing to let them do odd jobs for food and clothing. Both had learned to sew and to work hides, and Andy could butcher a kill as effectively as any of the men around them, but their education hadn't prepared them for life in the wilderness. Andy had lost the tips of three fingers to frostbite, while Iris had lost her left foot to a gangrenous wound the winter before. A concerned neighbor had taken her by snowmobile to a rural clinic that asked few questions and didn't try to collect on payment— the condition of her clothing was indication enough that she had no money.

Neither Varga had magical talent to speak of. The dragonscale wands they'd grabbed when they ran away from home had become firewood years before. Given their history, they were understandably reluctant to talk to a glowing stranger in their dreams, but with time and gentle persistence, Badger won their uneasy trust. Finally, they agreed to be evacuated, though without money or transportation, they had no way of meeting us. We'd have to go to them.

As the Vargas didn't have mobiles or even cameras, the best we could do was use satellite photography of the area around their cabin for reference. Duly armed, Badger and I drove to a quiet motel near Knoxville, just in case the Arcanum was monitoring fluctuations around Rigby. Early that evening, when the hallway outside our room was quiet, I opened a gate about a quarter-mile from the cabin. Though it was mid-afternoon in Alaska, the cold hit us like ice water to the face—the temperature had dipped below freezing, and snow blew into our room on a stiff, cutting breeze. We hurried across and sealed the gate, then marched through the woods toward the shack in the distance. An uncomfortable slog later, we shook off the worst of the snow on the Vargas' crude porch and stepped inside their hovel. It was as bad as Badger had described it, and I coughed with the smoke. "Best put that out," I wheezed, pointing to the fire tub.

Iris, bucket of snow melt in hand, hobbled across the warped floor and did the honors. "In case you didn't come," she explained. "We couldn't be sure."

The kids—young adults, really—were dressed in patched shirts and trousers beneath roughly made hide coats, which they wore with the fur turned in. Both were filthy, greasy and sooty from the fire, but then I supposed it would be painful to bathe in a room in which one could see one's breath. They carried few possessions—a small photo album, a bow and arrows, a Bowie knife—and looked at us with hopeful eyes. Iris even stuck out her leg to show off the leather wrappings she'd placed around her stump. "Ready to walk," she said, and smiled.

It was the childlike confidence in her smile that gutted me, but I held myself together. "No need," I said, and opened a gate back to our room. "This way. It won't hurt."

Once Alaska was behind us and the cold sealed out once

more, Badger leapt into action. She sent me for pizza—there was no need, she'd told me, to scare the kids with more magic than was necessary—then shooed the Vargas into the bath one at a time, ordering them not to come out until the water ran clear. Both took long, hot showers, wrapped themselves in the robes that Badger had stealthily "found" in the wardrobe, then sat on the spare bed and stuffed themselves with Domino's. When they were full, Badger asked if it would be okay for her to make them new clothes, and when they agreed, she started with pajamas and sent them to bed. They snuggled unselfconsciously, Iris spooning behind her younger, taller brother as if guarding him, and I wondered how many nights they'd slept like that for body heat.

The next morning, the Vargas dressed in their spellcraft-made jeans and jumpers—the latter of which they soon abandoned for T-shirts, citing the warmth of the Appalachian autumn—and Badger and I drove them back to Rigby after a stop, at their request, at that most wondrous of restaurants, McDonald's. Arnie had their tea ready when we arrived, and we pulled out the sofa bed, explaining that one of them was welcome to Amy's old room downstairs. But the Vargas wouldn't be separated, and so we made them comfortable there. As they'd grown marginally less skittish of magic, Arnie did his best to make a prosthetic foot for Iris, a flesh-toned construction that bent in multiple ways to simulate a natural footfall. She beamed and threw her arms around his neck even before he finished the fine-tuning.

When we shipped them off to Faerie the next day after breakfast, I was thrilled to see a small crowd waiting for them in Coileán's office: a doctor, a therapist, and many of the Canadian Fringers, come to welcome their own. Vivi hugged them both when they stepped through the gate. "As a former Alaskan," she said, grinning, "I'd just like to congratulate you on sticking it out that long. The interior is *not* forgiving."

Badger and I stood on the Rigby side of the gate to say

our goodbyes. As the doctor pulled Andy aside to give his maimed hand a preliminary inspection, Iris thanked us both again, then leaned close and asked, "You'll keep looking for our mom and dad, won't you? Please?"

"Of course," Badger told her, smiling tightly. "Rest, now, dear—you've earned it."

I contracted the gate and hid it again, pleased with our success. But when I turned around, I was alone in the room. I hunted through the building until I located Badger sitting on the side of our bed, gripping the duvet and staring at the rug. "Love?" I asked, taking a seat beside her. "All right, then?"

She said nothing for a long, *long* moment, and then, ever so softly, she whispered, "Where are they?"

"You'll find them," I said, pulling her against my side. "It's all a matter of time."

But she shook her head and turned her face toward mine, her brown eyes haunted. "What if they're dead, Seamie? What if they're all dead?"

"Mulligan wouldn't do that—"

"Wouldn't he? Look at what he's done already!"

I hesitated, gauging her mood. "Badge…"

"What if I'm hunting ghosts? What do I tell those kids— I wasn't quick enough?"

I couldn't answer that, and I certainly couldn't sleepwalk, but I could hold her for as long as she needed. "You're doing all you can," I murmured into her hair.

"It's not enough," she mumbled against my shoulder.

"It is. It's got to be," I replied, and sat with her as the sunlight crept up the wall.

NOVEMBER: COILEÁN

"Anyone I know?" asked Toula, cracking her knuckles.

"Not this time. I'm sure you've seen them around," I replied, "but this appears to be a new feud."

"Ooh, *lucky* you." She leaned against my bar and waited while I threw on a jacket against the morning chill. "And what, pray tell, set this one off?"

"As far as I can tell, swans."

Her brows rose in disbelief. "*Swans?*"

"Lia didn't invite Marelle to some party she threw, and so she set loose a flock of ill-tempered swans on Marelle's pond. For some reason, they had teeth."

"Mm. Creative."

"So Marelle killed them all and waited, and while Lia was out at a ball or some nonsense last night, she struck. I mean, I assume it was Marelle—I don't know anyone else with a grudge against Lia."

Toula grinned. "Which is why you have me. Get the gate open, and let's be done with it."

I started to comply with her order, then paused and considered her attire: leggings and a bright purple tunic, belted in black. "Don't you want a coat?"

"Nah." Her gelled spikes bobbed as she shook her head. "It's brisk, not horrible. I had breakfast on the balcony."

"Yes, well, all I had was a piece of Lia's mind. Shall we?"

I opened the gate and stepped through, unsure of what I'd find. Lia had complained that Marelle had altered her house in some respect—"That dog ruined my home!" she had shrieked, to be precise—but she'd been skimpy on details. What I saw in the middle of the formal gardens where Lia's sprawling brick manor home had been stopped me in my tracks.

Beside me, Toula began to laugh—a low, surprised chuckle that quickly burst into peals of giggles. "Are you kidding me?" she managed when she came up for air, her eyes streaming.

"Moon and stars," I muttered, "what *is*—"

"It's a giant bounce house, silly," she said, and grabbed my hand. "Come on!"

"Huh?" I asked as she nearly pulled me off my feet.

Toula spared me an exasperated glance as she tugged me toward the place where the front door had been. Instead of brick and graceful columns, the house had turned into a brightly colored balloon-like monstrosity, its walls replaced by inflated columns and panels of netting. A break in the net at the front suggested a door of sorts.

"You can probably run the spell from here," I said as we came to a halt. "Surely you'd see the culprit from this position—"

"Later."

I watched, perplexed, as Toula slipped off her shoes and opened the door. "You coming?" she asked, and climbed inside.

I wasn't sure that I wanted to, but I was sufficiently intrigued to kick off my loafers and join her.

The interior of the house was a massive floor of inflated segments, undulating where its parts were sewn together. The ceiling was another inflated piece perhaps fifteen feet above us. As I tried to find my feet, I heard gleeful shrieking and looked up to see Toula bounding across Lia's former foyer, or perhaps her ballroom. "This. Is. *Awesome!*" she crowed, timing her words with her jumps, and gathered enough steam to perform an ungainly midair somersault. She landed on her back, laughing, and scrambled upright to resume.

She was playing—actually *playing*, jumping and spinning

and throwing herself into the walls for the rebound. Her face was flushed, her shirt flying...

God, she had never looked so beautiful.

I don't remember the first time I looked at Toula and saw her as more than a spike-headed renegade. Yes, we'd forged our uneasy matricidal alliance, and that had developed into something nearing friendship while she'd served as the Arcanum's go-between. I mean, I had no choice but to get along with her—she was Val's little sister, after all. Now she'd been living in the palace for six and a half years, and somewhere along the way, I'd come to the shocking realization that I was *attracted* to her—that I wanted her for more than companionship.

It couldn't happen, I told myself. She'd been Meggy's friend, and again, she was *Val's sister*...and besides, there was no way she'd ever be with me. Toula had seen me at my nadir, broken and exposed—she'd have to be a fool to want any part of that.

But still, despite my internal warnings, I found myself drawn ever tighter into her orbit. The occasional dinner at her apartment became a weekly affair, then fell into a roughly three-day pattern. Game nights were sacrosanct on my calendar—stress relief, I claimed to anyone who questioned me, knowing damn well that I just wanted a few hours in her company, no matter how badly I lost. I began spending quiet afternoons with her, working on my petitions as she pored over books and made theoretical jottings on a thick notepad.

My feelings for Meggy had sparked into an almost instantaneous blaze. Toula had been a glow in the embers, but suddenly, I'd turned around and noticed a healthy fire. I was reminded of a frog in heating water, unaware of the change until it was too late.

As for Val...well, if he noticed, he held his tongue, and I was too embarrassed to broach the subject with him.

Toula, it seemed, had learned the trick to walking on the uneven floor, and she hurried back to where I stood near the door. "You look confused," she said. "Never been in a bounce house?"

"No…"

"They had one every year at the school Halloween carnival. *So* much fun. You get inside with a dozen of your classmates and go nuts, and at least one person ends the night with a black eye. Good times." She smiled wistfully, then glanced back at me, mischief playing at the corners of her mouth. "You're it," she announced, slapping me on the arm, and bounded away.

I had a grievance to settle. A court to run. A breakfast I'd never get around to eating.

I chased her.

Toula was faster than me and nimbler on the inflated floor, and I lost my balance several times trying to execute turns. The falls didn't hurt, though, and by the time I finally tackled her, we were both out of breath and laughing. I crawled off her to rest on the plastic-smelling red fabric, and Toula dragged herself out of the dip into which she'd fallen. When I sat up, I found her staring at me, mussed but still smiling. "I wish I'd known you when you were my age," she said.

That came as a twisting knife to the gut. I'd reminded myself many times that Toula had been involved with Mina, and Mina was older than me, but still…

Something must have slipped in my expression, as she added, "When the weight of the world isn't on you, you look like a big kid. I kind of figured that's what you were like before."

"I was pretty naïve at forty-four," I replied.

"Maybe," she said, and shrugged. "Still think it would have been interesting to meet that guy."

I hesitated, then heard myself murmur, "Could the current version be good enough?"

Toula pretended to give the matter serious contemplation, staring at the ceiling and rubbing her chin, then turned her gaze back on me and nodded.

We sat there together in that ridiculous inflatable mansion, neither speaking, and then Toula pushed herself off the floor. I followed suit, pausing to ensure my balance, and looked up from my unsteady feet when I heard her sigh. "Is something wrong?" I asked.

She'd folded her arms and was regarding me with a look of feigned annoyance. "Are you going to take your shot, or should I go for it?"

"What do you—"

She slid forward and kissed me with an unexpected strength, and I almost stumbled until I pivoted and sent us both falling. Toula landed in a seam, and I scrambled over her and resumed the interrupted kiss. "Toula," I whispered, "I—"

Look, she interrupted, speaking to my mind as she kissed me again.

She'd dropped her usual mental defenses, the sort of walls one puts up when surrounded by others with a talent for prodding, and having been given an invitation, I slipped into her thoughts.

It took me only a second to find what she'd wanted me to see. Against all reason, against her better judgment, she wanted me as badly as I wanted her.

I felt her testing my own walls and let her in. Connected, I sensed the relief rush over her when she saw my reciprocation.

When I came up for air, I propped myself atop the inflated segments between which she was pinned and studied her face as if seeing it for the first time. She had her mother's eyes, brilliant blue and thickly fringed—indeed, she had much of Mab's look about her—but there was a warmth in her smile that the old queen would never have been able to replicate.

"Are you sure?" I asked.

"Weren't you just in my head?"

"Yes, but—"

Her lips were soft and lightly chapped, and they moved

with practiced skill. I surrendered, then returned their ministrations as my hands began their own eager exploration.

When we slid out of the bounce house an hour later, Toula was flushed but wore a look of quiet satisfaction, an expression I was sure I mirrored. She put her shoes on, straightened her shirt, and ran one hand through her messy hair. "So, uh…I should probably run that spell now, yeah?"

"Screw it," I said, and with a wave, I sent the bounce house and its secrets back into the ether. "I'll just yell at them both until they cut it out. Any interest in brunch?"

"Mm. Sure. For some reason, I seem to have worked up an appetite."

I chuckled and started to open a gate, then paused as a thought occurred to me. "Uh…do you suppose that we could, um…"

"Keep this quiet?"

"How did you…*ah*," I muttered, raising my mental defenses again as she softly laughed. "Yes. It's not that I—"

"I get it," she cut in, saving me from that awkward explanation. "Yeah, it would probably be best for now if we kept this between us…more or less."

I cringed. "Val?"

"Let me handle him. And don't worry so much," she added, rubbing my shoulder. "I love him, but he doesn't get a vote in this."

"Does *he* know that?"

"I made that perfectly clear when I started seeing Mina. Just leave it to me, okay? And here." She smoothed my hair into place and grinned. "There, now. Secret's safe."

I kissed her once more—for luck, I suppose—and created a gate back to my office, then offered her my arm. "Come along, Glinda. I'm famished. Waffles?"

"Don't *start*, you," she replied, but wrapped her arm around mine and sealed the rift behind us.

MARCH: VIVI STOWE PERRYMAN

On the night before the seventh anniversary of the Unravelling, I was working late in my home office, polishing my remarks for the next day's memorial. We had reason to celebrate. There had been a few more arrivals, courtesy of the Virginia team, plus eight babies born in the last year. Several of the settlement school's earliest graduates had undertaken online college studies, and three were set to acquire their degrees in June. Most of the orphans who'd come of age had moved out of the dorm and into the apartments Robbie had designed with extra-thick walls and carpet resistant to beer stains, but a few lingered to help Rufe and Poppy, and all of them made occasional visits "home" for dinner. Toula had begun offering remedial education for the adult witches among us who'd received subpar training or wanted to brush up on their skills, while James did the same for the lesser bloods. Even Stephen, the once-reluctant debate coach, was sufficiently pleased with his students' progress to suggest adding mock trial in the fall.

No, we were no closer to finding our missing friends and family, but by God, we'd survived another year, and I'd resolved to do my best to see that everyone focused on the positive. If that meant a sleepless night and half a bottle of sparking rosé while I prepped, then so be it.

I was tweaking my notes for at least the eighth time when a knock at the door interrupted my train of thought. "Yes?" I called, trying not to sound irked. Hal had been working all day to keep me calm, and I assumed he was announcing his bedtime.

Instead, the door opened to reveal Ned, his face drawn. "You're needed," he announced, and beckoned for me to get up.

"Mind telling me why?" I replied, but did as he asked. Ned didn't stop by often, and he could play the "aloof eldest brother" role to perfection, but he never wasted my time.

"Defector," was all he said, and opened a gate.

I recognized the low settlement wall on the other side, lit by floating white orbs. Matthew and Harry stood nearby and watched as Ned ushered me through. "What's going on?" I asked them, tightening my bathrobe belt.

Matthew pointed toward the far side of the wall. "Mind having a word with her? She won't listen to us."

They stood aside while I stepped onto the bricks and peered out at the starry night, lit by my brothers' levitating lamps. Below me stood Connie Johansen, a defiant look in her eyes and a rucksack slung over her shoulders.

Shit.

"Hi, Connie," I said, keeping my tone conversational and my hands exposed, then jumped off the wall and landed beside her. She backed up a few steps, and I made no move to close the distance. "What's up?"

The tremor in her voice belied the steel in her gaze. "I'm leaving. I can't do this anymore."

She'd been on my personal watchlist for some time. Though she refused to speak about it to me, I'd heard from her friends that Connie had been the lone survivor of her family—that she'd come home from the grocery store to find her husband, their three daughters, their sons-in-law, and their infant grandson dead in the living room, the TV still blaring. I didn't know if Connie was in therapy—that was none of my business—but she'd become something of a recluse in recent years.

Connie had been in her early sixties when she was evacuated, so returning to the mortal realm wouldn't be an immediate death sentence, but still...

"You know you'll be on your own over there," I murmured. "Your house is surely owned by someone else now. You may have been declared dead."

She nodded.

"I know it's hard," I tried. "It's *so* hard. But you can make a life here—"

"Did you lose anyone that day?" she interrupted.

"Friends. Some are dead, some are missing."

"But you've still got your husband, don't you?" She glanced over her shoulder at my silent brothers. "Your family?"

"I know—"

"You *don't* know," she said, though there was no venom in it. "You can't know unless you've lived it." Connie hesitated, then stepped closer and squeezed my shoulder. "You're doing your best, honey, and thank you for that. But I'm ready to go home."

I might have been young, but I was wise enough to recognize a losing battle. "Where are you trying to go?"

"Battle Creek, Michigan."

The notion made me wince, and not just the idea of March in the Midwest. "We can't risk opening a gate directly," I explained. "There's one in Coileán's office that goes to Badger's place in Virginia, or there's a gate to Sedona. If you're set on this, why don't you go stay with Badger for a little bit, see how it goes?"

But she shook her head. "Sedona will be fine."

"Listen…Connie, was it?" Ned began, slipping over the wall to join us. "Why not wait until morning and—"

"No. *No*," she insisted, putting her hands up as a barrier between them. "I've done my waiting. Please, I just want to go home."

He looked her up and down, taking in her light jacket and small bag, and frowned. A heavy blue parka appeared over his arm, and he offered it to her with a matching pair of gloves. She cautiously took them from him and tried them on—a perfect fit, as expected—and as she zipped her coat, Ned extended a thick wallet. "You'll want to eat, I trust," he said. "And sleep beneath a roof. Ten thousand should see you to Michigan."

"Thank you," she whispered, tucking it into her bag.

"Can I at least give you Badger's number?" I asked Connie. "Just in case?"

Again, she shook her head. "I'll make it."

As I sought for the magic words that might convince her to change her mind, I caught my brother's eye again and heard him in my thoughts: *Your call, Vivi.*

This was my rodeo, and if I was going to be the coordinator, then I had to deal with the unpleasant parts. The boys wouldn't take her to the gate unless I approved it—I didn't need to be a mind reader to see that they didn't like Connie's plan any more than I did. But if I refused, then she'd slip off into the wilds of Faerie to search for her own way home, and I liked the odds of a lone witch at a Motel 6 much better than those of one up against the realm's more predatory fauna.

I reached for Connie's gloved hands and pressed them between mine. "Be careful, okay? And you can come back— just find Badger, and she'll help you."

I was still standing by the wall when Ned's quick gate to the natural Sedona gate closed behind the two of them. My brothers let me stare into space for a moment before Harry cleared his throat and asked, "What are you going to tell the others?"

I thought of my prepared, practiced remarks, the edits I'd been making to improve the flow of my jokes and bring out the best of our town's accomplishments over the last year. But that wasn't what the day was about, was it? No matter what sort of positive spin I tried to put on it, we were gathering to remember the missing and the dead.

Climbing over the wall again, I headed for the gate back to my cozy study. "Suppose I should think of something fitting to say."

—YEAR EIGHT—

MARCH: TOULA PAVLI

I lay in bed after our game night, unable to shut off and consequently staring at the immobile ceiling fan. My bedmate was a light sleeper, however, and when I huffed my frustration at the unyielding night one too many times, he mumbled, "Problem?"

I felt momentarily guilty for waking him—our quiet relationship was only four months old, and we were still figuring out each other's sleeping habits—but then I reminded myself that Coileán could conceivably go for days in an emergency. He enjoyed sleep as much as I did, but it wasn't an absolute *necessity*.

"Thinking," I said, rolling over to face him.

He chuckled. "Dangerous habit, that. What's keeping you up?"

His arm reached out to pull me closer, and I slid toward the middle of the wide mattress until we were almost forehead to forehead. "I hope Ellie's okay," I replied.

"Why wouldn't she be?"

"I mean, she's missed five game nights in a row."

"Don't be offended," he said, stroking my hair back from my face. "She's probably busy. You've heard her complain about petitions. And her court's the larger of the two, so she's got it worse than I do."

"Yeah," I muttered, "I know. But she was coming, like, *religiously* for months, and then all of a sudden...poof."

"Could have gotten bored."

I snorted my incredulity. "That woman has re-created every Catan expansion ever made, and she loves to win. I don't think the issue is boredom."

"Then perhaps Val and I don't provide a sufficient challenge," he replied.

"*That's* a given, but I'm a halfway decent player."

Coileán went quiet for a moment, then sighed. "Realm won't tell me anything. I get the feeling that this is none of my business."

"Doesn't mean it can't be mine."

His grip on my waist tightened. "And *there's* the Pavli."

"Shut up, you know you love the Pavli." Flopping onto my back, I said, "Last time I saw her, she seemed preoccupied. I won too easily, you know? Something's up with her."

He yawned. "As long as she doesn't take a page from her father's playbook and come after me…"

"I'm serious. Something's not right."

"What, beyond that little Arcanum situation?"

I sat up and slid out of bed, and I heard the mattress squeak as Coileán shifted. "I'm sorry, I'll be serious," he said as I fumbled in the darkness for my bathrobe. "What are you thinking?"

My fingers grazed the plush fabric, and as I dressed, I took an extra moment to fiddle with the belt, letting the silence stretch before I answered him. "You know that island jail she's been playing with for the last few years?"

"The archipelago?" he replied. "Sure."

"She's keeping everyone doubly bound, right? One to block their use of magic, the other to shrink them?"

He paused before responding. "That was my impression, yes. Why?"

"How many binds can you handle at once? I'm not talking about binding a mundane—how many binds could you keep going against targets that are actively resisting?"

The mattress creaked again, and I heard his footsteps shuffle on the rug. "Nightcap first."

I followed him out to the kitchen, where I made a cup of green tea while he plucked a generous double of bourbon from the ether. "Sorry," he said into his tumbler, "this subject—"

"Sensitive?"

"Makes me slightly squeamish, actually," he confessed, and leaned against the counter while I bobbed my teabag. "Sometimes," he said quietly, "I still get nightmares about that bind."

"I know."

His eyebrows rose, and a guilty expression flashed across his face before his cheeks began to redden. "Sorry, I didn't mean to disturb—"

"Hey. *Hey*," I said, rubbing his shoulder, "it's okay. Not like you can help it, eh?"

"Embarrassing," he muttered.

"Then just be glad you haven't been shacking up with your mortal enemy. But in all seriousness," I continued as he sipped, "what *could* you do in terms of binds?"

It took Coileán half the glass before he answered me, and even then, he didn't have much to offer. "I doubt that Oberon had anyone bound except me when he attacked, or if he did, it was a mundane. But we were evenly matched—he had experience and a little strength on his side, but not much."

"Let's say you weren't trying to bind another king," I replied. "Ordinary fae targets. Ballpark?"

"It would depend. Age, strength, any experience in repelling binds…" He frowned at the wall, then shook his head. "I'm sorry, but I don't know what to tell you. I mean, I've got far more power than the average faerie with the realm's boost factored in, but exactly *how* much more? I can't say, Toula." He paused to drain his glass. "You think Ellie's overextending herself?"

"Maybe. How many people does she have on that archipelago? And if she were getting close to her limit, don't you think she might have trouble concentrating on matters other than keeping the binds together? Like, oh, a board game?"

Coileán said nothing, but I could see his wheels turning.

"Why don't I go talk to her?" I said. "Or give her a call, see how she's doing?"

"That's not a good—"

"Yeah, I get it, *you* can't butt in. I'm not a queen, remember? I don't claim a court. Closest thing to a neutral party around here. Let me talk to her, find out what's going on, and if need be, you can take it from there."

He seemed to hesitate, but in the end, he set his empty tumbler aside and took my hands. "Let it go for now, okay? Please. The last thing I want is a war with Ellie, and if I back her into a corner, she might have to react with a show of force."

"*You* wouldn't be doing—"

"Just in case." I started to speak, but he beat me to it. "For me. Please, just wait it out. If the realm starts to complain, I'll tell you first thing, but until then…"

By rights, Coileán couldn't order me to do anything—he wasn't my king. But he *was* my boyfriend, and a request was a different matter entirely.

"Okay," I said, and sighed. "If it means so much to you, I'll stay out of it for now. But that doesn't mean I'm not worried about her."

"She's a big girl—I'm sure she's fine," he said, and wrapped his arms around my waist. "Thank you."

I leaned against him and closed my eyes. "Still don't know if I can sleep."

"Mm. Could I distract you, do you suppose?"

"That depends. What'd you have in mind?"

He kissed me—quickly at first, then longer and more deeply as his hands migrated south. My hands latched behind his neck, and he hoisted me off my feet. "How's this?" he murmured in my ear.

"Not a bad start."

"Ah, that means there's room for improvement, then," he replied, and carried me back to bed.

APRIL: AMY LEVEY

I'd just turned over the OUT TO LUNCH sign on the glass door when my phone vibrated in my pocket. The number was blocked, but in case it was a customer, I took the call as I headed toward the hidden apartment staircase. "Wilcox Webworks, Amy Wilcox speaking. How can I help you?"

There was a pause on the other end of the line, and then a male voice asked in Fae, "Is this Karl's granddaughter?"

Surprised, I stopped dead in the middle of the shop and thought of the many terrible ways such an enquiry could go. "Um…yes," I eventually replied, slipping into Fae as well. "Who—"

"Hugo. His brother."

His brother, not *your granduncle*. I wasn't surprised—the only highborn faerie who'd claimed me was Eleanor, and I didn't expect anything from her fully fae siblings.

"Oh. Hello," I said, turning toward the old oak counter instead of the kitchen and the grilled cheese I'd promised myself an hour before. "How did you get my number?"

"I told Eleanor I'd had time to think about it and wanted to thank you properly for the gift."

He sounded pleased with himself, and I assumed his excuse had been nothing but pretense. "No need," I replied. "You're welcome. Hope it helped."

"Why?"

"Excuse me?"

"Why did you do it?"

I sighed quietly and plopped into my swivel chair. "Because I felt sorry for you. You looked miserable in there, and I've got microfiber cloths to spare. You needed that one more than I did."

"But *why*?" he pressed. "That was nonsensical. You gained nothing."

Though I'd never had extended dealings with a full-blooded faerie, I'd been warned of the potential complications. "You've heard of the concept of altruism?"

"Of course," he said dismissively, "but never an explanation that made sense."

"And you're probably not going to get one today. Look...people help each other out, yeah? Like, you do something nice for your neighbor, and down the line, he'll probably do something nice for you."

"Reciprocity, you mean."

"It's understood, but yeah. There's not this formal contract or anything, it's just...you know, a norm."

"So this hypothetical neighbor isn't bound to reciprocate?"

"No," I admitted, "but most will."

"You might have done him a service, only to receive nothing in return."

I closed my eyes, searching for patience. "It's not about getting something back. If you do, great, but that's not the point. You do your neighbor a favor because that's what good neighbors do. Or you take clothes you don't want and give them to a shelter so someone else can use them. Or you give money to a charity that's feeding homeless dogs or tutoring underprivileged kids or whatever. It's..." I struggled, then said, "If everyone does a little bit of good, everybody ultimately benefits in some way. Maybe you don't get a tangible, direct benefit, but the net result is good for society as a whole. Does that make sense?"

Hugo snorted. "No, but I suppose it's all I can expect of you. Anyway, there's another matter I wish to discuss."

I propped my head in my hand. "What's up?"

"When did you last speak with Karl?"

At that, I laughed in disbelief. "The *only* time I've ever

spoken to him was the day we met. He doesn't want anything to do with me."

"So you don't know?"

"I mean, he tried to kill me twice—"

"*No*, girl. You don't know about the archipelago?"

I frowned at a display of cell phone cases on the far wall. "What archipelago?"

"*The* archipelago. My darling sister's chief amusement."

"Look," I told him, "I have no idea what you're going on about, so—"

"Shortly after you left that day, she imprisoned Karl in a terrarium, just as she had me," he interrupted. "After she tired of me and let me go, she decided to play with some of our other siblings. She discarded her individual terraria and built a miniature island chain. It's complex," he explained. "Storms, navigable stars, feral sheep—all within one of her parlors. It's an attraction of sorts."

"Jesus," I murmured. "That's…odd."

"She's left Karl there all along. He's been bound and imprisoned four and a half years for her amusement."

"Or maybe as delayed punishment for raping my grandmother," I offered, keeping my tone light. "Aunt Ellie didn't seem to take that news well."

"Four and a half *years*? For *that*?"

"I don't know, sounds fair to me."

Hugo muttered something under his breath—I couldn't be sure, but it sounded like *mongrels*. "Karl's not the only one. She's been collecting our siblings and a few others over that time. There must be a hundred people on the archipelago by now. No one has been released."

Was I imagining it, or did I hear an undercurrent of fear in his voice?

"And what would you like me to do about this?" I asked, drumming my fingers on the countertop. "Even if I wanted to, I couldn't bust anyone out of there."

"You have Eleanor's ear, do you not? Convince her to release her prisoners and destroy the archipelago."

"Why should I?"

That gave him a moment's pause. "You gave me a gift—"

"But I didn't push for you to be let out. What the queen does with the court is her business, and I'm not going to presume to tell her how to run her operation."

"You don't understand. She's imprisoning *us*," he protested. "High lords and ladies reduced to savages and caged beasts, huddling in shacks against the storms…"

"You seem to care. I'm surprised," I said, standing again. My stomach would be denied no longer, and so I headed upstairs. "I thought faeries didn't go for the whole 'empathy' thing."

Hugo sputtered as I mounted the staircase, then managed, "I don't care about her *current* prisoners. She can keep them as long as she agrees not to add to their number."

I opened the apartment door and nodded to Arnie, who was doing a crossword at the kitchen table. "I see," I said, holding the phone against my shoulder as I rummaged for the cheese singles in the fridge. "You want my help because you're afraid of being sent back, is that it?"

"Name your price."

I slapped the loaf of bread and mayonnaise on the counter and closed the fridge door. "What could you possibly give me?"

"What *couldn't* I give you?" he retorted. "Foolish girl, do you not understand—"

"I live with a faerie and two wizards. Tell me what you can do that they can't."

I had time to get the pan greased and heating before Hugo found a response. "Recognition," he said. "You said you've only spoken once to Karl. I can make him recognize you as his granddaughter. Isn't that what you'd like, to be a lady instead of a nameless mongrel?"

My shoulders tensed, but I forced myself to concentrate on the sizzling skillet to stay calm. A pity it was copper— we'd made as much of the kitchen as we could non-steel for

Seamus's benefit, but still, the thought of smacking Hugo upside the head with a proper iron frying pan made me feel marginally better.

"Funny you should say that," I finally replied. "Aunt Ellie recognizes me already, and that would seem to trump whatever's on offer from you. And I may be young, but I'm not so stupid as to think you could make Karl do *anything* he was disinclined to do. I'm Fringe, you know—what sort of idiot do you take me for?"

His voice rose in pitch and speed as his lies crumbled. "Listen, you don't understand, I'll see that Karl—"

"Pardon my French, but I don't give a flying fuck about Karl," I snapped. "And this mongrel is hanging up now."

I ended the call, cutting him off mid-squawk, and silenced the phone. By the time I sat down to eat, Hugo had stopped calling me back.

SEPTEMBER: VALERIUS

The secret to effective training is to know the trainee's limits. Run him until he can only walk, walk him until he can do nothing but crawl, and when his knees give out, demand one more step. It's brutal, I suppose, but effective, and my trainees have always been stronger for my methods.

Still, the boys looked as though they'd have liked to punch me if they weren't so exhausted.

I could seldom herd all three of my young students into simultaneous lessons. Aiden seemed to find problems with his computers that needed immediate correction, and he knew that I couldn't call his bluff. Joey tended to disappear with Georgie whenever my schedule cleared. As for my nephew, who was more in need of training than either of the others, Seamus insisted that he couldn't leave Badger for more than a few days at a time. I suspected that Badger could manage admirably without his assistance and told him as much, but coaxing Seamus over the border remained a difficult task. Having finally nagged him into returning for a week's work, I used his visit to lure Joey out to our practice ring as well. Preying on Joey's sense of pity was, perhaps, underhanded of me, but one does what one must.

While they rehydrated off to the side, I noticed a gate open out of the corner of my eye and beckoned for Toula to join us. "Perfect timing," I said as she strolled closer.

She cracked her knuckles. "Do my best. Did you tell them?"

"Not yet."

By then, the boys were giving her uneasy glances. "That's

completely unfair," Joey protested. "Don't make us fight *Toula*."

"I'd like to see you try, Percival," she taunted, and met his glower with a little smirk. "You'll be fighting wizards, but not this one."

"Huh?"

"Drink up, and you'll find out."

After a few seconds, I saw the light of comprehension dawn in his eyes, and his shoulders slumped as he turned to Seamus. "Projections," he muttered in English.

"Not *those* bloody things again," Seamus replied in kind, and swigged from his bottle.

If they thought they were having a private conversation, they were sorely mistaken—I'd picked up the language years before. Then again, perhaps it was a camaraderie thing. Joey could speak Fae passably well, but Seamus seldom used it, and as soon as one switched, the other followed. Not the best tactic for the heat of battle, particularly considering the opponents we envisioned—Toula reported that fluency in Fae was abysmally low among the Arcanum set—but for the moment, I was just pleased that they could work together. Joey's early training had been for solo combat, whereas Seamus's inclination appeared to be toward teamwork. I wanted Joey to improve his group awareness and Seamus to improve his practical skills, and the two seemed to be learning from each other. It helped that Joey viewed Seamus as an experienced elder. Seamus only had about twenty years on Joey, but with their youth, I suppose even that slight discrepancy still mattered.

While they quietly griped, Toula sloughed off her jacket and tied it around her waist. "Start with one and add?" she murmured, cutting her eyes toward the boys. "Or two? I don't care."

"How many can you control?"

"For simultaneous movement? Probably no more than four, but if you can keep my backups ready to go, I should be able to jump around as necessary."

I would have preferred conducting this lesson on my own. Creating a construct from enchantment to use as a sparring partner—Aiden had dubbed them "hard-light projections," whatever that meant—wasn't difficult for me, but then I'd had practice at the exercise and the strength of years to sustain my creations. The problem was that I had little fighting experience against wizards, and so I couldn't accurately mimic their techniques. While Toula was familiar with the Arcanum's fighting style, asking her to make the projections alone would have been unreasonable. She and I had thus come to an arrangement: joint constructions, powered by me and guided by her.

We anticipated raging headaches by the end of the day.

"All right, chumps," she called, signaling to our victims that the break had ended. "Let's see what you've got."

Enchantment is inherently messy, and two people attempting to make a unified result can lead to disaster. But Toula combined her talent with a wizard's precision, and when the construct materialized in the ring, it appeared solid and moved with fluidity. The wizard seemed nondescript: a man of roughly the boys' height, dressed in an unadorned blue robe over a black shirt and trousers, holding a dark-stained wand in his upraised right hand.

"Might want to shield," said Toula.

Her puppet struck hard and fast, but not with sufficient force to penetrate the shields that the boys hastily threw together. It shot again and again, moving in an erratic dance as it sought a gap in their defenses. Unfortunately for the wizard, the shield it had cast with its empty hand was small and weak, and Joey soon caught him off guard. "Good," Toula told him, appraising the smoking corpse in the dirt before it vanished. "Let's try something a little tougher."

A pair of wizards materialized that time—the first one, restored to health, plus a similarly proportioned comrade. The boys shielded, and as the wizards raised their wands, Seamus muttered to Joey, "Cover me."

Joey had barely said, "Yes, sir," before Seamus was

sprinting toward the wizards, putting everything he had into the shield. He drew their fire, then smashed into one, sending him down with a well-placed elbow and knee. Joey shot the distracted second wizard, and Seamus finished the first before he could rise.

"Unorthodox, but not too shabby," Toula decreed. "Ready for round three?"

Having twice triumphed, the boys traded confident grins as three robed figures appeared before them. That time, however, there was something different about the projections.

"No wands?" Seamus asked, already shielding.

"None needed," Toula replied. "You're fighting magi."

The bout was longer that time, and when Toula called it, Seamus had a broken wrist, Joey had a shattered leg, and the magi were closing in for the kill. "Decent attempt," I told the boys, tending to Seamus while Joey began weaving a healing enchantment around his own injury. "Good teamwork. Toula, did you—"

"Record it? Yes," she finished, flashing her quartz band. "Want to talk through the replay?"

"In a moment." I worked on Seamus for a time, then tweaked Joey's enchantment and brushed myself off as I stood.

"Where did we go wrong?" Seamus asked, cradling his bad wrist.

Toula pulled a bottle of water from the ether, took a long swig, and smiled grimly. "You tried to fight too many people outside your weight class."

His brows knit. "But they're just meant to be wizards."

"*Just?*" she echoed.

Realizing what he'd said, Seamus attempted to backtrack. "I didn't mean it like that, I—"

"I know what you meant," she interrupted. "And that's your problem. Wizards aren't all pushovers, and you, amigo, still have a long way to go. A magus your age has been training for forty-odd years. You've got some strength, but most of the rest of what you have is cockiness. And *you* know better," she added, glancing at Joey as he pulled together an ice pack. "If you don't believe me, I'll ask Arnold to come over and give you a demonstration."

Neither seemed keen to take her up on the offer. "So how do we beat them?" Seamus pressed.

Toula turned to consider our handiwork, frozen mid-step where she'd left them. "Honestly? You should run like hell and let someone more experienced take them on. But we could start a little smaller, if you'd like."

I felt her draw on my power once more. The trio of magi disappeared, replaced by a single figure: a middle-aged man in a red robe, his hair gray and thinning, his belly gone soft. Joey stiffened, and Seamus, noticing his reaction, turned to us for an explanation.

"This is James Mulligan," said Toula, folding her arms. "More or less. I've never studied him in combat, but I can approximate. You guys up for more, or would you rather let those breaks heal overnight?"

Before she'd finished, Joey had stood and created a crutch, and was limping toward the projection. "Show me how to kill him," he said softly.

I smiled to myself in quiet satisfaction.

My boys were growing up.

SEPTEMBER: ARNOLD LOWE

Even from the Joneses' ranch, it was a long drive to Houston.

We caravanned east, Zeb and Carey in the lead car and Badger and me following. The fact that we were keeping within a few notches of the speed limit irked my cousin, but then she wasn't the one stuck with the driving. While I listened to music at a low volume to keep myself awake during the overnight haul, she intermittently sleepwalked beside me, searching for the dim glow of our targets.

It had gone dark that morning, she said. Whether there were any survivors had yet to be determined.

As usual, Badger blamed herself for overlooking them, but it wasn't her fault. Though I certainly couldn't see what she could within dreams, I'd gleaned something of the experience from her: the dream space was a black-on-black landscape, and from a decent height, one could see lights shining below, gold for sleeping wizards and witches, white for faeries and their kin with diluted blood (and blue for Nath's people, though that hadn't been a problem since Badger sent them packing). For years, she'd scoured the globe in her sleep, hunting for Fringers in hiding and convincing them to let us help. We'd sent scores of grateful refugees to safety in Faerie, thanks to her work. I couldn't take much credit—I could drive and navigate, and patch up basic injuries, though my bit was nothing beside her tireless searching.

But there's a problem with searching from the air: the higher one goes, the brighter the light must be to catch one's notice. Badger had done her best, but the longer she searched, the more she discovered of the Fringe's fringe—the barely more than duds and the slightly fae who went unnoticed, washed out like faint stars by the suns of their more talented neighbors. She felt horrible about the situation, but what else could she have done? Our goal was to find Fringers and evacuate them, and we weren't choosy. There was no shame in going after low-hanging fruit. Moreover, there wasn't a full list of who might be in hiding—we didn't know how many had been snatched up by the assassin squads, nor did we know how many Fringers weren't registered on the network. Children, especially, had escaped everyone's notice—a blessing, maybe, since their absence from the network put them under Mulligan's radar. As the offspring of Fringers could easily tend toward the weaker end of the magical spectrum, Badger was only just learning how many people had been neglected in our recovery efforts.

She'd only noticed the Houston crew in late July, once it reached a critical mass and caught her attention. When she went in for a better look, she was stunned to find a dozen witches and lesser bloods, most of them barely more than mundane, sleeping together in an abandoned warehouse. The eldest didn't seem to be more than twenty, while the youngest were of primary-school age. All were small and somewhat emaciated, those lost orphans of the Unravelling. They slept on salvaged mattresses on a concrete floor, while behind them, a long table of wood planks and cinderblocks held several older-model computers and what appeared to be a few food boxes. Gutted, Badger had pulled the apparent eldest of the lot into the dream space and introduced herself, but the boy had been hostile and suspicious. Night after night she returned, trying to coax them into letting us help them, but to no avail. The boy, who called himself their coordinator, didn't know Badger and didn't believe her protestations that she wasn't from the Arcanum. And then he hit her with the question that sent us scrambling: if she was Fringe, then why wasn't she on the network?

The Fringe network—the *old* Fringe network—had been a ghost town for years. Mulligan had stolen credentials and access to everything in there, after all. Once the group in Faerie had come up with a new network, they'd left the old one untouched, partly in case someone reached out but mostly so that Mulligan wouldn't suspect the ongoing Fringe activity in the mortal realm. Seven years past the Unravelling, we barely glanced at the old network, perhaps once every few months, and always with Badger's "ghost mode" credentials, which had allowed coordinators to browse in peace without being mobbed by other users. The last time we'd looked had been in March.

Logging in upon awakening, Badger was horrified to see a post from April inviting Fringers to Houston. The so-called coordinator, who'd got on using his dead mother's credentials, offered his address and phone number to anyone out there. The comments that had appeared over the next weeks and months were from similar children, those who'd looked at the network on occasion but hadn't had the courage to post. When nothing bad happened, they were emboldened. They made plans to congregate and collaborate. In Houston, they set up their squatters' compound, poaching power and Wi-Fi from an unobservant neighbor and living off of food pantry handouts. Petty theft wasn't a lifestyle, but rather a means of survival. The original post remained on the network, augmented with more recent invitations to come shelter with the Houston crew.

Badger pleaded with the kids in their dreams, warning them of the risk they were taking by advertising their location, but they shrugged her off as paranoid—or worse, an Arcanum spy. Why else, their coordinator demanded, would she be telling them to scatter? That was what the

Arcanum wanted, wasn't it? To demoralize the ones remaining? Badger tried to tell them about the Fringers we'd seen killed years after the Unravelling, the ones we'd not got in time, but the kids were unmoved.

The night before, Badger had sleepwalked as usual. What was unexpected was when she shook me awake at two in the morning and told me to dress. "Bodies," she said as I fumbled for my shoes. "I haven't counted them yet, but there are bodies in the warehouse. We've got to get to Houston."

A call to the ranch warned the Joneses of our impending arrival, and I opened a small intra-realm gate from our garage to their driveway—a quick blip, hopefully too small to warrant the Arcanum's notice. With Seamus training in Faerie, it fell to me to drive. As we sped through the night, I tried to avoid sudden braking so as not to disturb Badger's concentration, but I could see little of her face in the blackness.

We parked two blocks away from the warehouse early that afternoon and climbed out of our vehicles, weary and worse for the long trip. At least the Joneses had slept in shifts— I'd been awake the whole time, and whatever sleep Badger had snagged hadn't been restful. Even still, we were wired…but then, Badger's latest findings had put us all on edge.

The bodies were gone from the warehouse. In their place were two men whose forms glowed brilliant gold in the dream space: wizards without question, assassins almost certainly. I'd been on the Council long enough to spot a cleanup crew. They'd been there when we rolled into town—waiting, certainly, but for what? Surely not *us*, I'd protested, as we'd given no indication that we were on our way.

Badger had regarded me with mild impatience as she gobbled a cheeseburger. "Someone must have escaped," she'd explained. "They're probably waiting to see if that one comes back to check on the others."

As we'd circled the warehouse at a few blocks' distance, Badger had sleepwalked one last time and found the wizards' prey. She hadn't tried to reach out to him—he was still awake when she saw him, crouching beside a broken window inside a small, abandoned office building—but she'd noted enough landmarks to guide us to his hiding spot. Nodding to Carey and Zeb, who had their wands drawn and ready, she quietly opened the door and led the way up two flights to the would-be coordinator.

He must have heard us coming, as he had his wand out and a weak shield in front of him when we walked onto his floor. "*Easy*, now," said Badger, showing him her empty hands. "We're here to help. Remember me?"

If he recognized her, he gave no sign. The boy's eyes were wide with terror, and his wand hand shook like there was an electric current running down his arm.

"We're not going to hurt you," Badger continued, taking a seat on the water-stained industrial carpet. "I'm Fringe, I swear it. We've come to get you out of here."

"You sent them," he whispered.

"Not sure which 'them' you're talking about," she said, keeping her voice calm, "but I *do* know there are two wizards lying in wait back at your squat. They came in the night, didn't they?" He nodded, and she sighed. "That's what I tried to warn you about. They used the network to rip us apart once—why wouldn't they keep checking it? There's a new network now, incidentally, but the people in charge of the tech side have left the old one untouched. Best to let the Arcanum think they have a window on our activities…or lack thereof, I suppose. But come on," she said, holding out her hand. "Let's get you out of here before those two start scouting."

The boy stared at us for a long, tense moment, visibly struggling, before his resolve weakened. "I've got to go back to the warehouse," he said. "It was chaos, they started shooting, and everyone scrambled. I...I ran, I don't even know how I got out, but I ran and hid..."

"Son—"

"I'm the coordinator," he insisted, his voice strengthening. "I should go back and check on them."

"You're not a coordinator," Badger replied. "But *I* am. And I'm telling you that you're the only one of that lot within a ten-block radius. I've been looking for survivors all night."

His face, which had momentarily hardened with his gathering resolve, crumbled. "You saw..."

She hesitated. When she spoke again, her tone had shifted toward professional yet sympathetic, and I supposed I was hearing Badger's best 'next of kin' voice. "I saw the bodies when I sleepwalked this morning. Everyone except you. They're gone now—the squad cleaned the scene—but the assassins are waiting for you to return. Maybe someone counted sleeping bags."

"But I..." His face reddened as his eyes welled. "We were fine, everything was going to be fine..."

"You're very young," she soothed, slowly going to her feet, "and you tried. Mistakes happen. I'm not sure if I'd have believed me, either."

But he continued as if he hadn't heard a word. "I...oh, God, I got them *killed*..."

My cousin knelt beside him and pulled him close while he sobbed, and his weak shield dissipated as his wand dropped to the floor. "It's okay," she said, rubbing his shaking back. "It's going to be okay. You tried."

Vivi was waiting in Coileán's office to receive the boy when we delivered him the next morning. She'd come with a therapist in tow. No one had to say the words *suicide watch*— it was simply assumed, and provisions were made to keep the new arrival under supervision and in counseling.

It was a bittersweet success, I told Badger, but a success

nonetheless. *Any* survivor had to count as a success. But she sat at the kitchen table with her laptop, ignoring me as she logged on to the old network with her coordinator credentials. The Houston posts remained on the main page like graffiti of a lost civilization.

"Scrub it?" I asked.

"No. They can't know we're watching," she replied.

"But if someone else tries to join the group in Houston—"

"We watch. And this time," she muttered, "I'll try harder."

OCTOBER: POPPY KANE

We sat on opposite sides of our bed, my husband and I, half-clothed after our night out. I'd kicked off my heels and tossed my pashmina onto a chair, but I had yet to change out of my dress. His sport coat had followed my pashmina, but though he'd unknotted his tie, it still lay around his neck like a lopsided scarf.

Finally, as the grandfather clock down the hall chimed the hour, I broke the silence that had hung between us since we got home to the dorm. "Are we going to talk about that shitstorm?" I asked, staring at the wall.

Behind me, Rufe muttered, "I'd rather not."

"You have to do something. She's your *friend*."

"She's my queen."

"*And* your friend," I insisted, turning to face him. "She's not well—you saw that, right? I'm not imagining things?"

He sighed, then turned toward me. "What would you like me to do? Confront her? Do you see that ending in anything other than disaster?"

I fought the urge to bare my teeth. "She wouldn't dare."

"As you said, she's not well." He reached across the bed and took my hand. "I'm not risking *this*. Not yet."

"We could go to Coileán," I suggested. "Ask him to intervene."

"Oh, yes, that would endear us to her forever. And he probably wouldn't do anything—he wouldn't make her lose face like that."

I huffed and squeezed his fingers. "Then what do we do? Because what I saw tonight...that ain't right, Rufe."

He didn't speak, but the look in his eyes said plenty.

Rufe had been surprised and pleased to receive a dinner invitation from the queen, whom he hadn't seen in months. I'd been invited, too, even though I couldn't contribute to their reminiscence session about the good old days of academia. I didn't care. A night out was a night out, and I hurried to line up babysitters to watch the dorm while we were away. As much as I liked the kids, I was eager for an evening of adult conversation.

The invitation hadn't specified a dress code, so we stayed on the formal side of dinner party attire, just to be safe. At the appointed hour—or its approximation, given how flexible clocks could be in Faerie—we arrived at the mansion's front door and knocked. An aide showed us inside and quickly escorted us to one of the smaller dining rooms, then scurried away.

Before I could consider that too closely, the queen arrived. "Ellie!" said Rufus, hurrying over to greet her. "So nice to see you, thank you for the invitation. We'd have asked you out sooner, but you can imagine what dinner in the dorm is like."

He hugged her warmly, but her eyes seemed distant, her grip perfunctory.

Filing that away, I waited for her to take her seat at the head of the table, then sat and smiled. "Great to see you again," I said, unfolding my napkin. "How's life?"

She gazed at the floral arrangement for a moment as if giving the question great consideration. "Oh, you know," she finally replied with a slight shrug.

Rufe cut his eyes across the table toward me, troubled. "Is everything all right?" he asked her.

Eleanor's movements seemed slower than usual, her face distant, and she barely spoke outside of a monotone. "It is now. Difficult morning. Problem resolved."

We kept our silence while an aide poured wine and

brought out soup—and hastened out of the room again. He seemed far more skittish than aides usually did in the queen's presence. For what I'd seen of her, Eleanor wasn't the type to explode on a whim, so why were her people giving her such a wide berth?

Despite the tension, Rufe did his best to keep the conversation light, though he and I carried most of it. Eleanor spoke only when politeness mandated a response, ate mechanically, and continued to stare into space throughout the meal.

By the time the port had been poured and the last of Luce's incredible bourbon-soaked bread pudding had been devoured—at our place settings, at least, as Eleanor had hardly touched hers—Rufe was obviously concerned. "You're not yourself tonight, Ellie," he said, looking her way until she met his gaze. "What's wrong? Can I help?"

She patted his arm and offered a brief smile. "Tired, I suppose. Nothing to worry about."

"You're not sleeping?"

"Not that." She lifted her port glass, held it close to her, but put it down before taking a sip. "I'm sorry, I should have cancelled tonight. It's been a trying day."

"How so?" I asked. "Really, can we help? Do you need something?"

"Peace," she said, barely nodding. "And I will *have* it."

That declaration set off all sorts of delightful internal alarms with me, and from the look on his face, I suspected that Rufe was likewise on alert. "Was there a fight today?" he asked her. "We don't get the immediate gossip in town, and the boys haven't said a word—"

"The archipelago."

I was grateful then that Eleanor seemed distracted, as Rufe's sudden expression made his distaste for her little penal colony crystal clear before he brought it under control again. My husband is many things, but a poker player isn't one of them.

"What," I said, sipping my port, "did someone try to

escape?"

"They started a *war*." Her shoulders tightened as she spoke. "By the time I arrived, several islands were on fire. Huts burned, food stores destroyed. Two little flotillas were on the water, shooting arrows at each other."

"What the hell happened?"

"Damned if I know. I sent them there to learn from their mistakes, to reform themselves, to obey my *simple* rules...well, it doesn't matter now," she said wearily. "They won't be waging war again."

I kept talking so that Eleanor wouldn't notice Rufe's look of horror. "Did you take away their weapons or something? You didn't kill them, right?" I asked, only half in jest.

"No."

She sounded too sullen for my comfort.

With a slight sigh, Eleanor pushed back from the table, and Rufe and I hastily stood with her. "Come along. See for yourselves," she offered, and left the room.

Trading uneasy glances, we followed.

Though Rufe had told me about the archipelago, I had yet to see it in person. I was prepared for the nearly invisible catwalks over the room-filling island chain. I was *not*, however, prepared for the gale-force wind that blasted forth as soon as Eleanor opened the door. I staggered back, almost knocked off my feet, but she ignored the storm and climbed onto the catwalk. Going higher seemed like an incredibly stupid decision to me, but Rufe and I followed...

...and the wind stopped.

"Apologies for that," said Eleanor, gesturing to the spiraled clouds covering the room below us. "The winds are rather strong at ground level."

"What's going on down there?" Rufe asked, clutching the railing as he tried to see through the cloudbank.

"Minor hurricane. Here."

She waved, and the clouds dissipated, revealing the devastation below. The miniature ocean was still wild, white-tipped waves slamming into the walls and washing over the little blobs of land. Some islands were nothing but projections of bare rock, while others still bore a few standing palms. Downed trees were scattered across the beaches and floating between islands, along with the detritus of what might have been a raft. And in the midst of it all, clinging to trees and driftwood, were the storm-tossed inmates—none of whom, strangely enough, so much as yelled for help.

"Dear God," I murmured.

"I sent them to a place of reformation," said Eleanor, glancing at the destruction below, "but not a *bad* place. They had food and fire, they built shelters. And still, they broke my peace. No more. From now on, they can learn to survive in a storm. Perhaps they'll be better students now."

"You're going to *drown* them," I protested.

But she shook her head, unconcerned. "No, the enchantments in this room won't allow it. They'll simply wash up, and if they can't swim to land, they'll just go under again until they figure it out. They can't *die* in here, but the hunger pangs might teach them a lesson. And I've taken their voices from them as well," she added. "They can contemplate their disobedience in silence. I suppose they're displeased with this turn of events, but I dare say they'll think twice the next time they consider breaking my peace." She gazed down on the archipelago, a tired smile playing on her lips. "I *will* have peace. What can they do now? They'll be too preoccupied with their base comforts to consider warring. And when they learn, perhaps I'll calm the storm." She looked back at us, her silent guests, then waved toward the door. "Again, I'm knackered. Let's call it an evening, shall we?"

I'd never been so happy to see a gate as the one Rufe opened ten seconds later, and I felt the wind begin again behind us as I slipped home to safety.

"She's gone too far," I told him from across the bed, "if not plain crazy."

"I know," Rufe murmured.

"How many *were* there? A hundred? Hundred and fifty?"

He hesitated before speaking. "Last I heard from Luce, the count's up past two hundred. He doesn't have an exact tally, but it's been growing faster of late. Folks are scared."

"Forget folks, *I'm* scared. Does Rohese know? What happens if Luce gets sideways with her and end up joining the hurricane party?"

"Please don't mention this to Mother. *Please.* I'll talk to Ned, see what she's heard. But Ellie likes Luce—I doubt she'd lay a finger on him."

"The Ellie you know, maybe," I retorted. "Was that woman anything like the one you remember?"

He sat in silence for a time, then rose and pulled off his tie. "I'll be back," he said, tossing it onto the chair. "Don't wait up, sweetie."

"Where are you—"

"Ned." He opened a gate at the foot of the bed and slipped off without another word.

Alone in our room, I changed into my pajamas, hung my dress back in the closet, and tried to wind down. The wolf was alert and pacing, however, and I knew I wasn't going to sleep until she had her way.

I needed to have a conversation, and considering the subject matter, I needed to do so face to face. Fortunately, Toula's number was saved in my phone. It was late, but not unreasonably so, and I sent her a brief message: *Awake?*

Yeah, came the reply a moment later. *Hi! How's it going?*

Can u meet me?

Where?

Orchard, I wrote. The trees behind Coileán's palace were a decent spot for a late-night rendezvous, but more importantly, getting there would give me a good run.

Leaving now, I added. *Going the long way. I'm going to need clothes.*

What's going on? she replied, but I left the message

unanswered. I sneaked down the stairs past the sleeping children, left my pajamas in a pile in the mudroom, and shifted in the dark backyard. The night came alive in an instant, a chaotic blast of sound and scent, and, resisting the urge to blow off steam with a howl, I loped away. Still, try as I did to let go and let the wolf do the thinking, the angry screams of the gale echoed in my thoughts, an arrhythmic counterpoint to my pounding feet.

FEBRUARY: COILEÁN

It was our first Valentine's Day as a couple, albeit a low-key, no-public-confirmation couple, and though we concurred that the holiday was stupid, we'd decided to have a nice dinner at Toula's apartment anyway. She could grill a steak to perfection—skill, spellcraft, or secret marinade, she wouldn't tell me—and I'd offered to pull a few of the older bottles out of my mother's stash and see if anything was worth sampling. That was all the plan entailed, but my gut warned me to do more—flowers, a gift, *something*. Unfortunately, Toula didn't strike me as the sort of woman to melt over a tennis bracelet, and so I pondered the matter as I halfheartedly held court that morning. Orchids? Or a necklace, perhaps? A piece in obsidian or jet? Maybe sapphires to bring out her eyes…

I envied Ellie as I listened to two of my more distant nephews argue over what amounted to a modest duck pond. Though we hadn't spoken much in recent months, I'd gathered that her people were largely behaving themselves—occasional quarrels, but nothing half so aggravating as listening to two grown men bicker over a pond that either could easily replicate. They were leaving my people alone, too, which was fine by me. I had enough intra-court refereeing to do as it stood, what with the ornamental lake war brewing before my eyes.

Maybe there was merit to the archipelago system, I mused. I hadn't been a fan of the idea at first. My holding cells remained occupied by Moyna's people, and the limiting wards on the prison allowed them to produce their own food and clean up after themselves, but little else. It seemed a fitting punishment: they weren't in pain, they were out of my sight, and they had each other for company, a special sort of torment. Upon first seeing the islands, I'd offered to help Ellie make her own set of cells, particularly once I learned that she was personally binding her captives. But she'd declined my offer, explaining that the public humiliation was an added deterrent. How better to threaten someone for whom status and appearance are everything than with a stint as a tiny tropical castaway, unable to enchant and forced to scavenge for coconuts in a homemade loincloth while passersby jeered?

But I'd come to share Toula's concerns. Toula, the prescient one of us, had seen what was happening to Ellie as she bound more and more reluctant inmates. Neither of us had spoken to Ellie in months or been invited to view the archipelago of late, but rumor suggested that matters had taken a darker turn. Poppy had even come to Toula a few months before with a disturbing report, but she'd been vague, insisting that she didn't want to reveal anything that would tie the story back to her and Rufus. "It's fucked up," she'd reportedly said, "but I'm not putting my husband at risk. Get Coileán involved, that's all I'm saying."

That wasn't an option. If I went to Ellie and demanded to know what she was doing, it would have made her seem weak. Unless and until I had proof that she was harming my court, I had no cause to confront her. We weren't complete novices any longer—I'd held my throne for nearly eleven years (even if I'd slept through one of them), while Ellie had kept hers for nine—and our earliest days of fumbling toward an arrangement were behind us. I had no right to tell her how to manage her affairs. Still, Toula's restless mind was keeping her up at night, and I couldn't say that I blamed her.

As my nephews yammered on, denouncing each other in the most pointed of terms, and I mulled over the ramifications of showing up to dinner with wine, flowers, *and* jewelry, the far doors of my throne room burst open, and a man sprinted up the blue runner, chased by two of my less experienced guards. Before I could so much as rise, Val had slipped in front of me, shield at the ready, but there was no need. The intruder tripped on his own feet and tumbled, coming to a stop a few yards from the foot of the dais. The pursuing guards grabbed him and frog-marched him forward, and while my interrupted nephews protested, I stared in astonishment.

"*Benatin*?" I said, leaning forward on my throne as the guards forced him to his knees.

For once, he appeared to me unglamoured. Instead of masking himself as a rosy-cheeked little boy, he showed me his true face, still bearing the slow-healing scars of the iron burns I'd given him years before. Yes, the fear in his eyes was familiar—our encounters had typically ended in pain for him—but as I'd set him on fire the last time we met, I'd never dreamed that he would seek me out.

He panted and rubbed his arms where the guards had gripped them. "Save me," he pleaded. "They're coming for me, please, my lord, save me."

The far doors opened again, more gently that time, and another pair of my guards escorted two of Ellie's toward the front. Benatin looked over his shoulder, flinched, then started crawling toward me. "*Please*," he begged. "Let me defect, I'll do anything. *Anything*."

Ignoring him, I held up a hand to stay the newcomers, then raised my voice to address them. "What's he accused of?"

"Party crashing, essentially," one of her guards replied.

"A prank," said Benatin, "just a little joke, no harm done to anyone—"

"My lady warned him," the guard continued.

I beckoned them closer, and as they neared, I took a good look at them. Both were relatively young—their eyes gave it away—and from his accented Fae, I pegged their leader as American-born. Judging by the set of their faces, neither was pleased with the retrieval assignment. I looked from them to Benatin, who seemed to be on the verge of tears, and sighed. "Is his the sort of offense punishable by death?"

"No, my lord," said the other guard—a Spaniard, perhaps. "Not unless something has changed overnight."

I looked down at Benatin. "Then you'd better give me a damn good reason why I shouldn't let those two take you back to your queen."

He scrambled closer on his hands and knees. "Please. Please, I don't want to go to the islands, don't let them take me, I beg you—"

"Enough," I muttered. "You break a rule and come to *me* for protection? Are you *drunk*?"

"You don't understand—"

I nodded to the guards. One managed to stun Benatin before he could get his shield up—he'd never been quick on the draw—and they dragged his slumped body toward a fresh gate to one of Ellie's white marble corridors. "Give her my regards," I told them as they departed.

Once they'd closed the gate behind them, I murmured, "Val?" He bent close, and I said, "Find an excuse to have a quiet chat with Nico, won't you?"

He nodded and departed.

That night, Toula and I had a pleasant dinner, and though she complained about unplanned gifting, the black opal earrings I gave her were a hit. We sat out on her balcony for hours, then retired to her room together. In the morning, as I was beginning omelet preparation, Toula answered a knock at the door. "Kitchen," she said. "Can I get you coffee? You look tired."

"Thank you, no," said Val, and I looked up from my egg cracking as he poked his head around the wall. "A moment?" he asked.

I followed him onto the balcony and closed the door.

"What did Nico have to say?"

"He wouldn't see me," Val replied, folding his arms. "Said it's not a good time. I tried a few others in that guard, but no one is speaking."

Unease prickled up my spine. "Any idea why?"

"No. I even stopped by the mansion last night on a pretense, hoping someone at the door would have information."

"No luck?"

"She's not admitting visitors," he murmured. "People go in, and they don't leave. The mansion's been locked down for a month, to hear the Stowe boys tell it."

I remembered that one of their clan was in Ellie's employ. "Lucian—that's her chef's name, isn't it? What's he saying?"

Val's face was grim. "Nothing. No one's seen him in weeks, and he does not answer his phone. His mother fears for him."

"*She* spoke with you?"

"They know I have your ear."

I leaned against the railing, feeling a chill deeper than the cold seeping through my bathrobe, and stared out at the frost-dusted morning. "I can't just break down the door and start interrogating her," I muttered. "You know that."

He grunted in acknowledgement and took a place beside me.

"Got any great ideas? I'm listening."

After a time, he said, "It might be worthwhile to send in a friend. Someone unlikely to antagonize her."

"You're not suggesting Toula—"

"Of course not!" he replied, aghast. "Why would you think—"

"I mean, she's a neutral party."

The look Val gave me spoke of deep disbelief. "Eleanor knows there's something between the two of you. Sending Toula would be a mistake."

"How does she know?"

He stared at me with an expression one might give a child confronted with an empty cookie jar and chocolate streaks on his fingers.

"Not exactly subtle?" I mumbled.

"No."

Val and I had yet to discuss my involvement with his sister—he changed the subject whenever we veered too close, which was fine by me. If he wanted to pretend for the rest of time that she and I were nothing more than two friends having breakfast together in our pajamas, well, I was in no hurry to disabuse him of that fantasy.

"So who were you thinking of?" I asked, steering the conversation away from the cliff's edge.

Fortunately for us both, he went along without complaint. "Amy Levey."

"The *crafter*?"

"And Oberon's great-granddaughter. Seamus mentioned that she's been over several times to see Eleanor—it might be worth trying," he said, and started for the door back into the apartment.

"She's a child," I protested.

"Do you think Eleanor would hurt a child?"

"I don't know, but seeing as she's sworn death to mine—"

"Moyna is homicidal," Val pointed out. "Amy makes wands. The two aren't entirely comparable. Your decision, of course," he added, and strode back into the house. "On second thought, coffee would be appreciated," he told Toula. "Cold morning. And will you be distracting him long?"

"Jerk," she said fondly, whisking eggs. "Pot's there, mugs are in that cabinet, help yourself. And *you*," she added as I latched the door, "are on dicing duty. I don't care how you do it, but I like my peppers finely chopped. Yeah?"

Val's little smirk spoke volumes. "I'll clean this and return it," he said to her, filling a mug, and took his leave.

When I'd acquainted myself with Toula's ceramic knives,

she turned on the burner and asked, "What was that all about?"

I considered lying—if there was one thing I knew about Toula, it was that she wasn't shy about taking matters into her own hands, and I didn't want her anywhere near Ellie if the queen wasn't in her right mind. In the end, however, the thought of Toula's reaction once she learned I'd lied to her worried me more.

"What have you heard from Ellie lately?" I asked.

She shrugged and topped up her coffee. "A whole lot of nothing, as usual. Why?"

I hesitated, hoping I wasn't about to make a grave mistake, then told her everything.

—YEAR NINE—

APRIL: AMY LEVEY

Surprise, Toula told me, would be the best approach. Aunt Ellie liked me, and if I showed up for a friendly chat, good manners would probably obligate her to invite me in. Personally, I didn't have much confidence in the idea—showing up unexpectedly on powerful faeries' doorsteps was a good way to get yourself killed or worse—but I tried to sound positive as I reassured Kip that I'd only be gone for a quick visit.

"But why *you*?" he pressed. "If something's wrong with her, then why don't they send someone who can make her own gates?"

I didn't have a good answer for that, largely because Toula had been spotty on the details. Since I couldn't block my thoughts, she gave me only generalities: no one had seen the queen in weeks, calls to anyone in the mansion went unanswered, and the Stowes were concerned about their missing brother. Hearing even that little, I recalled the strange phone conversation I'd had with Hugo a year before with a knot in my stomach, wondering if I'd ignored something important that had metastasized into a crisis. Guilt prodded me into agreeing to Toula's request that I stop by the mansion.

As usual, I got into Faerie via the gate to Coileán's office. From there, Toula created a gate to the edge of Aunt Ellie's parkland—an uncomfortable hike in my skirt and pumps, but necessary under the circumstances. She gave me a pair of tennis shoes as a parting gift, I stuffed my heels into my purse, and then I set off toward the mansion, telling myself that I was no more obnoxious than a Girl Scout offering Thin Mints. I'd even brought a little box of tea to smooth my way in—Badger and Seamus had taken to ordering high-end blends online, and having sampled their stash, I'd decided that no one could be angry if presented with chocolate-flavored black tea. I hoped they wouldn't miss it.

Half an hour's walk later, I finger-combed my hair and marched up the front steps toward the tall pair of closed doors. Pausing long enough to switch my shoes (and hide the new pair behind a potted rosebush), I gave my skirt a last smoothing and rang the bell.

Then I waited.

And *waited*.

I was about to walk around the building and look for signs of life when one of the doors creaked open and a guard stepped out. She looked strangely haggard, her green eyes sunken and shadowed, and she didn't smile. "Yes?"

"I, um…I've come to see the queen," I replied, trying not to falter under her stare. "If she's available. And seeing people, I mean. I'm Amy—"

"I know who you are." She paused with a vacant look on her face, then nodded curtly. "My lady will see you. I'll show you to her."

"Thank you—"

She bent close to me and gripped my wrist hard enough to leave the impressions of her fingers on my flesh. "Do *not* upset her," she whispered, then released me and disappeared into the mansion.

That was disturbing enough, but it was downright eerie to find the house shrouded in darkness—curtains drawn, shutters closed, lights dimmed or extinguished. Resisting the impulse to use my phone for a flashlight, I followed the guard upstairs into a wing of the mansion I'd never seen. "Where are we going?" I asked, jogging to keep pace.

"The queen's suite."

"Oh. Am I interrupting something?"

The guard stopped and lowered her voice again. "She's

not well. Hardly leaves her bed. She'll see you in the parlor off her bedroom."

My face must have betrayed my surprise, as the guard squeezed my shoulder. "None of that, now. Smile, keep a cheerful disposition. None of this is out of the ordinary, understood?"

I nodded, and we walked on.

When the guard rapped on the parlor door, I braced myself, not knowing what to expect on the other side. I heard Aunt Ellie's muffled voice, and with a last warning look for me, the guard escorted me in. "Lady Amy," she announced, and I tried not to gawk.

The room, a small space with a silk rug, a pair of overstuffed chairs, and a low table, was stiflingly hot thanks to the fire crackling in the grate. Heavy red curtains blocked the windows. Aunt Ellie was propped up in one chair, swaddled in a thick blue bathrobe and matching slippers. Her hair lay limp and greasy over her scalp, and her face seemed pinched, her eyes as exhausted as if she'd pulled all-nighters for a month. Her smile was weak, but she lifted one hand and beckoned me into the room. "Amy, darling," she said in a low murmur, "how nice. Do come in." She waited until I took the empty chair, then asked, "Aren't you cold? You haven't got a coat, girl."

Faerie's springs were typically pleasant, and having worked up a light sweat on my walk, a coat was the last thing I needed. "Oh, I'm fine," I said, forcing a smile. "Thank you. Warm-blooded, you know?"

"I can't seem to get warm," she replied, glaring at the fireplace. "Too much marble, I suppose. Holds in the cold air."

I fished in my purse and pulled out the tea. "I brought this, if you'd like to try it. Kept me warm all winter in the shop. It gets drafty in there."

Aunt Ellie accepted the box and considered it for a long moment, as if waiting for the words to make sense. Her eyebrows rose as recognition crossed her face. "Oh, this sounds lovely…" She turned to the table, frowned, then looked up as the door opened and a guard appeared in answer to her telepathic summons. "Nimalie, tell Jordan to bring the tea things."

As the guard escaped, I realized what seemed so off about the queen: her reactions were slow, and she spoke as if she were dreaming. "How are you doing?" I asked, hoping I sounded sufficiently chipper.

She contemplated the question. "Tired."

"Oh? Insomnia, huh?"

"No, I sleep. But…not fully. I can't." She turned the tea over in her hands, studying the label.

I risked it. "Why's that?"

When she looked up at me again, all I could think of was how exhausted she seemed. "Binds," she said softly. "The ones I've sent to the archipelago…they fight me. But I'm stronger. They will learn in time." She reached out and patted my hand. "You were concerned?"

"No one's heard from you in a while," I replied, which wasn't a lie. "You don't answer your phone."

Her response came out almost as a sigh. "Must concentrate…"

The opening door quieted her, and an aide scurried in with a tea tray. He winced when the porcelain cups rattled upon landing on the table, but Aunt Ellie waved to him in dismissal, and he slipped out as quickly as he'd come.

"Jordan," she said, rolling her eyes. "Clumsy. See to that, please."

I did as she asked—luckily, Badger had taught me the art of making tea. As I checked the color of the brew and doled out sugar cubes, I pinpointed something else that was bothering me: aside from the popping of the logs and the clinking of china, the mansion was virtually silent.

"Where is everyone?" I asked, handing Aunt Ellie a cup and saucer. "It's awfully quiet here today."

She sipped and shivered. "They keep their peace. Can't have noise. Distracts me."

I drank my tea in silence, waiting for the queen to take the lead. But as the minutes stretched between us, I decided to risk annoying her. "Spoke with Vivi Stowe the other day."

"Mm?"

"She said her mom is worried about Luce. No one's heard from him in a while. Do you know if he's all right?"

She held her empty cup in her lap and slowly blinked. "Luce…"

"Your chef?"

Understanding dawned. "Lucian. Yes." She closed her eyes and screwed up her face as if straining, then relaxed and held her cup toward me. "Top this up, won't you, dear?"

I'd just fixed her refill when the door opened and a blond man in kitchen whites slipped inside. "My lady," he panted, nodding toward her chair. "Sorry for the wait. What can I bring you?"

"Lucian," she said, taking her cup from me, "have you met my grandniece?"

"Amy. Hi," I said, lifting one hand.

He seemed more uneasy than winded. "No, my lady, we haven't met, but I've heard good things from my sister…"

"She said your mother is worried."

Luce's eyes widened. "You know how mothers can be," he replied in a rush, "worried over nothing—"

"Have you not spoken to her?"

"My lady…you prohibited phones, I—"

"Why do you not visit your parents?"

Luce swallowed hard. "My lady, you've been so busy, and I didn't want to bother you to ask about leaving."

She seemed perplexed in her dream-addled way. "But you should have time to yourself. Holiday time. Go, visit your mother."

His shoulders sagged. "You're certain? You won't need me for a bit? I can return in an hour—"

"Take the day," she mumbled. "Or…go to them. I will send for you when I need you again."

Saying that many words in quick succession seemed to

weary her, and she slowly turned my way. "Perhaps we could continue this later."

"Of course," I said, putting my teacup back on the tray with as little noise as possible. "Nice to see you. Let me know if there's anything I can do, okay?"

She smiled and nodded, and I followed Luce out into the hall. When the door latched, he leaned against the wall and clutched his chest, then put his finger to his lips for silence and ushered me out of the mansion.

Once we'd reached the front steps, he took me by the shoulders and whispered, "Who put you up to that?"

"Toula."

"Moon and stars." He released me while I retrieved my new tennis shoes from their hiding place, then ran his hands through his hair and slowly exhaled. "I'm going to have a *strong* word with Ms. Pavli," he said, and took my arm. "Come with me. You weren't planning to walk back to Lord Coileán's, were you?"

"Actually, if I could bum a ride, that'd be sweet. Would you mind dropping me off in town? I'd like to say hi to Vivi before I go home."

His response was a gate that opened onto a stretch of the low brick wall around the settlement. "Ladies first."

Once he'd sealed the rift behind us, he sank onto the wall and rubbed his face. "Are you all right?" I asked.

Luce looked up at me with incredulity. "My queen is *just* this side of fucking mental. No one goes anywhere near her unless summoned, and she blew up all of our phones, so no one's sent word out in months. And then you come waltzing in for *tea* and get me out of there. No, child, I am *not* all right."

I noticed a tremor in his hands, even as he gripped the edge of the wall. "What the hell is going on in there? It's something to do with the archipelago, isn't it? Hugo called and tried to warn me, but—"

His laugh came out as a short bark. "*Hugo?* He got sent back in December, I think. Did something to annoy her.

There were a dozen or so of her siblings trying to convince her to shut down the archipelago and let everyone out, and when they became sufficiently tiresome, she transformed them, too."

"Transformed?" I echoed. "You mean shrunk, right?"

"Shrunk, bound, silenced, and locked in a room with low-lying islands in the middle of a damn hurricane. Half of them are probably starving, and I wouldn't be surprised if a few come close to drowning every day."

"*What?*"

He nodded. "Our sentiment exactly, but one does not say such around the mansion."

"But...*why?*"

"Who knows?" he said, shrugging. "They squabbled, she got peeved, and presto. And then she shut down the viewing times—not much to see from above with the clouds in place, and I suppose it was distracting her to have visitors. You saw how rough she looked?"

I could only nod.

"She barely sleeps, and when she does, it's like a catnap. It takes incredible effort to keep those hundreds of binds intact—"

"Wait, hundreds?"

"She hasn't let anyone go. Just keeps adding to the population." Luce grabbed my wrist and squeezed. "Tell Coileán he must do something before this worsens. Everyone in the mansion lives in terror of setting her off."

"I will," I promised.

"Good. And I'll have a talk with Toula about sending unarmed witch-bloods into danger," he added, pushing himself off the wall. "Come along, I'll see you to Vivi's office..."

A brown-haired man rounded the corner and stopped in his tracks, and Luce raised a hand in greeting. With that, the two ran toward each other and met in a brisk, back-slapping hug. Moving closer, I recognized Ned, who by then was holding his brother at arm's length and speaking rapidly.

"It's okay," I said when Ned noticed me, "I'm just on my way to Vivi—"

Ned hugged me hard enough to make my ribs creak, then released me and shook his head. "Call her later. You're getting out of here now."

"But—"

He created a gate to Coileán's open front doors and pointed. "*Now*, Amy. I can't believe I'm saying this," he muttered, "but for the moment, you're probably safer in the mortal realm."

I surrendered and waved to the Stowes as the gate sealed, then turned to Coileán's curious guards and adjusted my shoe-stuffed purse. "Hi," I said with an uneasy smile. "Any chance I could get a word with the king?"

JUNE: BONNIE

Wizards, I'm told, begin formal instruction in spellcraft when they're ten. At least, that's when they're given wands and taught the basics concerning their use. Whatever instruction a young wizard receives before that time is surely piecemeal, and I'd imagine that much of it involves lessons along the lines of "don't get mad and set your brother on fire."

Those of us of the fae persuasion often start much younger, both for safety and as a matter of practicality. If our children's talent manifests early, it's usually stronger than that of a wizard of the same age, and as we don't use wands, there's no need to wait until a formal distribution date to begin teaching the elementary techniques of enchantment. So much of what we do boils down to picturing a result and sufficiently tweaking reality until it cooperates, anyway, and if a young faerie figures this out, then you've got a hellion on your hands. Little kids—even the good ones—are ruled by impulse and unchecked by the lessons of experience and caution, and so it's necessary to impress upon them at a tender age just how much trouble they'll be in if you catch them enchanting without your say-so. Honestly, it might be simpler to bind children until they're of reasonable maturity, but binding is a distasteful thing, best avoided if possible—and besides, lessons learned early are lessons internalized.

My Sammy was almost nine, and I'd been working with him since his cradle days. That summer, with school out and Audra busy with the calves, he was mine for hours at a time, and I did my best to make up for the lost months he'd spent with classes and homework.

Sammy was a decent student with me, attentive and clever. The problem, I came to understand, was that I'd put the fear of God in him a bit too strongly when he was a mite. Sammy *could* enchant—he just preferred not to.

"The Arcanum doesn't know you exist, baby," I said, sitting across from him at my old kitchen table. Before me was a ham sandwich on a paper plate—nothing fancy, just ham on wheat with a slice of provolone and a squirt of mustard. I'd set Sammy with the task of replicating it, or at least coming close. Honestly, if he'd produced something from the deli case and something from the bakery, I'd have been satisfied. But the boy eyed my plate like an injured lamb might eye a skinny coyote.

"They don't know I exist, either," I continued, though I didn't know if that was actually true. "We're so far away from Montana that they might as well be on the moon. They barely come out of their hole. No one's going to find out if you make yourself a sandwich."

"But what if they *do*?" he insisted, raking his teeth over his lip with worry. "What if they find out and come down here and get us?"

"I won't let that happen. Believe me, Sammy, I'm more than a fair match for some dope with a wand."

"What if they send *two* wizards?"

"Not a problem."

"Three?"

I sighed. "Honey, I can take whatever they send our way. And worst-case scenario, we'd go on the road. There are some folks in Virginia who'd help us out."

"What about Mama?"

"Mama would come, too. Now make your sandwich."

He wasn't satisfied. "But what if, like, they came in the middle of the night, and they got you, and then they went after Mama and me? And then Mama couldn't breathe?"

"Sweet boy." I looked him in the eye, calling upon

whatever reserves of patience I had. "First of all, your mama has a pistol and knows how to use it. Second, remember this?" I held out my hand, and my trusty yellow fireball blossomed in my palm. "Show me yours."

Dutifully, he called forth his own version, smaller and red.

"If you get in trouble," I told him, "and you can't run, you lob those. Shields break, Sammy. You remember that."

Though he still seemed uncertain, Sammy put out his fireball, concentrated, and managed to produce a respectable ham sandwich. The ham tasted more like turkey, and the cheese was rubbery, but it was a good effort, and I told him so. "Let's take a break," I offered. "Hop in the truck. What do you say to ice cream?"

His little face lit, and he ran out the door while I gathered my purse, keys, and protective driving gloves. I honked at Audra on our way out—Sammy and I knew better than to get close to her while she was trying to work the cattle, as we could spook anything—and I turned on the radio as I spun onto the main road.

The nearest ice cream option was a Dairy Queen fifteen miles away, but Sammy never seemed to mind the trips. That afternoon, however, he seemed quiet, and when we turned onto the state highway, I asked him what was on his mind. "You're not still worried about the Arcanum, are you?" I asked.

Having been staring out the window, he twitched, then looked back at me with hope in his eyes. "Miss Bonnie, if I get *really* good at sandwiches, can you teach me how to make Mama better?"

The question hit me like a sucker punch, and I flicked my gaze back to the road. Sure, eventually, with sufficient time and talent, he could learn to ease her pain and temporarily help her breathing. But enchantment alone couldn't fix Audra, and my girl, my sweet baby girl, got sicker every year.

But I couldn't tell Sammy that. And maybe, horrible as

it sounded, if he thought there might be hope for his mother, he'd overcome his fear of murderous wizards and learn the lessons I was trying to teach him.

"We'll see," I said, which wasn't entirely untrue.

Sammy smiled at that, and I bought him a large Blizzard instead of his usual small, an apology for the lie he didn't know I'd told him.

JULY: FAERIE

Ros had cried herself to sleep during the early evening. Even so, with the thin walls of the silo apartments, her grandparents argued in low voices late that night—or, more accurately, Rachel kept her voice down and occasionally reminded Howard to do likewise.

By most estimations, the afternoon had been a disaster. When Rachel took Ros to the silo's swimming pool, they only swam for a few minutes before a little boy was violently sick in the water. The staff cleansed the water with spellcraft, but Rachel preferred chemical measures and took Ros home. For their evening meal, Rachel made burgers, albeit of a plant-based meat substitute that apparently tasted little like beef, which left Howard in a foul mood. He grumbled about it being a holiday and him being entitled to a goddamn hamburger, and Rachel shrank into herself and murmured about little ears.

Rachel provided an apple pie for dessert—a reduced-sugar version, though Howard spoke neither in praise nor complaint as he shoveled forkfuls into his mouth. Ros finished quickly, swinging her feet as she waited for her grandparents to eat, and Howard noticed her squirming. "Going somewhere?" he asked.

Ros beamed back at him. "Fireworks tonight!"

"What fireworks?"

"Grandma said we could go—"

"They're setting some off at the state park just after sunset," Rachel interrupted. "You can see them from the trailers."

"I hate those stupid things," he muttered.

"I know, I know," she soothed, "but Ros was really excited when she heard, and I thought we might—"

"No."

Rachel gave Ros a warning look, bit her lip, then tried again. "You don't have to go, Howie. I'll take her topside."

"And how would *that* look?" he snapped. "I already get an earful from the busybodies on the Council about not going to enough of her damn school events—"

"Howard, *please*."

"—and I'm not adding fuel to that fire. Family outings or nothing at all."

"Then make an appearance," she cajoled. "It'll be good for you, and Ros has been looking forward to the fireworks all day."

He pushed back from the table and rose. "I have work to do tonight. No."

At that, the child could restrain herself no longer. "Please, Grandpa!" she begged. "It'll be fun, I'll be *so* quiet, I won't do anything wrong—"

The cold look he gave her silenced her wheedling. "Life doesn't revolve around what *you* want," he said. "And the sooner you learn that you can't always have your way, the better. Go play in your room."

Her lip quivered.

"*Now.*"

Ros looked to Rachel, found no ally there, and ran to her bedroom. Even with the door closed, the two left in the kitchen could hear her crying.

"Howie," Rachel murmured, catching his arm as he carried plates to the sink. "Howie, she's just seven. Don't be like this."

"Got to learn," he grumbled, dumping his load into the basin. "No one gives two shits what I want, but I'll be damned if the mongrel runs my life."

Rachel tidied what remained of the faux burgers—at least enough for a second meal, which must have displeased

Howard. "You know," she told him, "Helen loved fireworks. Couldn't Ros see them just once? She's old enough not to be scared by the boom."

"And maybe, if you'd ever said no to Helen, we wouldn't be in this mess now."

Her cheeks flared red. "That is *not* my fault. Don't you blame me—"

Before she could react, he wheeled and pinned her against the pantry door. "Are you saying it's mine, then?"

She struggled for a few seconds, then went limp in his grasp. "No, Howie. Of course not."

"Then I guess it's yours, isn't it?"

"Howard—"

"*Say it.*"

Rachel took a long, shuddering breath. "It's my fault."

"That's what I thought." He released her and stepped back, disgust creasing his face. "You can finish here. I'm going to the office. We'll talk about this later."

The slamming door rattled the picture frames—Howard and Rachel's wedding portrait, Helen's baby pictures, a photograph of Howard in his magus chain covering the spot where his son's picture must have once hung. As Rachel silently cleaned the dishes, Ros opened her door and crept back to the kitchen, startling her with a quiet, "Grandma?"

Rachel turned, her eyes red and watery. "Go to your room, baby."

"Please?"

"You heard Grandpa," she said stiffly. "Don't ask me again."

"But you said—"

"*Roslyn.*"

The child cringed at the tone of her voice, then slunk back to her room.

That night, when Howard deigned to come home, Rachel had recovered enough of her spine to quietly chide him for petty cruelty. "*She* didn't make herself," she said, pointing to Ros's bedroom door. "You don't have to love her, but don't make her suffer for Helen's mistakes. You're punishing the wrong person."

That small act of defiance made Howard's simmering anger boil afresh. While the two of them argued into the night, I watched the sleeping child, whose tears had long since dried on her face. I sent her dreams of fireworks, all of them plucked from her father's memories—the delayed sounds of the explosions echoing across the night, the warm breeze of the summer evening, the colored stars falling and fading, over and over, until morning.

JULY: POPPY KANE

I was already sitting at a two-top in my favorite of the settlement's cafés that Saturday morning when my lunch companion walked in. Even with the summer warmth, she wore a light white hoodie and green leggings—athleisure as camouflage. Spotting me, she waved, then wove between the tables and grinned as she plopped into the empty chair. "So great to see you, Poppy," she said, sliding closer and glancing at the laminated menu. "What's good here?"

"Everything except the quiche. And you can drop the hood," I said. "Looks a little weird, yeah?"

Liza hesitated, then flipped it back, revealing a long red braid. "Sorry, it just feels like I'm doing something naughty every time I sneak in here."

"You sneaked past the guys?"

"Okay, not *sneak*, but you know what I mean."

"Chill—you were invited," I replied, smiling as she flushed. "Good to see you, too. It's been too long."

Having found ourselves stranded together in Faerie years before, Liza Bell—Joey's great-grandmother—and I had struck up a friendship, made all the stronger once we'd teamed up to spy on Moyna. She'd volunteered to go in as a mole with her memory altered, Kuni had stowed away and hid among her things, and I'd waited, often with Rufe, to intercept his recordings. I'd also had a leg broken trying to get her out of harm's way, and Liza still joked that she owed me. Having settled in, we didn't run in the same circles—I was a Fringe-adjacent shifter, she was half fae and a lady by both courts' reckoning—but every so often, we made time to get together. Given the general Fringe mistrust of strange faeries wandering around the settlement, we usually met at Liza's house—which worked out well for me, as the woman could *bake*. That day, however, I had news, plus a craving for the café's berry chicken salad.

The waitress came over and took Liza's drink order, and I put in a request for crab dip. "Hungry, eh?" Liza asked. "Or is it that good?"

"Both. I've been wrangling kids all morning," I explained, sipping my lemonade. "I mean, they're growing up—the youngest we have in the dorm just turned twelve—but getting everyone up and dressed on Saturday takes some doing when most of them are teenagers. Wouldn't be surprised if half of them have gone back to bed since I've been out."

"Rufus isn't watching them?"

"Continuing education all day. Got to love summer teacher schedules. I told him I don't need seminars for PE beyond first aid. And he needs the distraction," I added, lowering my voice. "Luce has been hiding out at their parents' house, and everyone's a little twitchy."

Liza grimaced. "Archipelago?"

"You've heard about it, huh?"

"Word gets around."

"Talked to your aunt lately?"

"Not since last fall. I was going to reach out, but having heard the stories coming from that court...you know, maybe now's not a good time."

I'd hoped that Liza would have insider information—though she'd opted for her uncle's court, I knew she remained on friendly terms with Eleanor. "Fair enough," I replied. "I know Luce isn't getting near the mansion again if he can help it."

"I don't blame him." She leaned closer and murmured, "Permanent hurricane?"

"You didn't hear it from me."

She whistled low and shook her head as she straightened.

"Surely Coileán knows what's going on. I just hope it doesn't come to blows. The last thing we need is the two of them fighting."

I concurred wholeheartedly—no one in the settlement wanted to see the courts go to war with each other. "I may have mentioned it to Toula. She's staying in the palace, so I trust she's shared it with him."

Liza's mouth ticked into a secretive smirk. "*Staying*? Is that what we'd call it?"

"Something I should know?"

Once more, she leaned close to me and dropped her voice to a low murmur. "I didn't say anything, but Joey might have mentioned that Aiden told him that Toula and Coileán are what one might call an item."

"*Oh.*"

"Exactly. But you didn't hear that from me."

We pretended that nothing was amiss as the waitress returned with Liza's soda and a trivet for the dip, then leaned together again. "My understanding is that they're…what do the kids say, keeping it on the DL?" she said.

"Something like that." Appearances aside, Liza was older than Rufe and just slightly behind the times, but I couldn't fault her for trying. "I won't go spreading it, then. Maybe just Rufe."

"Atta girl." She unwrapped her straw and took a sip of her drink. "But on to more important matters. You said you had something you wanted to talk—*ooh*, that does smell good," she said, pausing as our appetizer arrived.

We tucked into the bubbling crab dip—Liza made faces to show her satisfaction—and when we'd come up for air, I said, "Yeah, I've got a bit of news."

She pushed her plate away. "Good news, I hope."

"I think so." Smiling, I pulled a photo out of my purse and passed it across the table.

Liza peered at the blurry black and white image for a moment, puzzling over it. "What is—"

"It's not great, I know. They don't have real imaging equipment around here, so that was the best they could work up with magic."

Her eyes widened as she realized what she was seeing. "*You?*"

I grinned and nodded.

She screamed and hugged me, dip forgotten, and the other patrons looked our way in alarm. "Oh goodness, *when?*" she demanded.

"Late December or early January, if all goes according to plan."

"And you aren't showing," she said almost accusingly as she glanced at my midsection.

I patted my loose T-shirt. "You're kind. Baby Stowe's gaining weight, or at least I am."

"As you should. Here, you need this more than I do." Liza pushed the crab dip toward me and took a second look at my makeshift fetal photo. "I'm so happy for you both, I truly am. Is this a secret, or can I tell the family?"

"I don't mind, but, uh…" I hesitated, trying to be judicious with my words. "I don't want to rub it in anyone's face."

There was a damn good reason why Rufe had yet to call Aiden with our news: manners would have dictated that such a call be followed by one to Joey, and neither of us could guess how he'd take it.

Liza knew what I was hinting about, and she patted my hand as she returned the photo. "I'll tell him myself. He's hurting, but that doesn't mean he won't celebrate with you. I think he'd be more upset if he were the last to know, in all honesty."

"We just don't want to make the situation worse."

She smiled, though there was sadness in it—Joey's missing daughter was Liza's great-great-granddaughter, after all. "This place can always use good news," she told me. "Especially now. Eat up, Mama."

The next evening, as Rufe and I cleaned up after dinner, the doorbell rang. One of our older teenagers ran to answer it, then returned with the visitor.

"Joey!" said Rufe, dropping the stack of clean plates on the counter. "Good to see you, man! Come in, come in. Have you eaten?"

"Oh, yeah, Sunday dinner at Mom and Dad's. She made lasagna," he replied, patting his stomach for emphasis, then extended a small white gift bag toward us. "And Liza told us."

Rufe handed me the bag, and I dug through the pale green tissue paper to find a fluffy stuffed lamb at the bottom.

"Liza said you didn't know the gender," he explained, almost in apology, "so I thought—"

I interrupted him with a hug. "It's adorable. Thank you."

The gesture had to sting—Joey and Helen had never had so much as a baby shower. But he hugged me back, and when we broke away, he was smiling. "Congratulations, guys. And, uh…at least you won't lack for babysitters, right?"

"Between the dorm and my parents, I think we're covered until the kid's grown," said Rufe, shaking Joey's hand. "But if you ever want to hang out and watch G-rated movies…"

"I just might take you up on that," he replied. "So I'll know what's cool when Ros comes home."

He left soon after, and we put the lamb in our unfinished nursery along with the growing pile of toys from Rufe's family. The firstborn grandchild, the only nephew or niece to an aunt and eleven uncles—our baby was going to be spoiled *rotten*. As I considered the empty crib, I absently rubbed the curve of my belly and tried to put myself in Helen's position, hoping that whatever bind they'd placed on her had completely knocked her out. The alternative was unfathomable.

While I stood there, Rufe wrapped his arms around me

and held on tight. It didn't take a mind reader to know where his thoughts lay that evening.

AUGUST: ELEANOR

My dearest,

Forgive me. I don't mean to neglect you. My mind is full, so full, and even important matters seem to slip.

I want to sleep. I cannot.

I can't remember when I last ate. Two days? Three? I think I called for Lucian, but I can't recall if he came.

Is this senility? Surely not. Who ever heard of a senile faerie?

Whatever befalls me, I take comfort in knowing that my plans have succeeded. There is peace in the court. I have given them peace, and they have accepted my gift. Those who would disturb it have been brought here into my safekeeping, rendered harmless to themselves and each other. They will eventually know peace on my terms. Perhaps someday, if they reform themselves, I will allow them to return to the outside world, but I must have assurances that doing so would not endanger the peace I have wrought. For now, my people live in safety and without fear, freed from that element of the court that seeks only to provoke and destroy for its amusement.

I used to hear complaints about incarceration, but no longer. The court sees the wisdom of my plan. Besides, we are all prisoners here, incarcerated by choice for the sake of Mulligan's hostages. There is such uncertainty outside our borders—the Arcanum's attacks, the whereabouts of the missing, the plans Moyna surely continues to draft to finish the work she started. It was that chaos that killed you, Walt.

I vow to keep it beyond our walls. My people will know the comfort of harmonious coexistence with each other here, where they are safe from the turmoil beyond the realm. If they refuse, they will be removed until they see the error of their ways. There will be no death in my court, no violence.

Only peace.

You would have been so happy here.

It's cold now. It's always cold. I want to sleep.

Forgive me. I don't mean to neglect you.

DECEMBER: TOULA PAVLI

As usual, I'd put up a skinny Christmas tree in my apartment for the holidays, a place to hang too much tinsel and strings of tacky lights. It was my sole concession to seasonal decoration, and it seemed even sadder as the backdrop to our first real fight.

"This has gone on long enough!" I protested. "It's been almost a year since anyone outside that fucking mansion has seen her. A *year*!"

Coileán stood behind a chair with his arms folded, our scheduled movie night forgotten. "I'm well aware of that."

"Then *do something*. If Ellie's gone off the deep end, you've got a responsibility to step in."

"Actually, I don't. The realm would have said—"

"Fuck the realm! This is a problem, and you can fix it!"

His hands clenched on the back of the chair, but I didn't care if he was losing his temper—mine was already boiling over. "It's not that simple," he said slowly through gritted teeth. "You know that. If I interfere, then we're probably looking at war."

"Against whom?" I scoffed. "Her people are terrified! Your court would have grown by half in the last year if you'd let them swear allegiance."

"Oh, right, because antagonizing Ellie is the way to solve this!"

I turned away and walked to the window, willing myself to calm down before I said something stupid. "If Ellie's really gone nuts," I murmured, staring at the reflection of the colored bulbs in the night-dark glass, "then that court is in danger. You have a responsibility."

"I can't just—"

"As a *decent person*, you have a responsibility. If she's truly insane, then she has to be removed from power."

He laughed aloud. "Do you hear yourself? You want me to kill her, is that your brilliant plan? I *can't*. The realm won't allow that."

"So they're all supposed to just live in fear forever, is that it?"

"I don't know. We don't know what's really going on in there—"

"But *someone* does," I snapped, turning around again. "Hey! Faerie!" I bellowed, glancing at the ceiling. "Show yourself! We need to talk!"

Coileán sighed and rolled his eyes. "That's not how it works."

"Then *you* make her come over."

"I don't control her."

"Well, then," I said, planting my hands on my hips, "if she can't be bothered, then it's up to you to grow a spine. And if you won't, I will."

His expression was dark. "Meaning?"

"I may not be a queen, but I *am* my father's daughter. So, what's it going to be?"

He glared at me for a moment in silence, then turned and stormed out, slamming the door behind him. With the plates still rattling, I sank onto the sofa, my heart pounding in my ears, and stretched out. Closing my eyes, I tried to take cleansing breaths.

"He's correct, you know."

I yelped at the unfamiliar voice and bolted upright to find a glowing, petite blonde in a silky periwinkle dress sitting in the chair beside me, watching me with her head cocked. "Who the—"

"You called for me?"

My eyebrows rose. "*You're*—"

"I'm unaccustomed to being *summoned* like a

misbehaving child," she admonished. "But nonetheless, you and I should talk."

The fact that the consciousness of the realm was sitting a few feet away did nothing to improve my mood. "Mind telling me what the hell is going on with Ellie?"

"She's testing her limits. Unintentionally, I suppose. Her father did worse when he was young—as did your mother," she added with reproach. "Ruling a court is a learning process."

"So, what—we're just going to sit here and act like nothing's wrong until she gets her head on straight?" I demanded, gearing up for a fresh fight. "Because I'm not okay with that."

"Good."

"That's not...wait," I muttered as the wind left my sails, "what?"

"Good," she repeated, folding her hands in her lap. "Coileán isn't pleased with the situation, either, but the rules of our arrangement put him in a difficult position. You, however..."

"You could just ease up on your damn rules and make an exception."

"I prefer to consider the long-term future of this realm. Remember that my memory extends *far* further than yours, child."

Something about her tone made me bristle. "This may all just be a blip on whatever epochal scale you're working with, but it's *our* blip, and—"

"As I said, good. You're concerned. Do something to address the problem, but be wise about it."

While I stewed on the couch, she rose and examined some of my Christmas ornaments. "Your instincts were correct about Eleanor. She's trying to control far too many binds simultaneously. The effort will break her in due course if she doesn't dissolve at least some of the binds."

"Why the lockdown?"

"Because the strain necessary to hold the binds together

has muddled her thinking. She hardly sleeps, takes little food…she can't abide disruption."

"Then if, say, I were to march over there tonight and distract her—"

"Remember that she's still a queen. I haven't withdrawn the power I've given her."

"Want to help a sister out?"

Faerie softly chuckled. "I have no cause to do so. Nothing she's done has violated our pact. Now, considering the circumstances, would you rather attack tonight or wait until she weakens further? Her prisoners are alive," she added. "Bound, tired, and uncomfortable, yes, but intact. They can't die in there. You've nothing to gain by striking now, but in a few months…if she keeps to this path…"

"But—"

"Apollonios's downfall was his haste, was it not?" she interrupted, turning back to me. "Be cleverer than your father. Think this through, Fotoula." She walked around the coffee table toward the couch, the better to stand over me. "Remember that you're not capable of miracles. You cannot singlehandedly take down the silo wards from this realm. You don't have the power. *Coileán* doesn't have the power," she continued as my mouth opened. "If it were possible, I would have directed you to the necessary information by now."

I gaped for a moment, then managed, "You couldn't have said something, like, eight years ago?"

"The research and practice were good for you. Educational. You're young yet, child—and you're welcome." She smirked as I floundered on the couch. "But you can stop Eleanor from destroying her own court, *if* you have patience and don't simply kick down her door tonight."

I folded my arms, but I muttered, "Okay, I'm listening."

"Good." She smiled and took a seat on the table. "Very good."

Coileán knocked as I was putting the coffee on the next morning. "Before you say anything," I began upon opening the door, "I'm sorry for yelling. You're doing your job, and the head bitch's rules are tricky."

"I'm sorry, too," he replied, and we hugged over the threshold. When we parted, he said, "She told me you spoke."

"Yep."

"Dare I ask?"

"Nope. Welcome to the land of plausible deniability, Gramps," I said, and swept one arm down the hall. "Join me?"

He frowned at me for a minute, perhaps looking for a way around my sudden mental wall. "Are you planning to kill her?"

"No."

After another long moment's silent thought, he surrendered and shrugged. "You know what? Fine. I can live with that," he said, and came in for breakfast.

JANUARY: RUFUS STOWE

The settlement's take on a hospital was more of a glorified clinic: half a dozen beds and one of a handful of medical professionals on duty, with the rest on call as needed. But then again, there was little need for an impressive setup. The vast majority of patients presented with scrapes, sprains, and fractures, the result of falls, sports mishaps, and one particularly memorable inebriated brawl in the stands during a pickup soccer match. Wraps, ice, and the judicious use of magic could fix most such complaints.

I was there that day for a very different reason. All three of the Fringe doctors had passed by our room, as well as the two nurses and their teenage apprentice, but not because of any emergency. Births were a time of celebration in town, and anyone with an excuse to be around the building during labor tended to stop by and lend a hand.

The only person who didn't seem thrilled that afternoon was the guest of honor, who ground ice chips between her molars and glared at the universe when her contractions hit. I'd done everything I could to numb Poppy's pain, but she was still uncomfortable as she paced the room in her bathrobe and stocking feet. Her discomfort was understandable—she looked as though someone had connected a helium tank to her abdomen and was trying to use her as a novelty balloon.

There were no fetal monitors in the clinic, none of the expected tools and paraphernalia of a maternity ward. One doctor and nurse, working in tandem, had developed a sort of visualization spell that could function like an X-ray, but their work was less than reliable and tended to fall apart if needed for more than half a minute. Thus, while they'd been able to assure us that Poppy wasn't carrying multiples, the baby's sex remained a mystery. I wasn't bothered by that—Poppy and I had whittled a list of names down to her favorites in preparation, and besides, it was perhaps five seconds' work to repaint the nursery. No, the worry that had stuck with us throughout her pregnancy concerned what, exactly, she was about to deliver.

No one I'd asked had heard of a pairing like ours, or at least not one resulting in children. The baby would defy classification: one-half shifter from Poppy, one-quarter fae and one-quarter mundane human from me. We assumed the child would look normal enough—it wasn't as if we'd thrown a merrow into the mix—but whether it would have any skill at magic, any ability to shift form, or any of my delightful metallurgic allergies were questions yet unanswered. Odds were that our child, whatever it was, would be mortal. That would mean vaccines if it ever left the realm…and what if, someday, it decided to go abroad and not return?

I'd begun, at least in part, to understand what my parents had gone through with Vivi.

But the what-ifs were a problem for another year. At that moment, all that mattered was Poppy, who gripped the windowsill and squeezed her eyes shut while she braced herself.

The baby was *big*—the visualization spell had revealed that much—but it seemed to be in a good position, according to the doctor's cheerful assurances. Position notwithstanding, I didn't envy my poor wife. Though I had little firsthand experience with late-stage pregnancy, I understood the basics of what was about to happen to her body, and I tried not to think too hard about the matter.

There were no formal prenatal classes in the settlement, nothing like the yoga sessions and Lamaze seminars I'd seen advertised around campus over the years, but there *was*

Mother, who was only too happy to prepare Poppy for the big day. After thirteen children, she knew a thing or two about delivering them—and seeing as Poppy was giving my parents their first grandchild, Mother offered to do whatever Poppy needed to be more comfortable.

Once, during the early months, while they'd chatted and Mother had told war stories, Father had pulled me into his study and closed the door. "Let me give you a piece of advice," he'd said. "If you like your body in its current configuration, don't offer unsolicited suggestions. If Poppy asks for your opinion, proceed with caution. And if she wakes in the wee hours craving chocolate and sauerkraut—"

"Ugh."

"Your mum has had some bizarre appetites. Just get her whatever she wants."

I'd laughed. "Yes, I'm aware. I'm not completely clueless."

"But this *is* your first," he'd replied, and patted my shoulder. "I've been in this game for five hundred seventy-four years, son. Let me help you."

By and large, I'd made it through the pregnancy without seeing Poppy's teeth—metaphorically, that is, as she hadn't shifted since the clinic confirmed her suspicions. Shifters refused to switch forms while pregnant, fearing that their physical realignment could hurt or kill the developing baby, even if their shifted form was bigger than their human body. Only once did I err by asking whether it might be more comfortable for Poppy to deliver in wolf form, considering the relative ease of canine birth. She'd stared at me with a mixture of horror and anger at the suggestion. "Why don't I just do it in the middle of the park?" she'd snapped. "Lick the baby clean? Eat the placenta?"

That was the last time I made *that* mistake.

With Poppy's labor underway, all I could do was stay close with the ice cup and administer the occasional massage as directed. She sat on an oversized ball, holding her swollen belly and grunting as I worked at the knots in her neck. "You're not nervous, are you?" I teased.

I'd expected a sharp answer, but instead, when Poppy looked at me over her shoulder, I saw tears in her eyes. "Terrified, actually."

I pulled up a chair and took her hands. "Sweetie, it's going to be okay—"

"I want my mom," she mumbled, trembling in my grip. "I want her here so badly."

We both knew that wasn't an option—Poppy had made her feelings about contacting her parents explicit—but still, she was on the edge of a deeply liminal place, afraid of what was to come, and I was no help. I kissed her, wiped her cheeks dry, and called Mother, who breezed in a few minutes later with a basket full of sweet-smelling candles and lotions and promptly kicked me out of the room.

Father was waiting in the lobby with a knowing smile and a cup of coffee. "Let the expert work," he said, gesturing to the seat beside him. "Join me."

I sat and produced my own coffee, but when I tried to drink it, I noticed that it seemed to slosh in its cup.

Father gripped my wrist. "You're shaking, Rufus."

"Not badly."

That merited a chuckle. "Nervous, are we?"

"I suppose it's contagious."

"Now, don't blame Poppy for *that*. Hell, if you weren't nervous, I'd think there was something wrong with you." He leaned his head against the wall and closed his eyes. "The first one is the most difficult because you haven't a clue about what you've truly done. They don't like to sleep, they're voracious, they constantly soil themselves, and if they're anything less than thrilled, they scream."

"Except me."

"Oh, of course," he said, his voice heavy with sarcasm. "You, the perfect little terror with colic for four months straight."

"I'm sure I couldn't help it."

"Mm. Just remember that fate has a way of repaying children for the trouble they give their parents," he replied, ruffling my hair. "And that it's now frowned upon to treat fussy infants with whisky."

The person in charge of the waiting-room television apparently had a fondness for *Law & Order: SVU* reruns, and Father and I were on our third "dead jogger in the park" story of the afternoon when Mother reappeared. "It's time," she told me. "She wants you in there."

I hurried back to Poppy's room and found her on the bed, flanked by nurses and resembling a wet tomato about the face. "Hello, gorgeous," I said, sliding into position at her side and taking her hand. "Still numb?"

She nodded. "Rohese does a better job of that than you do."

"She's had more practice," I pointed out. "Ice?"

Poppy's reply turned into a grimace, then a straining push as the doctor at the foot of the bed coached her. For the next few minutes, any conversation we tried to make was interrupted by similarly powerful contractions and the doctor's preternatural pep. "You're doing great, honey," she finally said, and smiled at Poppy over her belly. "I see scalp on the way. Hey, Rufus, want to come down here and take a look?"

No. I absolutely did *not* want to take a look. I'd seen my share of striking sights in the previous century, but I had zero desire to add a crowning baby to that list. But Poppy was nodding and giving me an exhausted smile, and the doctor slid her stool to one side, offering me a ringside seat. Reluctant but trying not to let on, I slunk down to the end of the bed, pausing just long enough for one of the nurses to whisper in my ear, "Don't lock your knees."

Swallowing hard, I glanced toward the main event.

It was…*something.*

I don't remember much of what happened in the next few seconds, only hearing the doctor say, "Here you go, dear, sit down, that's it. Let's scoot right over that way and get a good breath…"

And so it came to pass that while the nurse who'd suddenly become my new best friend kept me from falling off the doctor's stool in a dead faint, the doctor cheered Poppy through the grand finale. She reached in where I couldn't see—my viewing angle, I suspected, had been purposefully selected—and when she straightened, she was holding a red, wrinkly creature with a headful of fine, dark hair. It squirmed and mewled in protest as she wiped it down and placed it on Poppy's chest, and I tried not to think about the fact that the two of them were still *attached*.

But whereas I'd spent the last few minutes by turns lightheaded and embarrassed, Poppy was ecstatic, weary but crying with joy as she held the baby.

Our baby.

I watched them for a moment, mother and child, trying to process the enormity of what had just transpired, when the doctor crouched in front of me and grinned. "Hey, there, Dad. Feeling better?"

I think I managed to nod.

"Good. Want to come meet your son?"

My son.

I stood, tried not to wobble, and made it to Poppy's bedside. The smile on her face spoke of love—so much love.

I traced his little curled-up fist with the tip of my finger, completely in awe. At that moment, I didn't care what he was or who he would become—that was my son, my perfectly beautiful son, lying atop the most incredible woman I'd ever known.

"What's his name?" I asked.

She stroked his damp hair. "Malcolm."

"I love it. I love *you*."

Poppy pressed her palm against my cheek when I leaned down to kiss her, then reluctantly allowed a nurse to tend to the baby. "Go on," she said to me, "go tell them. Make it official. You know your mom must be dying for news."

"That's a great idea. Why don't you go see your family for a bit?" the doctor added, and gave me a meaningful look. "We're not *finished* here."

Though I wasn't quite feeling myself, I could still take a hint.

As I stumbled into the corridor, I looked toward the waiting room and, to my surprise, found the entire family packing the room to the twilit windows, all watching the homicide detectives. Mother was the first to notice my emergence, and she jumped up and waved. "Success?" she called.

I nodded. "Boy."

My brothers cheered, and poor Vivi, now even further outnumbered, huffed in mock exasperation. "Congrats," she said. "How's Poppy?"

"She's great," I replied, leaning against the wall for support. "Everything's great."

And it was, just then. The troubles of reality would return later. I was a centenarian first-time father of a newborn, in far over my head. Half of Faerie still lived in fear that Ellie had lost her mind inside that locked-down mansion. Luce was bunking with our parents and hoping not to be ordered back to work. And lest anyone forget, the Arcanum's thugs remained in charge on the other side of the border, the monsters who had orphaned the many children whom Poppy and I had been raising for almost nine years. Objectively speaking, there was plenty in the larger picture to keep me up at night.

But not *that* night. Hope endures while life does, after all.

While my brothers congratulated me, I heard my son begin to cry. "Healthy set of lungs on that one," said Leo. "Reminds me of his old man." He punched my shoulder and grinned. "Good luck, little brother. Sounds like you're going to need it."

"I think we'll be just fine," I said, and straightened. "Excuse me. I'm being summoned."

—YEAR TEN—

JUNE: VIVI STOWE PERRYMAN

I looked up from my computer that Tuesday morning at the soft rap on my door. "Miss Vivi?" said Angelique, my sixteen-year-old summer assistant, as she stuck her head inside my office. "You've got a visitor."

There was no one on the calendar, but that didn't matter. If I was in residence at our little town hall, then I was available, as far as the Fringe was concerned. Hell, even if I *wasn't* in residence, I was still on call. But after nine years at the helm, I'd grown accustomed to interruptions. "Sure, send them in," I told Angelique, then glanced at my clock. "And go ahead and take your lunch, hon. I don't want you getting busy and waiting until three again."

I'd just closed my computer in preparation for the impromptu meeting when Toula saw herself in. "Hey!" I said, rising to greet her. "How's it going? You're still planning to offer that intro to warding class at the rec center next month, right?"

"Eh…that may need to be postponed." She closed the door, then locked it. "Sorry to drop in like this, but I've got a proposal to run past you."

I polished my glasses on my shirt as she took a seat in front of my desk. "Sure. What's up?"

Toula leaned forward and steepled her fingers. "What would you say to taking in a few more refugees?"

The question took me by surprise—what else had we been doing since the Unravelling? "Of course. Why?"

"What if they weren't Fringers?"

I frowned. "Mundanes? Minor Arcanum?"

"Ellie's court."

She seemed unfazed by my incredulous laughter. "You're kidding, right?" I said.

"Dead serious."

"You want *us* to antagonize one of the two people keeping us in this realm?"

Toula paused, seemingly calm, but the way she drummed her fingertips together betrayed her agitation. "It's not antagonism, exactly. We'd just get the people at risk hidden away, unnoticed. Out of sight, out of mind, right?"

"Toula, I—"

"They've been coming to see Coileán," she pressed on, talking over me. "Even some of the ones who hate his guts. They've asked to swear allegiance. He won't take them—he doesn't want to anger Ellie—but he's disturbed."

"But—"

"He won't upset the apple cart, and I get that—everyone's got to save face and all. But you and I aren't bound by their rules, see? And with your help, maybe we can keep the rest of them from being sent to the archipelago."

"How many are we talking?" I reluctantly asked. "The half fae?"

"All of them, I was thinking."

"*All?* Even that lovely chunk of the court that looks at us like dog shit?"

"I mean—"

"You want me to risk my people's safety for *them?*" I demanded. "Because that sounds like a disaster all around."

Again, Toula paused, but I suspected she was refining her attack that time. "It's not ideal," she finally replied, "and I wouldn't ask it under ordinary circumstances. But you know this is bad. The tally's up over three hundred. She had five more dragged in yesterday, God knows why." She rose, pressed her palms against my desk, and stared me down. "Let them move into the settlement. We'll make sure everyone knows that if they screw up once, they're out.

They follow the rules here, they stay quiet, and maybe we can deal with Ellie."

"And what happens when she sends guards here?" I countered. "What if she gets pissed and drags my brothers in, huh?"

"The settlement is under Coileán's protection, too. And he's offered to send people to help guard the wall and keep order. Look," she said with a little shrug, "they've let you run this show from the beginning, haven't they? If people are here under your authority, and Ellie tries to bully her way in, then Coileán will be forced to get involved. Those two don't want a turf war over this place. And think about it," she added. "This is way beyond Ellie's territory. If her folks hide out up here, then maybe she'll overlook them."

"Oh, right," I snapped, "she'll never notice if everyone around her up and disappears overnight."

"Which is why we'd do it gradually. Move people a few at a time. You know she hasn't left the mansion in more than a year—it's not like she's making the rounds at night, checking beds. We move out the people most likely to end up angering her, we poke around, and maybe we get to the bottom of this mess. *Please*, Vivi."

I sat back in my chair, thinking over her proposition and all the many ways it could blow up in my face. "She's unwell, you realize," I told Toula. "Like, off her rocker or something. You really think she'd play by the rules if someone she wanted was hiding here and we refused to extradite? You want to bet our lives on that?"

"No," she said simply, "I don't. And I don't think she's crazy. But before I poke the bear, I want to reduce the potential collateral damage, and it's either stick her people here or in the mortal realm. You tell me which is the better option."

"What do you mean, *poke the bear*?"

Toula looked back at me in silence, and I knew I wouldn't be getting a straight answer.

"There are kids in that court, you know," she murmured.

"Not many little ones, but kids nonetheless. She's taken three already."

"There are kids here, too," I said. "My nephew among them."

"And I'm telling you that Coileán will have your back. I just need for you to let a few out-of-towners hang around for a bit."

We stared at each other, neither speaking, as the wall clock ticked closer to noon.

"Goddamn it," I finally muttered, and picked up my phone. "Ned's going to *hate* you."

The first moved in that evening, two sets of half-fae parents and their young kids—the baby couldn't have been more than eight or nine months old. While Toula and I went over ground rules with the adults in my office, Angelique, who was quickly becoming my favorite assistant ever, babysat in the conference room. Having grown up in the dorm, she knew how to keep kids entertained, and a quick call home resulted in three more teenagers, a stack of board games, and pizza.

As Robbie arrived to show the newcomers to their home sites—he'd taken the liberty of putting up basic houses, a canvas upon which anyone with a modicum of talent could easily work—one of the mothers clasped my hands. "Thank you," she said, a note of strain in her voice. "You won't hear a peep from us, we promise. If it's okay for the children to go to the park…"

"Sure, of course," I said.

"We'll watch them, they won't get into trouble." She paused, then quietly added, "If the queen comes for us, is there anyone who could take care of them? They have older half siblings on both sides, but just in case—"

"There's a facility. The Fringe has had its share of unaccompanied minors."

She seemed to remember, then, where she was. "Oh.

Oh, yes…I'm sorry, I forgot about—"

"Why don't you go get settled?" I interrupted. "One of my brothers"—Robbie raised an eyebrow—"uh, my *other* brothers will be out later to talk security."

They hadn't been gone for five minutes before Toula shepherded another group into my office. Having only just taken a bite of the pizza I'd snagged from the babysitters, I looked up in dismay and wiped my hands relatively clean. "I thought we'd chatted with all the incoming families for tonight," I said as Toula closed the door.

"Oh, we have," she said, breezing her way across the room. "Meet Ned's new reinforcements."

I gave them a quick once-over: three men, two women, none of them known to me. Before I could introduce myself, the door opened again, and a redheaded woman slipped in. "Sorry, *sorry*," she said, holding a slice of pilfered pizza on a napkin. "Haven't eaten, and someone left this unattended. Hi, Vivi."

"Liza," I replied, lifting my abandoned dinner in salute and grateful to recognize at least one face besides Toula's. "I didn't know you were a guard now."

She snorted and shook her head. "Hardly. None of us are. But it's not like Coileán could actually send *troops*, yeah? Might give Ellie the wrong impression." Using the pizza as a pointer, she went around the room. "Bon, Na, Ingulf, Pulen, Frances. A few of my more responsible cousins."

"Mina might disagree," Ingulf muttered.

"Yeah, well, Mina's not invited to this party, so we work with what we have. Everyone here has been involved with the field guide and mapping project," she explained to me. "These folks aren't trained guards, but they've fought off giant spiders and worse."

I was about to respond when Ned walked in, not bothering with a knock. "You rang?" he asked, picking Toula out of the small crowd.

She nodded. "Yup. Meet your recruits."

Folding his arms, he looked at each of them in turn—

and paused on Liza, who was unabashedly eating. "Right. Show of hands: how many of you have ever been any sort of soldier?"

They looked at each other, none volunteering. Finally, Pulen lifted a finger. "I, um...I'm just a botanist."

My brother sighed. "Okay. Step out to the conference room, if you will—I'll go over the schedule in a moment." Once they'd filed out, he gave Toula a long, hard look and murmured, "Just how am I supposed to keep the bloody court from turning this town into a crater? Tell that lot to go around asking nicely?"

"No," she replied, meeting his stare. "You remind them of the alternative. And with any luck, you won't have to put up with them for long."

His eyebrows rose. "Something you'd like to share with us?"

"Not tonight. Just do your best to keep the peace and leave the rest to me."

"Why you?" he said as she slipped out the door. "What aren't you telling us, Pavli?"

She turned and smiled. "I'll tell you the same thing I told Coileán: this is plausible deniability. See you tomorrow, Vivi," she said, and walked away.

I looked at Ned, who'd closed his eyes and was massaging his forehead. "You okay?" I asked.

"Did he really say he's a botanist?"

"That's what I heard."

My brother groaned and saw himself out. "Might as well call Stephen and Leo as this lot. Bloody useless *botanist*," he grumbled, and stalked off to meet his new guards.

DECEMBER: TOULA PAVLI

She had to notice eventually. Even distracted by the binds, she *had* to notice when things got too quiet.

I'd expected blowback during the summer, while we methodically moved her court into the settlement, or at least by fall, with two-thirds of her people hunkered down out of sight. But either the binds were taking more of a toll than I'd imagined or else her guards saw what was going on and didn't hate the plan, as we made it to early December before they came knocking.

Ned called me to the settlement's front gate early one Wednesday morning—fortunately for me, a day that Coileán had opted to skip breakfast for coffee in his office. "Get down here," was all he said, and I threw on a jacket and took myself over. When I arrived, I found him, two of his more martially competent brothers, and all six of Coileán's volunteers blocking the break in the wall— posturing, surely, as the wall was only three feet high and easily climbable. On the other side were two of Ellie's younger guards, neither looking pleased to be there.

"What's going on?" I asked, zipping my jacket against the wind.

Ned pointed to the guards. "The queen's summoned one of her sisters and won't say why. I've explained that if she wants to talk extradition, she'll need to make an appointment with Vivi."

"Hmm. Well?" I said, turning to the guards. "Is that the case?"

"It's not our place to question her," one of the pair

replied, though his words seemed forced. "Lady Dionne—"

"Has been a perfectly law-abiding guest for the last four months," I interrupted. "She and her little boy. Either Ellie can explain why she's ordering Dionne to come to court, or she can try to work something out with Vivi, but we're not sending Dionne without a damn good reason."

The guard nervously licked his lips. "Let's be reasonable—"

"*Reasonable*? Come on," I snapped, "you know as well as anyone that nobody leaves the mansion."

By then, the other guard's look of professional resolve had begun to crumble into something more closely resembling panic. "We can't go back to her with that answer. She...we can't upset her, you don't know what it's like—"

"We're only doing our duty," said his calmer companion. "If we return empty-handed..."

She'll send us to the archipelago was the unspoken end of that sentence, and we all knew it.

I looked at Ned and his band, some of whom had only just graduated to swords, then at the guards. "You're not going back," I told them. "Stay here. I'll deliver the message myself."

Ned grabbed my shoulder before I could take two steps. "Are you insane?" he demanded, giving me a good shake. "You're not strong enough to face—"

He flew a good ten feet at my whispered command, then skidded to a stop in the grass and stared up at me, dazed.

"I'll be back," I said, and glanced at the others. "Does anyone else have something to say about this plan?"

Ellie's guards gaped, and their leader managed, "But...but I thought you were witch-blooded..."

I cracked my knuckles. "Yeah. And I've been doing little but study and train ever since we got here."

"Just be careful," Liza cut in before anyone else could quibble. "If you don't come back, how long should we wait before telling Coileán?"

"The realm will handle it," I replied, then cut my eyes to Ned, who was climbing to his feet. "Sorry about that. I'll make it up to you," I told him.

He staggered back toward the wall. "Toula, wait—"

But I wasn't in the mood. I waved open a gate to the mansion's front door and marched through before good sense could get the best of me.

Having had my ass handed to me by my classmates in combat practice all throughout school, I learned a valuable lesson at a tender age: if you talk a big game, you make yourself a target. The kids who bragged about their skill were the ones everyone loved to beat. Bound as I was, I knew that I couldn't pull off the bolts or shields that my peers could, and so I kept my head down, tried not to antagonize anyone, and worked overtime on my own to improve my speed and stamina through technical methods. By graduation, I could barely hold my own, but my classmates were too busy fighting each other for bragging rights to understand the feat I'd accomplished. They still laughed at me for being on a dragonscale wand, looking right past the fact that I was winning perhaps one bout in three. They had strength on their side, whereas I had a slew of focusing techniques at my fingertips, practiced to the point of instinct.

And then, suddenly, I had strength, too—strength far beyond that of a thirty-something wizard, even one from exceptional stock. My parents' gifts didn't clash in me—they *worked together*, giving me a talent that was, conservatively, well beyond magus-level. What's more, like all talents, it was growing. Greg Harrison had quietly taken me into a practice room several times over the course of two years to test my limits, and he'd shown me my growth curve against that of the typical wizard. I was strengthening exponentially faster than I should have been, which was shocking to me until he showed me what he'd had to do to tabulate that result. The base curve he'd showed me was an extrapolation, as my starting point at age thirty-five was roughly where an ordinary wizard would have landed around, oh, age three hundred. On top of *that*, my attack style was still highly focused, the internalized result of all those formative years fighting with both hands tied behind my back. In Greg's hyper-technical estimation, I'd grown into a "scary bitch."

But I didn't make a big deal about it—I didn't go around demanding rematches or conspicuously flexing my newfound muscles, aside from the work I did on the silo wards (and yeah, the dozens of assassins I had to kill that once). In general, I stayed quiet and let others think what they would, and I continued to appraise the people around me with a practiced eye.

He might have had his qualms, but in a fair fight, I was no match for Coileán. I'd seen what he could do at full strength—*angry* full strength—and we weren't even close. The guy was a bruiser, plain and simple. Nor would I have wanted to go toe-to-toe with Val, all else being equal, as he had both strength and experience on his side. At forty-seven, I was maybe the equivalent of a decently talented five-hundred-year-old wizard, had such a thing existed, able to throw around the occasional faerie and hold my own against the Arcanum's worst. When I employed my focusing techniques, my power virtually doubled—and so much of what I'd done since the Unravelling had been research into focus and speed. Not too shabby, all things considered, but still not a real threat to a faerie backed by the realm under ordinary circumstances.

These Ellie's guards, however, were anything but an impediment.

I strode up to the mansion, where a pair of them waited outside the doors, eyeing me. "I'm here to talk to the queen," I announced, not slowing. "Do you want to let her know I'm here, or should I see myself in?"

The guard on the left took a step forward and held up

her hand. "My lady isn't receiving visitors—"

I flung her off the stairs and into the grass with a wave of my hand. "This is not negotiable," I told the other guard, whose eyes had gone wide in surprise. "I'm here to discuss the archipelago, and I'd hate to hurt you."

He cut his eyes toward his colleague, who was moaning and rubbing her head. "What about the archipelago?"

"How quickly it can be dismantled. Do I need to toss you, too?"

After a brief pause, he shook his head and stepped aside. "Don't harm her."

"I'm here to *help*," I said, then slipped past him into the mansion.

The marble hallways were usually cool, but with every door and window shut, the place was dark and unpleasantly chilled. "Ellie!" I bellowed, my voice echoing through the corridors. "It's Toula! Where are you?"

I listened, then heard soft shuffling in the distance and headed toward it with a shield up. "Ellie! I just want to talk to you! This has gone on long enough!"

When I reached a staircase, I wasn't surprised to find her captain, Nico, and a handful of other guards blocking my way at the top. "Hi," I said, and dropped my shield. "I come in peace. Let me through."

"I'm afraid I can't do that," Nico replied, though he sounded genuinely sorry. "The queen isn't receiving visitors."

"No shit."

He flashed a brief smile. "I'm sworn to protect her, and I will."

"Then we have the same end goal," I replied, showing him my empty hands. "I've come to save her from herself. Look me in the eye and tell me she's doing just fine, Nico."

He ignored the request. "Does your brother know you're here?"

"Nope. Not his fight. And before you ask, Coileán doesn't know, either. This is all *me*," I said, patting my chest.

"Let me see her. I can help."

A green flame bloomed in Nico's outstretched palm, and he began tossing it like a tennis ball. "I appreciate the offer, Fotoula. Honestly, I do. But we are sworn…"

Seeing his jaw go slack, I turned and found Faerie standing behind me with her arms folded—still petite, still wearing an impractically diaphanous dress, but glowing like a miniature sun in the darkness of the corridor. "Hi," I said, nodding in greeting. "Fancy meeting you here."

"Toula," she replied with a slight dip of her head, then turned her attention to Nico and the other guards. "Stand aside, children. Let her pass."

The rest of the guards began to shuffle away from the center, but their captain held his ground. "Whoever you are," he began, "you're not—"

He collapsed, unconscious, and rolled down a dozen stairs to the first landing. Faerie flicked her fingers toward the other guards, who retreated, then gestured toward the staircase. "As you were."

"Thanks." I started up, then turned back as the glow behind me vanished. "Oh, come on, really?" I said to the empty room. "That's all the help I get?"

I could have sworn I heard her laughing as I stepped over Nico and continued my search.

When I eventually found Ellie, she was alone in a sitting room, propped up in an armchair by a roaring fire. She seemed almost skeletal in the flickering light, her face gaunt, her eyes deeply sunken, her hair dull and brittle. Most of her was hidden from view, swathed in plaid afghans, though the room was warm enough to make me sweat. The only true sign of life in her was the spark in her green eyes—dim, yes, but flaring as she noticed me in the open doorway.

"What…" she croaked, and struggled to rise. "What are you—"

"Let's chat," I interrupted, closing the door. "Your court

is terrified, word on the street is you're off your rocker, and from what I'm seeing, you're killing yourself. Sheesh, woman, have you looked in a mirror in the last year?"

Her pale lip rose into a snarl. "How dare you."

"It's time to shut down the archipelago," I said, moving closer. "For your own good, and for the good of the court. You can't keep this up, Ellie."

When her blankets fell away, I barely had time to gawk at her emaciated frame before she'd found her feet. Anger was a good motivator, I mused, calling forth my best shield, then braced myself against the sudden volley of lightning.

Had the queen been at full strength and wanted me dead, she could have just stopped my heart. That she was resorting to missiles of any sort told me my hunch was correct.

"That the best you've got?" I taunted, feeding my shield against the onslaught. "Come on, I thought you were supposed to be a queen! If you're going to hit me, hit me!"

Fire flew with the lightning that time, driving me to one knee. "You're weak!" I shouted, pouring my strength into the shield. "It's the binds, Ellie, can't you see that? If you want to fight me, you'll have to break them!"

I don't know how long I knelt on the rug, praying that my shield would hold. My arms trembled, and I know I squeezed my eyes shut at one point, finding sight to be a distraction. Ellie didn't close the distance between us, but she kept up her attack, fueled by rage and whatever madness was driving her.

But then, ever so slightly, I felt her begin to waver—a suggestion of relief like the hint of a breeze on a humid July day.

Yes, anger is a good motivator, but it's a temporary solution. Ellie was burning hot, a rocket blasting off and rapidly expending its fuel, and she was starting to weaken. The fire flew less frequently, the lightning decreased in intensity, and I watched as she finally staggered back and fell into her chair, panting and wide-eyed. "How?" she gasped.

"How are you still…"

I stood, shield battered but strong, and dragged myself across the room. "Tell you later," I said, and without hesitation, I slapped my hands on either side of her head.

Coileán wasn't the only one who could force sleep on another person. My way was closer to pure spellcraft—go with what you know, and all that—but it did the trick. Ellie's eyes closed, and she sagged to the left, almost falling off her chair. I tucked her back into place, dropped my shield, and collapsed, dripping with sweat as my heart hammered on its adrenaline high.

I was still on the floor when Nico forced the door open. "My lady!" he cried, running across the room, and pressed his fingers against her neck. Satisfied that there was a pulse, he stared down at me and my shaking arms. "What have you done?" he demanded.

I laughed weakly, too exhausted to rise. "Naptime. I knocked her out."

"*Why?*"

In response, I cocked my head toward the open door…and the sounds of excited voices echoing up from below. "She can't hold all those binds together if she's fully unconscious, now can she?"

He realized what he was hearing and gasped. "Moon and stars—"

"Might want to go coordinate the exodus, eh?"

Before he could answer, voices in the hallway began to shout my name, and I turned and smiled as Val and Coileán burst into the room. "*Toula!*" Val cried, ignoring the sleeping queen as he scooped me off the floor. "What were you *thinking*, she could have killed—"

"Oh, *shit*, Ellie's not dead, is she?" Coileán interrupted, hurrying past us. Nico shook his head and stepped between them, and Coileán stood down. "What happened?"

He pointed to me. "Ask her. A glowing stranger overpowered me, and when I woke, I found those two like this."

"Congratulations," said Coileán, "it sounds like you met the realm. Are you hurt?"

"Bruised," Nico muttered.

"Your pride, perhaps," Val added, holding me like an overcome damsel on an old paperback romance. "The queen is sleeping?"

"So *she* says," he replied, gesturing toward me. "And it sounds as though the archipelago's inhabitants are moving about, so I assume she's sleeping deeply."

"Right…" Coileán murmured, and looked around the room. The fire died with a flick of his hand, and the curtains opened wide as the windows rose, admitting a blessed blast of cool air. "Put Ellie to bed," he told Nico, "and I'll see that no one downstairs disturbs her. If you need reinforcements, say so. I don't want her to come to harm."

"And put me down," I told Val. "Before the party gets up here…"

He and Nico shared a long look, and both nodded. As Nico floated Ellie out of her chair and into the next room, Val lowered me to my unsteady feet, then stormed into the hallway, bellowing for Nico's underlings.

Coileán caught me before I could collapse and put me in Ellie's vacated seat. "You're insane, Glinda," he said, holding my face in his hands. "You know that, right? You're absolutely *insane*."

"But effective," I pointed out.

He stared at me, flabbergasted, then drew close and kissed me with the urgency of a man who's just pulled his beloved off the edge of a cliff. "What am I to do with you?" he murmured when he broke away. "You didn't even tell me you were—"

"Because you would have flipped out," I interrupted. "And I needed to do this."

"This is what you and the realm discussed?"

"More or less. How'd you find me, anyway?"

He swore and glowered at the ceiling. "Damn it, Toula, she could have killed you. And Liza called me, thank goodness."

"Snitch. But look, no harm done. I'm still here," I replied, and smiled. "And if you go nuts someday, well, I'll do the same for you."

"Why *you*? The realm couldn't have done it alone?"

I shrugged. "Don't think she would have. Something about your agreement. And as for me," I added, trying to find the strength to get out of the chair, "you know how it is. Sometimes the situation just calls for a Pavli."

"*Toula.*"

"I'm an improvement over the last one, right? No one's dead this time!"

With a deep sigh, Coileán hoisted me into his arms and opened a gate to my bedroom. "You're going to take a nap. I'll be here with Ellie."

"Yeah, sounds good," I said, leaning against his shoulder. "Don't even have to knock me out this time. You may not have noticed, but I'm just about dead on my feet."

He grunted, then waited as the covers turned themselves back and the pillows fluffed. "*Rest*," he ordered, pulling off my shoes. "And let me see about that jacket…"

Perhaps he removed it then, or perhaps he returned later and peeled it off of me—I couldn't have said. Within seconds of hitting the sheets, I passed out, falling into a dreamless sleep for the next two days.

Well, almost dreamless.

I found myself sitting in the old folding chair outside my father's cell, facing him once again. Same old, same old: yellow jumpsuit, short black hair, twisted nose, dark, sunken eyes that bored into mine. But I wasn't a little girl or a teenager any longer—I was myself, already five years older than he'd been when he was executed.

"Hey, Dad," I said, crossing my legs. "So, how'd I do?"

And for the first time in my life, I saw him smile at me.

DECEMBER: FAERIE

As intimately connected with Eleanor's mind as I was, it took me almost no effort to decorate our meeting space with familiar furnishings: an antique sofa, an expensive silk carpet, a mantle decked with pine and holly boughs, a tastefully appointed fir by the window. I laid a fire on the hearth—a tame little blaze, unlike the bonfires she'd kept burning of late—and beyond the window, I painted the sky black and added fat, falling snowflakes.

Eleanor came to on the sofa, sat up, blinked in confusion at her surroundings, then saw me standing by the grandfather clock in the adjoining dining room and gasped. "*Walt!* It's..." She paused, frowning warily. "No, it *can't* be you...and we can't be here, the house burned to the ground," she added, turning to take in my handiwork. "What the devil..." Her voice trailed off, and a sick look creased her face. "Oh, God, am I *dead*?"

"No," I said in Walt's borrowed voice. "And in the strictest sense, this place does not exist. You're in your own head, Eleanor. But as you've had a difficult few...well, years, I thought something familiar might be a comfort. No?"

"You're not Walt. Who are you?"

I shrugged and returned to my typical form. "Better?"

"*Ah*. Somewhat." She rose and leaned on the fragrant mantle, running her fingers over one of the needlepoint stockings. "What happened? Why are we here?"

"What do you remember?"

Her brow puckered as she stared into space. "Toula," she finally murmured. "Something to do with Toula...but

I..."

She stiffened, then cried out as I replayed the last moments in her mind's eye. "Remember that?" I asked.

Eleanor stared at me, horrified. "I...no, I couldn't have..."

"Sit."

She returned to the sofa, regarding me warily. "I'm trying to recall what happened, but it's like there's a cataract over so much of late."

"Exhaustion," I explained. "You haven't had true sleep in years—not with those binds to maintain. The archipelago is being vacated as we speak, by the way. You're finally unconscious, the binds are breaking, and your guards are seeing the inmates out. I believe Coileán is sending reinforcements to keep order."

"Binds..." she mumbled.

"As of this morning, you had three hundred forty-seven people silently enduring a months-long hurricane in your parlor, many constantly on the brink of starvation or drowning. That's far too many binds to manage, even for you."

She sat in silence for a time, her face shifting as she combined the information I'd given her with her fragmented memory. "I...I just wanted to keep the peace," she said softly. "Bring order to the court. It worked with Karl, and then Hugo attacked Amy, I had to do something, and the riots..." She looked up at me with plaintive eyes. "I never wanted this throne. I didn't ask for it. All I wanted was to be left alone with my Walt and be happy, and...and I *killed* him, and I swore there'd be order, nothing like that would ever happen again..."

I sat beside her and produced a handkerchief as her eyes brimmed. "Child," I said, dabbing at her face, "the courts are but a veneer of structure over chaos. Our people cannot be fully tamed. It goes against our nature. But there *can* be order and peace, within limits. It's not easy, and they will try your patience, but you can rule them without resorting to such…*creative*…measures." I passed her the handkerchief, and she blew her nose. "Your father didn't want the responsibility, either," I said. "He wanted the power and the glory, but none of the work, and he chafed when called upon to restore order. You, now, you wanted none of it, but you're trying to do your duty. You're already a better ruler than he was."

Eleanor's expression spoke of deep incredulity. "Three hundred forty-seven islanders might say otherwise. And why didn't you *stop* me?"

"A learning experience," I replied, and held up a hand to silence her protestation. "You needed to know why mass binding isn't the answer, especially not against talented targets. Lock the troublemakers away, if you must—build cells like Titania's. But you cannot personally control the actions of every member of the court. You've learned that now, I trust."

"I barely remember the last year," she said. "And before that…bits and pieces, but…" She frowned as she puzzled through the detritus. "Why did Toula come today?"

"She and Vivi have been slowly moving your people into the settlement, just to take them away from your notice. You had an idea about Dionne—paranoia, nothing more—and sent guards to fetch her. They knew she was in the settlement, and Toula decided to handle the matter."

"I could have killed Toula."

"You owe her thanks, and perhaps an apology. But that's a matter for another day," I said. "You're absolutely exhausted. Three months of sleep should set you to rights."

"Three *months*?" she exclaimed.

"Trust me, child. It's for the best. You'll feel much better once your thinking clears—no more castaways, hmm? Hear petitions, decide them, move on," I suggested. "Accept that there will always be pettiness in the complaints you receive. But if you can learn to rule—to guide and lead without oppressing—then you'll have something close to peace." I rose, smoothed my dress, and rested my hand on her shoulder. "You've wondered for some time what Walt would say about your little archipelago project. If I may hazard a guess?"

She nodded.

"Something along the lines of, 'Free them, Richard.'"

Eleanor closed her eyes against fresh tears, but she faintly nodded.

"They are alive," I told her. "Excited to be free and terrified that you'll change your mind, but alive. When you wake, I would suggest that you construct proper cells for future incarceration. Yes?"

"Yes."

"Good. Now, before I let you rest, do you have a preference as to who runs the court during your convalescence? A sibling, perhaps?"

She gave the matter a moment's consideration, then asked, "*Must* it be a sibling?"

"No. This is only a three-month regency. I'll share enough power with that person to maintain the peace and withdraw it once you wake. Any thoughts on the matter?"

"Rufus," she replied. "I trust him. He'll hold the wheel steady."

"He's been slightly busy," I cautioned. "Did you know that he has an infant at home?"

"Who, *Rufus*? No!" she cried, shocked. "When? He and Poppy?"

"Last January. The boy's almost a year old."

Eleanor stared at the fire, mouth agape. "How the hell did I miss *that*?"

"You'll have plenty of time to make up for it," I assured her. "And if Rufus is your choice, I'll see to the arrangements."

Though still unsettled, she nodded. "Thank you. Please, ehm...convey my apology, won't you?"

"If you like. It's time for you to rest." The room dissolved around us, leaving us in perfect blackness. "I will wake you soon," I promised. "Incidentally, your father and

I went through this when he was young and inexperienced. He was worse than you."

"Oh? What's worse than an eternal hurricane?"

"Statuary," I replied. "He had a garden full of frozen people—most in compromising positions, as I recall. At least they were insensate. They woke a few years later, unaware of the missing time, when he pushed himself so far that he lost consciousness. It almost killed him, and he slept for nearly a year. That's why I sent Toula in after you."

"That's *horrid.*"

I smiled. "And you're learning. Good."

With that, I left Eleanor and allowed myself to take in the rest of the realm. The captains had her security under control, and word had reached the settlement, passed along through the cafés and across the parks by excited whispers. Toula had sunk into untroubled sleep—the girl was a marvel, I had to admit. I located Rufus in the dorm with Poppy, Malcolm, and a huddling knot of their worried young charges, hiding from Eleanor's wrath. He and I would speak momentarily, I decided, but first, there was one other matter to address.

I sent part of myself through one of the smallest of gates into the mortal realm to the place where Walt—or his essence, perhaps—waited, wringing his hands. "She'll be much better now," I told him. "Resting. She's horrified with herself, but that means she should learn far more quickly than her father did."

His shoulders slumped with relief. "Thank you."

"I told you, it was all a matter of waiting her out. She'll be a better queen for it." I considered him—a stooped, aged man in a tweed jacket and pleated trousers, with glasses perched on the end of his nose. "She will be fine, Walt. You need not keep vigil."

But he shook his balding head, as I'd suspected he would. "Tell her I love her, won't you?"

"I'll see that she knows," I replied, and watched as he faded away.

MARCH: RUFUS STOWE

Aiden, who'd been down this road, had prepared me for Ellie's awakening. "You're going to feel like you've been hit by a truck," he'd said, "while simultaneously been getting over the flu. Uh…exhausted and drained," he'd clarified as my brow wrinkled. I'd been fortunate to never endure the former, and while I understood the flu to be quite unpleasant, I'd also never been sick. Aiden, on the other hand, had grown up practically mundane, and I trusted that he spoke from experience. "And she probably won't wean you off it, either," he'd added. "It's like, 'okay, you're done.' *Boom.* There's no trick—just endure it, and it'll get better eventually."

The realm hadn't confirmed or denied his prediction at the time, but Aiden had been spot-on. I knew the instant that Ellie woke because my legs grew wobbly and I slumped to the floor. Fortunately, Mal was sitting in his playpen and not in my arms at the time, and he regarded me curiously as I caught my breath. "Dada?" he asked, scooting toward the netting.

"Dada's okay," I assured him, hoping that sounded convincing, and tried to catch my breath.

I was pushing myself back to my feet when Poppy came into my makeshift office with sandwiches. "Honey? What happened?" she said, dropping the lunch tray on the coffee table. Her arms were stronger than mine at the moment, and I leaned into her as she dragged me toward the couch. "Did you trip? Hit your head?"

I held up a finger to ask for a moment's patience, waited

for the vertigo to pass, then muttered, "She's back."

"Oh. *Oh*," she said, realizing why I was a sudden wreck, and wrapped her arm around my shoulders. "Are you all right? Should I get someone?"

"No, it...it's passing," I replied, and managed a weak smile. "At least it's over."

"You can say that again." She kissed my cheek and moved lunch within reach. "Eat up, mister. Luce brought out the jamón."

I sighed. "Ham on wheat. It's not a complicated sandwich."

"Stop complaining. You could do with a little frou-frou in your life, especially when it tastes like this," she said primly, and took a bite from hers. "Ooh, arugula."

"Enjoy." Standing, I tested my balance. "I'd best see to Ellie. She'll want a report."

"*She's* the one who thrust the court in our laps," said Poppy. "She can wait. Eat your lunch first."

"True. But the sooner we're square, the sooner we can go home. How about it, buddy," I asked Mal, who'd returned to haphazardly stacking blocks, "are you ready to go home?"

Our son didn't seem to care, but then again, he was fourteen months old. Molars were a more prominent concern of his than where we put his crib.

"Back soon," I told Poppy. "Here's hoping we can pack today."

She'd been a real trooper, my wife. We'd been hiding in the dorm with Mal and the kids, holding our breath like the rest of the settlement, when I'd heard a strange voice at the back of my head: *Eleanor needs a favor. She asked for you.*

The question I'd been forming had emerged instead as a scream as the power slammed into me. When I'd returned to full awareness, I was on my hands and knees, and Poppy had shepherded the kids to the other side of the room, where they'd watched with terrified eyes. I couldn't fault them for that—I *was* glowing.

With the worst past, the voice had introduced itself properly. And with that—and quite without my say-so in the matter—I'd been handed the court for the next few months and told not to mess it up too badly.

I'd quickly reassured Poppy that I wasn't dying, then ran for my home office, pulling up Aiden's number on the way. As soon as I'd babbled something like an explanation, he'd come over, locked us in my office, and more or less forced me to meditate until I could think clearly—not an easy task with the realm still camping in my mind. "You'll get used to it," he'd insisted. "And the rest. But for now…you know, try to keep calm. You might be testy for a while."

I'd had the advantage on him there—unlike Aiden, I'd grown up fully aware of the problems with a fae temper, and I'd learned to control mine. Still, Aiden's warnings had spooked me. I'd asked Poppy to take Mal to my parents' house for safekeeping, then left her to see what had become of the mansion after Toula's visit.

The place had been chaos, a dazed crowd milling around the halls and finding its way out into the sunlight. A few of the more coherent ones had been sprinting away over the lawn, buck naked, when I'd arrived. I'd seen myself in, looked around for the person in charge, then spied Nico, who'd seemed to be giving orders. "Uh, hello," I'd said when he eventually noticed me loitering behind his guards. "I—"

"Not a good time," he'd snapped.

"Oh, yes, understood. I'm subbing for Ellie."

A slight, controlled surge had restored my weird corona, and Nico had stepped back in alarm. "My…erm…"

"'Rufus' is fine. I'm no lord," I'd told him, and watched another pair of former inmates hurry for the door. "So, uh…what can I do to help?"

Not much, as it turned out. While his people and some of Coileán's guards had dealt with the newly freed, I'd looked in on Ellie, then obliterated the archipelago. That had been my first act as regent, and perhaps the one of which I was proudest.

On my way to Ellie's suite, however, I wondered if she'd feel the same way. Three months was a long time for a nap, and the realm hadn't bothered to tell me whether my queen was cranky before the voice finally left me in peace.

I found a pair of guards stationed in the corridor, but they nodded and allowed me to pass. At the end of the hall, Nico himself stood watch at her bedroom door. "Is she in any condition for guests?" I asked, keeping my voice low.

"No, but I suspect she'll see you." He rapped twice at the door, then cracked it open, showing me a sliver of daylight on the other side. "My lady? Rufus is here."

"Send him in, please," she said, her voice a weak croak.

With a warning glance, Nico stepped aside.

I gently closed the door behind me, then turned and spotted Ellie, propped up on pillows and buried beneath her thick duvet. "Good morning, sunshine," I said, keeping my distance. "Feeling better?"

"Rufus." My name emerged as a sigh. "I'm so sorry. She asked me for my preference, but she didn't give me a chance to ask *you*, and—"

"It's okay, Ellie."

"No, it's not. But I knew you wouldn't destroy the court, so thank you for proving me correct. I owe you a *great* deal."

"Hey," I replied, shrugging, "you've been out of sorts—"

"You have no idea," she muttered. "I owe you, I owe Poppy, and…belated congratulations are in order, are they not? You're a father now?"

I grinned. "Little guy's walking, and he's into everything. Your house is lovely, but I think we'll all sleep better once Mal's back in a place with fewer marble surfaces."

"Mal…"

"Malcolm."

"*Ah.*" She hesitated, then asked, "Is he…okay?"

She didn't have to clarify the question—I'd been receiving more or less polite variants of it from my fae acquaintances for the last year. "He doesn't have the metal allergies," I replied. "No immediate signs of talent, but he might be a late bloomer. And we won't know if he can shift until he hits puberty, so that'll be something to look out for. But he's healthy, he's growing like a weed, and he's a clever little fellow, if I may brag. We'll keep him around."

"Glad to hear it," she said, though she sounded morose. "As for the court, can you bring me up to speed? And sit, please," she added, gesturing toward the chair by the window. "No need to lurk in the doorway."

I took a seat and considered Ellie for a few seconds before I began. She looked nervous, I realized, drawn about the eyes and mouth, as if she'd prepared for a punch.

"Things are calmer than they were," I told her. "No rioting now—not that there *was* rioting, I mean. Nico's done great work, and Val's team was very helpful."

"So Coileán has been involved?" she interrupted.

"Advice and extra manpower, but that's all. He's got his own fires to smother, you know?"

"Too well," she muttered. "And, ehm…Toula?"

"Perfectly fine," I said, and a modicum of tension drained from Ellie's shoulders. "She's been checking in. Actually babysat for an afternoon to give Poppy a break—I've been next to useless at home with the court on my plate," I explained. "But no lasting harm done to Toula. Put that out of your mind."

"But the court?"

I thought briefly, trying to slot the facts into the order least likely to upset her. "As I said, things have been relatively calm. A few of the expected squabbles, but no homicides to deal with, so that's always a plus. Um…I took the liberty of dismantling the archipelago—"

"*Good.*"

I tried not to let her see my relief. "Now, some people have moved back into their homes—"

"Wait—*back*?"

"You don't remember?"

"It's patchy," she admitted. "Who's moved where?"

"Last June, Vivi began allowing the court to move into town. Not everyone, but…uh…"

She watched while I struggled for the best phrasing. "Go on."

"She and Toula worked with a few of your siblings to figure out who was most likely to set you off, and they were evacuated first. By the time you sent guards after Dionne—"

"I did *what*? Why?"

All I could offer her was a shrug. "Dionne doesn't know, either. Anyway, the idea was that conceivably, Vivi could say that the people in town were under her protection, and Coileán would back her up against forceful removal. Honestly, I don't think Toula ever imagined it working out that way. She and Vivi got people out of your sight, and you were too preoccupied most of the time to remember them. When it got to the point that the guards would have to tell you what was going on, Toula took the fight here instead."

"Good," she murmured. "That…that was wise of her. But you're telling me that a significant portion of the court has…what, defected?"

"Not exactly. It's complicated. Plenty of them tried to swear for Coileán"—Ellie cringed at the news—"but he wouldn't accept them. They're still yours, technically, but they're hiding out in town for the time being."

"You were unable to reassure them?"

"I'm just the seat warmer, and they know it. They need to hear it from you," I replied. "And if you're smart about it, you'll work with my sister. Be gentle."

She nodded, then produced a cup of tea and took a long sip. "Rufus?" she said softly.

"Yes?"

"There's something wrong with me."

I tried lamely to reassure her. "You just got in over your head—"

"No. I mean, *yes*, I did, but that wasn't the problem." She drank again, staring into space. "I allowed myself to slip. To become so obsessed that I didn't weigh the costs against progress...or *perceived* progress..." Slowly, she looked my way again. "I did something horrible. But in the middle of it all, it felt...right. Justified."

"You're not the first."

"Maybe, but you never think about it being *you* who's halfway to madness and blowing up the world in quixotic pursuit of some illusory 'greater good.' I made that damned archipelago, and I let it overwhelm me. *I did that*, Rufus. And now I know what I'm capable of. Without even realizing it, I let myself become something monstrous. Where the hell do I go from here?"

"I don't know, but out of bed might be a good beginning."

"I'm serious." She finished her tea, and the cup disappeared. "Honest answer: when I showed you the archipelago for the first time, what did you think?"

"I, um...I found it somewhat concerning."

"*Honestly?*"

"Appalling," I confessed.

"And that night when you and Poppy came to dinner...that was the day I added the hurricane, wasn't it? It's all a blur."

"I believe so, yes."

"You were horrified. I saw it in your face, but I pretended not to."

I couldn't deny it. "Wasn't your greatest idea."

"May I ask why you didn't tell me I'd gone too far?"

There was earnestness in her expression, but I couldn't help but laugh at the absurdity of the question. "You were sending anyone who displeased you to the archipelago, Ellie. I'd have been a fool to open my mouth."

"I see." She picked at the duvet for a moment in silence, then said, "I know I've asked much of you already, but might I add one thing more?"

"If I can do it."

"I trust you," she murmured. "Perhaps more than I trust myself right now. And I need someone who isn't afraid to look me in the eye and tell me I'm speeding toward an event horizon I'd rather not cross. Can you do that for me? If I…" She hesitated, struggling. "If I go too far again, will you tell me? Because what happened…what I did," she amended, "cannot happen again. I need to know that I can ask your opinion and get an honest answer. In case my version of reality stops synchronizing with everyone else's. Please?"

"You have my word," I replied.

"Thank you." She ran one hand through her filthy tangles. "How do I look?"

I thought quickly. "Is this a test, or would you like reassurance?"

"Say no more—you pass," she muttered, and pushed back the blankets. "I'm going to shower, and I don't plan to come out for half an hour, at the very least. Would you ask Lucian if…" She froze, struck by a thought. "Did he move to the settlement, too?"

"He came back with me. In the kitchen, last I saw. I don't know if he's aware that you've awakened. Are you hungry?"

"Famished." She eased herself to her feet. "Would you be so kind as to give him my sincere apologies for whatever I did and ask that he send anything edible and close at hand upstairs? I'll speak with him in person later, but I'd probably be less offensive if I were clean."

Ellie was stalling—she could have willed herself presentable, as I'd done many a morning to sneak a few extra minutes in bed—but I didn't call her out on it. "Will do. And after that, if I may make a suggestion…"

"Please."

I pulled my phone from my back pocket. "Call Vivi. I'll help."

It took some work to coordinate the affair that afternoon,

but to her credit, Ellie did everything by the book. I escorted her to the gate outside the settlement, and she waited until Vivi met her and invited her in. Ned's augmented security force had coaxed the remaining members of the court to come to the town auditorium, and Ellie addressed them quietly, simply, and apologetically. "I was not myself," she said—perhaps not entirely the truth, but close enough that night. "What began as a plan to bring order turned into chaos. I assure you that the archipelago is gone and will not be rebuilt."

She paused, letting that sink in. "If some of you still wish to swear loyalty to Coileán and he'll have you, I'll not stand in the way. I haven't earned that right. But for those willing to return with me, I promise that things will be different. I'll give your petitions due consideration...and fair punishment as needed. We start afresh. But whatever you choose, it's time to leave this place to the Fringe. Either join them and submit to their laws or move out of the settlement."

A week later, the court's neighborhood was a ghost town. Robbie removed the more ridiculously ostentatious homes and contracted the wall, and my neighbors breathed a sigh of relief. I could be tolerated, more or less, but my full-blooded peers made everyone nervous. As Coileán refused to take any of them in, they returned to Ellie's control, some willingly, some with reluctance. But since the alternative was to take orders from the Fringers, whom most of the fully fae considered little better than mundanes, there was no real choice in the end.

And Ellie was true to her word. The mansion's doors were opened once more, and she held court for hours, leaving her throne only for five-minute breaks throughout the long days and evenings while she heard complaints, mediated the pettiest of disputes, and listened to concerns. When the rush slowed, she invited the former castaways into her office one by one to apologize, particularly to those who'd done nothing so severe as to warrant a stay on the archipelago. Her apologies mollified some and confused the rest. Still, Ellie felt that they needed to be said, and I saw no reason to tell her otherwise. She was trying to begin to make amends. It would take time, naturally—I couldn't imagine that some of the long-term inmates were at all pleased to see her awake again—but time was one thing we had in abundance.

I stopped by the guards' common room after one of those long days of court, having come over to check on Ellie, and found Nico drinking with a few of the others. We'd become almost collegial by then—he knew I was liable to vomit at the sight of gore, which knocked me down several pegs in any guard's estimation, but he recognized that I was trying to do right by the queen.

"Honestly, it's going better than I'd anticipated," I said, joining them at the table with a beer. "I'd expected more blowback."

Nico laughed softly. "That's because you're young," he replied, trading looks with several of the senior guards, "and you never had the privilege of living here under Lord Oberon."

I frowned in bemusement as his fellows made faces. "Sorry, you've lost me. I thought he was more of the hands-off beach bum type."

"For a time, there, at the last. He shirked so many of his duties in the end. But before he left the realm, when I was your age…" Nico glanced down the table at one of the women, who was nodding along. "You were here for the tar pit, weren't you?"

"Oh, yes," she said, eyebrows rising. "And the years of the stocks? The racks in the dungeon? Put one in and leave him there for months?"

"I remember those well." He caught my sick look and smirked. "It wasn't the archipelago that concerned me—I saw worse punishments from her predecessor. I was concerned because the queen was, shall we say, losing control of her rationality." I continued to gawp, and he chuckled and refilled my drink. "When Lord Oberon was annoyed, or sometimes just bored, he could be deviously creative. The part of the court that's panicked in recent years is too young to remember how things were before. Don't worry so much—those of us with longer memories have been explaining to you children how this is a marked improvement."

"How so?" I mumbled.

"Simple." He drank and set his mug aside. "The king *enjoyed* it. I remember fewer petitions in years past because people feared what he would do if he were displeased. I know Valerius has conveyed the same to Coileán," he added, and grimaced. "You know what Titania did to Coileán, yes?"

"I've heard bits…"

"Solitary confinement for about fifty years. It's a wonder he emerged with his sanity."

"We hope," one of the other guards muttered, and the rest laughed.

I'm sure I looked horrified, as Nico pointed to my beer. "Drink up, boy. And as my lady is apparently trying not to be her father," he said, raising his mug, "I'll join you."

Time would tell, I supposed. Time always does. And while those in the realms with memories measured in centuries might see a grander picture of events, back in town, the only thing that seemed to be on anyone's mind was that the calendar was turning over once again. Every year's passing was an occasion for solemnity, but this was a big anniversary: ten years since the Unravelling, and no sign of justice for the Arcanum.

I wasn't sure what to expect. Tears? Tirades? A demonstration against the current settlement regime? But five days after the last of the court departed, my sister took to the platform and gave her commemorative speech. She spoke with a confidence born of practice, naming the murdered and the kidnapped, reciting family histories and past deeds. She recalled the parents who had sacrificed themselves so that their children could run. And then she concluded with a simple promise: "We endure. And we will find them. If it takes another ten years or if it takes ten thousand, we *will* find them."

People clapped, friends hugged, and the bells tolled for the dead and the missing.

And then, as it always had, life went on.

The restaurants brought out the massive picnic they'd coordinated, the kids ran and shrieked as they played in the park, and I chased after Mal as he toddled toward the middle of a soccer game.

It wasn't perfect. Life never was.

But we endured.

—YEAR ELEVEN—

MARCH: HELEN CARVER

How do you lose a decade in the dark?

"Stuart says that Ros is doing well this term," said Badger, the only voice of comfort I had known for ten long, lonely years. "She's still not making many friends—some of the magus brats in her class are little beasts, to hear him tell it—but he's keeping an eye on her."

Ten years. My baby was a child, well on her way to womanhood. She'd be ten in October. The big double-digit birthday. I hadn't been there for a single one of the others, and at the rate things were going, I'd miss her tenth, too.

"And Aiden saw her two nights past. She's worried about giving a book report, but she was able to rattle most of it off for him, and he says she sounds fine."

Of all the godparents we could have chosen for our baby, my little brother and Stuart freaking Purcell would never have topped the list. And yet, somehow, they'd stepped up and done right by Ros. At least there was someone around her who loved her, who showed her kindness.

Did she ever think of me? Did she wonder about the person who'd given her life, who would have done anything to protect her? Did she miss me?

Did she *hate* me for not being there?

"Oh, Seamus saw Joey yesterday," Badger continued. "Training time with Val. I don't know what they get up to, but Seamie was black and blue when he came home last night. He says Joey is…not well," she admitted, "but he's holding on."

Did Joey remember my voice? My face? Or had I become little more than photos and memories to him?

"He sends his love. *Always*, he sends his love." Badger let slip a soft sigh. "I spoke with Toula recently. She says the realm told her more than a year ago that taking down the wards remotely is impossible. She's still been plugging at it, but I think she's admitting defeat."

Defeat? *No*, I wanted to yell, beginning to panic, *she can't give up! I'm still here, damn it! Help me!*

"No one's giving up on you or the Fringers," Badger hastily continued, almost as if she'd heard me. "We just need to go about this another way. Someone sufficiently strong on the inside might be about to sabotage the wards—the problem is finding such a person. But no one's abandoning you, love," she said, patting my cheek. "I'm so sorry it's taken this long. I…" She struggled briefly, then said, "I look for them. Every time I visit you, I scour the silo for them. Not a trace. They *must* be here, but I'll be damned if I know where. I don't suppose you could tell me, hmm?"

I said nothing. Not like I had a choice, even if I'd known.

"I promise you this: we will find them. If it takes me the rest of my life, I'll see that they're found. And then we'll get the lot of you away from there. Joey's waiting for you, Helen. He's not giving up, either." She sighed again, then laid her hand on my shoulder. "I'd best be going. Keep hope alive, my dear—we'll free you, I swear it."

I wasn't sure if I had any hope left. An ember, perhaps, a dull red glow instead of the roaring fire it had once been. Part of me was afraid to fan it because of how much it hurt every time I tallied the days and weeks and months in which my hopes of rescue had been dashed. But what was the alternative? All I had were my thoughts and time, and the blackness rising to cover me once more.

Maybe I could dream of hope, though dreams were scarce in my private hell.

Please don't forget me, I begged into the unresponsive void, then surrendered once again.

ACKNOWLEDGEMENTS

Thank you, dear reader, for coming along with me to this point. Writing is a bit like chucking a message in a bottle into the sea and hoping it reaches another shore. Thanks for picking this particular bottle out of the surf.

As always, I'm grateful to the wonderful ladies of the Novel Chicks. Adam Domby's feedback has been invaluable, and a thank-you back here can't fully convey my appreciation.

And yes, here's to you, Mom and Dad.

ABOUT THE AUTHOR

When not writing fiction, Ash Fitzsimmons is an appellate attorney and an unrepentant car singer.

Find her online:
www.ashfitzsimmons.com